Advance Praise for *Man in the Blue Moon*

"Michael Morris has been one of my favorite Southern writers. His new novel is reason for great celebration. *Man in the Blue Moon* is a beautifully wrought portrayal of small-town Southern life where poverty, tragedy, and human love engage in a ritualistic dance. His portrait of Dead Lakes, Florida, is one of the best portraits of a small Southern town I've ever encountered. His main character, Ella Wallace, is fascinating, and Mr. Morris is one of those rare writers whose females are as fully formed individuals as his males. Buy it. Read it."

PAT CONROY, *New York Times* bestselling author

"Michael Morris is a wonderful writer with a unique gift—he can break your heart and mend it, all in the same sentence."

PATTI CALLAHAN HENRY, author of *Coming Up for Air*

"The magic of turn-of-the-century Old Florida, in all its pain and natural beauty, has found its voice with native son Michael Morris in his latest novel. Told in a multitude of voices, all desperate, all determined, *Man in the Blue Moon* spins a delicate, unforgettable family drama of abandonment and grit and redemption from unlikely sources. Morris describes with a pitch-perfect ear a vanishing rural culture of timber-cuts and bank foreclosures, where hard-held faith was not a luxury but a necessity for survival. Florida is lucky to have him."

JANIS OWENS, author of *My Brother Michael* and *The Cracker Kitchen*

"Now that I have read *Man in the Blue Moon*, I'm suffering anxiety pains waiting for a publication date. Our book clubs continually select Michael's titles, and [this] is his best work by far. Every member of our staff will 'dig' this delightful story of an innocent time in the South and the marvelous characters that delight and disappoint."

JAKE REISS, owner, The Alabama Booksmith, Birmingham, AL

"This new novel by Michael Morris not only effortlessly transported me to Apalachicola, Florida, but back in time. . . . The characters are all so believable. . . . Morris is such a visual writer that I could see the story unfold in my mind like a movie as I read it. . . . I can't wait to sell this wonderful novel to all my customers who love fiction."

MARY GAY SHIPLEY, owner, That Bookstore in Blytheville, Blytheville, AR

"*Man in the Blue Moon* is incredible. This novel will appeal to a wide range of readers. I really loved this book!"

KARIN WILSON, owner, Page & Palette, Fairhope, AL

"I loved *Man in the Blue Moon*! Finished it Saturday and have been thinking about it ever since. . . . One of the keys to hand-selling is the story behind the book, and Michael Morris has got a doozy with this one! . . . Make no mistake—his storytelling is original, compelling, and extremely descriptive."

SALLY BREWSTER, owner, Park Road Books, Charlotte, NC

"As a Southern bookseller, we have missed the voice of Michael Morris since *A Place Called Wiregrass* and *Slow Way Home*. *Man in the Blue Moon* is another of those stories from a true Southern writer with a keen sense of a good story."

TOM WARNER, owner, Litchfield Books, Pawleys Island, SC

"If ever there was a perfect book for my book club it would be *Man in the Blue Moon*! It's all about the story for me and this one is pure MAGIC! We have characters that we develop a vested interest in [and] enchanted storytelling at its finest! . . . A real page-turner and one that will keep the home "book reading" fires burning!"

KATHY L. PATRICK, founder of The Pulpwood Queens and Timber Guys Book Clubs

Man in the Blue Moon

MICHAEL MORRIS

Tyndale House Publishers, Inc.
Carol Stream, Illinois

Visit Tyndale online at www.tyndale.com.

Visit Michael Morris online at www.michaelmorrisbooks.com.

TYNDALE and Tyndale's quill logo are registered trademarks of Tyndale House Publishers, Inc.

Man in the Blue Moon

Designed by Stephen Vosloo

Published in association with Laurie Liss of Sterling Lord Literistic, Inc., 65 Bleecker Street, New York, NY 10012.

Man in the Blue Moon is a work of fiction. Where real people, events, establishments, organizations, or locales appear, they are used fictitiously. All other elements of the novel are drawn from the author's imagination.

Library of Congress Cataloging-in-Publication Data

Morris, Michael, date.
  Man in the blue moon / Michael Morris.
    p. cm.
    ISBN 978-1-4143-7330-0 (hc) — ISBN 978-1-4143-6842-9 (sc)
    1. Single mothers—Fiction.   2. Right of property—Fiction.   3. Apalachicola (Fla.)—Fiction.
I. Title.
    PS3613.O775M36 2012
    813'.6—dc23   2012016147

Printed in the United States of America

18   17   16   15   14   13   12
7   6   5   4   3   2   1

Also by Michael Morris

A Place Called Wiregrass
Slow Way Home
Live Like You Were Dying

In memory of Curtis *Papa* Whitfield—

a storyteller's storyteller

1

While world leaders stood on platforms and predicted the end of World War I, Ella Wallace stood behind a cash register in a country store and knew without a doubt that her battle was just beginning.

Through the open door Ella could make out the calico-colored cat she constantly shooed away from the store. It climbed down a cypress tree draped in Spanish moss and was careful not to step into the murky water at the edge of the low-lying lake that gave Dead Lakes, Florida, its name.

The cat then trotted across the dirt road and dashed in front of a wagon loaded with sacks of horse feed. It paused long enough to rub its back against the lowest stair leading into Ella's store. It looked up and turned its head as if it knew Ella was watching.

Chimes shaped like Chinese lanterns hung above the store door. They twisted in the late-May breeze and called out as the cat entered. It arched its back and pawed at a clump of tobacco-stained sawdust on the floor.

Ella didn't take a step toward the cat. She wondered if she could move at all. In all her thirty-five years, she never thought she would wind up on the verge of financial and emotional collapse.

Staring back at her in the glass window etched with the words *Wallace Commissary* was a reflection Ella no longer wanted to acknowledge. Hints of gray were beginning to streak her black hair, and weariness was settling in her blue eyes. Only the full lips that her husband had once called "deliciously pouty" remained of the seventeen-year-old girl who, against her aunt's wishes, had wed Harlan Wallace in the parlor of a circuit judge he'd once beaten in a poker game. Ella had ignored her aunt's warnings at the time, but there was no denying them now. "He's a gambler at best. A con artist at worst," her aunt had said of the handlebar-mustached man who snatched Ella away from her dreams of studying art in France. Ella's aunt had known the French consul back when the country had an office in Apalachicola. Her aunt Katherine had planned the trip to study abroad the same way she orchestrated everything else in Ella's life. Now that dream, like the country itself, was ravaged.

Eighteen years later, here Ella stood, struggling to keep the store she had never wanted from being foreclosed on and trying to support the three sons who were still at home and depended on her.

Ella gripped two letters, one from the Blue Moon Clock Company and another from Gillespie Savings and Loan. Watching the minister's wife, Myer Simpson, finger through a stack of cloth, Ella held the letters flat in her hands like weighted tarot cards. She hoped one would outweigh the other and give her an indication as to which to follow.

Ella could either scrape together enough to make a partial payment on the second mortgage her husband had taken out on their property, or she could gamble on paying the freight charges for a clock her husband must have ordered before he disappeared.

Myer Simpson held up daisy-printed cloth and popped it in the air. Dust danced in the light. Ella used the clock-company envelope to shade her eyes from the early-morning sun that seeped in through the windows. Her thoughts were as scattered as the dust.

With the clock, she stood a chance of selling it and making a profit. The letter didn't say that freight charges for the delivery were covered, only that the clock itself was paid for in full. She hoped if she pulled aside some money to pay the freight, she could sell the clock and use the profit to make a higher payment on the past-due loan. *"You're robbing Peter to pay Paul,"* Ella heard her fearful aunt Katherine call out in her mind. For the past three months, the bank loan had been paid in portions that never equaled the total amount due.

Clive Gillespie, the banker, had made it clear to Ella that she was legally responsible for her husband's bad decisions. "The eyes of the law have no cataracts," Gillespie continuously reminded her before pushing her to sell him the property.

The land that her husband had taken over as his own was the last possession she had left of her father's. His gold watch, the diamond-studded tie clip, and the curls of hair that her father had maintained until death belonged to President Lincoln—they had all been sold, one by one, to cover her husband's debts. The tract of land that sat on the Florida panhandle was thick with pines and cypress. An artesian spring fed a pool of water that local Indians claimed could remedy gout and arthritis. The acreage had been in her family for two generations. Before her parents had died of typhoid fever, her father had given her strict instructions to use the land but never to sell it.

Ella had been only eleven when her father died, but whenever she thought of him, she still felt the grip of his fingers around her wrist as he leaned up on the side of his deathbed. His words were tangled in the bloody mucus that was suffocating him. Ella struggled to turn away but his bony fingers dug deeper into her. "Hold on to your land," he wheezed. "It's your birthright. Don't forget whose you are and where you come from."

But that was long ago. That was before she met Harlan Wallace and accepted his proposal to join their lives and livelihoods together. That was certainly before she had learned through Mr. Gillespie that her husband had taken out a second mortgage on the property. The banker never seemed to believe her when she told him that Harlan had forged her signature.

"How much for this red polka-dotted one?" Myer Simpson held up the cloth with the edge of her fingertip. She eyed Ella through the tops of her glasses. Her pointy nose and collapsed chin always reminded Ella of a hedgehog. "It's got a nick at the bottom," she added.

"Does a nickel sound fair?" Ella asked.

"Three cents sounds fairer."

As she paid for the cloth, Myer Simpson used the newspaper with President Wilson's picture on the front page to fan herself. "You heard about Judge Willughby's son?"

"So sad," Ella said. "So young."

"They tell me he died in the middle of the ocean. In a submarine. Can you imagine? Losing your boy in a contraption like that . . . in the middle of the ocean, no less." With her fingers spread across the face of President Wilson, Mrs. Simpson lifted the edge of her straw hat and fanned her scalp. She paused long enough to point toward the spot on the shelf where bags of sugar had once sat. "When in the world will you get some more sugar?"

"I can't get a straight answer. All I hear is not to sell more than half a pound a week, and I can't even get the first pound."

Myer Simpson frowned and fanned faster. "The way this war is going on, if I ever see sugar again, it will be a miracle. President Wilson keeps talking about peace, but I don't know what this world is coming to. Wars and plagues . . . well, just last week I received a letter from my sister in Kansas. She says hundreds of boys at Fort Riley came down with some sort of flu. Strapping boys dropping dead . . . just like that." Myer Simpson swatted the air with the folded newspaper. "Mark my word, we're living in the end times."

A breeze swept in through the store door, and the chimes called out, soothing the air. Ella welcomed the distraction. She was anxious enough as it was. She didn't need the added burden of dire revelations.

Myer Simpson smiled at Ella in a way that made her feel uncomfortable. It was an expression that Ella took as a show of pity. "We've been missing you at church. Do you think we'll see you this Sunday?"

To avoid Myer Simpson's stare, Ella looked down at the counter.

"Now, Ella, not to pry," Myer said, moving closer, "but you know what Reverend Simpson says: we can be bitter or we can be better."

Ella felt a panicked grip on her chest. Her eyes landed on the Blue Moon Clock logo on the envelope in her hand. It was a cartoonish drawing of a full blue moon shaped like a man's smiling face. "Mrs. Simpson, would you have any need for a clock?"

Myer Simpson recoiled backward. "What? No. Now I'm talking to you about—"

"I have a clock being delivered by steamboat to Apalachicola. It's beautiful," Ella said without knowing anything about the item her husband had ordered. "Handcrafted. Walnut, I believe. I just thought that maybe you'd . . ."

"Where's it coming from?"

Ella flipped the envelope back over and looked at the return address. "Bainbridge, Georgia."

"What use do I have with another clock? I've got a fine clock sitting right on my mantel," Myer Simpson said while placing her purchase in a wicker bag. When she got to the edge of the door next to a barrel of apples, she paused and lifted her finger. "My daughter, Mary Francis, might be interested, though. When you get it, I'll take a look." She stepped outside and then came back, leaning halfway into the store until her drooping bosom brushed against the peeling doorframe. "If it's a grandfather clock, I especially want to see it. I've always wanted one of those."

Ella didn't even bother to put the Closed sign up on the door when she locked it. She snatched the Blue Moon envelope from the counter and yanked off her apron.

On the back porch of the store, Ella tried to step past Narsissa, who was sweeping sawdust into an organized pile. A Creek Indian, Narsissa had shown up at the store with all of her possessions wrapped in a gingham quilt, wanting to work until she had enough money to buy passage to Brazil. Six years later she was still living in a converted smokehouse behind Ella's home. She stopped sweeping and stuck out her boot. "Where are you running off to?"

"I've made up my mind. I'm getting that clock." Ella stepped over Narsissa's boot and walked down the wooden stairs and toward the white clapboard home that was guarded by a sunflower garden. She didn't have to look back to know that Narsissa was shaking her head in disapproval. Her braided hair, as thick as a horse's tail, would be swinging back and forth.

Narsissa had made her opinion known about the mysterious letter last night at supper. "The last thing you need to go and do is upset that bank man. He's told you and told you—he will take this place. He's not playing, either." Ella tried to forget the words of caution. Besides, Narsissa was too cautious for her own good. If she had been of a nature to gamble for something better, she would have left a long time ago for Brazil in search of the husband who supposedly awaited her.

It was just a clock, Ella kept telling herself as she walked through the back door of her home and smelled the turnips that were stewing on the woodstove. If nothing else, she could give it to Mr. Busby, the picture taker, and let him take it on his circuit. He could sell it just like he had all her father's other possessions, and she could split the money with him again.

Ella reached for a log that was stacked atop a pile in the corner, and a lizard ran out. She snatched it up by the tail and jerked open the screen door. As she threw the lizard outside, Ella was sideswiped by the fear that she, too, would be tossed out of her home. She pictured the fear that had become a constant tormentor as a black mushroom clamped to the side of her brain, a deformity of sorts that she had begun to accept as her lot in life. She put another log in the stove and poked at the embers extra hard, causing sparks to fly out. She never paused to realize that before Harlan's afflictions, the idea of catching a lizard by the tail would have caused her to shiver.

"Samuel . . . Samuel, are you here?" Ella could smell the salve from the hallway. She followed the scent to her youngest son, Macon. He was propped up on the bed, his throat swollen and blisters the size of quarters covering the outside of his lips. Sweat lined Macon's forehead, and when he turned to look at Ella, his cheeks seemed gaunter than they had the day before.

"Did he eat anything?" Ella asked her other son, Keaton. Then, not wanting Macon to think that she thought he was invisible, she turned to him and wiped his brow with the rag that was in the basin next to the bed. "Baby, did you manage to eat any breakfast?"

Both boys shook their heads at the same time. There were seven years between them, yet Macon looked more like he was three instead of six. The virus that wouldn't let go had caused him to seemingly shrink until there were nights when Ella dreamed that she walked into his room and found nothing more than a son the size of an acorn.

In desperation, Ella had even used some of the mortgage money to hire an internist from Panama City to make a house visit. The doctor had arrived with a medical bag made of cowhide. When he set the bag on the edge of the bed, Ella noticed that it was ripped in the corner, revealing discolored cardboard. The doctor spread his tools across the nightstand next to Macon's bed and anointed Ella's oldest son, Samuel, his assistant. "I take it you're the man around the place now that your daddy has run off from the henhouse," the doctor said without looking at Ella. Samuel rubbed the sparse goatee that he was trying to grow on his sixteen-year-old chin and nodded.

When Keaton stepped forward to get a closer look at the scratched silver tools on the nightstand, Samuel jerked his brother away and shoved him back toward the spot where Ella stood at the bedroom door. While the doctor prodded and poked Macon, he rambled on about a weakened constitution caused from parasites.

"You know how boys this age can be. He'll eat the dirt and anything that's in it," the doctor had said. "A virus in the chicken pox family," he declared. "He's still puny because the illness is aggravated by his asthma. He'll be back to running around in no time." Ella followed the doctor's instructions to the letter, preparing coffee so thick that it looked like mud. She mixed in the powder that the man had magically pulled from his bag. Macon gagged and vomited when she fed it to him. By the fifth day, she had heeded Macon's plea to stop making him sicker.

"Well," Ella said as she sat on the side of Macon's bed. "What if I get you some candy? Not that cheap candy from our store . . . genuine salt water taffy from the dock." She watched her ailing son's eyes light up. He loved the taffy that came straight from the boats that docked in the bay at Apalachicola. Back when times were better, he'd gone with his father to town every chance he had.

"We're going to town today?" Keaton, the middle son, asked. There was a stitch of hair above his lip. It was a constant reminder to Ella that he was a boy trapped inside a body that was becoming a man.

"I've decided to go ahead and pick up that shipment from the clock company."

Keaton jumped up from the wooden chair and shuffled his feet in a playful way that made Macon laugh and then grimace in pain. Before Ella could touch Macon's forehead again, her youngest son sighed, expressing the frustration they all felt toward the illness that not even Narsissa with her herbs and chants could eradicate.

"Where has Samuel run off to now?" Ella asked. Since the day the doctor had prescribed him the role of head of the household, Samuel had taken the responsibility with a seriousness that at first made Ella proud. Now his arrogance was irritating. It was, she realized, the same overconfidence that had first attracted her to his father.

"Samuel is still out squirrel hunting," Keaton said. His eyes were green like her father's had been. Of the three boys, Keaton was the one who felt most like hers, seemingly untainted by the troubled blood of her husband.

"Please get him. Ask him to hitch the wagon. And ask Narsissa to come inside. She can stay with Macon until we get back from town."

Inside her bedroom, Ella looked into the spider-veined mirror above her dresser. Pulling her hair into a twist against the nape of her neck, she snatched out a gray strand. She put on the earrings Narsissa had made for her out of baby mockingbird feathers and oyster shells. Fingering the dangling earrings, she felt that by wearing them she somehow paid homage to the young woman she used to be. That young woman, who had been sent to attend finishing school in Apalachicola by the aunt with dreams, had become nothing more than a mist that sprinkled her memories. For some odd reason, Ella could still recite bits and pieces of a poem from English class. A verse about the eyes being the mirror to the soul. Pulling back the skin around her forehead and causing the wrinkles to momentarily disappear, Ella studied her eyes. There was dullness now that resembled the marbles her sons played with in the dirt. She snatched up a doily that her aunt had knit years ago and flung it over the mirror.

After she had dressed in the last gift her husband had given her, a dropped-waist lilac-colored dress shipped from Atlanta, Ella kissed Macon on the forehead and tried not to look at the open sores lining his swollen lips. Narsissa sat in the chair next to the bed. She had brought the butter churn inside and with a steady rhythm pumped the wooden handle.

As Ella rose up from kissing her son, loose ends of Narsissa's hair tickled her arm. Narsissa leaned close and whispered in that graveled voice that always made Ella think she was part man, "Don't pay that steamboat company one cent until you see what you are getting because—"

"Narsissa, please don't." Ella pulled away and straightened the top of her dress. "Don't patronize. Not today."

Narsissa leaned back in the chair and made a mulish huffing sound. She flung her coarse braid and continued churning the butter.

"When I come back, I'll have that taffy for you, and a surprise," Ella told Macon. "I'll have a surprise waiting."

Macon tried to smile, but his chin quivered. Kissing her finger, Ella pointed at her son and then kissed it once more and pointed at Narsissa, who pretended not to notice.

Outside, Samuel was squinting as he jerked the halter on the draft mule and led the wagon closer to the back of the store. Ella saw her oldest son watching her, studying her through the gaps in the tall sunflowers she had planted years ago for beauty as much as for a border between their family life and the life meant for income.

"Mama, can I go to the picture show?" Keaton asked as he climbed into the back of the wagon.

"We'll see."

Samuel climbed up on the wagon, and Ella felt his leg brush against hers. At least he didn't pull away. Keaton leaned in from behind and jabbed Samuel. "Clayton Carson says there's one playing about a preacher . . . I mean a priest. See, he protects these people over there in the war. The people over in France. He protects them from the Germans."

Samuel shrugged Keaton away. "We won't have time to go to no picture. We need to just get this package that we're probably paying too much money for and get back to the store."

"You're beginning to sound as crotchety as Narsissa," Ella said.

"As it is, we're missing out on the busiest time of the day." Samuel popped the reins, and the mule bobbed his head.

"Need I remind you, the letter said that the package was paid in full? If we have to pay the freight, so be it," Ella said, trying to convince herself as much as Samuel. "And another thing . . . we work at that store six days a week from sunup to sundown. It won't kill anybody to have an afternoon off."

"*The Cross Bearer*—that's the name of the picture. *The Cross Bearer*," Keaton said.

The rocking motion of the wagon seemed to pacify everyone but Ella. She kept toying at her wedding ring, flicking it around her finger until it threatened to rub the skin raw. Her thoughts and fears alternated back and forth between her son's disease and her husband's desertion. No one spoke for the remainder of the thirty-five-minute ride to Apalachicola.

Along the way they passed the few buildings that made up the Dead Lakes community. A church with a weathered cemetery and a schoolhouse that rested on cinder blocks marked the official spot where Dead Lakes was noted on the Florida map. The store, like Ella herself, was distant from the center of the village. Ella enjoyed the wide porch that swept around the side of her clapboard house and the acreage of timber that obstructed her view from neighbors on either side. There were the occasional visitors to the aquifer spring that the Creek Indians vowed had healing properties. Sometimes during summer evenings when Ella sat on the porch rocking in the chair that Harlan had ordered for her special from North Carolina, she could hear muffled voices and splashing water from the hidden pool. Even Harlan had heeded Narsissa's warning that calamity would fall on his family if he barred access to those he deemed superstitious fools.

Although Ella had privacy on either side of her, the front of her house was clearly visible to the neighbors who lived across the road. When times were good and her worries fewer, Ella used to pity her neighbors for their lack of privacy. Their houses were built so close to one another that Mrs. Pomeroy, the doughy-cheeked woman who lived with her middle-aged husband in the house with the red door, routinely came into the store complaining about the eavesdropping Myer Simpson, who lived with the reverend in the parsonage next door.

When the wagon passed the gray-shingled house that belonged to the woman who had once been Ella's confidante at finishing school, the mule bowed his head and chewed harder at the bit. Neva Clarkson was now the teacher in Dead Lakes. Washtubs filled with pansies covered the front lawn. Neva had been Ella's best friend until Harlan redirected his affections from Neva to Ella. Behind her back, the townspeople called Neva a certified old maid. There was a time when Ella had felt sorry for Neva. Now she envied her. A chill snaked down Ella's system and settled so deep that not even the spring sun could thaw it.

They made their way around the low-lying lakes and cypress trees draped in Spanish moss and headed toward the red clay fields, plowed and ready for planting. An island of trees and kudzu sat in the middle of the beekeeper's farm. Ella shaded her eyes and looked out at the land, wondering if Harlan had taken refuge in a place like this and was weaning himself off the opium. Maybe he had been hired on as a laborer at such a property and would come to his right mind when the poison cleared his system.

Harlan might have surrendered himself to the powdered substance, but Ella had not. Her emotions tilted back and forth between anger, despondency, and love for her husband. The only thing she knew for certain was that a part of her felt sorted through and broken, just like the field they passed.

The mule's hooves kept an uneven pace against the clay-dirt road. The wagon rocked and chains rattled. A hush settled over Ella and her sons.

Ella clasped her hands and pictured her husband passed out on a red velvet sofa stained with human liquids in one of the Chicago opium dens she read about in the newspaper.

Keaton leaned against the backboard of the wagon and pictured a dramatic priest pulling a sword from beneath his robe and defending people in a land unknown to him before the war.

Samuel gripped the reins tighter and pictured their store windows covered with plywood, a foreclosure notice dangling from the front door.

But none of them could fully picture the box with the logo of the Blue Moon Clock Company that awaited them or the ways in which opening that crate would forever change the direction of their lives.

2

As they approached Apalachicola, the county seat, salt air tickled Ella's senses and caused her to canonize the past, the same way it did every time she came upon the white pine Episcopal church at the edge of the city limits. Tucked alongside a bay on the Florida panhandle, the town marked the spot where the Apalachicola River emptied into the Gulf of Mexico. One of the largest export centers of cotton before the Civil War, the city of two thousand now drowsed in a state of neither sleep nor vigor. Empty lots tangled in overgrown weeds, sandspurs, and vines were lingering imprints of a fire that had ravaged the city eighteen years before. The cavities competed with the surviving Georgian structures that still beckoned for the days when the French government housed a consulate in a brick building overlooking a saw-grass island in the bay. Wide streets edged the bay where pieces of cotton once sprinkled the banks like fresh snow. Now there were only four warehouses that guarded the waters. They stood like oversized mausoleums with sun-bleached walls bearing the faintest of letters that spelled out the names of cotton brokers from long ago. Oyster shells piled high as sand dunes filled the vacant spaces.

Women of color, dressed all in white, sat on the porches of the Victorian homes the wagon passed. The women fanned, gossiped, and guarded the children in their hired care. A trio of white men in black bowler hats glided across the sidewalk in front of the J.E. Grady hardware store.

Ella took it all in and longed for the days when she lived in the dormitory at Miss Wayne's School for Women. An automobile blared its horn, and she flinched. Ella turned and watched as the car rattled and then gained traction past their wagon. At the corner, massive oak trees lined the park where she had first met her husband at a town dance. Harlan's black mustache had glimmered underneath the gas lanterns that hung from bamboo poles that night.

Two weeks after the dance, Ella became intoxicated by Harlan's ability to fan money across the table to pay for oysters and French champagne. Childhood promises made to her father and the cautions of Aunt Katherine, the spinster who had raised her, became nothing more than nuisances that competed with her infatuation. Before she knew it, she had caused her aunt to take to the sickbed when she decided to marry Harlan and cancel her plans to attend art school.

Two children later, she was living in a home next to a store that she was forced to manage. By the time there was a third son to care for, Harlan had shaved his mustache and was sipping whiskey, first only at night and then every morning, to help soothe the back pain caused when a filly he had tried to break threw him against the side of a fence.

Harlan knocked the drinking problem and the back pain thanks to a doctor's suggestion that he take opium. "Miracle worker," he declared, and gave the doctor a gold-tipped walking stick. Within three weeks, Harlan began ordering mass quantities of the miracle drug, and within four months he no longer pretended to function. He sat shirtless on the steps of the store, spat tobacco at the cat, and watched the crossroads community of Dead Lakes, Florida, pass him by. Then, a month before Easter, when the air was still cool, he slipped away with the fog of early dawn. If not for his debts and the sons he left behind, a visitor would never have guessed that he had ever really existed.

When their wagon passed the brick building with the words *Gillespie Savings and Loan* above the archway, Ella felt a knot tie her stomach. She wondered how many times she had passed the brick building as a young girl in town, never once guessing that one day she would be groveling for her future with a man who pasted thinning hair to his scalp.

"Mama, can we get cherry lemonades?" Keaton asked as Samuel tied the wagon to the post in front of the drugstore. A little girl in a pink linen dress stood on the sidewalk and looked up at them before a woman put her arm around the little girl and shepherded her away.

"We're broke. Flat broke," Samuel said between locked teeth. "What is it about that that you don't understand, Keaton?"

Ella pulled Samuel away from Keaton and handed the younger boy two coins.

"Mama," Samuel protested.

"There's money enough for you, too," Ella said. "I'll be in to get you directly."

Samuel stood in the doorway of the pharmacy and looked at Ella and then at the savings and loan building across the street. A man wearing suspenders with one brace broken and dangling at his protruding belly shuffled around him and slipped inside the pharmacy. Ella waved to her son, turned her back so he couldn't see the anxiety she knew she wore on her face, and walked across the street. Unlike her husband, she never had a poker face.

Clive Gillespie was leaning against the marble counter of the teller station when Ella walked into his bank. A white-and-red framed print with a sketch of a freckle-faced boy holding a dollar hung on the wall behind the teller: *Raise Your Children Right. Teach Your Son to Save.* Clive glanced her way before finishing with the teller.

Never formally acknowledging Ella, he motioned for her to follow him inside an office with a frosted glass door. Blades from a wicker ceiling fan sliced the thick air. The edges of a newspaper on his desk lifted with the breeze.

He tossed a pad onto his desk. "Ella, have you come to your senses and banished that deadbeat husband's mistakes by letting me buy your land?"

"Good afternoon to you too, Mr. Gillespie."

"Good afternoon." Clive sighed and massaged his chin. Scars from youthful acne still lined his middle-aged face. "I hate that we've come to this. I really hate it."

"*Hate* is such a strong word."

He fingered the handle of the adding machine that sat on his desk. "I'm sure you didn't travel all this way to town just to talk semantics with me."

Ella pulled an envelope from her purse and slid it across his desk. "I was hoping to leave this out front with the teller. But there you were, and so . . ."

He flipped open the envelope and smiled at her in a way that made her shift her weight in the chair. "Ella . . ."

"See, I have this delivery I'm picking up today, and when I sell it I will . . ."

He sighed again but in a way that caused Ella to think that maybe he really did have sympathy for her cause. "This is not even a quarter of the month's payment."

"It's coming. Really. Summer is right around the corner, and there will be a crop."

"If I recall, the crop last summer was supposed to come in too, but it didn't. And if I'm not mistaken, that's when your husband lost his automobile."

Ella leaned forward and touched the edge of Clive's polished desk. "That was . . ." She fingered the desk like she might have been inspecting it for dust and then leaned back against the chair.

No matter how challenging life with Harlan might have been, Ella never talked about her marital troubles in public. It was not becoming.

Clive sighed once more. When he shifted his weight, the springs in his chair creaked. "We both know who got you into this mess, precious. Now I want to help you, but I'm beginning to get offended. You don't seem to want my help."

"That land is all I have left of my daddy . . . all I have that is outright mine. I want to exhaust all possibilities before—"

"I applaud your persistence. Really, I do." Clive picked up an unlit cigar and ran the tip across his pouting lips.

Ella wondered if he was making fun of her. Her racing heart kept beat with the clicking sounds of the adding machines out in the lobby.

"Ella, precious Ella . . . nostalgia is fine and good as long as there's money to back it up."

Ella glanced around the room and settled her eyes on an amber-colored water pitcher near the corner of his desk. Clive Gillespie picked up the newspaper and gestured with it toward the pitcher. The middle section containing the society page cascaded to the floor.

"Look at these," Clive said, holding up the front page. "This entire column is filled with foreclosures I've had to make. Do you see these? Now, I have been patient with you. I've been more than patient. Under your circumstances, I know how hard this must be."

"I have a clock coming."

"Excuse me?"

"There's a clock . . . a grandfather clock that I'm picking up at the dock today. It's paid for and everything. I can sell it and give you the rest of the month's payment."

Clive laughed and Ella's desperation turned into a flash of anger. "Please don't make this personal, Clive."

"Beg your pardon?"

"No one made you take Harlan up on that bet, you know. No one put a gun to your head. Please don't take your vengeance out on me."

It was the first time Ella had acknowledged what everyone in town knew and whispered about behind Clive's back. Harlan had lost ten acres of the land that Ella's father had left for her, and then, in showman style, he won it back for all the town to see. The first time Harlan lost the land to Clive was at the Mardi Gras horse race while holding a Mason jar filled up to the ring with bourbon and molasses. Never acknowledging that the land was his wife's inheritance, Harlan had signed the deed over to Clive against the stirrup of a sweat-stained horse saddle. Harlan's silver tie, blemished from one too many mint julep spills, was twisted to the side as he walked into the house that afternoon. He never slurred in delivering the news. He shared the misfortune in a matter-of-fact style, the same way he might if a shipment of insured merchandise had been lost with a sinking steamboat. Ella had stood at the doorway of the kitchen and then leaned against the wooden frame, still gripping the knife she had used to cut collard greens. For the first time that day, the pungent smell of the collards simmering on the stove made her want to vomit. But all she could do was stare at the stains of liquor on Harlan's tie and watch as he tore it from his neck in one yank.

Months later, when Harlan mentioned to her that there would be a poker tournament on a steamboat docked at Apalachicola and that he would be spending the night in the port city, Ella folded his undergarments and placed them in the leather overnight bag. "Will Clive Gillespie be playing?" she asked.

Harlan never stopped shining his shoes from where he sat on the corner of their bed. "I imagine," he said.

Ella stared into the insides of the bag that smelled of damp socks. "I'm not begging you, Harlan. I'm entrusting you. Entrusting you to stay sober long enough to get my daddy's land back. That is the one thing I ask." The land taken from her might be nothing but swamp with a spring that bubbled eternally at the surface, but it was hers alone to lose. In the end, when the last hand was dealt, Clive had to publicly sign the deed back over to Harlan on the torn green velvet that covered the steamboat poker table. Everyone said it was the repetitive public humiliation that hurt Clive the most. Once again Clive had lost to the charismatic man who first beat him all those years before when he stole Ella's schoolgirl affections.

In his office, Clive leaned forward and rotated his head in a way that made Ella think of a reptile. He bit the cigar, spat the end to the floor, and laughed. "Do you really think I'd put so much energy into a piece of swampland for the sake of revenge? Ella . . . precious . . . you're much brighter than that. It's business. Pure and simple. Now if I let you pass, I'll have to let all the others out of their debts too. And my shareholders wouldn't be too pleased with me, now would they?"

"All I know is that shame has a way of festering."

"Now let's get something straight, Ella Wallace. You're one of many . . . just an account with numbers."

Ella got up from the chair and pulled her shoulders back the way she had learned to do all those years before at Miss Wayne's school. Her back was turned to Clive Gillespie when he said the words that caused her to grip the door handle tighter.

"You know, when my father started this bank, your aunt was one of his best customers. Lord rest her soul. Miss Katherine was a good woman. A measured woman. And man alive, was she ever proud of you." Clive tapped a pen against his desk. "If I had a half-dollar for every time she told me what a gifted young lady you were . . ." Clive's words became a chuckle. "And what I'm sitting here trying to figure out is, what exactly happened to that young lady with so much potential?"

Ella opened the door. Her voice cracked, but she said the words loud enough for the tellers out front to hear. "You'll get your money, mark my word."

Outside on the sidewalk, Ella leaned against the brick wall of the bank and struggled to catch her breath. Across the way stood Miss Wayne's school, the cold stone building where Ella had been polished into a lady. Shuffling through the people on the sidewalk, Ella cursed Harlan Wallace and Clive Gillespie all in the same breath.

At the drugstore she found her sons sitting on the burgundy stools by the soda fountain. Ella stood in the doorway watching them and refused to hurry them along. There was something about the way they both held their glasses and the way Samuel licked the rim of the glass that comforted her. They were still boys. When Keaton dropped his napkin on the black-and-white tiled floor and bent down to retrieve it, he saw her. "Are you about ready to pick up our surprise?" she asked.

Along the dock where the river met the sea, shrimp boats with tall skinny masts competed for space with steamboats. Black smoke drifted from the steam engines and created a haze over the workers who moved through an obstacle course of fish, blocks of ice, and crates stamped with the names of exotic ports of call. Boys the size of men gathered nets, and old, weathered sailors cussed them for not moving faster. The smell of rotting fish and urine caused Ella to cover her mouth, but then, fearing she might seem vulnerable, she quickly pulled her hand away.

The blue moon-shaped logo with the face of a smiling man was stamped on a seven-foot-tall crate. It sat in a warehouse that still had faded, peeling letters that read *Bailey's Cotton Exchange* on the brick wall. A cast-iron cage separated the shipping clerks from the chaos of the dock.

A clerk with a crooked nose and wiry eyebrows flipped through a stack of receipts. "Parcel paid."

His monotone words caused Ella to breathe deeper than she had all day. She loosened the grip on her purse and lowered it to her side. The money she had held back to pay for shipping was still hers for now. She turned and smiled at Samuel, who darted his eyes away from her. Keaton nodded and said, "Paid for. Told you so." Ella hushed him and signed the papers releasing the delivery to her care.

The words *Blue Moon Clock Company* ran down the side of the crate along with the crudely written instruction in red chalk, *This Side Up*.

During the drive home, Keaton continued to run his finger down the side of the box. "I told y'all it was a grandfather clock. Didn't I?" he kept saying.

The sun was sinking lower when they passed the swamp where the cypress trees loomed like giants wearing moss for armor. Ella felt chilled and rubbed her shoulders. Samuel pulled off his jacket with one hand and held the reins with the other. Without ever taking his eyes from the road, he balanced the jacket on Ella's shoulders. She studied him and the way his chin was beginning to take the square shape of his father's. "Thank you," she whispered. She offered the words as much for his thoughtful gesture as for the times past when he had defended her against her husband's tirades.

Narsissa met them as they turned the bend at the farm. She stood on the porch with a broom propped against the side of her hip. "How much did it cost?" she yelled out.

"Not a cent!" Ella shouted and laughed when Narsissa jolted backward in surprise.

The box was heavy enough to require all four of them to unload it. While Samuel used a crowbar to pry the box open, Ella stood over it like it was a birthday cake and wished for a walnut clock. Mrs. Simpson's dining room table was walnut, and Ella knew a matching clock would be an easier sale.

"Hurry up," Keaton said, licking his lips and dancing a jig.

"Give him time," Ella said. "I do not want it nicked."

"This thing stinks to high heaven," Narsissa said, covering her mouth and moving closer.

Samuel swung the crowbar with the purpose of a full-grown man. Pieces of jagged wood flew from the box and landed at Narsissa's feet. She leaned closer, peering into the part of the box that was exposed.

A man's muddy boot kicked out from the end of the box. Narsissa screamed and ran toward the house. Samuel stumbled backward, rebounding with the crowbar held over his head. Keaton ran and hid behind the mule that darted to the side and kicked at the dirt. But Ella was frozen. If she still had been the girl from Miss Wayne's school, she probably would have fainted.

"Don't be scared," the man said, waving the end of his boot. He held up his hand through the ripped opening and attempted to wave. He finished what Samuel had begun and pulled the broken wood back until he could climb out. His blond, curly hair was slicked with sweat against the nape of his neck. Green eyes shone from his dirty face. A cocktail of waste and perspiration glued his clothes to his skin. He groaned as he rose up from the box. "I'm the one your daddy is waiting for."

Narsissa ran out of the house carrying a double-barreled shotgun. The man stumbled over the box, landed on one knee, and held up a crumpled paper like a shield. "Don't! Please don't shoot," he said. "I'm the man from the letter. I'm the man from the Blue Moon."

3

It wasn't until the man handed Ella a copy of the letter that had been sent to her husband that Narsissa finally put down the shot-gun. The date on the letter was February 28, a week before Harlan Wallace left his family.

"Harlan's daddy was my mama's first cousin," the man kept repeating as he marched his legs up and down, trying to wake the muscles that had become locked from the tight confines of the crate. He kept his hand held high as a sign of surrender.

"We don't want trouble," Ella said as she took the letter. "We don't need trouble," she kept saying as she read the words.

"I promise I'm not bringing trouble," the man said and offered a second letter. "This right here is from the sheriff in Bainbridge, Georgia."

As Ella reached for the second letter, she tried to push down the crowbar that Samuel kept held over his shoulder. Samuel ignored her instruction.

While Ella scanned the notarized letter vouching for the character of the man who stood before her, she asked without looking up, "That letter was from a clock company. We expected a clock. If you're so upstanding, then why did you arrive here like this . . . in this crate? Nothing good comes from secrecy."

"I'm a victim of circumstance," the man said. He used the inside of his elbow to wipe the side of his head. A cluster of curls broke free from the grime in his hair.

"Ummm. Victim of circumstance," Narsissa mumbled.

The man's green eyes darted from Ella to Narsissa and back to Ella. "My friend who knows the truth helped me. He got the stationery from the clock company. He mailed that letter to this store . . . mailed it directly to Harlan. My friend even got me shipped out on the steamboat."

"I don't like this," Ella said. "I don't like this one bit."

"Look, now, I'm speaking the truth. My wife took her own life. Her family never did see it that way, though." He raised his hand higher, begging more than surrendering. "You got to believe me. They're out to get me."

"That's it," Ella said and handed the papers back. "I've heard enough. I want you to leave."

Samuel leveraged the crowbar higher above his head, and this time Ella didn't try to stop him.

The man shuffled the letters in his hands and stammered, "Now ma'am, I settled all this with your husband. Like I told you, Harlan is my cousin. He knows all about me. If you just go get him, then—"

"We don't know where he is," Keaton said from behind the mule.

Ella stomped her foot, and the mule moved to the side, exposing Keaton. "Hush," Ella said.

"What you mean?"

Samuel stepped closer with the crowbar. "Ain't none of your business."

Standing behind Samuel, Narsissa roped her thick hands around the crowbar and fought to pull it out of Samuel's hands. She tossed the bar to the ground. "Watch yourself," Narsissa whispered as the crowbar landed on pieces of broken oyster shells.

"My husband is not here. That's all you need to know, Mr. . . . whoever you claim to be," Ella said.

"Lanier Stillis," he said. The man ran his hands through his chin-length hair, and more curls broke free. He pulled on a left ear that was disfigured and jagged in shape. "I'm not bucking your suspicions. I reckon I'd be suspicious too, but I am not lying to you. I am kin to Harlan." His words seemed to plead more than state the fact. "Harlan gave the all clear for me to come down here. Just think about it this way: if he didn't know about all of this, then would I be crazy enough to go to such lengths?"

"Like being packed like a rag doll in a box ain't crazy enough," Narsissa hissed.

As Ella and the others darted their eyes away from the visitor, Keaton stepped closer. He was fingering a rip in the sleeve of his shirt. "If you are kin to us, then what was my daddy's mama's maiden name?"

Lanier looked up at the trees. A flock of chimney swifts darted down to the oyster shells that were scattered along the side of the store. "Keaton," Lanier said. "Her name was Keaton. She grew up in Tempest, Georgia, up in the mountains . . . just like your daddy and me. Your daddy left home when he was fifteen to jockey racehorses in Kentucky. The last I'd heard from him, he'd polished himself up and come to Apalachicola to run a horse track so that all the rich people making their way to New Orleans would stop off and make bets on the evening races. That's just how he told it."

Ella tried not to let the man see her flinch. Harlan Wallace had indeed owned a racetrack when she met him. It was only after she had signed a marriage license that he lost it to the steamboat owner who had helped finance the venture.

Keaton looked up at Ella and then back at Lanier. "Do you know where our daddy might be?"

"Keaton, enough," Ella said.

"No, son," Lanier answered. "Believe me, right about now I wish I did know."

"Well, if all this is like you say, then how long was you planning on being here?" Narsissa asked the question like she already knew the answer.

"Probably not as long as you've been here." Lanier's answer caused Narsissa to take a step toward the crowbar. "My cousin told me that there was a Creek woman on the place. Said something about her planning to go to Brazil but never seemed to get there." Lanier locked eyes with Narsissa and raised an eyebrow. "He said folks around here wouldn't think anything about one more showing up to work in the store for extra money."

"She's been here six years," Ella said. "You've been here six minutes. Narsissa's more family to me than the filthy man I'm standing here looking at."

"I think it best if you keep on heading to New Orleans," Samuel said.

Lanier tried to brush the dirt from his hands. Flakes of dead, soiled skin fell to the ground. "I don't mean no harm. I just . . . I just need . . ."

"You just need to leave," Ella said.

The man looked down and kicked at the box he had arrived in. The steady thumping noise rose up like a drum beat, and Ella suddenly realized that they were all exposed, out in the open.

"Would it be too much to ask to let me stay the night?"

"Yes," Narsissa answered.

"Just until I can get a ticket to New Orleans?" Lanier reached inside his boot and pulled out a wad of money secured with a silver clip. The silver shone brightly against the dingy color of his clothes. "I've got money to pay you."

Ella stopped short from saying that her home was not an inn. The mule stomped the dirt again and looked over at the barn where his hay awaited him. Lanier followed the mule's gaze and pointed in the direction of the barn. "I don't mind sharing a stall with a jackass. I've slept with worse."

Keaton laughed. Ella wrinkled her brow and shot her son a look of disapproval. Over Keaton's shoulder Ella saw Myer Simpson and her husband, Reverend Simpson, rounding the corner of the store.

Myer Simpson clutched a rose-printed parasol with one hand and her husband's arm with the other. The reverend's stomach poked out over his belt. The end of his wrinkled shirt protruded from his pants. He pulled away from his wife long enough to fan away gnats.

"Well, there you are," Myer Simpson said. "I told Reverend Simpson, I said, Reverend, let's take our afternoon exercise over to Mrs. Wallace's store and have the first peek at that clock."

Ella walked toward them and pulled the edge of her dress out like she might curtsey. She hoped without reason that she could pull the dress out far enough to hide the man who had arrived in place of the grandfather clock.

"As soon as she saw the wagon turn the bend in the road, she has spoken of nothing else. I told her, woman, let's get on with it and see that clock." The reverend stopped swatting when he noticed Lanier.

"I have already moved my parlor furniture, marking the spot where that grandfather clock will go," Myer Simpson said. She twirled the parasol and giggled until her bosom shook. "But of course if it's not a grandfather clock, then our daughter . . ." Her voice faded as she looked at Lanier. "Oh."

"The clock," Ella said in a singsong fashion, hoping to make them think she was cheerful. "That clock . . . that clock. It was so gashed up that I just refused. I flat refused to pay for that clock. I refused right then and there on that dock."

"I see you have company." Myer Simpson raised the handle of her parasol and pointed it at Lanier.

Lanier stuffed the letters assuring good character inside his pants. He nodded and bit the edge of his lip.

"That's . . . ," Ella said. "He's . . . he's a worker who has come to help us out."

"I didn't realize business was so brisk," the reverend said.

"From the looks of him, you've been working him but good," Myer Simpson added.

"He's here to get the crop going again. He's just here to help out. So . . ." Ella's voice trailed off. The chimney swifts dipped down toward them and then darted back to the trees.

"Mrs. Simpson, now you have me out here to take exercise," the reverend said. "If we don't get back to our walk, I'm afraid I might sit down on Mrs. Wallace's wagon, and you won't be able to budge me."

The reverend took a step forward, but Myer Simpson continued to stare at Lanier. She stumbled a bit before letting the reverend lead her away. "Good evening," the reverend said as they continued their walk.

"Evening," everyone said, even Lanier. But Myer Simpson didn't say a word. She just clutched the arm of her husband and turned her head ever so slightly, examining the man who looked like he had been dipped in dirt.

It was only when the reverend and his wife had walked past the magnolia tree that stood between the store and the main road that Ella let go of her dress. She felt her boys, Narsissa, and this so-called relative staring at her, pinning her into making a decision. If only Myer Simpson had never come into the store. If only Ella had never mentioned the clock. "You can stay one night in the barn," Ella said without turning around to face them. "And not one hour more."

Lanier unfurled a couple of bills from his money clip and looked at everyone before handing the money to Samuel.

As Narsissa walked back into the house to check on Macon, she passed Ella and mumbled, "This is trouble. Mark my word."

Ella closed her eyes, felt her pulse race against the side of her neck, and once again fought the fear that had tried all day to overtake her.

After the supper dishes had been dried, Keaton stood behind the living room curtains and looked out toward the barn. He strained to see the movements of the visitor, whose silhouette flitted back and forth beneath the gas lantern that hung on the barn door.

"Get away from there," his mother said and pulled Keaton back from the window. "Now quit studying that man. Go get ready for bed."

But Keaton ignored his mother's instructions. Instead of following Samuel into the bedroom, he darted to the side hall and eased out the back door. He used the tip of his boot to lift the bottom of the door and keep it from squeaking against the floor.

Outside, Keaton followed the swaying yellow light of the lantern. The flickering light stretched out from the barn like fingers, waving him closer.

Keaton peeked around the doorframe of the barn and watched the man.

Lanier was washing his dirty clothes in a barrel that had once been used to water the horse that had long been sold. He had already changed into the clothes he had brought with him in a tote bag made from speckled hog skin. His hair, still wet from a bath, hung in loose blond curls. He wrung out the remaining water from his shirt. When Lanier looked up, Keaton tried to dart behind the door.

"Evening," Lanier yelled.

Keaton stepped forward and brushed the end of his nose, striking the beginning of a mustache. "I was just . . . just making sure that you knew the boat to New Orleans leaves at two tomorrow."

The mule, in the stall next to Lanier, kicked the stall door. Lanier snapped the shirt again and put it on a stack of fence posts. "Appreciate it."

Keaton turned to leave but stopped. "And I . . . I just wanted to see how you were making it?"

"Doing better than I was when I was folded up in that box."

Keaton looked at the broken top of the Blue Moon Clock crate that had held Lanier. "How long were you in that thing?"

Lanier hooked his thumbs inside his pants and glanced up at a cobweb that dangled from the crossbeam in the barn. "About ten hours, give or take."

"You scared?"

Lanier slung his head sideways and drips of water scattered from his hair. A strand of hair clung to the top portion of his left ear that was mangled and partly missing. "I'm done through being scared."

Cautiously flicking a piece of splintered wood on the crate, Keaton turned his head and studied Lanier. "If you ain't done nothing wrong, then why did you hide in this box? Do you need you a lawyer?"

"I'm done through with lawyers, too." Lanier looked at Keaton, and for the first time he smiled. "And let me tell you, son, innocence and justice sometimes don't go hand in hand."

Keaton jerked a portion of wood from the crate and then bent down and stuck his head inside. "Looks to me like you'd suffocate in this thing."

"Way back when people were slaves, some of 'em got free. Their friends shipped them up north like cargo. You ever heard of the Underground Railroad?"

Keaton tossed the sliver of wood to the ground, where it landed inches from the tip of Lanier's boot. "How come you know all that? You're not that old."

Lanier laughed for the first time since being nailed into the crate. "No, I ain't that old." He reached into his bag and pulled out two books, one made of black leather that was frayed at the corner and another with an orange cover. He dusted the orange one off and placed it on top of a hay bale. "I just like to read. How 'bout you?"

The mule grunted and rubbed his back against the boards that separated him from Lanier. Keaton picked up a rusted pitchfork that was turned sideways on the ground. He scooped up hay from a pile in the corner and tossed it in the mule's stall. "When's the last time you saw my daddy?"

With his head dangling sideways and water dripping to the sand, Lanier didn't bother to look up at Keaton. "You sure do ask a lot of questions."

Keaton kicked at the sand until it covered the wet stains that Lanier had left on the ground. He decided against asking Lanier how he ended up with a left ear that was shaped like a cauliflower that had been cut in half. "I was just wondering . . . how long it's been since you've seen him."

Lanier smoothed out the wrinkles on his shirt. "I'm figuring it was twenty years ago." Lanier stopped and looked back up at the cobweb. "Yeah, twenty. I was about ten or some'rs around there. But when I got into . . . well, when trouble started brewing for me, I sent him some letters. We corresponded, you might say."

"What was he like . . . you know, back then?"

Lanier stopped working on the clothes, shook his head, and laughed again. "Your daddy had just gotten back from riding the horse of a rich man from Atlanta. He'd placed in some big horse race, not the Derby but some big one. All us kids crowded around him, even the grown folks. He was carrying on like some banty rooster."

"Back before he started . . . well, we used to have horses," Keaton said. "And cows, too. This one time . . . this one time I was riding out with Daddy, and we were rounding up the cows to worm 'em. Daddy saw this big ole rattler way off in the field. The thing was eight feet long, I'm not joking. Boy, Daddy took off on his horse without even holding on to the reins. He held his gun in one hand and a bullwhip in the other." Keaton stretched his arms up over his head. "Daddy took that whip and popped that snake's head right in two." He snapped his fingers and widened his eyes. "I'd show you the head if we still had it. Samuel kept it in a jar of vinegar underneath the bed until Mama found out and made him throw it away."

Lanier folded his arms and widened his stance, the same way he might if he'd been talking on a street corner to a grown man. "Harlan was the first person we'd heard tell of who left that mountain and didn't wind up working in the factories."

"Did you ride horses too?"

Lanier walked over to the empty stall where he would sleep and shut the gate. "No, I whittle here and there. I make things out of wood. When I heard that your daddy had set up this store down in Florida, I sent him a letter asking him to sell my things—dolls, clocks, cabinets, such as that. He sold a fair amount of my work, and then I got on with the Blue Moon Clock Company." Lanier's voice trailed off and then he leaned down so that he was eye level with Keaton. "Hey, why don't you remind your mama of that . . . you know, of me selling my work in the store."

Just beyond the barn door, light from a gas lantern hung in the night air and moved closer. The shadow of Narsissa's tall figure soon stretched out across the barn floor. She never had to tell Keaton to leave. She simply motioned with her chin toward the house, and he obliged.

While the crickets chirped in an uneven rhythm, Narsissa and Lanier stood there staring at one another. There was hardness in Narsissa's black eyes.

Holding the lantern up to her face, Narsissa casually lifted her other hand. The tip of a jagged hunting knife shimmied against the flame.

Lanier stepped backward and felt the stall boards press into his thigh. The mule kicked the stall. Lanier turned to see if he was being ambushed. When he looked back at the door of the barn, the light from Narsissa's lantern was gone. He edged closer to the door and heard an owl call out. The moon cast a dim light across the patch of sunflowers and the house, but Narsissa was hidden somewhere in the darkness of the woods that bordered the property.

Lanier unfurled the torn quilt that Ella had given him to use, laid it on the ground, and propped his head against the horse blanket that still smelled of the sweaty mule. He looked out into the dark and could feel Narsissa's eyes out there, searching him, knowing him. She was the guarding, jealous presence that Lanier would never overpower.

4

The past caught up with Lanier in his sleep. Kicking the quilt until it balled at his feet, he fought the demons that had driven him to extremes.

No longer picturing Narsissa standing outside the barn ready to slice him with the hunting knife, his mind replayed the events of yesterday.

If only in his dreams, Lanier was once again at the Blue Moon Clock Company with his friend Dave Hinshaw. The first person to befriend Lanier when he stepped off the train in Bainbridge, Georgia, Dave had also been the first to warn him against getting involved with the clock company owner's daughter, Octavia. "She's mixed up. Not right in the head," Dave had said as the wood shavings piled at his feet. Smoothing his hand against the shell of wood that was to become a clock, Dave looked up toward the portrait of the factory's owner, Reynolds Troxler, a sharp-nosed man who owned a textile mill along with the clock company. The painting hung above a window that had been blacked out. "You poke around a hornet's nest long enough and you're apt to get stung."

A month later Dave declined to meet Lanier and Octavia in the neighboring county at the courthouse. He refused to be a witness to the ceremony that would cause Octavia's oldest brother, J.D., to knock Lanier from the porch with an iron cattle prod after the happy couple returned home with news of their union. Dave had children to feed, and his wife was pregnant again. He couldn't risk losing his job. It was the first time Dave refused to help Lanier.

Soon it was Lanier who was moving away from Dave. "If my daughter chooses to marry a jackass," Mr. Troxler told him as he handed him the key to the office with *Superintendent* on the door, "then it's my job to turn him into a thoroughbred." The transformation included a home with a new icebox, weekly trips to the barber shop, private lessons from an old-maid schoolteacher who taught him how to lose the choppy sound of his North Georgia roots and to properly loop his cursive writing, and a brand-new Buick Roadster that took him to dinners in fancy homes. Each morning as Lanier shaved, he would look in the mirror and imagine parts of his old self being scraped away as easy as a snake shedding its skin.

Despite his efforts, none of the Troxlers ever recognized the person he tried to become. Least of all Octavia's brother J.D. or his wife, Camilla, who refused to give up her seat next to Octavia at the weekly family dinners on Sundays.

"I want a baby," Octavia said one day in the same tone she used when she placed an order at her favorite store in Atlanta. Lanier had smiled and embraced her. Nine months later he stood at the front of the Presbyterian church holding his son, who was dressed in a lace garment that seemed more fitting for a girl.

By then Lanier had not talked to his family in a year. The last time was during Christmas, when he traveled back into the Appalachian

Mountains of North Georgia to prove his worth to his mother. He drove his automobile around the mountain and down into the valley that revenuers could never find. He gave his mother a clock with a gold-encrusted sun on the top. But she seemed more interested in the money tucked inside the red velvet sack that he had also given her. She held the crisp bills up toward the sun as if to see whether they were real. "I won't ask how you come by this money," she said. "I learnt long ago not to ask questions I don't want to hear answers to." Her stooped shoulders carried her burdens and her new money into the kitchen, where she hovered over the gift like a dog hiding a meal from her pack. Dirt from her fingers soiled the crisp bills as she counted them and then stuffed them inside the waist of her skirt.

No one in the community came out to hear him talk about life in the city. No one wanted to hear about a clockmaker. "What was you expecting?" his mother asked. She sat on the porch, rocking in the chair Lanier had made and smoking one of his cigars. "It ain't like you been off racing horses like your cousin. You happened to get by on your looks long enough for a rich girl to marry you is all. Anybody can get married, don't you forget it. No telling what curse will come out of this unequal yoke of yours. The Bible says you ain't supposed to mix tribes. A poor boy ain't got no business in a rich tribe. No business a'tall."

Three years later Octavia was dead, and Lanier was carrying the blame. It was then that Lanier stopped cutting his hair in what he saw as a revolt and a demonstration of some sort of Samson-like strength that he hoped would empower him to stand up against the Troxlers.

After Lanier was vindicated in court, one of the less intelligent Troxler brothers, Cecil, had tackled Lanier in broad daylight in front of the post office a block from the courthouse and slashed off a piece of his ear with a switchblade. Later Lanier stood on the back porch of his old friend's home with a bandage over his left ear. As Lanier pleaded his case with Dave, he could hear his mother's words of prophecy playing in his head. Dave whispered in the cold night while a dog barked in the distance. "You gotta get out of here. Those Troxler boys killed a colored man one time in Sasser County just to see if his blood was red." Smoke bellowed from Dave's mouth and drifted off with the damp February air. "I'm telling you, you've got to run. They're apt to kill you just as soon as they figure out a way to do it without the law pinning it on them."

Peering through the slits in the crate Dave had built for a custom-made clock, Lanier watched his friend nail the cover. He felt he was being put into a coffin and fought the urge to slam his forearm against the top of the crate. Every time Dave pounded the lid with the hammer, there was a shock to Lanier's system. Maybe he would have been better off dead.

Lanier thought he had seen a vision of his son standing behind Dave. The boy was three, the same age he was when he died, and was wearing that christening gown. His brown eyes shone through the slits in the crate like some sort of beacon that led the way. Lanier reached his finger through the slit. Dave's hammer pounded down on him. Pain ran up to his head and a blaring scream jarred his ears. The scream from all those nights long ago when croup had taken hold of his son and Octavia had run around the house holding the baby by the legs, claiming that the croup would leave his body this way. The scream roared in his ears, snatching him back to reality.

Lanier shot up from the hay. The scream was so shrill and anguished that at first he thought it might be a panther. When he heard footsteps, Lanier ran barefoot out of the barn and into the darkness.

Through the mist Ella came running toward him. Her hair was wild and draped down the side of her face. She was carrying Macon. His lips had lost the shine of the salve and were now blue. "Narsissa," Ella screamed. "Narsissa . . ."

Samuel and Keaton ran shirtless behind Ella. "Mama, is he dead?" Keaton asked. "Is he dead?"

Ella gave no recognition that she saw Lanier standing there as she ran past. He reached out and brushed the edge of Macon's hair. The boy's eyes had rolled back into his head and were fluttering.

Narsissa ran out of her cabin. The strap of a thin shift was dangling from one shoulder. She motioned for Ella to bring the boy inside.

"Mama, is he dead?" Keaton's words could be heard outside.

Inside, Narsissa reached for a tiny bottle above the stove while Ella, Keaton, and Samuel stood over Macon. The boy lay on the bed, where the sheets were still disheveled from Narsissa's awakening. No one noticed when Lanier walked in.

"God have mercy," Ella screamed and shook Macon. The springs on the bed screeched from the weight, but Macon didn't move.

Narsissa shoved Ella out of the way and stuck the bottle she was carrying under Macon's nose. He gagged, and for a moment the air of tension evaporated. Then Macon rose up in pain and gurgled, clawing Narsissa's face so hard that she jerked away.

Lanier moved forward and gripped the boy's hands. Macon arched his back in terror.

"What are you doing?" Ella shouted.

Lanier never looked at any of them. He kept his eyes closed and his hands gripped on Macon's wrists. He moved his lips as if reciting a silent chant.

"Let go of him," Samuel yelled.

Then, as if consuming the boy, Lanier leaned down and put his open mouth onto the sore-riddled mouth of Macon. The boy wrenched a hand free and pulled a clump of hair out of Lanier's scalp. He gripped the strands in the air like a trophy from battle.

Ella pulled at Lanier. "You're suffocating him!"

Samuel pounded his fist into Lanier's back. Lanier flinched but never took his mouth away from Macon's.

A branch screeched against the window of the cabin. Macon quieted and Ella screamed again. She sank down to the floor, catching a piece of her gown on the ends of the bedsprings.

Lanier rose upright, and Macon inhaled loud enough to make his mother look up. At first his breath was shallow and unsteady. Then his eyes opened.

Moving back, Lanier let the family examine Macon. They brushed the boy's sweaty hair, rubbed his arms, and kissed his forehead. Only Narsissa remained at the foot of the bed. Her mouth was slightly open, and a trickle of blood marked the spot where Macon had clawed her. She studied Lanier in a way that she hadn't before. When the bottle of smelling salts fell from her hands and hit the floor, she never flinched or even bothered to pick it up.

Walking back toward the house, Ella carried Macon and covered him in kisses, sores and all. "Are you all right, Macon?" Ella asked. "Thank you, Mr. Stillis. Thank you," she chirped all the way to the barn.

Lanier never asked Ella to call him by his first name or even acknowledged her gratitude. He simply walked into the barn and lay back down against the horse blanket. He could hear them all outside—Narsissa, Ella, and her boys. Words from the conversation on the front porch drifted down to the stall.

"Beyond belief," Ella proclaimed.

"Lifesaver," Keaton repeated.

"Voodoo," Narsissa speculated.

The speculation continued well into the morning as the sores on Macon's lips began to close and fade.

Narsissa had been by Macon's side since daybreak and came to the store to give Ella hourly reports. "It's not natural," Narsissa said as she stood at the cash register with her wrist against her hip.

Ella smiled when Mr. Purvis, the beekeeper, entered. She nodded like it was an ordinary day. The man pulled out a notepad, flipped to a page that listed needed items, and then walked to the end of the store, where cans of paint were stacked against the wall.

"That man is a witch doctor. You mark my word," Narsissa whispered.

"Hush," Ella said.

The beekeeper rolled his eyes toward Narsissa and then returned his focus to his notepad.

"All I know is that my son had sores in his throat so bad that he was choking to death. That man saved his life. That settles it with me," Ella whispered.

Watching Narsissa march out of the store, Ella did not feel the tightness of fear that usually accompanied Narsissa's warnings.

By noon, the only sores that remained on Macon's face were the ones dotting his upper lip. Ella stood in the doorway of the barn and watched as Lanier used a pitchfork with a missing spike to arrange the scattered hay into piles.

He stopped when he saw her. "I hope you don't mind. . . . I just . . . I saw that the hay . . ." Lanier wiped flecks of hay on the side of his pants. "Just earning my keep, so to speak."

"I think you've more than done that," Ella said. "Mr. Stillis . . ."

"Lanier," he said. "If we're close enough for me to straighten up your barn for you, then you can surely call me by my first name."

Ella nervously played with the bow of her store apron. "All morning I've been thinking about what happened last night. You don't know how relieved I am."

"I'm glad I could help," Lanier said. "Your other boy . . . Keaton . . . he said Macon was healing."

"Yes," Ella said. "He does . . . he does seem . . . Listen, how did you do that last night?"

The mule stopped eating and kicked the stall. Neither Ella nor Lanier took their eyes off the other.

"I don't like to get into it." Lanier lifted a bale of hay and placed it in the corner with the others.

"Well, I'm sure you can understand my curiosity. . . ."

"You mean Harlan never talked about it? The healings, I'm talking about."

"Healings?"

"Back home there were a few who could heal. My grandmother was one. She said if you were a fatherless man, then you'd be more likely to heal certain things."

Ella folded her arms. "You mean like those men who pass through and put on the tent meetings?"

Lanier stopped moving the hay around and stared at her. "Nothing like that. Some people from the mountains where I come from have the gift for healing. They can heal a person after a bad fire has got on them. They can heal a person when there's a bad bleed. They can even heal a boy from thrush, I reckon."

The intensity of his green eyes caused Ella to rub the back of her neck. She hoped he wouldn't see the flush of embarrassment she could feel on her face. "I'm just not familiar with such. Where I come from . . . well . . . let's just say that people don't put their mouths on a boy and make him better."

Lanier walked toward Ella, and she lifted her shoulder to let him pass. She hated the way she felt vulnerable with this man, whose almond-shaped eyes sparkled with either hope or mischief.

He prodded the hay with the pitchfork.

"Will it come back?"

Lanier stopped and turned to her. The sweat from his work clung to his shirt. "Pardon?"

"The condition. Will it come back when you leave?"

"Uh . . . no. If I did my part, then it will stay away."

"I don't know if I feel any more comfortable about what went on last night. But I'm appreciative just the same. At this point, any good fortune is welcome." Ella balled her fists and forced herself not to look away from Lanier. "I wish I could do more to help you, but with things the way they are right now . . ."

If Lanier heard her, he gave no indication. He just continued to stack the hay and wait for the hour of his departure back to Apalachicola to catch the boat.

Before she had made it to the barn door, he called out. "I am a good man, you know."

Ella never turned around. She just kept walking back to her proper place behind the cash register in her store. The less she knew about Lanier Stillis, the better.

The clock on the store wall read half past twelve. Ella ate the biscuit stuffed with sausage that Narsissa had brought her and listened to the latest progress report on Macon. "He's out of bed," Narsissa said, not able to hide her enthusiasm any longer. "He's out playing ball with Keaton and that man from the box."

Ella walked over to the window that overlooked the front of her home and the rows of pine trees that bordered the yard. She grabbed Narsissa's shoulder. "I don't care if you call it hoochie-coochie medicine or not. Macon is out there in the pines, playing ball and laughing. That's good enough for me."

Myer Simpson came into the store, declaring a miracle at having seen Macon playing in the side yard. Ella smiled and felt downright giddy in front of the sanctimonious woman. "A miracle. Yes, a miracle," Ella repeated.

Samuel came in and gathered the mail that he would be taking to Apalachicola along with Lanier Stillis. "What time did you tell him you'd be leaving?"

Samuel didn't look up as he flipped through the envelopes before placing them into the mail pouch. He never did pay any mind to Ella's complaints that the US mail was confidential.

"What time did you say you were leaving?" she asked again.

"One o'clock," Samuel said. "Let me go and hitch the wagon."

As Samuel walked out through the back of the store, a sheriff's deputy, Ronnie Eubanks, came in through the front door. He took off a felt cowboy hat. An indented ring on his forehead marked the spot where it had sat upon his head.

"Afternoon, Ronnie," Ella said as lightly as she could. She darted her eyes out toward the lawn, where Macon, Keaton, and Lanier were still throwing the baseball. Watching her boys playing so carefree, Ella kept telling herself that if seriously bad news were being delivered to her doorstep, it would come from Sheriff Bissell, not his deputy. *Ronnie is probably just passing through and decided to stop for his usual cheese and crackers.*

"I bet you we break ninety today," Ronnie said and used a handkerchief to dab at his freckled forehead.

Ella stood in front of the cheddar cheese and lifted the cake lid that protected it. "How's your mama doing?"

"Improving some every day. I appreciate you asking." Ronnie tucked his handkerchief into his back pants pocket and pulled out a white envelope. "No thank you, Ella. I'm going to pass on the cheese today."

For an instant Ella hoped it was only notification that her husband had been found, probably in an opium den where he had overdosed.

"I hate to be the bearer of bad news." Ronnie sighed and laid the envelope on top of the register.

Ella ripped into it the way an anxious child might open a birthday gift. She pulled out the official notification with the clerk of the court's signature and stared. She had tried to prepare herself for this day. Many were the nights that she had woken up drenched in sweat, picturing in her mind's eye the type of print that would inform her that she was losing everything to foreclosure. But to hold the actual papers and to see the way the swirled, bold print spelled out the details in the King's English still caused her knees to buckle. She leaned against the counter and felt the edge of the nail where her husband had instructed her to hang shopping baskets.

"I'm sorry, Ella," Ronnie whispered. "He didn't have to send us out here to deliver these to you but he's a snake enough that he did."

Ella flipped through the pages to find Clive Gillespie's signature at the bottom of the documents. The scent of cigar smoke was embedded into the document, and suddenly Ella felt nauseous.

After she had managed to stand on shaky legs long enough to collect money from her neighbor Mrs. Pomeroy for a package of Cheek-Neal coffee, Ella went outside. She leaned against the railing and sank down to the porch step. She watched her sons run and jump for the ball that Lanier kept tossing in the air. His laughter echoed up to the porch, and she wondered how a man this seemingly carefree could be running from anything. She imagined him being loaded onto the steamboat back in Georgia, stuffed in that box like cargo. She couldn't help but feel envious that he had managed to escape his tormentors. If only she could be irresponsible and flee. The thought both terrified and angered her.

Voices from Ella's past, present, and future played in her mind. "Throw it to me," Macon yelled as he ran past Keaton. "Catch," Lanier Stillis said as he threw his arm back and tossed the ball. *"I've been more than patient,"* Clive Gillespie called out in the darkest corner of her mind. "Throw it to me," Macon repeated. *"Whatever you do, don't sell that property,"* her father whispered in her head. *"Either you sell me the land, or I'll take it on the courthouse steps,"* Clive hissed. *"Remember who you are and where you come from,"* her father said again.

"Throw it to me," Macon called out from the side yard. Lanier threw the ball to him. It flew far into the sky, over Keaton's grasp and past the reach of Macon. Ella watched as the ball landed in between the pines that were shrouded in vines of kudzu. *"Use it as a resource, but don't sell it."* She heard her father's voice one last time and stood up.

The bit of salve that remained on Macon's face glimmered in the sun, and he fanned his hand across his forehead when he looked up at her. "Did you see me catch it, Mama? Did you see me?"

Gripping the foreclosure notice behind her back, Ella marched toward them and never took her eyes off of Lanier Stillis. "My husband used to talk about his daddy taking him out of school to help cut timber. He claimed it was why he hated the man. And why he had to teach himself everything he knew."

Lanier leaned down and picked up the wayward ball. "All right."

"Did you cut timber like that growing up?"

"We all did. We all got took out of school to cut the timber when it was time to sell."

"I'm taking you at your word." Ella stared at Lanier and twisted the foreclosure notice up until it took the shape of a thick straw. "I couldn't pay you up front, but if I gave you a percentage, would you stay and help me cut this timber?"

As soon as Lanier offered the slightest nod to her question, Ella pointed the bound document at him. "I need your word," she said. "I don't need any more trouble."

"Uh, yeah . . . I mean, you have my word," Lanier said. "Like I said, I'm family."

Ella had already made it halfway back to the store when she called back to him. "We have to have it all cut and sold in forty-five days. You can do that, can't you?"

The bridle and harness had already been put on the mule. Lanier shook his head and stretched his head back toward Samuel. Ella cleared a path of grass as she walked past Samuel.

"Did you tell him to come on?"

"He's not leaving," Ella said, never stopping long enough to register Samuel's disbelief. "You're taking him to town. Buy every saw, chain . . . every piece of equipment that he tells you to buy. I'm going to give you Aunt Katherine's pearl necklace to sell." The necklace and her wedding ring were the last pieces of real jewelry that Ella still possessed.

"What?" Samuel shouted. "You told Mr. Busby in front of God and everybody that you'd never sell that necklace."

Ella bounded the steps two at a time. When she swung the store door open, the cat that had been hiding behind the sewing samples ran down the stairs, past the mule that kicked at it, and circled Lanier before disappearing deep within the thicket of pines.

5

Myer Simpson stood at the window in her parlor where the grandfather clock might have been placed. Sunlight streaked through and fanned out across the room to the walnut desk, where her husband sat working on his weekly sermon.

"Don't you think it curious?" Myer asked as she fingered the lace curtain.

Not looking up from his papers, the reverend grunted.

"How this man just shows up out of the blue to help Ella Wallace."

The reverend reached up to the bookshelf above the desk and took down a book of Greek translation. "What man?"

"What man?" Myer Simpson repeated and turned toward her husband. The light from the window cut across her face and caused the vein in her neck to look even bluer. "The *man* we met the other day when we were out taking exercise. What man? The very notion that you'd forget such a sight."

The reverend never turned away from the pages he flipped through. A long gray hair fell from his beard and floated in the air before landing on the cuff of his shirtsleeve.

"That *younger* man, I might add. He's at least ten—well, maybe five—years younger than Ella Wallace. Don't you think it curious how this woman who is about to lose everything suddenly has this man show up at her place? This woman—this *married* woman, I might add—has a man living at her place. In the barn, supposedly."

"Maybe he's an answer to prayer," the reverend said. "Lord knows she could use the help."

"Reverend Simpson, must you always be contrary when I speak my mind? The woman has three impressionable boys living on the place."

If the reverend heard her he didn't let on. He simply flipped through the Greek translation, searching for the original meaning of the word *pardonable*. All the while, Myer Simpson fingered the seam of the lace curtain and watched as the townspeople made their way down the dirt road to the store that Ella Wallace struggled to keep open.

By the third day of gripping the handle on the snarl-toothed saw blades to rip through pine bark and swinging a machete to slice through the vines of kudzu that hid the trees, every muscle in Ella's back ached. She worked alongside Narsissa and Lanier without ever voicing uncertainty or fear. She fought the clumps of briars and a swarm of hornets that tried to keep her from the pines. She sliced her machete through palmetto bushes deep in the woods, all the while staying on alert and ready to kill a rattler like the one that had struck at Narsissa two days earlier as she stepped over a dead log. Even though Narsissa kept looking at Ella in a cautionary way as if she might break at any moment, Ella marched forward, deeper into the rows of pines. She swung the axe until her fingers were numb and wore stains of dirt and pine tar on her face like war paint.

"Everybody okay?" Lanier would call out, his voice echoing against the trees. "Fine," Ella would yell, knowing full well that the question was intended for her.

By the end of the first week of cutting timber, even the Watkins liniment that Ella sold to customers in the store by guaranteeing its ability to replenish tired muscles had stopped working. She went to bed each night too sore to move and too tired to let the pain keep her from sleep. Ella made certain that her sons would not see the blisters that had burst and turned bloody. She wrapped her hands in bandages that she claimed helped her to grip the axe handle tighter. When the dirt and blood stained the bandage cloth, she put on the leather riding gloves that her aunt had given for her eighteenth birthday. Any appearance of normalcy was important to Ella, now more than ever. It helped to keep her sane.

Ella even tried to convince the customers that her sons' increased activity in the store was all part of a grand plan. "We forget how important apprenticeship once was in this country," she said to casual inquiries about her children's role in the business. "They are learning the trade from the ground up."

Keaton had become the official store manager, Macon, whose face had now healed, was the clerk, and Samuel was the logger learning to follow Lanier's instructions. Naturally Samuel rebelled at first. But after he didn't move fast enough and a loblolly pine missed driving him into the ground by mere inches, he began to follow Lanier's plan.

As the evening sun turned the sky orange and the mosquitoes swarmed the heavy air, Samuel, Narsissa, and Ella carried tools and chains along the path that had emerged from their boots and the wagon wheels. Lanier pulled the mule by the harness. The animal tried to shake his head as if saying he was too tired to pull the last load of timber that filled the wagon behind him. With a nudge of Lanier's elbow to his neck, the mule bellowed and then stepped forward.

After the timber had been mostly stacked, Ella wrung the red handkerchief that she kept tied around her neck. Sweat dripped from the handkerchief like water. She ran her hand through her hair, trying to comb out the bark, ticks, and chiggers that had accumulated. Narsissa had used alcohol to help draw out the last two ticks on her scalp. Ever since, the hat and handkerchief had never left her head.

The fear that Ella had pictured attached to the side of her brain now ran wild through her system. "We're not going to make it," she declared, lifting her head toward the tops of the trees. The mass of pines stood like lean, defiant soldiers who would not be taken without a fight.

Lanier stopped unloading the timber. Samuel dropped a line of chain he'd been wrapping around his forearm. Narsissa let go of the axe she'd been cleaning.

"What kind of talk is that?" Lanier stepped forward and took off his hat. Strands of curly wet hair hung over his mangled ear, and the side of his neck bulged.

"It's reality," Ella said.

"It's a give-up spirit," Lanier said. "I don't like quitters."

"No, you just like those who run away, I reckon," Narsissa added.

"Look," Lanier said, "we're all tired. I understand that. I'm tired too, but we can't just walk away. We've cut—"

"We've cut hardly anything. Look at this pitiful mess." Ella pointed toward the small stack of timber that lay scattered and twisted next to the road.

"We'll make it," Lanier said.

"Stop lying," Ella said and threw her hands up in the air. "We won't make it. You know it's the truth."

"Now you listen to me," Lanier said. "I am starting from scratch here. I got nothing to lose. And if I'm not mistaken . . ."

Ella kicked over the water bucket. Clouds of dust twirled up behind her as she marched toward the house.

"And you'll lose everything you got unless you straighten out that attitude," Lanier yelled.

Narsissa got so close to Lanier that he could make out a black mole under her right eye. "I've listened to you just about as long as I intend to. Step to the left. Saw more in the middle. Break away to the center. . . . But so help me, I will not stand here and listen to you yell at her. Make no mistake—I can get the sheriff over here anytime I want to."

Lanier reached down and picked up the bucket. "Go ahead then. Nobody's stopping you."

Samuel moved from the side of the wagon and brushed his hands against his overalls. Crickets began to break the silence. "He's right," Samuel said. "We're in just as deep as him."

"He's blackmailing us," Narsissa shouted.

Samuel shrugged. "What you want us to do? Give the place over to the bank? My daddy ain't coming back home and finding out that I let the place go on my watch. No, ma'am."

Narsissa picked up the axe she had been using and slowly wiped the blade on the side of her denim work pants. The blade left a gluey smear of pine tar on her leg that shimmered in the fading sunlight. When she swung the axe over her shoulder, Lanier stepped backward. She never said a word as she walked back to her cabin.

Samuel continued stacking the equipment and didn't notice Lanier unfastening the mule from the wagon. "I'll water the mule," Lanier said. Samuel gave no indication that he heard him. It was only after Lanier had watered and fed the mule that Samuel offered his opinion. Walking past the sunflowers that had begun to unwind their petals for evening, he spat a stream of tobacco at the nearest bloom.

"She's wrong, you know," Lanier called out.

Samuel stopped and turned. The light from the barn caused Lanier to seemingly glow.

"Hear me out. I'm not blackmailing anybody. Family is family. I want this just as bad as y'all do."

Samuel pulled out a pocketknife, examined the tip, and flung it at the water pump where Lanier stood. The knife stuck out of the side of the water bucket like a wild hair. "You ain't no family of mine. I just want to keep my property."

Yanking the pocketknife from the wood, Lanier folded the blade up and tossed it back to Samuel.

Samuel caught it with one hand and spat a line of tobacco juice from the side of his mouth. "And hear me when I say I'm gonna be watching you," he said.

Around bedtime, Ella stood in the doorway of her bedroom with drips of water falling from her dark, wet hair. "You're going to skip school, you say?" Ella said after Samuel had informed her of his decision.

"Either me and Keaton stay out of school and help, or we'll all go to the poorhouse. You said as much."

"Don't you sass me." Ella closed her eyes, wishing she could take back her moment of weakness when she had let the fear manifest itself in front of her sons. "Skipping school is not an option."

"There's no option to it," Samuel said. "There's only two weeks left till school lets out for the summer anyway." Muscles flinched in his forearms and beads of dirt dotted his neck like a necklace.

Ella no longer saw a boy. The thought scared her just as much as Samuel's ability to convince her that he was right. She stammered the words. "You will go back to school after summer. Promise me that."

From her bedroom, Ella could hear Samuel explaining his plan to Keaton and Macon. His words were low and hushed as if a secret were being offered.

Not wanting to hear any more, Ella followed the sounds of the clock and walked into the dining room. She stood in the spot where her cherry buffet had once sat. The one that had been taken away in Mr. Busby's wagon after the picture taker had found a buyer for it in Albany, Georgia. She tried to think of happier times, of holidays when the family sat alongside the dining room table decorated with branches of holly berries. But all her mind would play was the scene from the day when Samuel was forced to become a man.

It was the night before Harlan left. Ella had met Clive Gillespie at the store earlier that day. In ignorance and desperation, she had tried to sell him a new derby hat when he walked through the door of the store.

"No, I'm afraid I'm not here for shopping," Clive had said. "Is Harlan here?"

Ella fiddled with the edge of the derby hat and then placed it back in its proper place on the shelf. "No, I'm afraid he's off . . . off picking up new merchandise." She couldn't very well say that Harlan was in bed, hallucinating that he was riding a cloud.

"There's an issue with payment." With those words, Clive Gillespie introduced Ella to the world of banking and finance. He opened the doors to a knowledge that she had otherwise just as soon not known.

"This isn't even my signature," she had said whenever Clive pulled out the document verifying the loan and specifying the payment that would be required each month, the same payment that she learned was overdue.

"The law is black-and-white. Just like this piece of paper, Ella," Clive said. "Now, I'm not here to get into marital squabbles."

Ella had repeated the words back to Harlan that night when he went to take another hit of opium. The dinner dishes had been cleaned, and she was in the kitchen drying them when he staggered in through the back door.

"I can manage without an interfering wife," Harlan said while knocking his pipe against the stove.

"Well, evidently you can't," Ella shouted. "You lost some of my land once already. Now I find out that you've gone and forged my signature for a loan. A loan on property that belongs to me?"

"What are you going to do, Miss Debutante? Huh? Are you going to put that finishing school education to use and get yourself employed?" Harlan threw the pipe into the eye of the stove and circled Ella.

"I have a job. I have to run that store you cast aside the same way you do everything else you touch."

Then Ella saw the click in his eyes, the glazed narrowing that indicated he was at his breaking point. The point at which her husband transfigured out of the graciousness used to manipulate others. As Harlan moved past the kitchen sink, he snatched a butcher knife that she had used earlier to slice a chicken. Strips of milky-white fat and blue veins clung to the blade. Before Ella could see what was happening, Harlan was standing behind her, breathing on her in a musky scent. His breath was hot against her skin, and the blade cold as he held it up to her throat. "I'll run this straight across those pouty lips. We'll see how good you can sass then."

Ella felt a trickle of urine run down her leg. From the corner of her eye, she saw Keaton and Macon in the hallway. Without lifting her hand away from her dress, she managed to motion with her index finger, shooing them away. When Harlan laughed, she elbowed his groin and ran into the hallway, screaming, "Get out of the house, Keaton. Get Macon out of here. Run."

Keaton jerked Macon's arm and ran out of the door without closing it.

Ella darted into the dining room with Harlan running, stumbling behind her. "I'm going to cut your lips off," he yelled, holding the knife high over his shoulder. Spit flung from his mouth, and strands of his hair hung over his eyes.

Ella dashed around the dining room table and through sheer agility managed to keep away from his grasp. When she stopped at the head of the table, Harlan stood facing her with the front door at his back. He held the knife higher. The dark eyes that she had grown accustomed to seeing in a state of opium-induced glassiness were now piercing with an intensity that terrified her.

Through the front door, Samuel eased into the house. Before she could scream for him to leave, she saw Samuel shaking his head, instructing her to be quiet. Ella obeyed. She never even flinched as he lifted a two-by-four, and she certainly never uttered a sound as the tip of the board brushed against the chandelier, causing it to chime.

Harlan halfway turned, following the noise from the chandelier. Before he could turn completely around, the two-by-four landed against the side of his head. He fell backward against the china cabinet, causing the dishes to rattle and a decorative china bird that Ella's aunt had given her to fall and crash to the floor. Pieces of china scattered around Harlan's body, which lay in a ball on the floor. His eyes fluttered and skin unfolded on his forehead. A stream of blood darkened the floor and the pieces of white china.

That night after Harlan was sewn up, Ella put him to bed in a stack of hay inside the barn. She awoke the next morning expecting to find her husband mournful and ready to repent. Instead there was only the indentation of his body on crushed hay. Harlan had seemingly disappeared into the ground. At the breakfast table, none of the boys said a word about what they had witnessed the night before or if they expected their father to return. They left for school through the front door, leaving Ella sitting at the dining room table with shards of china strewn before her, working to glue the pieces of the bird back together.

Ella tried to walk away from the preoccupying memory, and without ever realizing it, she had ventured outside in her bare feet. The earth was cool with dew, almost soothing. She dug her toes into the soil. The dampness soothed her aching calves and tickled the length of her spine. She tried to let the moment envelop her, but the sweetness of the earth could not ease the sting of the fear that whipped at her mind. She wondered what would become of her if she lost the farm. Visions from easier days fluttered about, tempting her to give up and walk away. If only she could go back in time and lounge in her aunt's parlor listening to proper ladies in her aunt's reading group, the Philaco Club, debate the social perils of women's suffrage. This time she would have opinions of her own.

The Philaco Club met monthly in the home of Ella's aunt Katherine. The women sat in a semicircle in the parlor, where dried red rose petals and crystal rabbit figurines were scattered across a marbled fireplace mantel. It was Ella's young and foolish friend, Neva Clarkson, who suggested reading *The History of Women's Suffrage*. Ella could still see Neva's round face turn as crimson as the rose petals when Sadie Donohue, a former schoolteacher herself and wife of the former mayor, reprimanded Neva's mother for allowing her to read such propaganda. "Mr. Donohue says that women have no business getting mixed up in politics. A turn of the ballot will be a loss of purity in the home. Why, it will be a loss of the home itself, you mark my word." Sadie's arthritic and shaking finger pointed straight at Neva until the girl seemed to fold into the wingback chair. Her posture reminded Ella of one of the rabbits on the mantel, bent and ready to jump.

Now, all these years later, it was Ella who felt pressed to the point of shattering. With the newspaper declaring that it was only a matter of time before women cast their votes, Ella wondered if Old Lady Donohue had been right after all. Maybe it was an omen, like the kind that Narsissa cautiously delivered to her during breakfast after a restless night of dreams. Maybe she had been brought to this point of homelessness as a punishment by God Almighty for having secretly agreed with Neva that women had a rib as strong as Adam's and a voice beyond the walls of their homes.

As Ella circled the magnolia tree, she was lost in the tortured thoughts that flashed in her mind like gray charcoal drawings: images of her standing by the lamppost at the corner of Commerce Street and in front of mounds of tattered fishnets at the docks in Apalachicola, begging with cupped, callused hands, relying on those who no longer recognized her as the niece of Katherine or the wife of Harlan.

Ella gripped the collar of her robe and hurried away from the scent of magnolia leaves. She made her way down to the stack of timber that lined the edge of the road. Crickets and bullfrogs called out from the thicket of pines yet to be touched. She pictured the pines all cut down to the low-lying ground covered with water and cypress trees, land so marshy that not even Harlan had been able to gamble its value. Harlan never did believe the spring that rose up in that section had the magical properties that Narsissa proclaimed. He couldn't care less if Indians trekked four counties over to soak in the water. He saw no value in an artesian spring that was guarded by palmetto bushes, scrub oaks, and a vine-covered magnolia tree whose branches shaded ferns along the ravine.

When she turned to walk back toward the house, Ella paused at the barn. The Little Dipper lined the sky above the barn door, and she held her breath, hoping to hear Lanier inside. She pictured him sleeping, his curly hair hanging from the top of the pallet. There in the night air, warmth covered her body. Lifting the collar of her robe, she wondered how she might sketch Lanier in slumber. Embarrassment and sensation confused her. She barely knew this man, this drifter, after all. He was a distant relative of her husband, she told herself, nothing more. He would help her until the timber was cut, and then he would be on his way. She had no business getting mixed up in his troubles. *Funny,* she thought, *he's already mixed up in mine.*

A bat swooped down and then jetted over the top of the barn, barely missing the rooster-shaped weather vane. Ella stared at the barn door. Even though she wanted to move away, she couldn't. She could not walk away from the hope that Lanier Stillis was so distant from her husband that he might be a good man after all. She stood there for a while longer, toying with the notion that Lanier was the man he claimed to be. Whether she would admit it or not, Ella needed for him to be something more than just a mere man running from trouble.

6

Keaton stood outside the one-room schoolhouse, hoping to avoid facing his teacher, Miss Neva Clarkson. Leaning against the peeling white fence that opened to the schoolyard, he picked at a piece of flaking paint and prayed that Macon would be one of the first ones to exit. The door swung open, and the Flander twins bounded down the steps. Keaton's prayer, just like the one he prayed for his father to stop taking opium, was not answered. Watching the others walk toward the gate, Keaton pulled his cap down low. The last thing he needed was somebody asking questions.

Marla Davis, a girl with a missing front tooth, stopped and looked at him. "How come you ain't been at school?"

"Been busy," Keaton answered and looked up at the door, hoping to will Macon out of the schoolhouse.

Red Kennedy stopped long enough to adjust the strap tied around the books he carried. "You mean you been busy cutting pines like a pulpwood ninny."

Marla laughed and covered her mouth. "Who's that man staying at your house?"

"My daddy's cousin." Keaton planted his hands in his pockets and looked back at the door.

Red looked at Marla and laughed. "That's what his mama tells him. She tells him that so that he won't question why she's got a man living there. Shacking up like white trash."

Just as Keaton balled his fist and took a step toward Red, Miss Clarkson stepped out of the door with Macon trailing behind her.

"What's this fuss?" Miss Clarkson called out. She had auburn hair and a round face that made her seem heavier than she was.

"He was trying to pick a fight," Red yelled.

"Keaton Wallace. It's not bad enough that you skip school, but you show up and cause trouble on top of it."

"No, ma'am," Keaton stammered. "He was—"

"He was picking a fight," Red yelled again.

"Enough." Miss Clarkson swiped her hand across the gray skirt that she wore, and a mark of white chalk was left on the material. "Red, Marla . . . get on home."

The others wasted no time in leaving the schoolyard, but Keaton was reluctant to walk beyond the gate. Miss Clarkson motioned with her finger, and he slowly moved forward. Keaton could see into the school and tried to make out the cursive words written on the chalkboard. He feared that before the pines were cut he would forget everything he had learned and would be forced to repeat his grade.

"What is this business about you and Samuel skipping school? I know sickness, and sickness doesn't linger with brothers for two weeks." Auburn strands stuck out from the bobbed hair on her head. All Keaton could hear were the taunts that others in his grade made behind Miss Clarkson's back. Taunts about the hairstyle making Miss Clarkson look like a little boy.

Macon looked up at her and then down at the wooden sidewalk patched together with rusted nails. Keaton followed his gaze and then, thinking that Miss Clarkson would believe he was lying, looked back right into her eyes. "We've been helping Mama."

"I suppose cutting trees is more important than passing grades."

"Yes, ma'am. . . . I mean no, ma'am. Ummm . . . I was wondering if I could keep up with my lessons while I'm out. I can come get Macon after school and find out what everybody did that day and . . ."

"Those are privileges for students who cannot come to school because of afflictions. Not for those who choose to play hooky." The sternness of her voice caused Keaton to put his hands back into his pockets. Miss Clarkson clicked her heels together the same way the girl did in his favorite book, *The Wonderful Wizard of Oz.* If only he could do the same and disappear.

"Now your mother knows better than this," Miss Clarkson continued. "Ella, of all people. If she would have kept after her own education, then she wouldn't . . . well, let's just say she knows the importance of being educated."

"We have to cut the timber to pay the bank back," Macon quickly said. Keaton wanted to punch him for telling their personal business. No matter how bad it had gotten, their mother had told them to always hold their heads high and say nothing.

"I can appreciate that, but I understand there is a man at your house who can do such work. And speaking of this man . . . who exactly is this person?"

Keaton stared hard at Macon as if to tell him in some telepathic way that if he said another word, Keaton would punch him but good. "He's my daddy's cousin," Keaton said just like Ella had told him to if anyone asked about the man in the box. "He's come to help out for a while."

Miss Clarkson rose up on her toes and brushed the chalk stain from her skirt. "Mm-hmm."

Keaton felt an invisible force pushing his shoulders down. He kept thinking that if his father had never gotten sick and started taking the opium, none of this would be happening to them. He hated the opium and pictured himself jumping up and down and crushing all of the glass vials that his father had tucked inside his pants pocket over the past year. Then he'd click his heels and make an invisible wall around the store, a fortress that would never let any opium enter.

Walking back home with Macon in his care, Keaton didn't punch his brother for telling their secrets. Keaton didn't say anything at all. He just slowly walked down the dirt road dotted with clay-covered rocks and dried moss and pretended to listen as Macon rattled on about a new marble he'd won during recess. Unlike times past, Keaton didn't bother to chase away the feeling of hatred for his father. Today he let it seep in and settle inside his soul.

The lunch crowd was just beginning to thin out of the Owl Café in Apalachicola as Clive Gillespie walked past. The top of his derby hat brushed the shoulders of the business owners who filed out. The men nodded reluctant pleasantries to Clive, whose popularity among the citizens matched his stature. He stood five foot six. Looking up to the men coming out of the restaurant and tilting his chin back with authority, Clive had no way of knowing that two of the men whose businesses were being foreclosed on had just finished off two dozen oysters and talked about doing the same to Clive. He was on a tear, calling in loans, turning a deaf ear to financial hardships, and taking over prime downtown real estate. "It's all within the law," he would answer to the few who threatened to challenge him in court.

Inside the office of the *Apalachicola Times*, the new city reporter, a boyish man who still had polish left on his shoes from his graduation ceremony, sat with his long legs stretched across a desk piled high with yesterday's newspapers. A small open window sat above the printing press that was still smoldering from use. Every time the hot breeze swept in from the window, the curtains parted, revealing a flock of seagulls hanging in midflight above the dock outside.

When Clive opened the door and the bell rang, the young man didn't even bother to lower today's edition. He held the paper up in front of him like a blockade. "What might you need?"

"I thought lunch hour ended fifteen minutes ago."

The sound of Clive's voice caused the young man to jump and the paper to rumple. He tossed it to the desk and sprung up, straightening a faded blue necktie.

"Yes, sir, Mr. Gillespie. Have another foreclosure for me to list?"

Clive half grunted and half laughed. "That's yesterday's news."

The young man sat back down at the desk and dug a notepad from underneath the stack of papers.

"Is Levitt here?" Clive asked.

"No, sir, he's over in Carrabelle today, covering the new train route that's coming through."

"Well, he and I have been talking for some time about a series of . . . not stories . . . but I guess you could say . . ."

"Editorials."

"Why, sure. *Editorials* would fit the bill. We were talking about a series that calls the townspeople out of this malaise. To remind them of what this city once was . . . what it can be again." Clive massaged the acne scars on the side of his face. "Yeah, I am confused. We keep talking, but he never starts writing."

The young man scribbled notes on his pad. "People want progress here. The government keeps talking about putting a ship-building plant here. You know, with the war and all."

"Somehow the words *government* and *progress* don't excite me. No, what I'm talking about is huge." Clive unbuttoned the top of his jacket and bent down closer to the young man's face. "I'm talking about an event that will generate so much revenue, it will make King Cotton look like a pound of mullet. I'm talking about a national figure coming to Apalachicola and making claims that have never been made before. A theologian, you might as well call him. A man who is set to make a revelation about a piece of land in our county that no other place in the world can claim."

As the young man scribbled on his pad, Clive reached down and pulled the pencil from his fingers. "I'm talking off the record for now. But you need to build this event. If you start a whole series about this area needing an economic lift, well . . . just maybe you'll get one too." Clive winked, and the young man's eyes widened. Clive picked up the pencil and tossed it on a stack of papers with yesterday's news. "Off the record. I'm about to fill you in on something the likes of which Franklin County has never seen."

On a Saturday morning when the daylight air was already thick as wool, Ella took the newspaper that she hadn't had time to read and wrapped the pages around the sandwiches she'd made for that day. The headline "Apalachicolans Looking for a Miracle" and part of the column listing the latest foreclosures covered a ham sandwich. She tucked it inside the tin pail along with the others.

After the sandwiches were eaten and the paper wrappings balled up and trashed, neither whipping nor pulling could make the oxen or mule move. Ella, fearing what the community might say if she continued to cut her timber on Sundays, heeded Narsissa's warning that the defiant animals were a sign. "If God can make a jackass talk like the Good Book says, then He can sure have His way with yours, too." Tomorrow would be the first Sunday since Lanier had arrived that they didn't cut, stack, and count timber.

"If we don't wind up walking the streets, it'll be a miracle," Samuel protested that evening as he flung rusted chains back into the pile of equipment. Ella, frozen, stood at the barn door, feeling sweat run from her hair and cascade into her ears. She pretended not to hear him and forced an awkward smile at Lanier, who stared at Samuel.

Daybreak on Sunday cast a weak glow across the inside of the barn. The mule plowed at the dirt and knocked his head against the stall door. After Lanier had fed and watered the animal, he put on the shirt he washed the night before and slipped out through the barn door. He eased past the pair of oxen that were standing in the pen Samuel had built.

By now he had learned all of their schedules. Narsissa would wake first and then Ella. Together they would prepare the breakfast, and Samuel would come out to pump water for the morning. Lanier didn't want to be around them this morning. There was a stamp of darkness on him again. He had feared that it would return. For a while he had succeeded at keeping it at bay, but this morning he had awoken with its grip around his neck again. It was an iron yoke that Old Lady Cash, the woman who wore a man's torn felt hat and her deceased husband's dungarees, had called a generational curse. She had informed him of his curse on a summer's day years ago when he had skipped school and was down by the edge of the creek, cutting the water with thrown rocks. As he picked up a piece of slate with a green streak down the middle, he felt someone grab his wrist. Three teeth stuck out from her mouth, and her gray eyes had a wildness that caused Lanier to look back toward home. She stood over him the same way the lush mountain in the background towered over her.

"Your mama know you out here?"

"Yes, ma'am."

The grip tightened, and when she turned her head, the old woman's felt hat tipped farther to the side. "Don't you tell me no story."

Lanier had heard that she was a witch who could read minds. "No, ma'am. She don't know."

"Just what I figured," Old Lady Cash said and released his wrist. She groaned when she reached down and stuck a wooden bucket into the creek. Water rushed against the sides and into the bucket. The woman held the side of her hip when she lifted the bucket back up. "A sorry liar. That daddy of yours was right up yonder with the Prince of Lies. You no different, I reckon."

Lanier was ten. Even though his mother forbade him from mentioning the father he could only recall through broken memories of wayward grins and screaming fights, others had gladly told him at school. A rapist. A murderer. A caged beast. A dead man walking in the Atlanta prison. Lanier had heard them all, the taunts told right to his face and those whispered behind his back.

"They might tell you you're a fatherless child, but that ain't nothing but a lie. That man's seed got aholt of you, and there ain't nothing you can do to stop it," the woman said. Water sloshed when she walked away. "He killed my sister, and he'll pay for that the rest of his life and on until the next. The den of hades has his name on it. I know, 'cause I seen to it. I cursed that daddy of yours the day they hauled him out in front of the judge. Right then and there I cursed his whole generation. Ain't a thing you can do to stop it neither." When she got to the top of the bank, she laughed and dipped her hands into the water. She flicked her fingers at him, and water hit his face. Lanier flinched but didn't blink. He let the cool water soak into his skin the same way he soaked in his father's shame.

As Lanier walked deeper into the brush, past where they had cut timber the day before, a branch from a scrub oak slapped his face, stinging him back to the present. Old Lady Cash's words were as heavy on him as the day they had first been delivered. *Forgive me my trespasses as I forgive those who trespass against me,* he kept repeating in his mind. But no matter how many times he recited the words or closed his eyes and pictured them scribbling across a blank page, he could never relieve himself of the sins of the father. The past shaded his mind until at times he was certain darkness had overtaken him, had sought him out the same way he figured it had eclipsed his father.

Lanier walked deeper into the brush, jerking the branches and vines as hard as he wanted to snatch away the torment that he pictured as vines around his brain.

A palmetto shrub tangled around his ankles. A thick layer of vines partly shielded his view of the water and cypress that lay ahead. Out in the dark lake that held knee-deep water, tall weathered trees rose up from the mud. Their twisted gray limbs made Lanier think of a witch with pointy fingers, buried deep below the lake's surface and reaching up, trying to claw her way back out again. A chill ran down to his core, and he pulled back a hickory limb that tried to block him from moving ahead. Ella's property seemed far away now, and for an instant he wondered if he had left Dead Lakes far behind him.

When he walked into a spider's web, Lanier stopped to peel away the layers. It was then that he heard their voices. Beyond a curtain of kudzu, Lanier could make out Narsissa sitting on the edge of the water. Her hair was free and the leg of her pants was rolled up to a fat knee.

"You haven't used that ointment I made for you, have you?"

"I used it some," Ella said.

When Lanier stepped closer he could make out Ella's back as she stood in a pool of water. The edges of the water were lined with palmetto bushes and a magnolia tree whose blooms fought to break free of the wild vines that tried to suffocate them.

Lanier stepped closer and crushed a moss-covered branch. The popping sound ricocheted down to the water, and Narsissa stopped massaging Ella's shoulder long enough to look in his direction. Lanier held his breath and stood frozen behind the branches of a pine sapling.

"Your shoulders are going to be as big as Samuel's before we are through with all this cutting."

"Please don't mention that boy's name. I was just beginning to feel some peace."

Narsissa playfully slapped Ella on the shoulder. "You hush. Besides, what would you have done without him?"

"Samuel might be sixteen, but he's still a boy—don't forget it. A boy can do heavy lifting but not heavy thinking. Besides, there's Lanier. You're forgetting Lanier. . . . He would have shown up to help me."

Narsissa sighed and shook her head.

"He was meant to pass this way. He was."

Narsissa laughed. "You're acting like a foolish schoolgirl."

"What? You can't possibly still think I'm a fool for letting him stay. Now you just can't."

"That man is up to something. I can sense it," Narsissa said. "Argue with me all you want."

"And you call me the fool? Now I want you to hush with all that."

"I'm telling you, I sense something, and it ain't good."

Ella balled her fist and hit the water. "You and your senses. I wish you could have sensed when Harlan was fixing to run off. Or maybe when he took out that loan? That would have been a good time to have your senses. Or how about when your own husband took off to Brazil? So I guess we see how good your senses work."

Bubbling water and the cry of a blue jay broke the silence. Ella never looked up from the water. She reached up and tried to squeeze Narsissa's hand.

Narsissa pulled her fingers out from her grip. "And I did sense it when my husband left. I felt it in my chest like an itch that couldn't be scratched. I knew it was the way he felt. His family didn't want him on account of marrying me. The town didn't want him on account of marrying me. He couldn't stand it. He opted to run off to a make-believe world. . . . I know what I know."

Lanier stood watching them long after Narsissa had stopped massaging Ella's glistening back. He couldn't turn away when Ella climbed out from the water and wrapped herself in a towel. A burning from the grip on his neck ran down his body. Fear and temptation tangled together. He closed his eyes and felt the racing pulse in the vein of his neck. He was tired of fighting the curses thrown at his father's generation. Evil was pumping through his body, he was sure of it. It was the fury of his bloodline that scared him. A tortured beast he could no longer harness.

7

The calendar with a sketch of a redheaded girl holding a bottle of Coca-Cola hung from a nail on the wall behind the store cash register. Ella began each morning by drawing an *X* through yesterday's date, signifying another day completed with the timber cut. There were eleven blank dates remaining on the calendar before the thirty-first was circled, indicating the last date before the bank would take ownership of the store and farm. With the help of Keaton and Samuel, they were making progress. Pine bark and tar-tipped stumps now marked the path they had made across the land. The low-lying bed of water and the cypress trees were now visible through the gaps in the pine trees that remained to be harvested.

Ella shielded her eyes from the rising sun and counted the timber stacked along the edge of her property the same as she did every morning. The muscles in her shoulders, neck, and back still ached, but there was lightness in her bearing that she hadn't felt in some time. Avery Herndon, a wide-faced man with a potato-shaped nose, came by from the lumber mill. He scratched figures and ran his finger across the lines in the tree trunk.

"I beg apologies for coming so early. Hope I didn't get you out of bed," Avery said as he looked down at the palm-sized pad where he did his figuring.

Ella cocked her head to the side and stopped short of asking if he was joking.

"Good wood," the lumberman said and ripped out the ticket with his figures. "The Army is after us for more yellow wood like you got. Pine is treasured right now with all the building of training camps and so forth. I want to work with you."

Ella grabbed the ticket and breathed deeper than she had in ages.

After he had driven off with pine straw and tree bark raining down from the flat bed of his truck, Ella quickly tucked the estimate inside her hat. A piece of the paper broke away and stuck to the gluey pine tar that she could never completely remove from her hands. Fear whispered to her that if she held the dollar amount too long between her fingers, the deal might evaporate. So with her fingernail she scraped the sliver of paper off her index finger and quickly stuck it in her pocket.

When Ella looked up, the schoolteacher, her once close friend Neva Clarkson, was making her way along the side of the road to the one-room schoolhouse. Neva's cheeks seemed plump and pristine, her complexion milky like those illustrated in advertisements for beauty products. Pulling the collar of her work shirt up against the side of her face, Ella hoped to hide the tanned, leathered evidence of her work out in the sun. She stared at Neva's rounded, porcelain-colored face. She had never noticed her skin being so perfect, so dainty. She wondered whether Neva's skin would still be so taut if she had ended up marrying Harlan like all had thought.

If only for an instant, the women who had once shared secrets and a room at Miss Wayne's school locked eyes. Ella could feel Neva's reprimand for having allowed Keaton and Samuel to miss the last weeks of school. It was a severe gaze offered with a tilt of the chin and a quick bat of the eyelashes.

"Morning, Ella," Neva muttered before adjusting the books she carried and rotating on her heels. With the back of her fair neck facing Ella, the woman walked up the road in the direction of her life's work.

Ella opened her mouth and let go of the shirt collar. Words she had meant to compose in a letter to Neva explaining the circumstances and pledging her commitment to educate her sons became tangled on her tongue. "Morning," she finally stammered. Right then she wished that the pine tar on her hands would cover her entire body, shellacking her like an amateur painting, creating a glossy shield behind which all of her shortcomings would be disguised.

The sound of a tambourine provided Ella an excuse to look the other way. From the opposite end of the road came the village eccentric. High-stepping in front of the beekeeper's home, wearing white shoes, was Ruby Tucker, the sixteen-year-old daughter of a man who stayed drunk half the time and trapped fish the other half, when he was sober. Ruby held the tambourine high in one hand and used her baton like a walking stick in the other hand. She wore a green turban with red sequins shaped like cherries. If she had been any other girl, Ella would have thought she was glamorous.

Ruby stopped and looked at the timber. She brushed the sweat from her brow with her forearm, and the tambourine chimed. "That sure is a lot of wood, Miss Ella." The girl's teeth were bucked, and the words sounded slurred.

"How are you making it today, Ruby?" Ella rubbed her index finger against the side of her denim pants.

"Fine. I told Daddy I was late with the parade. I know y'all been thinking I wouldn't come this month." Ruby toyed with a thread of cloth dangling from the tambourine.

Giving up on trying to remove the tar on her finger, Ella looked at the girl and smiled. "You're a welcome distraction." Ruby made it to town at the end of every month, pretending that she was leading a parade down the dirt road of Dead Lakes. "But it's not the last Friday yet," Ella said with a lift to her voice, trying to sound playful.

Ruby turned her head and studied Ella. Fury overtook her narrow eyes. Mrs. Pomeroy was coming out of the store and just about to walk over and speak to Ella when Ruby screamed, "It is so Friday!"

Mrs. Pomeroy stopped, and two men who were sitting on the porch steps stood up. Ella reached over to pat Ruby's arm but was pushed away. Ella looked at those staring and tried to whisper. "I just meant it's not the last Friday of the month. No need to get upset."

"I always have my parade on the last Friday of the month." For good measure, Ruby stomped her foot, and a rock hit Ella's leg.

"Ruby, now there's no need for all that."

Ruby bolted toward Ella and poked her chest with the baton. "My parade is the last Friday of the month. It is the last Friday of the month," she screamed.

Ella tried to push the baton away.

Spit flung from Ruby's mouth. "You and Daddy. Neither one of you want me to lead my parades. But Mr. Clive does. Mr. Clive likes my parades. He likes how high I can lift my legs." As if to prove her point, Ruby yanked her dress up to her knees and kicked out her legs. The ends of her faded red dress unfurled to reveal torn beige underwear.

Ella took a step backward and suddenly felt more vulnerable. When she had spoken to Ruby's father about her frightening customers with the flamboyant way she led her make-believe parades around the store, she never guessed that he would reveal it to his daughter, who had the curvy body of a woman but the underdeveloped mind of an eight-year-old.

"Mercy," Mrs. Pomeroy said. She leaned over the store railing and peered down at Ella. "Should I go get the law?"

Ella shook her head and then smiled at Ruby. "You're right, Ruby. You're exactly right. Today is your parade day."

Ruby gradually moved the baton away and straightened the turban on her head. As Ruby marched on, shaking the tambourine and pumping the baton higher in the air, Ella tried to reassure Mrs. Pomeroy that no harm was done.

"She's like a stick of dynamite just waiting to explode," Mrs. Pomeroy said. "Juanita told me she found that girl plundering around in her garden shed last week. Looking for something to steal, I have all idea." Mrs. Pomeroy fumbled with her wicker basket of shopping goods. "I don't care what her daddy says about not being able to control her; he ought to keep her locked inside the house. Nothing but white trash."

"It's difficult to raise them on your own . . . let alone raise a child who is touched in the head like her."

Mrs. Pomeroy swung the wicker basket across her forearm. "That might be the case, but with all of your trials and tribulations, we don't see your boys running wild that way." Mrs. Pomeroy turned to leave and then glanced back at Ella. "Bless your heart."

Watching Mrs. Pomeroy walk away toward her house, Ella didn't know whether to be honored or insulted.

"Now that girl with the stick was a sight," Lanier said as he put on his work gloves. He had appeared from behind Ella, and as usual she had not heard him walk up.

Ella fanned her hand across her bosom. "I declare. I didn't know you were standing there."

He began pulling out the tools from a steel box. In the distance the mule honked at the sound of the tools being jostled. "I was thinking I was going to have to break the two of you apart. That ole gal looked like she was ready to jump you."

"You mean Ruby. She means no harm. Just a little touched in the head. At the end of every month she marches up and down this road and sometimes all through the store, pretending that she's leading a parade. She has it in her mind that today's the last Friday of the month. So much for me setting her straight. I don't know who's sillier, me or her." Ella laughed.

Lanier stopped working and looked at her. His eyes narrowed and seemed even softer. "I don't think I've heard you laugh once since I've been here. You've got a nice laugh."

Ella felt a streak of fire run up her neck. She massaged the place where her embarrassment had shown and looked away from Lanier.

Narsissa plodded forward with chains balanced on both shoulders. "Samuel is bridling up the mule. That animal is acting more ornery than usual today. He kicked at me twice."

Lanier never looked away from Ella as Narsissa unfurled the chains across the ground. Narsissa looked at him and then at Ella. "What did I miss?"

Ella put on her work gloves and grabbed the end of the chain, pulling it out straight. "Ruby. She's come to town today for her parade. She's a week early, but she wouldn't believe me." Ella laughed again, but Narsissa only shook her head the same way she did whenever she thought Ella was acting childish. "I wouldn't play with her if I was you," Narsissa said and then tucked her coarse ponytail underneath the collar of a plaid work shirt. "Say what you will, but that girl's got the devil in her."

By lunchtime, Lanier had led them deep into the woods by the water's edge. He had taught all of them how to scout out and avoid cutting the diseased pines until most of the path back to the house was nothing but pine-straw-scattered sand dotted with decayed and rotting trees. While Ella handed out biscuits and Narsissa opened up a jar of honey, Lanier and Keaton sat against what remained of a beetle-infested tree with half of its top missing.

Samuel busied himself with watering the mule that stood with one leg half propped up. "His left leg is acting up again. See how he's giving on it," Samuel said.

"He'll be all right," Ella said. "Come have a biscuit. You need to eat."

Narsissa stood leaning against a pine. She looked out toward the cypress trees lining the low-lying water. "We don't need to get much closer to the water."

Lanier looked at her and then at the water's edge. "I don't expect we'll have to. With the progress we've made, I think we're doing good."

"Why, Narsissa?" Keaton asked, licking a drop of honey that was wedged between dirt and a piece of bark glued with tar to his thumb.

"Because she's scared of the bougars that will come out of the water and eat her," Samuel yelled over his shoulder. The chain on the mule rattled.

"Samuel, hush," Ella said. "Lanier will be scared of his own shadow."

"Yeah, I might decide to quit," he said and then smiled at Ella.

In frustration Ella spat out her words. "What she means is that there's a wives' tale about the water down there."

Narsissa looked Lanier up and down. She spoke her words cautiously, the same way she might if they were coming out of her mouth with pine needles attached. "No wives' tale to it."

"What's a wives' tale?" Keaton asked and pulled at the bark that was stuck to his thumb.

Narsissa threw the chain into a pile with the others. "It's not the time for us to work down there."

Ella yanked the belt tighter on her work pants. "Well, what time of day does your sixth sense tell you that I'll be moving into the poorhouse, Narsissa?"

Keaton looked up at Ella with surprise. Bits of biscuit fell from his bottom lip.

"Come look at the mule," Samuel called out. "I think we might need to dress his hind leg. It's swelled."

Just as Lanier was getting up, the sound of a whip cracking rang out in the distance. Keaton jumped up and pointed. Out from the brush a snake with its head raised high was moving so fast that it appeared to be running. Lanier stumbled trying to get up, and Ella knocked over a jug of turpentine. The mule darted to the side and the wagon tilted. The animal then kicked with its hind leg and twisted it in the chains used to pull the wood. Just as the mule cried out in pain, Narsissa screamed. The snake had wrapped around her leg, biting at her pants and whipping her leg with its tail.

Lanier grabbed a machete and ran toward her. Narsissa pulled at the snake, which kept twisting its head and snapping at her. Lanier pulled her hand away and then grabbed the snake by the back of its head. With a swipe of the blade, the snake's triangle-shaped head fell to the ground and blood splattered across Lanier's hand. The body of the snake still gripped Narsissa's leg. Out of reflex, its coarse tail whipped her once more before finally breaking free.

While the boys stood over the headless snake that still flailed and switched, Lanier examined Narsissa's leg. The mule called out and pranced to the side, farther away from the snake. A trio of crows cried out from one of the trees. The sound of their cawing grew louder as Lanier moved closer to Narsissa. Jagged marks ran down the side of her calf and ankle. Beads of blood began bubbling at the surface of the broken skin. Narsissa flinched whenever Lanier brushed his finger down the markings left by the snake's platted tail.

"Narsissa, are you all right?" Ella eased toward her as if another snake might be hiding and ready to strike.

"Coachwhip," Samuel said, leaning over the decapitated serpent. "It's a coachwhip snake."

Lanier seemed to envelop his torso over Narsissa's leg. His breathing was deep, and he mumbled something that was muted by the crows' cries and the boys' chatter over the dead snake.

"I've never seen one move that fast," Keaton yelled and kicked at the tail of the lifeless snake. "It just came out of nowhere."

Samuel reached down and picked up the snake's body. He dangled the black tail that looked like shrunken alligator hide in the air. "Look out," Samuel yelled, and Keaton jumped backward, tripping over the mule's feed bucket.

"Samuel, act right," Ella shouted. She turned away to reprimand Samuel further, and Lanier breathed directly onto the wounded flesh of Narsissa's leg. Jerking away from him, Narsissa pulled her leg, knee first, closer to the folds of her stomach. She stared at the streaks on her calf that were now seemingly nothing more than crooked lines that a child might have etched on her skin with a pencil.

When Ella returned to Narsissa, she bent down and lifted the edge of Narsissa's pants cuff with her pinky finger. "It's not as bad as I'd feared. I'm sure it stings like the devil. Should I get one of the boys to take you back home?"

Shaking her head, Narsissa studied Lanier. She watched him wrap the mule's leg and then playfully prod the boys back to work by tossing them axes.

That evening Narsissa stood on her porch with a piece of pine straw dangling from the side of her matted hair. She propped her boot up against the side of a rail and unfurled her hair. Wood chips, chiggers, and straw floated to the mismatched porch floor.

With hair hanging in tangles around her eyes, Narsissa quickly swiped the hair back over her head and then straightened the chime of shells that hung by her cabin door. It would be days before she confessed to Ella that an icy tingle came over her when Lanier touched her after the snake flogging. She would certainly never use the word *heal* or admit that there ever was blood on her skin.

Down at the barn, Lanier was unloading the equipment from the wagon. Holding two crosscut saws, he stopped and turned in Narsissa's direction. When she saw him watching her, she flicked at the chime, twisted her hair back into submission, and disappeared into her cabin.

The bronze letters *JWC* glistened between the two smokestacks on the *John W. Callahan* as it glided into port at Apalachicola. Smoke billowed from the steamboat, and a whistle on the deck sounded. Two black men with matching rubber boots helped to secure the boat's bow to the side of the dock. Their forearm muscles protruded against the rolled-up sleeves of their shirts as they secured a wooden plank with the painted words *Welcome to Apalachicola* against the side of the steamboat. The plank made a screeching noise as the boat rocked against the painted wood. A flock of seagulls suddenly took flight. "The *John W. Callahan*," one of the black men shouted.

"Coming to port," the other one added, as if not to be overshadowed.

The first to step off the boat was Brother Mabry and his wife, Priscilla. Standing at six foot six and weighing nearly three hundred fifty pounds, Brother Mabry towered over his wife, who looked more like a little girl than a woman in her late thirties. His mere appearance suddenly made the steamboat seem like a toy.

Before stepping onto the plank, Brother Mabry brushed the lapels of his signature crimson velvet jacket. The coat had become a brand of sorts for the man, an evangelist who traveled the country holding tent revivals and promising a mixture of redemption and reversal of fortune. "I advertise salvation, and this coat is my calling card. Crimson, like the blood of Jesus," he would tell reporters when asked about the custom-made jacket.

He had been born Alfred Mabry, the son of shoemakers in Brooklyn. After losing the family business, he had found his way again through a street preacher who had convinced him that he had the call to preach the gospel.

By the time Brother Mabry had grown a church from a few who met in an abandoned home into a congregation that assembled in a stonemasonry masterpiece on Columbus Square with pews for thousands, he had managed to marry Priscilla, the translucent-skinned daughter of an industrialist. She brought to the marriage a trust fund, a weakened constitution caused by childhood rheumatism, and a Victorian mansion in Chautauqua, New York.

When the couple stepped onto the dock, Clive Gillespie emerged from the crowd that awaited the boat's arrival. He motioned for a teenage boy with reddish-orange hair to retrieve the luggage trunk that had been placed by a pile of fishing nets.

"Brother Mabry," Clive called out with open arms. Sunlight glistened off his waxed hair.

"Mr. Gillespie," Brother Mabry said in a voice loud enough to match his stature. As the two men clasped hands, Priscilla stood nearby, holding a handkerchief to her nose.

"May I introduce my wife, Priscilla," Brother Mabry said with a wave of the hand.

Priscilla managed to nod at Clive. She pointed toward a warehouse next door with piles of empty oyster shells stacked twenty feet deep. "I don't recall the smell the last time I was here."

"Please excuse the aroma," Clive said with a laugh. "Oysters are high commerce here nowadays. When was your last visit to our town, Mrs. Mabry?"

"Thirty, maybe twenty-five years ago," Priscilla said and then placed the handkerchief back over her nose. With her hand she motioned for Brother Mabry to get moving.

Brother Mabry pulled Clive by the arm, saying, "Are we all set up at the inn?"

"Yes, indeed," Clive said. "Come this way, and I'll drive you. I know you will want to rest before dinner."

"Rest is for the deceased. I'm famished," Priscilla said and promptly put the handkerchief back over her nose. Passing by a group of children playing marbles by the door of a warehouse, Priscilla reached out with her free hand and brushed the head of a towheaded boy. "I was about his age when I came here and that Indian led my father to this place . . . this magical place. I wonder . . . I just wonder if that old man is still alive. Might he be alive, Mr. Gillespie?"

"If he is, then by pete we'll find him. Now I'm sure you see how Apalachicola has progressed since your last visit, Mrs. Mabry. Back then you probably had numerous train changes and the like. Now it's comfortable travel on steamboat. One thing I'd like to point out to you is the number of steamboats we have running here. Perfect for drawing in those needing water therapy. I'd say in the past five years, we've had an increase of travel from northern ports by . . ."

"Do you have the water?" Priscilla asked, as if suddenly realizing why she had made the journey in the first place.

"I have a container waiting for you at the inn." Clive smiled a toothy grin and then reached for the door handle of his automobile.

Priscilla paused before climbing in. "I wonder if the water will be as favorable to me outside of its natural habitation? What do you suppose, Brother Mabry?"

Brother Mabry placed his wide hand against Priscilla's cheek. His thick, long fingers eclipsed the paleness of her face. "Now, now. What did I tell you on the boat? Faith and the Lord's water healed you the first time, when that Indian brought you to this place. Faith will heal you again."

The smell of fried fish clung to the air at the local café in the port city. Waiters wearing black vests with stained aprons carried platters of food while bamboo fans rotated overhead. After being properly welcomed by the mayor, Brother Mabry, Priscilla, and Clive Gillespie took their seats at a corner table.

Dimitri, the café owner, was of Greek descent and had the leathered skin born of hard labor. He gently pushed the waiter aside and squeezed in next to the table. "Ah, Brother Mabry," the owner said in accented English. "We are honored to have you and your missus. Anything I can get you. Anything. You let me know."

Brother Mabry nodded and unfurled the white napkin. When he tried to tuck it inside his collar, fat rolled over the edges of his shirt.

Priscilla wiped the edges of a water glass with her handkerchief and then took a sip.

Clive Gillespie hunkered down and leaned over the table. "Dimitri there," Clive said, motioning his head toward their host, "came to town ten years ago to sponge fish, and now he's raking in the money with this restaurant. I tell you, he's a smart man. This town is growing by leaps and bounds. An ideal setup for our resort," Clive said.

"Retreat, Mr. Gillespie," Brother Mabry corrected and then broke off half the loaf of bread. "A retreat of spiritual and physical nurturing."

"Certainly," Clive said. "Retreat. Um, Mrs. Mabry, I never asked your husband, but exactly how did you come to find the springs out near Dead Lakes?"

Priscilla folded her handkerchief and placed it next to the silverware. "My father. He was the head of the Chautauqua festival in New York. Have you ever heard of it, Mr. Gillespie?" There was a sliver of preeminence to her voice.

Clive closed his eyes and smiled. "Certainly."

"Well, then you know that a little town not too far from here has the sister festival each winter."

"DeFuniak. DeFuniak Springs is the town," Clive said.

Priscilla turned her head. "Why, yes. Charming little village. Anyway, my father brought my sisters and me along with him to the festival the year I was thirteen. My doctor thought the warmer climate would be beneficial for my rheumatism."

"She's a walking miracle," Brother Mabry added. Crumbs of bread fell from his mouth. A man seated at the table next to them jumped at the sound of Brother Mabry's booming voice.

Priscilla cleared her throat and folded her napkin into a perfect square. "If you're familiar with the conclave, Mr. Gillespie, then you know that the participants are scholars always in search of knowledge. Experts in all fields come to share. The year we were attending, an Indian chief presented on his culture—very dramatic, with burning sage and chants and so forth."

The waiter came to take their order, and every person in the restaurant turned to stare. Clive turned and waved the waiter away. He also raised an eyebrow toward the other patrons around him, as if daring them to approach his table.

"Anyway, my father was so intrigued that he hired the Indian to take us to this supposed pool of water that he said had helped many in his tribe. Even his own granddaughter, he claimed." Priscilla fanned her face and took a sip of water. "It's so warm in here with all these people surrounding me, I'm feeling a bit flushed."

Clive reached for the paper menu, folded it in half, and began fanning it in Priscilla's direction.

"Thank you," Brother Mabry said.

"What a gentleman," Priscilla said with a smile. She patted her brow with the handkerchief.

"Are we okay now?" Brother Mabry asked.

Priscilla closed her eyes, dramatically inhaled, and smiled.

"And so what exactly did he do when you got to the spring?" Clive asked.

"Well, naturally, in my weakened state, I had to be eased into the water just so, you know. Much like you'd place a baby into a warm bath. Except the water was not hot like the springs I had been accustomed to. Even though it was January, the warmth was pleasant. Room temperature, I'd say." Priscilla pointed to the empty water glass in front of her. Brother Mabry and Clive motioned for the waiter both at the same time. He tripped over a lady's parasol trying to get to them fast enough.

"And were the results instantaneous? I mean, did you feel . . . ?"

"I felt warmth all over my body," Priscilla whispered. "It was the most intoxicating, exhilarating feeling I've ever known. Papa had the Indian man wrap me in a blanket after I'd been dipped, but I didn't need it. There was a glow all in me. We returned home on the train the next day and . . . I never shall forget it. Right after the conductor said we were nearing Tennessee, I leaned against the window and looked down at all those trees that ran down the side of the mountain and knew that I'd been healed."

"She just knew," Brother Mabry said.

"See, Mr. Gillespie. That is why I need this water once more. The doctors have given up hope on me. Terminal, they call this disease, this horrific disease that I have. Cancer." Priscilla whispered the word the same way she might if she were cursing in public.

Brother Mabry engulfed her hand in his. "The doctors say . . . but what does God say?" He massaged his lips with his tongue and studied Clive. "Do you believe in miracles?"

Clive flinched and stroked his chin. "Why, certainly. Absolutely." He reached for his glass of water and took a sip.

"Good," Brother Mabry said. "I knew when my man told me he had found the person who could help me develop this land that we had found an answer to prayer."

"Yes, of course," Clive said with a strong voice suited for a stage actor. When Brother Mabry's attorney had contacted him after researching the deed holder of the land with the spring, Clive was officially the owner. He refused to let the opportunity slip away from him now simply because Harlan Wallace had gotten him drunk one night. A scribble of his name on a bourbon-stained slip of paper at a poker table meant nothing. Even if the paper was witnessed, it was not a genuine deed in Clive's estimation. Besides, one way or the other the property would be his again anyway. "I want us to use the land for good. I want to help those who are in need. As soon as you mentioned building this resort—this retreat—I knew that I had to work with you. People from the North, the West . . . they'll be pouring in."

"I want to begin my water therapy immediately," Priscilla said.

"Absolutely," Clive responded and lightly tapped his knife against the table. "Now, I've taken the liberty of securing a young architect from Tallahassee to develop some plans . . . in keeping, as you suggested, Brother Mabry, with the Victorian theme."

Brother Mabry looked at Priscilla. "We want the retreat to be based on Wetherford Place, Priscilla's home."

"Absolutely. A fine home, I'm sure."

"I'm going to use every resource out there to get the word out," Brother Mabry said.

"Yes, absolutely. Get the word out."

"I want to begin my water therapy tomorrow, Mr. Gillespie," Priscilla said and balled up her handkerchief.

Clive rubbed his chin. "Well, now it's not an easy path to the spring, Mrs. Mabry. With all these afternoon thunderstorms this time of year, it might be a rough journey for someone in compromised health. I'm working on having my men clear the way through the overgrowth out there."

Brother Mabry reared back in the chair. "What's this?"

"I want to begin tomorrow," Priscilla said again. "Tomorrow at noon. The same time of day as when I was healed the first time."

Clive smiled and waved the paper menu, calling forth the waiter. "Knowing the urgency, I arranged for barrels of the water to be shipped to the inn for you. You can soak in the water in your private bath . . . you know, until you are stronger from the travel. Let's order, shall we?"

Priscilla leaned forward and the cuff of her silk dress dipped into the empty plate. "Bath? At the inn?"

"Absolutely," Clive said. "It will be an exact replication of that spring. I'm sure Brother Mabry can bless it and so forth and so on."

Brother Mabry reached over and rubbed her arm. "Mr. Gillespie has a point, sweetness. Your body needs to adjust to the climate, not to mention the long trip. The spring will be there when you're rested."

The waiter pulled a pad from his back pocket and walked toward Clive Gillespie. He sidestepped Dimitri, who was barking orders at the kitchen door near where Reverend Simpson, Myer Simpson, and Neva Clarkson sat.

Saturday was the day that most citizens in the surrounding areas would come to Apalachicola to make purchases of products that were not available in the small commissaries, such as the one Ella Wallace ran. But Brother Mabry, the famed evangelist whose picture had appeared in the papers and the newsreels that played at the theater, had made the normal downtown crowd swell threefold. Dimitri had hired two off-duty policemen to stand outside just to keep the curious from placing their hands on the restaurant windows and peering in.

Myer Simpson had even purchased a new red hat with a white egret feather rising from the back. "A circus over a mortal human being. I can't imagine making such a fuss." Myer glanced over at the table where Brother Mabry and Priscilla sat. Then she gasped and picked up the paper menu and held it to the side of her face as if to block them from seeing her. In a stage whisper she said, "Don't look now, but when you get a chance, I want you to look at his wife's shoes. That preacher's wife is wearing leather shoes. *Leather,* mind you. With all the rationing going on with the war, leather shoes are running fifteen dollars a pair. I know what I'm talking about. I've seen them priced in the catalogues. What preacher's wife can afford leather shoes in this day and age?"

Reverend Simpson was hunched over a plate of oysters. He picked up a half shell and tossed it back in his mouth the same way he might if he were taking a dose of medicine. "Well, certainly not the preacher's wife sitting at my table."

Myer Simpson looked at Neva Clarkson and rolled her eyes. Then she reached over and wiped away crumbs from a saltine cracker that had collected in the reverend's beard.

"Well, one thing about it," Neva said and dabbed a napkin at her lips. "All the racket over this preacher's visit will silence the talk about the man who appeared at Ella Wallace's doorstep."

Myer Simpson shook her head, and the feather waved back and forth. "Not for long. Nothing will stop the questions there as far as I'm concerned. I tell you . . . the reverend won't pay me any mind, but I tell you it is queer that this man shows up out of the blue. It's as if that man at Ella's walked right out from the fog."

"People come and people go," Reverend Simpson said and slurped down another oyster. "It's a port city."

"And when I tried to ask Narsissa about him the other day when I was leaving the store, she was just as rude as can be. You know she's always been an uppity thing to have no standing. Why, she practically gruffed at me, didn't she, Reverend?"

The reverend half nodded and jabbed his fork into a piece of fish on Myer Simpson's plate. He didn't seem to notice when Myer motioned with her pinky finger toward the spot in his gray beard where a sliver of an oyster lay.

Myer Simpson rolled her eyes and turned her attention back to Neva. "Now, am I crazy, Neva? Tell me it's not queer."

Neva looked down at the morsels of cheese grits and hush puppies left on her plate. "Ella certainly has her burdens. I just wish she didn't have to use those boys the way she's doing."

"What about that?" Myer Simpson rested her index finger on her chin. "The very notion . . . well, desperation will make you do desperate things. Neva, I'm just glad you didn't get strung along with that Harlan Wallace. I know you were sick at heart over him marrying Ella back in your growing-up days, but look at everything now. Well, just think . . . it could be you out there working like a pulpwood roughneck."

Neva pushed her plate to the side of the table and looked out the window at the townspeople who walked by, all of them craning their necks toward Brother Mabry. "What is it you say, Reverend? About the Lord being gracious in all His ways."

"Amen," Myer Simpson said and then shoved her plate away from Reverend Simpson's reach. "Now, Neva, what was it you were about to tell us about Ella using her boys?"

Neva fanned her hands in the air. "Oh, nothing. I just wish Ella would not have taken Keaton and Samuel out of school to help her cut the timber. Especially Keaton. He loves school as well as any student I have."

Myer Simpson made a clucking sound and shook her head again. "I tell you the truth, it's plumb pitiful. Her in that fix she's in and ruining her boys' morals with having that man live with her."

"Now hold on," Reverend Simpson said with a cracker in hand.

"They tell me Clive Gillespie offered her a fair price for the place," Myer said. The feather on her hat waved as she shook her head.

"Huh. I doubt it was a fair price if Clive Gillespie offered it," Reverend Simpson said as spit and cracker crumbs flew out of his mouth. "The only thing fair about him is his skin."

"What in the world is that girl thinking?" Myer said, ignoring her husband. "Oh, me. What a mess. And if Clive hadn't been out there gambling, he would have never lost all that property down by the river to Harlan in the first place."

"Now Mrs. Simpson," the reverend said.

"Don't you *Mrs.* me," Myer said. "Clive Gillespie is just as crooked as Harlan Wallace. The only difference is that he's dressed in better clothes. I've thought a number of times that he turned out the way he did because his mother left him before he could speak."

Reverend Simpson licked his lips, managing to strike the bit of oyster that clung to his beard with the tip of his tongue. "The things that occupy your mind." The reverend laughed, but no one followed, and he soon coughed into his napkin.

"Why, Miss Emmitt's wash girl used to work for the Gillespies. She said that the Gillespie woman never paid a bit of mind to that boy. She didn't even want to hold him after he was born." Myer Simpson leaned down until the roll of fat that clung to her midriff balanced on the edge of the table and whispered, "Miss Emmitt said that Clive, with no mother to count for, started calling the colored wash girl *Mama*. You can't tell me that such maternal desertion doesn't lead to problems in the head."

"I think it's probably more a problem of the heart," Reverend Simpson said.

"I wonder what became of her? Mrs. Gillespie, I mean. Where did she go?" Neva asked, glancing over at the table where Clive and the celebrated visitors sat.

"She was from South Carolina, if I recall," Reverend Simpson said, massaging his beard and removing another sliver of oyster meat.

"Georgia," Myer Simpson corrected with a cluck of her tongue. "She was from a big wheel family in Savannah. Spoiled rotten, they tell me. She took the first boat out of here after the Jones boy shot that man in the head in her husband's bank."

"Mercy," Neva said. "I'd forgotten all about that."

"Mm-hmm." Myer Simpson poked her tongue against the corner of her cheek until the side of her face poked out like a bump. "The Jones boy claimed the man had stolen his cattle. And come to find out he did. They settled it right then and there. No charges were filed. The Jones boy walked away scot-free. But the Gillespie woman was never the same after that day. Bad nerves, they tell me. Well, nerves or no nerves, you don't desert your family. You certainly don't break your biblical oath to your husband and just leave town."

The young waiter appeared and refilled Myer Simpson's glass. She pushed back against the chair as tea splattered to the table. "I declare. Pay attention." The waiter mumbled apologies and darted back toward Clive Gillespie's table.

Reverend Simpson looked directly at Neva. "I always said that she should teach history in your school. She can remember trivial details better than anyone I've ever known."

Neva picked up her handbag from the table and placed it in her lap. "Well, there you have it. Ancient history. I guess Ella and I were jinxed from the start. Harlan at first wanted to marry me, and Clive wanted to marry Ella. Either way, we both lost."

"You didn't lose, my dear," Reverend Simpson said. "Let's not forget that there is something to be said for never marrying."

Myer Simpson slowly turned her head toward the reverend. Her mouth twisted to the side, causing her face to seem even sharper.

"Well, just look at the apostle Paul. He never married," the reverend said.

"Poor Ella," Myer Simpson said. She looked up to the ceiling as if she might be at a loss for words and then she sighed. "Bless her heart. I always said Ella was petted too much by that hedonistic aunt of hers . . . all those art lessons and talk about painting in Europe." Myer Simpson giggled and rolled her eyes. "Now look at her. And what if she would have married Clive Gillespie? She wouldn't have been much better off. He practically drove that bank his daddy built into the ground."

The reverend tossed an empty oyster shell onto the platter that sat on the table. "Now I will give you that much. Clive Gillespie ruined everything his father worked for. The father was decent, from all accounts."

"Remember, right before his father died, Mr. Gillespie had to sell the family home place over in Baldwin County just to keep the bank from going under?" Neva asked.

"Just plain sorry. . . . I don't care how much money they had at one time. He is just plain sorry," Myer said.

"Who knows why certain humans are decent and others like Clive are . . . well . . ." Reverend Simpson rolled his shoulders into a shrug. "It's one of the mysteries that I chalk up to God."

Neva closed her eyes and leaned closer to the reverend. "Something is bothering me, Reverend Simpson. My cousin—the one I visited in Pensacola—well, she said I should come right out and ask you about it."

"What?" Reverend and Myer Simpson asked at the same time.

Neva licked her lips and opened her eyes. "Reverend, have you ever heard of the sort of healing that the man staying at Ella's place is reported to have performed?"

Myer Simpson clutched her chest with one hand and gripped Reverend Simpson's arm with the other. Her knobbed and curved arthritic fingers seemed like claws.

"You mean Mrs. Pomeroy didn't tell you?" Neva asked.

"Ever since she left the church to go associate with that Pentecostal bunch, I don't pay that woman any mind," Myer Simpson said.

"Mrs. Simpson," the Reverend said in a long sigh. "No, Neva, we've not heard about any healings."

Neva bit her lip and rubbed the corner of her napkin.

The reverend and Myer Simpson both leaned closer until the tip of Myer Simpson's feather touched Neva's hairline.

"Now, I don't know all the facts, but the children at school were talking about Ella's youngest son. He was sick—desperately sick, as you well know—then . . ."

"Then he was well," Myer Simpson added. "I saw him outdoors playing ball."

"Yes, and then all of the sudden he comes to school perfectly fine.

After I heard him telling the students on the playground about this visitor who healed him I—"

"Healed?" Reverend Simpson repeated.

"Macon said—and again, this is from a child, but it has bothered me enough to bring it up—Macon said that the man . . . this man they call Lanier . . . well, he put his mouth on Macon's and then he healed him."

Myer Simpson jerked backward against the chair, and her hat became askew.

"Good heavens," the reverend said.

"Now I'm talking behind a boy who is six," Neva said with a cautionary wave of her hand.

"Breathed on him?" the reverend asked.

"Kissed him on the mouth," Myer Simpson said twice.

"No," Neva said with her hand raised higher. "Now, he never said the word *kissed*. The boy said he felt that he was drowning and that this man cleared his lungs. All I know is that the day I took his lessons over to him, the poor little thing had blisters all over his lips and even in his mouth. Then he shows up at school perfectly fine."

The waiter, a mere boy himself with the beginning of a mustache, approached and cleared the plates from their table. Against a background of lunchtime chatter and clanking silverware, the three of them sat in silence, each looking in different directions. Neva leaned back and sighed. "Please don't repeat what I've told you. Again, he's just a child. You know how children are."

"None to worry, dear." The reverend patted Neva's hand.

"Why, of course not. You can't take children at face value. I wouldn't dare say a word," Myer Simpson said and adjusted her new hat.

8

Neva Clarkson was an invisible apprehension that rode on Ella's shoulders from the time she woke in the morning and felt the knots in her shoulders to the time the back of her sweat-soaked blouse stuck to her flesh out in the woods. Her onetime friend weighed on Ella as much as the axe she swung and the chains she dragged. No matter how many times she chastised herself for worrying with notions of Neva when she faced losing all that she owned, the burden would never leave her. Try as she might, Ella couldn't toss aside the chastening look of her former friend. Neva's judgment was as heavy as the rusted chain Ella lugged through a sandy path of palmetto bushes. She could feel it like metal digging into her collar, trying to pull her back. Ella imagined Neva's disapproving comments being sung throughout Dead Lakes with all the townspeople joining in to share their shock and disdain. The voices buzzed in her ear the same as the mosquitoes. *"What has become of Ella Wallace?"* she pictured Neva asking each and every one of them. *"What would her aunt think about her now?"*

The mule kicked his leg at the log closest to him, and the chains rattled in a rhythmic way that made Ella think of her aunt reading poetry to her on Sunday afternoons. She could still see in her mind's eye the way her aunt's long, thin fingers would fan out across the cover of the book as she held it. Dickinson was their favorite, and the lines bubbled to the surface of Ella's memory. *"'Tis dogged does it,"* her aunt chimed. Gritting her teeth, Ella lifted the axe high above her head and swung it into the tree in front of her with a ferocity that left a cat-face-shaped scar on the bark of the tree.

The mule kicked faster, now with both hind legs, and the chains sounded as if they might break apart.

Samuel's voice broke through the rhythm of Ella's memory. "The mule's got a lick on his leg," he yelled. He was hunched over the animal examining the injured spot. Blood was beginning to spew from the mule's ankle.

"Is it broke?" Keaton asked.

"I don't think so, but it's sure bleeding," Samuel said.

They all dropped their equipment and fussed around the mule, examining the creature for further injuries. Only Narsissa looked straight ahead toward the swamp water.

By the time they had made it out of the woods and back to the stack of timber in front of the house, the mule's leg was bleeding profusely. Worry had settled over Ella. If the mule was out of commission, the remainder of the timber would go uncut. The man from the lumberyard had included the uncut timber in the estimate for payment that she was to receive. Promises had been made. A gentleman's agreement, the lumberman called it.

"How bad is it?" Ella stroked the mule's mane while Samuel lifted his hind leg. The mule whinnied in a high, pierced shrill and darted to the side. Lanier moved to take a look, and Samuel stomped harder than the mule had.

"That's right. Go ahead and take over. You seem to know everything." Samuel marched off toward the barn and didn't turn around when Ella called out to him.

"Let's see what we got here." Lanier lifted the mule's leg.

Ruby was marching back and forth down the road, carrying her baton. Two men who had been sitting on the store porch were now walking toward them. "You got a hurt mule?" the one with the suspenders asked.

Mrs. Pomeroy came out of her home and called to Ella, "Is everything all right?"

All the while, blood poured from the animal. When the mule stepped to the right before walking unbalanced and falling to the ground, everyone stepped closer. "Is it dead?" Mrs. Pomeroy asked.

"Is it dead?" Ruby said in a mocking tone.

Lanier hovered over the leg while Keaton massaged the mule's neck and whispered to him. Ella pulled off her gloves and massaged the callused places inside her left palm. The people moved closer to her, and she felt as if they were stealing the air away. She struggled to breathe while she looked at the mule and then back at the timber.

Wrapping his hands around the mule's leg, Lanier gripped tighter when the animal tried to kick. Eventually the mule quieted and let Lanier take control of his injury.

Narsissa watched closely as Lanier bowed his head, the curls of his hair hiding much of his mouth. She couldn't make out what he was mumbling but she could tell that he was moving his lips like he had done earlier with her. When Lanier let go of the mule's leg, Narsissa stepped backward. The blood on the animal's leg was gone, completely washed clean. Lanier and Keaton pulled the mule up by his bridle.

"Is it a permanent injury?" Ella asked.

"He'll be all right directly," Lanier answered. But there was no waiting for healing. The gash in the mule's leg had disappeared as fast as the injury had occurred.

"Look-a there," the man with the suspenders said. "That mule's not giving on that leg one bit."

"Was it that leg that was cut?" the other man asked.

"I don't think it was so much a cut as it was a scrape," Lanier answered.

Ella looked at Lanier and opened her mouth to speak but didn't.

"Scrape? That poor animal was liable to bleed to death. There was blood everywhere," Mrs. Pomeroy said, gripping the buttons on her blouse.

"Blood everywhere. Everywhere blood," Ruby said.

"I don't see no blood now," one of the men said.

"What? What happened here?" Mrs. Pomeroy asked and then stepped backward, bumping into Ruby, who was marching in circles.

"For he's a jolly good fellow," Ruby began to sing.

"That mule was bleeding profusely," Mrs. Pomeroy said.

"He was about to bleed out, looked like it to me," the man with the suspenders said. The sun caught one of the brass buttons on the suspenders and it sparkled for a moment. The man looked at the mule and then back at Lanier.

"Now look at that mule, walking around like nothing was wrong," the other man added.

Keaton and Samuel led the mule back to the barn. Lanier wanted to feed the animal and put him back in the stall just like he had every night since he'd been in Dead Lakes. He hoped that the crowd would move on and go back to normal conversations about the weather. *They'll forget about this soon enough,* he kept telling himself.

"For he's a jolly good fellow," Ruby sang. "For he's a jolly good fellow that nobody can deny." Her singing echoed all the way down to the barn.

When the crickets called and the slivered moon first appeared that evening, Lanier came out of the barn carrying the tray that Narsissa had brought him for supper. She had piled the plate high with extra pieces of fried chicken legs.

As Lanier rounded the garden of sunflowers, he looked up and found Ella sitting on the porch steps of the house. She had a sketchbook on her lap and was bent over, intensely gripping a yellow piece of chalk. Sheets of papers drawn with sunflowers scattered the porch steps.

"I didn't know we had an artist on the place."

Ella jumped and folded the pad shut. She tossed it to the side and the yellow chalk rolled down the first porch step and lodged against the corner of the banister. "Let me get that for you." Ella stood and took the supper tray from Lanier. Their hands brushed against each other.

Lanier felt the cool of the sweat on his back again. "I'm sorry. I didn't mean to interrupt your work."

"Work? Hardly. Play, more or less."

"I wouldn't say that." Lanier leaned down like he might pick up one of the drawings. "Can I?"

"I'd rather you didn't."

"Sorry," he said, stepping aside, brushing against the azalea bush. "I learned to like art back in Bainbridge when . . . well. How long have you been drawing?"

Ella set the tray down on a small wicker table next to the front door. "Since I was a girl. I'd never thought about it . . . about how long it's been."

A dragonfly paused in midflight in the space between them and then moved closer to the bush.

Ella rubbed the back of her neck and looked around the porch floor, searching for the chalk. Lanier picked the piece up and handed it to her. This time he purposely brushed his fingers against hers. "I like to whittle dolls," he said. "I have done that since I was a kid too. Looks like we have something in common after all."

The sun sank until it became an orange glow beyond the tops of the trees. Lightning bugs were called out in time for the first evening star.

"I'd like to paint again, but for now . . ." Ella shrugged and laughed. "Why am I feeling like such a schoolgirl right about now?"

"You tell me." He studied her full lips and the white tips of her teeth. He liked the way she would lightly roll her tongue across her lips whenever she finished a sentence. Her blue eyes swam in tiredness, making them seem even more translucent.

Ella looked over Lanier's shoulder at the road where Ruby had led a make-believe parade in Lanier's honor. "Lanier, may I ask you a personal question?"

He laughed and looked up toward the sky that was now dotted with more stars. "After the way I showed up here, I figure I'm pretty much an open book now."

Ella smiled and shook her head. "I'm being serious. I need to settle something in my mind. What happened today . . . what happened with Macon and then with Narsissa and the snake . . . well . . . do you consider yourself to be a Christian man?"

Lanier's laugh turned into a sigh and he looked back up at the evening sky. He pictured the words handed down by Old Lady Cash raining down upon him.

Ella reached out her hand. The tips of her fingers brushed against his forearm. "Now please don't take offense. The reason I'm asking is . . . well, out there today, with people seeing you that way with the mule and all of these signs and symbols . . ."

"Signs and symbols?"

"Look, Narsissa has been scaring me to death with her talk. She thinks . . . I don't know . . . that there is some black magic to all of this stopping blood business."

"I guess she thought it was on account of signs and symbols that that snake let go of her leg, too."

Ella pulled at the cuff of her shirt. "I shouldn't have said that. . . . It's just that with all of the people standing around today, I know there will be talk."

"You know, after all my book learning, I've really only learned one thing I know to be a fact. What folks might think of me is none of my business." Lanier turned back to the barn. "Thank you for supper. Have a good evening." He raised his hand as much to say good-bye as to register his frustrations.

A sunflower leaf slapped across his shoulder as he called out, "I think the thing for me to do is to move on from here." With each step toward the barn he felt the anger and heaviness of his time in Bainbridge boiling to the surface. The ugliness of his past, all of the things that he was running from, were finally catching up with him.

The quiet dawn was cut by the squeal of the whistle from the steamboat *John W. Callahan* as it made its way back upriver from Apalachicola and onward to the next port of call. The bronze star and eagle on the boat's bow were darkened black from the smoke that billowed from the two tall pipes. As the boat made its way around the bend of Dead Lakes, only a speckled hound noticed. He ran down the riverbank, barking at the boat and swinging his head at the sound of the whistle. By the time the boat made the corner and grazed the tips of moss that hung from a low-hanging tree on the bank, the dog had gone back to sniffing for the smell of fresh ham and bacon that hung in the air. He trotted past the church and school and paused in front of Ella's store.

Ella came out of her house carrying a tray, and when the dog trotted toward her, she carefully balanced the tray and tried to shoo the dog away all at the same time.

The same tray that Lanier had left on her porch last evening now held a plate of biscuits and ham. She stepped across the yard carefully, watching the coffee slosh around the edges of the cup. Lanier's declaration from the evening before had echoed in her mind and tied up the muscles in her body, strangling the desire for rest. She needed Lanier Stillis to stay and help. She desired him to stay.

The kerosene lantern still burned at the barn entrance. Lanier sat on the feed crate. Wood shavings littered his boots. He glanced up at Ella and continued whittling. "Some folks pray before they start the day. I whittle. But I guess that's not surprising with me being a heathen and all." He stopped long enough to look up and offer Ella a sideways smile.

"I am sorry about how we left things yesterday evening." She lifted up the tray of breakfast as if it might be a peace offering.

Lanier brushed the wood shavings from his pant legs and stood up. "I could smell the ham out here about as good as that hound that was following you."

Ella waited for Lanier to move a bridle from the workbench and then set the tray down. When she moved past Lanier, he could smell her lavender scent and was reminded once again that beyond the checkered work shirt and denim jeans was a lady. When she turned toward him and offered the cup of coffee, he feared that she had caught him staring at her.

"Here's to a snakeless and a cloudless day," he said and offered a toast.

"You know, about what I said last evening . . ."

"Let's not study all that again."

Ella held up her hand. "No, I want to say something. Now, in all fairness to Narsissa, I said what I said because of people knowing about . . . well, about your special . . . abilities or gifts or whatever."

"So I really am special after all?"

"The healing is what I'm getting at."

"Oh." Lanier sipped the coffee and playfully winked at Ella.

"Must everything be construed into a silly joke?"

"The way I figure it, better to joke than cry."

"I've thought more about what you said last night. And I want to say that I'm glad you can afford to turn a blind eye to what others might think of you, but in my defense, I have a business to run. I don't have the luxury of being so lackadaisical about perceptions."

"Perceptions?"

"Yes. People around here know what you had for breakfast by lunchtime."

He sipped the coffee and looked away. The mule kicked the side of the stall and without putting the cup of coffee down, Lanier grabbed a bale of hay with one hand and tossed it into the mule's stall. "I know you've got a lot on your mind. You've managed better than most. What you've been through would have broken many a man."

"That's just it," Ella said and leaned sideways. "If I were a man, I wouldn't have to be so concerned with the impressions of others. I could run around God's creation at will, run up gambling debts, and people would say I was just being a man . . . a sorry man, mind you, but a man all the same."

A chimney swift swooped down low through the barn door and then back out again. Ella never flinched.

"I have been running this place for months whether anybody knows it or not. Harlan left this place long before he walked away."

Lanier held up the biscuit in the air. Crumbs fell from his mouth and the mule raised his head from the bale of hay. "I'm starting to feel like one of us is saying the wrong things again. This time I think it's me," Lanier said and wiped his hands on his trousers.

"It's different for you than it is for me. And don't get it in your mind that I'm seeking sympathy. I am certainly not. I'm just explaining it to you. I have children. Whether it is justified or not, what is said about me in this community affects them. I have obligations beyond myself." Ella walked to the barn door and looked out at the orange colors that were beginning to spread in the sky over the oak trees. Frogs were still calling out from beyond the swamp. "And another thing. I cannot have you eating out here like some hobo drifter. You are going to get a cut of this timber. The way I see it, that makes us partners."

"Partners?"

"Business partners, don't you think? In fact, that's what I told the timberman when he asked about you."

"I thought you told him I was a hired man."

"He said no man works that hard unless he's getting a cut." Ella stopped at the barn door and halfway turned. She pulled a red handkerchief from her pants pocket and tied it around her neck. "Plan on coming inside for supper tonight."

"Is that an invite or an order?" Lanier licked his lips and took another sip of coffee.

The mule brayed and Ella offered a smile before turning to go.

"All right. But what will Samuel say about all this?"

Ella spun around. One eyebrow was arched higher than the other. "I'll have you know, Mr. Stillis, that I still sit at the head of the dining room table."

"I'll try to remember that," Lanier said, but Ella never heard him. She had already made it past the sunflowers and was halfway back to her home.

At the close of the workday, after Brother Mabry and Priscilla were tucked away in the suite at the inn, Clive Gillespie sat on the front porch of his home down by the dock in Apalachicola. The soft clanging noise of the boats rocking on the water swept through the city park across from Clive's house and rolled up the porch steps to pacify him. Clive struck a match against the stone on the pillar closest to him and lit a Cuban cigar. The porch ran down the front of the clapboard building and was held up by four stone columns that had been specially crafted by Clive's father to resemble the pyramids of Egypt. Inside were five bedrooms, all empty except the main one that Clive occupied. His wife had died giving birth to their last son, who was now eleven and like the other three sons was in a military school in Alabama.

A man wearing suspenders, a drifter who had once worked for Clive's bookie in New Orleans, meandered up the stone pathway to the home. He had his hands in his pockets and whistled as he walked. His boyish posture would never indicate to anyone that he had slashed the throats of an insurance executive and a whore—who just by happenstance had been picked up by a man who failed to make good on his bets.

"Evening," the man with suspenders called out.

"Evening," Clive said. "What you got for me, Roy?"

Roy wasn't the man's real name. It was Gunther, but Clive's bookie had been stingy with details. The bookie simply promised that his man would do the job and then disappear, and that was good enough for Clive.

The man pulled at his suspenders and laughed. "It looks like you had yourself a day of it. Hauling that preacher all around. Did you find religion yet?"

"No," Clive said and blew cigar smoke right at the man. "But he thinks that he's found the Garden of Eden, and that's good enough for me."

"It won't be long now," the man said and planted his hands back inside his pants. "I was down there the other day. Me and my partner . . . you know, checking the scenery out and so forth. They're fixing to have that place cut clean."

"Yeah, and who knew she'd have a boyfriend to help her out."

The man licked his lips and twisted his hands inside his pockets. "That man ain't right."

"Is he going to be trouble for you?"

"No, I don't figure he will." The man glanced up at the frosted glass above the front door of Clive's home. "I've seen a lot in this world. I ain't but thirty-six. Some say I've seen enough to be seventy-six. But one thing I've never seen me is a man who could make a lame mule walk again just by laying hands on him."

Clive leaned up from the rocking chair and held his cigar up like a torch. "What are you carrying on about?"

"We was down there the other day when they all came out of the woods with this crippled mule they work with. The leg was pouring blood. Blood all over the hind leg. Blood all over the grass."

"I didn't think a jackass would give you this much trepidation."

"What I'm saying is the man that's been helping your lady friend cut all that timber put his hands on that mule. Next thing you know, the skin—skin that was ripped near to the bone—was made new."

Clive glared at the man, blew smoke from the side of his mouth, and snorted.

"Laugh all you want, but we seen it. Some old lady saw it too. She and this silly girl with her went to gawking and carrying on." The man pulled his hands out of his pockets long enough to take the money that Clive had removed from his shirt pocket.

"See if this won't help take care of your haints," Clive said. "You're still man enough for the job, aren't you?"

The man tucked the wad of bills inside his pants and grinned like a shy boy. "If you don't know the answer to that by now, then you ain't as smart as you think you are."

Clive blew a fresh ring of smoke, and it danced around the man's shoulder. He drew the cigar from his mouth and stared at the growing ash. "Just see to it that you don't kill her."

9

Five days before the timber cut was to be completed, a late-afternoon storm broke the humidity as much as it did the productivity. With the progress they had made, Lanier promised them that they would finish on the lumber mill's deadline. "We don't need to get somebody killed from lightning," he screamed as he pulled the oxen into the pen. A clap of thunder caused the mule to dart to the side.

Samuel stood holding the chains and raised them up as if in defiance to God as much as in protest to Lanier. "They tell me lightning don't strike the same place twice. I hope that's the case. We don't need another drifter showing up." They all ignored him and scattered, carrying the saws and tools back into the barn. One by one they headed into shelter, Narsissa into her cabin and Keaton running toward the house.

As drops of rain dripped from the brim of Ella's hat, she watched from inside the barn while Lanier finished penning up the oxen.

Samuel flung the chains against the side of the house, cussed with words that caused her to turn her head, and stomped toward the porch.

The mule tossed his head and took a clump from the hay that Ella had put inside the animal's stall. He looked up at Ella and smacked his mouth. Strands of hay fell from his mouth, and he appeared to be smiling at Ella, as if to tell her that God was on his side and knew that the animal needed rest. Ella fought the urge to pick up the shovel and knock the mule on the side of the head.

The pressure had mounted on Ella in a loaded weight worse than the one she imagined the mule thought he was bearing for her cause. Sleep had become nothing but intervals of dreaming. Images of her family living in a makeshift tent in the public park in Apalachicola played in her mind the same as if she were viewing a horror picture at the Dixie Theatre. And each time she dreamed, Ella would awake in a spasm of twitching muscles. The torment had become such that Ella would climb out of bed, tearing and clawing at her chest, trying to free herself from the nervousness that pressed against her. Red claw marks lined her chest the same way scratches from the pine tree limbs appeared along her cheeks and wrists. She envisioned the winged demons illustrated in her aunt's family Bible as living creatures who had taken up residence in her mind. They hid in dark corners and whipped sections of her brain with the same leather whips as shown in the Old Testament illustrations. It was no wonder Harlan had turned to opium. She feared that if she ever found a hidden stash from his collection, she might break down and do the same.

Lanier came into the barn and tossed his gloves into the broken crate that he used as his wardrobe drawer. Ella tried not to look at him. She ran her hand against the brim of her hat, and water ran down the side of her shoulder.

"It's pouring out there," Lanier said.

"Of all the times . . ." Ella took the hat off and beat it against the side of the stall. The mule stepped away. "I'll go on and start washing. At least this won't be a total waste of the day." Ella looked down at the wooden dolls that lined the ground next to the barn wall. The doll at the end had eyes marked in chalk, and its hand was touching a torn and aged spiderweb at the edge of the wall. Ella thought that it resembled a small child with an eternal look of wonder coming from its eyes. "How do you have the energy to make these things? At the end of the day I'm so tired I can't think straight."

Lanier wiped bark from his pants. "That right there is what keeps my mind balanced."

Ella picked up the doll with the chalk eyes and replayed in her mind what Lanier had just said. "You mean, what you find relaxing?"

A clanking noise rang out as Lanier tossed a chain into a pile with the others. Ella flinched and put the doll back on the ground.

"No, I mean balanced." Lanier rotated his neck, and his joints made a popping sound. He ran his hand through his wet hair. Ella felt flushed with a sensation that scared and enticed her.

"Sleep quit being my friend," Lanier said. "My mind seems to be my undoing. I mean, well, when I whittle these dolls it frees up my thinking somehow. Sounds crazy, I reckon."

"No," Ella whispered. "Painting used to do the same for me."

"I could tell when I came up on you drawing that evening," Lanier said.

A bolt of lightning struck beyond the pen of oxen. Ella flinched and tucked a strand of hair behind her ear.

"When I first saw you, I figured you to be somebody who liked to do such," he added.

Ella looked up at a weathered brown wasp's nest hanging on the beam of the barn and laughed nervously. "The manure is thick enough in the stall. We don't need any more." Ella turned her head and before she could stop it, a smile formed.

"You notice things that the others don't. I can tell when you notice them too . . . like when you noticed a hummingbird dart past the other day when none of the rest of us saw it. You pointed straight at it, and your eyes just went to dancing. You've got nice eyes, if you don't mind me saying. Forgiving eyes."

"Now you're just telling me what you think I want to hear."

"No, I mean it," he said. "I see the way even when we're out there working to the bone you look up and tell us to notice a pair of redbirds. And how when we stop to eat, you reach down and touch the bloom on one of those wild lilies out there."

Ella pulled at the collar of the coat and looked around the barn, searching for another topic for conversation. Her mind told her to leave, to run out into the driving rain, but her heart wouldn't cooperate.

"Take it," Lanier said and motioned with his chin toward the doll. "Go on. I want you to have it."

When she hesitated, Lanier walked over and picked up the doll. He brushed against Ella's shoulder, and she did not bother to step aside. There was weariness in his green eyes that she recognized and appreciated. She saw the heaviness in her own eyes each night when she looked in the bedroom mirror on her chest of drawers. Looking at him now, she felt as if she was seeing a fraction of herself, a tired and frightened part that she could not reveal to anyone, least of all to this man, whom she pictured as layered with complications, if not lies.

"I don't know . . . ," she stammered.

"There's nothing to know," Lanier said and opened her hands. He placed the doll in her palms. The legs and head dangled over the sides. "If you can't paint right now, then keep on painting in your mind. Don't let all this mess stop you from that. . . . Don't let it win."

Ella cradled the doll against her stomach. Her breathing became shallow, and she reminded herself that she was the one in control.

Drips of water still fell from the ends of his hair that curled tighter from the rain. She saw a crack on his lip. A bloody spot that reminded her that this man who could heal boys and mules was human after all, the same blood as her husband. A shiver ran over her, and she pulled the coat tighter. Ella turned and saw the calico cat, its fur wet and matted, dart across the yard and under the store. The cat pierced its ears back as if angered by the inconvenience of the rain.

"Thank you," Ella said. She sighed and reached down for the pile of clothes wadded into a ball on the workbench next to the barn door.

"I see how this works. I give you a gift and you take my clothes," he said with a laugh.

Ella thought it intriguing how this man could find any humor in their circumstance. It was another dimension of him that interested and confused her.

"What's one more pile to add to the wash?" Ella never turned back to face him. "My aunt always told me to return kind gestures. Since you've been so helpful it's the least—"

"Partners, remember?" Lanier lowered his chin and stared at her, seeming to dare her to blink away from his gaze.

Ella shuffled the clothes from hand to hand and finally looked away. "Partners," Ella murmured, hating once again the circumstance that required her to partner with a man who caused her such confusion.

She put the hat back on her head, stuffed the doll into the big pocket of the work coat that had once been worn by Harlan, and cursed under her breath. Lanier was of the same dangerous bloodline as her husband, and the darkness in her mind would not let her forget it. She ran out into the rain, feeling the pellets beat against her head and picturing the demons being jolted, unlocking their grip on her mind.

On the porch Ella found Keaton and Macon playing marbles. A round circle had been drawn on the porch floor with chalk. Macon picked up the piece of chalk and hid it behind his back. His eyes were wide as he held her gaze. Ella never mentioned the chalk or the ring that had been drawn on the boards of the porch. Her body was on the porch, but her mind was still back at the barn.

Pulling the coat off, Ella placed it on the back of a high-top wooden chair that she had not too long ago sat in and watched the sun set over the trees that were quickly being chopped down. She dismissed the memory and placed Lanier's soiled shirts and under-garments into a small mound of clothes by the wash pump at the other end of the porch.

Samuel came out of the house, pinching morsels of snuff from a red tin can. He motioned toward the pile of clothes with his chin. "What? You're now his washwoman on top of it?"

"Don't start," Ella said. She tossed the wet hat against the butter churn that was by the door.

"Wait till people hear about this. It's bad enough he's sitting in our house, eating at our table."

"People won't hear a thing unless we run our mouths," Ella said.

"Oh, is that the fairyland you live in?" As Samuel walked past, his thigh brushed the edge of the chair. The tip of the head on the wooden doll hung slightly from the coat pocket. He sat on the porch step and stared at it, never seeming to care that he was exposed to the weather. Rain gathered at the tips of his boots, washing away the red clay of his work.

"Samuel," Keaton said and then tossed a cat's-eye marble into the ring.

"What? I'm just telling the truth. Somebody needs to face the truth around here."

"The truth is we're going to see that note paid off in full," Ella said, trying to lift her words the way she was taught at the finishing school.

The attempt at optimism was wasted on Samuel. He stuck his leg farther out into the rain. Water covered the ankle of his pants leg. He motioned toward the coat with the doll in the pocket. "What?

He giving you pretties now? Huh. . . . Paid off or not, our name is ruined around here."

Ella took a bar of soap from the washer and began scrubbing one of Samuel's shirts. "You're just like your daddy. Never knowing when to stop."

Macon struck two of Keaton's marbles out of the circle and scooped them up. He held them up high as if they were trophies.

"Quit washing his shirt," Samuel said with an authority that both startled and angered Ella.

"What?"

Macon pulled down his marbles and stuck the winnings in his pants pocket.

Samuel stood up, water still running down the side of his leg. "I said, *quit* washing his shirt."

Ella stood with the shirt in her hand, as startled as if she had just noticed a water moccasin at the foot of her porch steps.

"Ain't it bad enough the whole town is going behind your back, ruining your name on account of him? Now he's got you taking care of him like he owns you."

Keaton stood up. "If that snuff won't fill your mouth long enough to shut you up, then I will." Chalk stained his balled-up fist.

"It's about time we had us a family meeting," Samuel said, wiping pieces of the tobacco on his pants leg. "You can call that hobo your partner, your hired man, your whatever, but you need to know what folks are calling you."

Keaton stepped closer. Lightning flashed in the yard and a clap of thunder called out beyond the sunflowers. "Shut up!"

Samuel paid no attention to Keaton. He kept his eyes locked on Ella. "You feed him, you wash his clothes. . . . I wouldn't be surprised if you go in there and bed down with him. At least that's what everybody says you're doing. They say you've turned into a—"

Keaton ran across the porch and slammed into Samuel from the side. The tin of snuff flew up in the air and landed on the step. Samuel fell backward with Keaton on top of him, and they landed in a pool of mud in front of the porch step. Keaton managed to punch Samuel in the face before being blocked by Samuel's grip.

"Get off me, you pissant," Samuel yelled. He flipped Keaton onto the ground, pinning his chest and arms. Keaton thrashed his legs in the air and made gasping sounds as he struggled to regain the breath that had been knocked out of him.

Ella ran down the steps two at a time, still clinging to the bar of soap. She pulled Samuel by the shirt collar. "Get off me," Samuel screamed louder.

When she finally managed to pull Samuel up by the back of his shirt collar, Ella spun him around and slapped him square in the face. The sound, as loud as thunder, ricocheted up to the porch, where Macon still hovered over his marbles. Ella shoved the bar of soap deep into Samuel's mouth until he gagged.

Samuel spat out clumps of the soap, bent over, and vomited.

Ella balled up her fists, ready for Samuel to strike back. But there was no need. Samuel simply stood there, dazed, with a kernel of soap clinging to his upper lip and water running down his forehead and into the thick eyebrows that Ella used to say reminded her of her father's.

Keaton heaved for air, and Ella helped lift him up. Keaton brushed away Macon's attempt to help him back up the porch steps. Before going back into the house, Ella flung her arms, and flecks of water landed on the floor. She looked down at Samuel, who still stood in the rain. His drenched shirt clung to his barreled chest. "And it was your shirt," she said. "It was your shirt that I was washing."

That evening rain continued to tap the tin roof of Ella's home, an unrelenting caller reminding her of timber deadlines yet to be met. Samuel managed to come out of his bedroom, mumble that he was sorry at the dinner table, wash his supper plate, and then excuse himself. Sitting at the desk where he'd once been forced by Ella to do school lessons, he let free all of his thoughts about the drifter and his mother's lack of judgment in a letter addressed to his father. He licked the flap on the envelope, rearranged the pencil between his fingers, and finally flipped a coin. Heads, New Orleans; tails, Chicago. His father had visited both cities and had shared stories to prove it. The penny landed tails up on the notepad with an Indian chief on the cover.

Neither Lanier nor Narsissa joined the family for supper that night. Ella couldn't help but think that the absences were blessings. The last thing her nerves needed was a repeat performance in front of Lanier. While Keaton and Macon sat at the kitchen table working on an arithmetic problem for Macon's schoolwork, Ella wrapped two biscuits in wax paper and placed them in a basket along with a small jar of honey. "I'll be back directly," she said and put the work coat over her head as she stood at the door. "I'm going to run this out to Narsissa."

The kerosene lamp that sat on a milk jug inside Narsissa's cabin door flickered through the small window. As Ella ran past the sunflowers that drooped beneath the raindrops, she could see Narsissa walking around in the cabin. Ella ran faster and felt that the amber-colored light in the window was a beacon that could safely satisfy her longing to escape.

Inside the cabin, Narsissa sat down in a straight-back chair lined with the skin of a buck Samuel had killed when he was thirteen; she listened to Ella unfurl her feelings. Occasionally Narsissa ran the tortoiseshell comb Ella had handed down to her through her hair.

"I never would have believed that my own son would have said such to me. It's as if . . ." Ella watched strands of black hair fall as Narsissa combed her hair. Then, fearing she was not being listened to attentively enough, Ella looked up toward a damp crack in the ceiling that had been filled with a gray plaster made from newspapers and oyster shells. ". . . as if he's two people all of a sudden. He's listening to what people in this town are saying about me. He's believing them over me."

Narsissa placed the comb in her lap and tapped her thick, nicked finger against the side of her cheek. She sighed and stared out into the rain that fell outside the window. "I gave up trying to figure out why the people we love the most can hurt us the worst." Narsissa groaned as she stood up. She held the side of her hip and walked across the room to where a photograph sat next to her bed.

Ella took the picture when Narsissa handed it to her. She had seen it many times before. Inside the smoky glass frame was a photograph taken soon after Narsissa had married. Her husband, David, was a thin man with a widow's-peak hairline and a sharp chin. He stood holding a silver-tipped cane in one hand, the other hand propped on Narsissa's shoulder. She sat in a Victorian velvet chair, just as stone-faced as her husband and dressed in lace with a piece of pearl jewelry placed on her neck. The formality of the photograph had always struck Ella as foreign to the Narsissa she knew.

"I know all about scandal," Narsissa said. She took the photograph back, dusted it off with the back of her hand, and set it in her lap. She looked down at it as if reading a book.

"My grandfather always told me that nothing good would come out of marrying a white man. You heard me say it before, and I'll say it again. He was a wise man, that grandfather of mine. But I was too young to know better. Young and in love." Narsissa snorted and shifted the picture sideways. "Whatever love is supposed to mean.

"There was nothing doing but to marry this white boy who hung on to notions of moving to Brazil, where his father's people had run to before the War between the States. They didn't fight, because their conscience got the better of them. They ran so they could keep living a way of life they saw passing away. They turned this little corner of Brazil into their own little world. A make-believe world, if you ask me." Narsissa shook her head and then looked sideways at Ella. "You never knew this ole gal married into money. You never knew that, did you?"

Ella clutched her hands and placed them in her lap. Shame wrapped around her like a shawl, and she could only shake her head that she did not know. How could this woman who had helped to care for her children, work her farm, and nurse her back from pneumonia two winters ago be so unknown to her? Ella had relegated Narsissa to an extension of the store, a business item of Harlan's that up until his undoing was of little interest to her. Ella's aunt had always labeled Harlan as too self-involved to ever be devoted; now she realized that the same could have been said about her as well. Wanting to look away, Ella forced herself to stare into Narsissa's eyes.

"White trash, my grandfather called David's people." Narsissa got up and put the photograph back on the nightstand. "This from a man who couldn't be buried next to a white man, mind you." She took a seat again, shifting her weight as if trying to find a spot of comfort.

"I thought you said they were people of means," Ella whispered.

"You know well enough that money and decency don't go hand in hand." Narsissa stared toward the window that was now opaque with rainy mist.

"David's mother took to the marriage about the same as my grandfather. She cut off the purse strings when he married something dirty like me. David always was petted by her. Especially after his father died when he was just a boy. I knew that much about him when I met him at the cane grinding down at the Summerville place that night in January. Some of my people told me he was touched in the head. They warned me, but I didn't believe . . . couldn't believe it. I didn't even want to believe it when he jumped out of bed that night, claiming that Moses had come to him, telling him to go find his father's people back in Brazil. Said that's where we'd find the Promised Land with the milk and the honey and the gold and the . . ." Narsissa waved her arm and fluttered her fingers as if there was such a thing as magic. "He even described the homes his people had built down there . . . described them right down to the brass doorknobs shaped like hawks. 'Dreaming,' I kept saying. 'You're just dreaming.' But he was already gone, in his mind at least. It was two months later when he left for good." Narsissa wrapped herself with her arms. The chair creaked when she rocked.

Ella reached out to touch Narsissa, but when her hand brushed against the side of her shoulder, Narsissa shifted away from the embrace.

"I kept hoping that the note David left would tell me how to find him . . . tell me to sit tight until he was ready for me to follow behind him. But all that note amounted to was gibberish, symbols and numbers, with that old hawk from his family's crest printed at the top. I interpreted it the way I wanted. I told so many people that David was setting up a new life for us and would send for me, that after a while I started believing it."

The rain beat down harder on the roof, and a slow drip began to fall from the plastered spot on the ceiling. "What about your mother or your father? Couldn't they have helped?" Ella asked.

"Father . . ." Narsissa grunted out the word and coughed. "He died a drunk, and then my mother headed out west. She was good enough not to take me with her. After my grandfather died from the TB, the woman who sold herbs next door didn't mind telling me that I could find my mama selling herself in San Francisco. Went out there chasing the men who found gold. Whichever way it went, who's to know?" Narsissa shrugged and rolled her shoulders back. "But don't you feel sorry for me. I didn't tell you all this so you'd be favoring me."

"No, of course not," Ella said, pressing her back against the chair, wondering if Narsissa could tell that she was lying.

Narsissa lumbered over to the side of the bed. She pulled back the woven rug that she had first brought to Ella's home when she claimed she could work twice as hard as any man. Pulling a knife out from underneath the mattress, she used the tip to lift up a piece of wood from the floor. Narsissa withdrew a small croaker sack tied at the end with frayed string.

"You told it to me straight that day back at the spring," Narsissa said, looking Ella straight in the eye. "I've been hanging on to notions that I need to let go of."

"Now, I had no business saying such." Ella fanned the air, trying to dismiss the charge as much as cut the tension. "That was just me being melancholy. You know how I can be."

Narsissa handed the sack to Ella. Rain rattled against the rusted tin roof of the cabin, and Ella clutched the bag, not knowing what she should do.

"I've been hanging on to pipe dreams that ain't nothing but rust now. All this talk about the bank taking over made me realize that if we lost this place, where would I go? Huh? Brazil? And what would I do once I got there? Hunt down a husband who probably wouldn't recognize me if he was to lay eyes on me? Even if he had a piece of his mind left . . . even if he's still alive. No . . ." Narsissa shook her head. A piece of bark fell from her hair and onto the bedspread. "For all his faults, Harlan Wallace was good enough to give me a place to stay. No matter what . . . I'll always be grateful. He let me turn this smokehouse into a home, more or less."

"Yes, I know," Ella said, turning her rigid head to the side and raising her eyebrows. "I'm the first to agree. There's good and bad in everyone. Even in those who forge your name and gamble away your possessions." Her words hung in the air. Drops of rain kept tapping at the roof. Finally slumping forward, Ella deflated with a sigh. "Truth be told, there are parts of him—parts of us, I should say—that I can't let go of even though I know I should. I'd only say this to you, but some mornings I drag out of bed and peep out from the curtain, thinking he might've come to his senses. I look out that window half-expecting to see him walking up the drive, coming back for the sake of my boys if for no other reason. I guess there's enough fool left in me to believe he'll be cured or something and find his way back home."

Narsissa looked away from the bag and halfway smiled. "Well, now here I am. And no matter what anybody says, this *is* my home." She reached down and pulled open the string on the sack. "Here's what I'd been setting aside along and along. There ain't much, but you take this money and put it—"

"Now, Narsissa, I can't take your—"

Narsissa squeezed Ella's hand and leaned down lower until Ella could see the dark hairs that grew from the corners of her lips. "Don't make me tell you twice, Ella. Now you take this money, and put it toward keeping our home."

Ella sat stunned, holding what would amount to a fraction of what was owed to the bank. Her aunt had taught her that servants were to be considered, even valued, as distant kin, but never adored. Up until now Ella had held the notion that Narsissa fell into that category. For the first time Ella spoke the words that she had been too guarded and protected to offer. "I love you, Narsissa. You know that, don't you?"

Narsissa stopped straightening the rug back over the secret spot. She turned, and the amber light from the lantern caused her weathered face to soften, to appear almost youthful.

Ella stood at the door holding the bag, fighting the urge to run out the door and hide the tears that burned her eyes. An emotional cocktail of shame and guilt spilled inside of her. When she spoke, her voice cracked. "Narsissa, you're braver than me."

Narsissa picked up the photograph once more and studied it. "Somehow and someway, we'll still be here long after that bank shuts its doors." She ran her finger down the side of the picture frame and then turned it facedown on the table.

During the early hours of the next morning, right before the sun broke out across the sky, Samuel stood at the door of the house before any of the others inside had awoken. He pulled the small red tin of snuff from inside his boot. He used his fingers to delicately pinch out a bit from the can and tucked the grainy snuff inside his mouth, behind his lower lip.

Lanier watched him from the barn door and wondered how long the boy who thought he was a man would be a problem. Torment and burden had become tattooed on the boy's face, with lined creases between tired eyes that would be better suited to a man three times his age, one who had been ravaged by misfortune and lost love. Samuel reminded Lanier of his dead wife, Octavia. The boy was twisted in a spell of anger and confusion. Lanier was satisfied that Samuel was a dangerous threat. He could imagine Samuel winding up like Octavia, a victim of circumstances.

An owl called out one last time from within the trees, and Samuel turned. He walked to the edge of the porch closest to the barn. Lanier stepped to the side, hidden by the barn door. He picked up the end of an axe nearby and wondered if Samuel would trouble him at the start of a new day. A rabbit hopped through the sunflowers, and when it did so, the branches rattled. The animal stopped long enough to look up at Lanier and then ran off underneath the porch where Samuel stood. The boy's weight landed against the oyster shells that were scattered on the ground, and he kicked a shell toward the barn.

Lanier gripped the handle and felt a burning sensation snake from his fingers to his groin. His heart began to race with the familiar click that always caused him to think he would break free and give way to the generational curses put upon him by having his father's blood in his veins. The rabbit now sat at the edge of the house on its hind legs, its ears twitching. In the darkness, the animal would be the only witness to the justice Lanier was going to serve Samuel once and for all.

When Samuel got to the pen, the oxen turned toward the entrance of the farm. A wagon being pulled by a Clydesdale horse with a tangled, yellowed mane rattled toward him. Samuel stopped and turned toward the road.

The wagon was covered with a moss-colored tarp with foxtails dangling from each of the four corners. A colored man wearing tall leather boots, a jacket with a checkered patch sewn to the pocket, and a floppy felt hat drove the wagon. He pulled up right next to the oxen pen and nervously rubbed the graying beard on his chin.

"Bonaparte," Samuel called out. "What's the matter?"

"I'm sorry to show up so early like this but I got serious trouble." He jerked the reins, and the horse stepped to the right. "Is that man still 'round the place?"

Clutching the axe tighter, Lanier moved closer to the wall of the barn.

Samuel reached down and pulled a weed from the ground. "How come you're asking?" He took the end of the weed and stuck it in the corner of his mouth.

"It's my baby girl. My wife was blanching some sheets last night out in the yard. My baby girl fell backwards into the pot. Like to have burned her legs off. Doctor's over in St. Joe for the night tending to a woman with pneumonia. Folks said . . . said that man here can heal people."

"People been saying a lot of things lately," Samuel said. "Ain't much that trash can do but breathe on people."

"Whatever he did, it took to that mule and that brother of yours. Look, I can pay whatever the man say . . ."

Lanier stepped out from the barn and tossed the axe at Samuel. It landed blade first, a foot from where he stood. Jumping to the side, Samuel yelled a high-pitched squeal.

"Where's the girl?" Lanier asked.

As Lanier climbed onto the wagon, the horse moved to the side and blocked Samuel from stepping in front of them. "We're a day late on the cut as it is," Samuel said. "You ain't no doctor, you know."

Bonaparte Ruston popped the reins and then shook Lanier's hand. With foxtails dancing from the roof, the wagon turned at the fork in the road past Ella's store and bounced over the ruts in a red clay road that ended up at the south end of the county. The wagon flew past palmetto bushes that lined the edge of the narrow road. Green leafy branches became tangled inside the spokes of the wagon wheels, and the sound of the branches shredding by the force of the wheels made Lanier think of a pit of hissing snakes.

Lanier ducked to keep a low-hanging oak limb from hitting his head. Moss fell from the tree and draped one side of his shoulder. As he flung it to the ground, he saw the morning sun casting a pink glow against a camp of weathered cabins. At the end of the road a small fishing boat with peeling green paint rocked at the edge of the river. Cypress trees, their branches dressed in layers of moss, guarded the boat and the small shanty that stood out over the river on battered stilts. A shirtless boy, no more than ten, ran out of the house and up to the wagon. As he grabbed the horse's halter, he looked up at Bonaparte, wild-eyed and nervous.

"Come this way," Bonaparte said. He motioned for Lanier to follow him past a clothesline decorated with the drying furs of foxes and rabbits. A rusted horseshoe was nailed above the front door of the house.

A woman with cornrow-braided pigtails, wearing an apron stained with lard and blood, met them at the door. There was an urgency in her eyes that was as unmanageable as that of the boy who had taken control of the horse. "Help my baby," she said, pulling Lanier into the house by his arm.

The house was all of two rooms. A lifeless fireplace and a rusted oven sat across from each other. The woman led Lanier by the shirtsleeve into a room with yellowed pages from a Sears and Roebuck catalogue pasted on the walls. She stood in front of a cracked page advertising a modular home and closed her eyes like she might be struggling to recite a poem in school. "I had a pot out in the yard, fixing to blanch some clothes. . . ." The woman's voice trailed off. She moved to the side, never opening her eyes. Her wide hips blocked a full view of the young girl who lay on the bed covered in mismatched colorful quilts. The woman only moved when Bonaparte put his hand on her shoulder and nudged her closer to the catalogue picture.

Lanier felt once more the burning sensation he had felt when he saw Samuel that morning. He tried not to look away from the little girl lying on the bed, shaking with a fever so forceful it caused the bedsprings to moan. She gripped the edges of the quilt that was made of red-and-white cloth. The tips of her fingers were squeezing so tightly that her skin had gone from black to the color of warm milk. The girl looked up at Lanier and then at her father. She moaned in a throaty, deep sound more fitting a grown man.

"It gonna be all right now," Bonaparte said. "This the man who fixing to make you better." He turned and looked at Lanier, and so too did the girl. The smell of cinnamon and aged grease hung in the air.

"Jesus, help my baby," the woman called out. The sway of her apron as she walked back and forth in prayer kept Lanier distracted from the half-dollar-sized boils that covered the girl's legs. The skin, tight and discolored, shimmered with the lard that the mother had placed on the burns.

"Go on and get in the other room," Bonaparte shouted to the woman walking back and forth.

"Jesus, come on now. Heal this baby," the woman said louder, continuing to clutch her hands and walk back and forth at the foot of the bed. A rocking chair placed at the other side of the room slightly swayed whenever she brushed past it.

Lanier placed his hands over the girl's legs, and she flinched. "Easy, now," Lanier whispered. "I'm not here to hurt you. You believe me?"

Sweat ran from the girl's temples. She bit her lip, moaned, and then nodded her head in agreement.

"Come, Jesus," the woman murmured from behind them.

"Quit with your foolishness!" Bonaparte said in a stage whisper.

"She's still got fire in her," Lanier said, half turning his head toward Bonaparte. "The fire is still burning in her."

"Unhhh," the girl cried.

"Jesus," the woman said.

"You expect you can do something about it, can't you?" Bonaparte asked. He put his hand on Lanier's shoulder. "You can do something, can't you?"

Lanier never answered. He bowed down next to the bed and smiled at the girl. Her teeth rattled, and she closed her eyes whenever Lanier placed his hand on her brow. The skin was as hot as the boiling water he imagined her falling into. The tingling sensation ran down to his core again, and he shook until Bonaparte steadied him by placing his palm on Lanier's shoulder. He closed his eyes and leaned his head back.

"Jesus, You healed the lepers from their sores," the woman sang out. "Heal this baby."

"Woman, I done told you to get in the other room."

Lanier moved his hands down over the girl's body, careful not to touch her. When his hands were over the top portion of her legs, he began to tremble again. Heat ran all over him, and he tried to picture the water that lined Ella's property. He pictured the glassy surface of the water and how the living things of nature surrounded the edge.

"Jesus, You the great doctor," the woman said in her deep, throaty voice.

"Quit your carrying on before I give you something to really carry on about," Bonaparte yelled.

"Unhhh," the girl said. "It burning me bad."

"What you doing to her?" Bonaparte asked.

Lanier didn't answer. He just shook with a rage that caused Bonaparte to grip him with both hands.

"Jesus. My precious Jesus. Come on," the woman hollered.

Lanier heard her words and felt them as much as he felt the burns of the skin. Sweat ran down his face and caused the shirt he wore to press against his back. He shook harder and repeated the words that had alleviated suffering in the past. He murmured the words first in his mind and then through his lips. The woman stomped harder and shouted with gripped fists in the air, fighting and praising something unseen. Lanier felt himself shrinking as he repeated in his mind the words he had been taught long ago. As the verses scrolled through his mind and grew larger in the size of their letters, the burning intensified against his hands. Balling his fists, he envisioned himself shrinking into the fire that raged in hellish flames beneath the girl's skin. He felt the words rolling off his tongue and pictured them spewing out of his mouth on a twisted, heated fork. Falling backward to the floor, his foot knocked the rocking chair over, and the woman screamed. The girl sat up and shook one last time before crying, "Daddy."

Bonaparte ran to his daughter and looked at her legs and then down at the floor at Lanier, who was lying prostrate with balled fists. "Lord have mercy," he said.

Outside the cabin, the boy, who had tied the horse to a railroad post by the river, stood with the others out by the clothesline and was the first to hear the girl's final scream. Bottles in pastel colors tied to the branches of a dogwood tree chimed in the morning breeze. A woman wearing a dress held at the breast with a safety pin put her hands on the boy. He pulled away from her.

"Jesus, heal my baby." The words rolled from inside the house and out into the yard.

As if in a chorus, the women standing outside by the clothesline replied, "Yes, Jesus." The one wearing an alabaster turban jumped in a circle.

A man spat a line of tobacco juice toward the lowest hanging bottle on the tree.

Some hummed hymns, others called out in prayer, and some just waited to see what the white man who had healed the mule could do. But none of them said a word when Lanier walked out of the house.

When Lanier came outside, he used his forearm to brush away sweat that caused his hair to stick to his forehead. He pulled at the wet shirt that chilled his skin. A pair of blue jays swooped down, seemed to spar with one another, and then squawked as they flew away. Bonaparte followed Lanier out the door. He raised his arm in victory but no one in the crowd cheered. They shifted across the yard as if the misfortune that had fallen upon the house was contagious and settled at the riverbank. The green boat sloshed in the current and lightly banged against a cypress tree.

"Thank You, Jesus," the woman said when she ran out the door. She raised her hands and shuffled her feet in some sort of dance. "Thank You, Jesus. My baby's sores done dried up," the woman proclaimed. "Dried up, I say!"

The boy ran and untied the horse. Lanier climbed onto the wagon. Bonaparte followed suit and then took the reins from the boy. The woman shouted her praises again, and the crowd moved on, some walking toward the house to see the girl for themselves and others off down the road, going about earning their daily fare, debating whether the white man was an apostle. Whether silent or opinionated, none of them took their eyes off the wagon carrying Lanier Stillis. They kept watch over him long after the wagon had turned the corner and disappeared from view.

10

Ella had pondered how she would feel the day they finished their work. She imagined the day while pulling the end of the jagged cross saw or carrying the buckets of water to the group while the blazing sun, so strong that she thought it was riding her back, pounded down on her. Naturally relief came the day the last pine fell and green pine needles fanned out in submission on the ground, but still, Ella did not feel as satisfied as she thought she should. The sun still beat down upon her, and damp undergarments still clung to folds of her skin.

She and Lanier stood there looking at the stumps that rose up from the earth like crude sores on infected hide.

"A lot of timber," he said, surveying the work with his hands on his hips, his tall body slightly leaning to the right.

"I can't take it all in," she said. And since she couldn't, she repeated her declaration twice. She pictured her nerves just as prickly as the ends of the pine needles on the ground. Joy, no matter how abundant that day in August, only danced around her like the little dots she would see whenever she closed her burning, tired eyes at the end of the workday. Jubilation that was so easily recognizable on the faces of her boys, on Narsissa, even on Lanier, was a mere mask on Ella.

No matter how hard she smiled that day, or laughed, or even raised her arms in victory, she could not escape the unsteady feeling that caused her to want to vomit, much as she had during the early days when suffering heatstroke. Darkness stretched out across her mind to keep her guessing when the next disaster would strike. Somehow it was easier to stay in the shade of doubt rather than give way to the momentary light of wishful thinking.

With eleven days and twelve hours to spare before the bank note was due, the calls of celebration from the others could be heard past the store and to the fork in the road. Myer Simpson, awoken from her afternoon nap, cracked her door open, grimaced at them, and then disappeared back inside her home, pulling the shade down over her parlor window. Mrs. Pomeroy, from across the road, came outside and pretended to check on a dying tomato plant on her porch. She fanned herself with the purple satin fan she had purchased from Mr. Busby the peddler. Circling the plant three times, she finally waved the fan at Ella.

Mr. Busby, a photographer as well as a peddler, later claimed that even he could hear whoops of their cheer as he came across the fork in the road. He snapped the reins against his wagon, instructing Old Blue and Miss Maggie to take his portable shop faster to Wallace Commissary.

The only picture taker to grace Dead Lakes, Mr. Busby traveled South Georgia, Alabama, and the northernmost corners of Florida. He was not only the recorder of people's profiles but also the collector of their possessions. Copper pots originally given to a man and wife in Elba, Alabama, as wedding gifts had been secured for a price less than wholesale when the man's crop of peanuts didn't make. The freshly polished pots, as good as new, dangled and rattled from the top of Mr. Busby's wagon. The feet of an emerald-colored wingback chair, purchased from a woman in Blountstown, Florida, whose husband had suffered a stroke while sitting in the very same chair reading the newspaper, stuck out over the tailgate.

Mr. Busby wiped a drop of bourbon from his chapped lips and smeared the whiskey across a cheek lined with purplish veins. Tucking the genuine silver flask with another's initials back into the pocket of his vest that was missing a button, he popped the reins and guided the wagon toward the piles of timber. The pines looked like five stacks of giant, worn pencils. Shavings of bark, pine straw, and crushed pinecones carpeted the ground.

Macon ran up to the wagon, jumping up to the breast of the horses. "We did it, Mr. Busby. We did it." One of the horses snorted, shook sweat from its head, and champed at its bit before trying to bite Macon, who darted away.

Mr. Busby pulled the wagon to a full stop right in front of the highest stack of timber. The copper pots made a clanging sound. "Did what?" Mr. Busby inquired.

Narsissa, pretending not to notice Mr. Busby's arrival, licked her thumb and then proceeded to wipe a stain of pine tar from Keaton's cheek.

Ella plopped, if not collapsed, right down on the ground. "Saved the store," she yelled.

"We saved the store. We saved the store. We don't owe the bank no more," Macon repeated in song as he danced a jig around the wagon, farther away from the reach of the horses.

"I see some changes around here," Mr. Busby said. He looked down at Macon and then at Ella, who sat cross-legged in a dusting of wood. On his last venture through Dead Lakes, Mr. Busby had taken a photograph of the sheriff's family and given Ella the split he'd made for selling the locks of Abraham Lincoln's hair to an insurance man in Thomasville, Georgia. Trying to encourage Ella at the time, he kept his eye on the white china plates displayed on a glass shelf behind the store window. He had hoped to make her a price on the gold-trimmed plates with little red birds painted at the edges. It was the least he could do to help with the reversal in fortune.

Samuel tossed his head back and howled so loud that the horses twisted and pranced to the side. Mr. Busby put the brake on the wagon, groaned as he pulled himself down, and began to riffle through the wagon for his camera equipment.

"I'd like to be a fly on the wall when you hand Clive Gillespie the money on that bank note," Narsissa said.

"I never met a banker I could like, let alone trust," Lanier added.

Mr. Busby stopped what he was doing and turned to Lanier. His pensive look said it all.

"This is . . . ," Ella stammered, motioning toward Lanier.

"Just Lanier," Keaton said.

Mr. Busby brushed his hand against his pin-striped gray pants. A marking of dust lined his thigh. "Well, pleased to know you . . . just Lanier."

They laughed and Ruby Tucker marched toward them with her baton.

"Let's have a parade," she yelled and pumped her baton high into the air.

"What timing," Ella said.

"Last Friday of the month," Ruby said. "Last Friday is parade day."

"Honey child, more than you know," Ella said.

Mr. Busby pulled a bedpan from the wagon and then a child's pink step stool shaped like a piglet. "Let me see now," he said. "Here we go." He lifted a tripod camera from the side. The body of the object was as big as the stool. The black flap that hung around the top of the camera was frayed at the ends. "A day of celebration deserves recording," he said.

"Don't start with that picture-taking around me," Narsissa gruffed.

"Oh my, no. I look a mess," Ella said and yanked off the sweat-stained work hat. The band of the hat left an indentation around her tanned, wet forehead.

"Ella Wallace," Mr. Busby said with eyes closed. "I'll have you know that I am more than some circuit photographer who goes around making pictures of fat women with even fatter babies propped on their laps. I am an artist. *We* are artists." He raised his gray eyebrows and nodded. "So you of all people know artists thrive on capturing authentic moments. So put that hat back on your head."

After he used more of the same cajoling and convincing that made him a more successful peddler than photographer, the group relented and let Mr. Busby take a photograph for their "family history." Setting up his equipment at the edge of the road, Mr. Busby motioned for the group to move closer to the highest stack of timber.

Ruby marched back and forth behind Mr. Busby, swinging her baton and singing "Happy Timber Day to Ella" to the tune of "Happy Birthday." Keaton and Samuel laughed while Ella pointed her finger at them to hush.

They bunched closer together. Everyone smiled, except for Lanier, who fidgeted with the brim of his hat, taking it off and then putting it back on. "Stand still, Mr. Just Lanier," Mr. Busby directed as he stuck his head underneath the black drape and peered into the camera. When Mr. Busby said, "Three," the camera flasher let off a bright light and a trail of smoke. Lanier jumped away from the group and moved closer to the store. None of them, not even Ella, noticed that his hands were shaking long after Mr. Busby put his equipment back into the wagon next to a table carved in the shape of a sundial.

An afternoon shadow fell over the side of the store, covering the piles of timber. Samuel sat on the store steps, attempting to smoke a cigar while Keaton and Macon played a round of marbles next to a barrel and counted the number of times that Samuel coughed. Inside the store, Narsissa helped Mr. Busby set up his makeshift studio, complete with a gray curtain that they nailed to the back wall next to the supply of paint. Ella watched Mr. Busby move his camera to the left and then shift it to the right. He had set up his studio in her store for the past two years, usually at the end of summer and during the two weeks before Christmas, just in time for the start of school and the celebration of a holiday. No one gave a second thought to Lanier, except for Sheriff Bissell, who walked in behind Ruby. He took off his hat and moved to the side to prevent getting hit with the baton that she still pumped. "Careful," Ella called out, but Ruby paid her no attention. She just marched to the side of the store where a brass-colored birdcage hung.

"Afternoon, Sheriff," Ella said, wanting to lead him outside and point to the side of the store where the land had been swept clean until almost nothing was left but a sandy floor with scatterings of palmetto bushes. She dared him to speak of Clive Gillespie or the pending foreclosure that his deputy had personally delivered. "I haven't seen your deputy in a while. How's Ronnie getting along?"

"Good, good. I'm keeping him busy," the sheriff said. He took off his hat and fanned himself with it. A sweat stain on his shirt revealed a protruding belly button. "I mean to tell you, you flat-sure are tough to be able to work out there in that heat. Many a man couldn't have held up like you've been doing."

Strands of Ella's dark hair were glued to the side of her neck. She nervously picked at a dented spot on the wooden counter and smiled.

"Of course with all the men off over there fighting in the war, the ladyfolk are having to pick up the slack. I hate to see it, but I guess we all got to sacrifice." The sheriff licked away a bead of perspiration from his upper lip. "At least that's what President Wilson keeps telling the newspapermen. Keeps saying we all got to sacrifice." Sheriff Bissell snorted his displeasure. "I'm sorry, but it's not right to see natural-born ladies like you out there working like they're on a chain gang."

"Natural or not, I finished the job," she said, trying not to sing the words. "We might have worked like dogs, but we finished." She swept her hand to the side as if the sheriff could see through the curtain that Mr. Busby had hung in front of the store window.

"Ain't that something," Sheriff Bissell said in the way that he might say to a child who had just performed a somersault for the first time. "Well, now. I thought there was an extra sparkle to those pretty blue eyes of yours."

The smell of damp talcum powder clouded the room. The sheriff unfurled a handkerchief from his back pocket, folded it in half, and dragged it across his brow. "How 'bout a slice of that cheese and maybe a couple of saltine crackers?"

Ella lifted the wax paper from the block of cheddar cheese. She felt the sheriff looking at her with the same pity as Deputy Ronnie had before she had cut the trees. "What is it with cheese and crackers and lawmen? Ronnie comes by here and practically makes his noontime meal out of them."

Sheriff Bissell placed a cut of cheese onto a saltine and chomped down on it. He leaned over as crumbs tumbled to the sawdust-sprinkled floor. He ignored Ella's attempt to chitchat and looked to the part of the store where Mr. Busby was busy setting up his studio.

"To the left," Mr. Busby yelled. "Move the chair a little more to the left." Narsissa, his impromptu assistant, slammed the chair against the wall and stormed out of the store.

"Mr. Busby," Ella said, "would you please use your inside voice."

Mr. Busby didn't acknowledge the reprimand or Narsissa's departure. He simply moved the chair back in front of his camera and adjusted the dark curtain that was his backdrop.

"Sheriff Bissell," Ella said, "now, your wife asked me to let her know the next time Mr. Busby passed this way. I think she wants a new family portrait made with that grandbaby of yours. How old is he now? A year? Year and a half?"

"Some'rs around there," the sheriff said, balancing another slice of cheese on a cracker. He chewed and talked at the same time. "Oh," Sheriff Bissell said as if he might have forgotten the reason for his visit, "about that fella you got hanging around here like a stray looking for milk . . ."

Ella shifted her weight and leaned against the store counter. "Mmm-hmmm." She wanted to shove the cheese farther down his throat and garble the words that she expected him to say. Doubts about Lanier that had tormented her now rose from the black corners of her mind. She didn't bother to brush the thoughts away.

"What's this business about him going around healing folks?"

"He just . . . he just helped a child. . . . Children get better. Like a doctor, I suppose."

"Must be some kind of doctor. Must be some kind of animal doctor too. I heard how he stopped that mule of yours from bleeding to death. They tell me he laid hands on him."

"He's Harlan's cousin from Georgia. From up in the mountains. He grew up cutting timber and knows how to work animals. I'm just so grateful for all he's done."

"Oh yeah." Sheriff Bissell practically sang the words. "I mean to tell you. He has flat-sure been a help to you." A flake of cheese collected at the tip of the sheriff's dimpled chin. "But this doctoring business . . . sort of peculiar, don't you think?"

"Beg your pardon?"

Sheriff Bissell motioned toward the door. "Folks been saying some awfully peculiar things. Saying how those sores the boy had cleared up in a day. Cleared up like a miracle or something." The sheriff leaned closer over the cash register and in a stage whisper said, "Now, Ella, you know me. I speak my mind and the next man speaks his.

So I might as well go on and say it. Folks are saying he kissed the boy in a way not fitting for public conversation."

"Kissed?"

Sheriff Bissell glanced over at Mr. Busby and then leaned down until the crumb on his chin fell to the top of the counter, next to the cash register. His eyebrows rose into perfect arches. "Folks are saying he put his mouth right on your boy's mouth. Same as he would a woman. Now I'm not saying whether he did or didn't, I'm just saying—"

"Well, he did not." Ella stood upright. Her face flushed, and she stammered, "What you're repeating . . . what you're circulating is a lie."

Mr. Busby stopped fussing with the backdrop, and Ruby looked away from the wooden doll with blue chalk eyes that Lanier had made.

"Now I'm not here to get into beauty-parlor gossip," the sheriff said. "My job is to uphold the law. I got to clarify . . . you know . . . clarify what people are accusing."

"Who's accusing?" Ella asked.

The sheriff closed his eyes, shook his head, and fanned his hat. "Like I said, I'm not getting into all that. I just don't want somebody around here that might have unnatural tendencies."

Ella walked from around the store counter. She stood so close to the sheriff that she could make out a stye underneath his eyelid. "If there's anything unnatural here, it's the unusual amount of attention that people are paying to me lately. Now let me tell you one thing, Charlie Bissell. I was standing right there in that room when Macon was treated by that man, and there was nothing perverse about it."

"Enough said." Sheriff Bissell smiled and brushed crumbs from his hands. "No need to fly off the handle. We're just sorting it all through."

"Oh, you're right. There's been more than enough said," Ella added. "I am the boy's mother. Husband or no husband, I am still able to keep watch over my children."

"Now, Ella. May I say this." Sheriff Bissell held up his stubby fingers with flakes of crackers on his thumbs. "Folks just want to make sure you and these boys don't get hurt. You know, there is such a thing as being too trusting, even if somebody's claiming to be kin."

As Sheriff Bissell walked out of the store, Ella stared at the damp khaki material that gathered in the seat of his pants. She noticed how he patted the side of his waist where a pistol hung from a holster. "Now, you call if you need us. And I'll tell Lovey that the picture man has come to town. She always was the craziest thing over a picture."

Ella leaned against the barrel half-filled with watermelons that were becoming too ripe to sell. Her breathing was sparse, and she felt the rage of her pulse. She fought the urge to run after the sheriff and plead her case in front of the people who milled about in front of the store.

"Ella," Mr. Busby said. He barely touched the sleeve of her shirt that was still stained with pine tar.

"I'm fine," she said and pulled away.

Ruby marched up to them carrying one of the dolls Lanier had made. It was painted with a white beard that he had modeled after the Uncle Sam poster that hung on the store wall, advertising the need for war recruits. She hummed "The Star-Spangled Banner" and used the arm of the doll to imitate a salute. The sound of her song wore on Ella's nerves as much as the words handed down to her by the sheriff.

"Are you sure?" Mr. Busby asked. "You look peaked."

Ella nodded and then watched Ruby stomp back to the birdcage. The sound of her humming seemed to grow louder.

"I am perfectly fine," Ella said.

"You might be weak from all that work. Have you eaten?" Mr. Busby turned his head as if examining Ella.

Ella nodded once more, and Ruby began tapping the beat to the song against the birdcage.

"Ruby, will you hush with that humming!"

Mr. Busby took a step backward, and Ruby dropped the doll on the floor. She stared at Ella and then thumped the birdcage with her thumb and forefinger.

Elroy Purvis, the beekeeper, came in wearing a wide-brimmed hat with lifted veil. He looked at Mr. Busby, then at Ruby, and finally at Ella. "Afternoon," the man said.

"Afternoon, Elroy." Ella moved away from Mr. Busby and the barrel of melons. "What can I do for you?"

While Ella rang up the case of Mason jars that the beekeeper wanted, Mr. Busby busied himself by selling a portrait to a woman who was new to the area. "You can't spend enough to capture precious memories," Mr. Busby said after the woman told him she had two children. "They grow up so fast," he added. Ruby sauntered about the store, running her baton against one of the watermelons before returning to the birdcage, where Lanier's dolls were displayed on a shelf below. Pulling the ends of her dress up to her waist, she grabbed the Uncle Sam doll and shoved it into her underwear.

"I tell you what we can do," Mr. Busby said. "I'm so confident you'll be pleased, I'll go ahead and take your son's photograph. And then we can settle on an amount you think fair."

The woman twisted her mouth and said, "I just don't know." She looked to the side and then back at Mr. Busby. She pointed toward Ruby. "Oh my stars," she whispered. "That girl . . . that girl just put a doll in her unmentionables."

The beekeeper lifted the crate of Mason jars, thanked Ella, and turned to leave. Ruby swung the baton over her shoulder and marched directly into the man. The crate fell to the floor, and the sound of breaking glass filled the room. Ruby screamed and tried to run out the door. Mr. Busby grabbed her by the arm, and the baton fell and then rolled out onto the porch.

"Let go of me," Ruby screamed. She kicked and leaned down, trying to bite Mr. Busby.

"It's in her unmentionables," the woman kept saying, pointing at Ruby.

Ruby thrashed and tripped over the crate of broken Mason jars. Her dress rose up, and the foot of the doll stuck out from the hem of her underwear.

"Look," the woman said, moving closer.

They all stood over Ruby, and when she scampered to get up, Mr. Busby grabbed her by the wrist again.

"You never were nothing but trouble," the beekeeper said and left to get the sheriff, who was standing at the intersection, listening to an old man complain about his neighbor's wayward cattle ruining his garden.

As the sheriff pulled Ruby out of the store, promising to take her back to her father, they all agreed that she was in need of better supervision. "I've been telling that daddy of hers," the sheriff said. "I been telling Earl she was going to wind up in a mess. He won't hear of it."

"Earl ought to lock her up in her room or something," the beekeeper said. "Instead of staying drunk half the time, he ought to be looking after that simpleton."

Ella stood at the door with her arms wrapped, massaging her elbows. The new customer, the beekeeper, and Mr. Busby stood behind her, shaking their heads. Ella kept telling herself that the sheriff would take care of it. The incident was only a momentary setback in returning to normalcy. She watched Ruby kick and listened as the sheriff warned her not to make a scene. But the time for warnings was long past.

Myer Simpson, Neva Clarkson, and the other ladies who fought the afternoon heat by sipping tea poured from a glass pitcher all leaned against the Simpsons' spooled porch railing, craning their necks toward the parade that the sheriff led. Everyone within shouting distance of the intersection could hear Ruby screaming.

That night Ella stood at the bedroom mirror with her hair draped over her shoulders. She brushed it and watched as slivers of pine and bits of spiderweb fell to the floor. *This too has passed,* Ella thought of the wood that seemed to multiply inside her black locks. She sat on the edge of the bed, massaging her shoulder, and then looked toward the window. The thin lace curtains revealed the shadow of the tin roof on her barn. She stepped closer and lifted the edge with her fingernail that was still sticky from the turpentine that no amount of kerosene seemed able to strip away.

There was no light from the barn or across the way where Narsissa's cabin stood. A whip-poor-will called out from the night, and Ella felt satisfaction at the sound that typically made her feel melancholy. Even if she couldn't make out the stacks of pine at the edge of her drive, she knew they were there, served up from land that had saved her, just like her father had promised in her youth. Lying on the bed, Ella reached over and turned down the kerosene lamp. She could hear Samuel snoring in the room next to hers. If she hadn't known better, she would have guessed that the noise was coming from an old man. Sleep found her before she could pull back the covers.

The darkest hour of the night fell on Ella Wallace's property. An owl swooped down to snatch away a field mouse that the calico cat chased from a tree stump to the pile of timber. The cat looked up just as two men arrived. The tallest man was dressed in suspenders and the other in knee-high boots. The cat twitched its tail and darted across the road, but the men didn't seem to notice.

The one wearing the boots carried gallon jugs of kerosene, and the other held a shotgun and two torches. The man with the suspenders whistled and motioned with his chin at the pile nearest the sound of crickets chirping. Splashes of kerosene landed inside the broken-off places of the stacked pine and dripped down along the rings of the tree trunks. The owl circled overhead as the men lit torches and flung them as they ran. Fire sparked and spread across one pile and then to the next. The men ran past a stray hound that scavenged in a pile of trash behind the Simpson home. They headed north toward Neva Clarkson's house and the schoolyard. Jumping into a pickup, they never looked back at the flames that grew taller and would eventually reach the height of the rooftops in Dead Lakes.

11

Charred devastation blanketed the ground where the pinewood had been stacked. Black soot now spread out across the property. Smoldering smoke rose up and twisted through the crowd that had gathered in hopes of getting a glimpse of Ella as much as what was left of the blazing commotion that had awakened them in the first hour of that Saturday.

Ella sat next to the store on the stacks of croaker sacks filled with feed. She hadn't heard her neighbors' words of sympathy, even though they stood right next to her, patting her and awkwardly trying to hug her. They were only mumbles against the roaring fire out in her yard that had awoken her. Hours later, all she could hear were the crackling sounds of wood that disappeared in what seemed only seconds. She looked like a rag doll, slumped against the side of the store, never bothering to adjust the patchwork quilt that had fallen down the side of her shoulder. Ella stared at the fiery ashes as if peering into a crystal ball in search of direction.

Keaton was the first to see the blaze. He had stepped out into the thick summer air to relieve himself in the outhouse. Standing on the front step of the house, he rubbed his eyes and slapped himself. He looked into the fire and was certain he saw the red haints that Narsissa always said guarded the water. Inside the blue blazes, they danced on top of the hissing pines, swaying and reaching up toward the sky.

Keaton ran screaming toward the barn, snatching up a bucket used to water the oxen. Pumping the handle to the water pump, he screamed, "It's burning. It's burning to the ground."

Lanier came hobbling out of the barn, pulling up his boots. His shirt dangled from his chest, and he jerked it free, running toward the pump and taking control of the handle. "Go," he yelled as he handed the filled bucket to Keaton. Water sloshed over the edges as Keaton lifted the bucket chest high and ran.

Narsissa's hair frayed out at the sides as she clambered to the water pump with two more buckets. Samuel grabbed the wheelbarrow and tried in vain to get the water to the fire faster. Macon came out of the house barefooted and followed his brothers toward the fire that continued to rise. But Ella stood frozen on the porch, watching them run in circles. The feeling that had warned her that something worse was headed her way pierced through the armor of optimism she had pretended to wear. She tried to run. She wanted to run. But her body forbade it the same way her aunt had forbidden her to play outside when the temperature reached its noontime peak.

Now her body was slumped on sacks of feed. She looked at the smoldering ash and wished Lanier could touch it and restore the lumber back. Maybe he could.

Mrs. Pomeroy hovered over Ella and whispered words of comfort in a tone more suitable for soothing a baby. With arms so flabby and dewy that they were like damp towels, Mrs. Pomeroy attempted to hug Ella. "Bless it," she whispered.

Ella jerked away and stared at the old woman's kernel-sized yellowed teeth.

"Now, don't move about and overtax yourself. You're just all to pieces, I can tell," Mrs. Pomeroy said.

Ella reached for the porch rail and pulled herself up from the sacks of feed where she sat. She marched past the oxen that circled and snorted in fear, brushed against the sunflowers she had planted on a carefree day, and stomped a path toward the water pump. The patchwork quilt Mrs. Pomeroy had placed around her shoulders tumbled to the ground. That quilt, stitched with gold thread in the shape of stars, landed in a puddle of mud. Priming the handle so hard the squeaking sound of the handle turned to a hum, Ella grunted the same way she did when she swung the axe into the base of a pine.

"We tried," Lanier mumbled to Ella. He stood in front of her coughing and wiping the sweat from his eyes. His forehead looked as if he had just stepped out of an Ash Wednesday service.

"Would you like for us to help you inside and pray?" Reverend Simpson's musky breath cut through the smell of smoke.

Mr. Pomeroy reached for Ella as if he might pat her on the shoulder but then stopped. "You worked it as good as a man," he said and then swiped sweat and water from his arms.

"Who would do such a thing?" Neva Clarkson asked and reached out to brush the hair from Macon's eyes.

"I don't think it coincidence that Ruby was caught stealing red-handed right before all of this," Myer Simpson said as she pulled at the collar of her floral-print night coat. She made a clucking sound, and the beekeeper joined along.

"If Earl was a decent man, he would've locked that girl up a long time ago," the beekeeper protested. "He's nothing but a drunkard.

A drunkard with a simpleton for a daughter. What's to be done with the both of them?"

"I have said all along that the girl should be in Chattahoochee, where she can be seen after proper," Myer Simpson said. "Remember, Neva? Remember me telling you that girl needed to be in the nervous hospital?"

"I knew she'd wind up doing something dangerous," the bee-keeper said. "We're lucky this fire didn't burn down all of our places."

"Now, nobody knows for sure what happened," Neva said.

"Don't tell me." Myer Simpson smacked her lips.

"With all due respect, Miss Clarkson, you weren't in that store when Ella caught her stealing. She was fit to be tied. That gal had a crazed look to her. Looked like some wildcat or something." The beekeeper stretched his neck out and bugged his eyes.

"And Mrs. Pomeroy . . . you heard for yourself how she was curs-ing and yelling." Myer Simpson pointed down to the intersection where the incident had taken place. "Cursed Ella for all she was worth. Didn't she, Callie?"

Mrs. Pomeroy tucked her head and offered a nod to her husband. "I'm going to Apalachicola to get the sheriff," Mr. Pomeroy said as he turned away from the crowd.

"Bless your heart," Mrs. Pomeroy said. She stepped forward but stopped. Doughy skin rolled up over the tops of her black slippers.

Ella kicked the water pump, primed the handle again, and then stuck her head underneath. She rose up, and strands of wet hair whipped the air. Lanier never moved away even when water splat-tered against his face.

Ella stared at him, daring Lanier to offer her words of hope. "What do you suggest we do now, Mr. Stillis? Can't you breathe on the fire and make it go away?"

"We have eleven days," Lanier said.

"Ten," Samuel yelled from the stump he sat on.

"We could sell the oxen," Keaton said.

"Huh," Samuel spat out the word. "We'd be lucky to get the worn-out things to stand upright long enough for somebody to bid."

"You have that sack of money I gave you," Narsissa added.

"It's over," Ella yelled and dusted her hands in the air. "Over!"

Macon flinched, and a flock of crows cackled out in the field mangled with tree stumps.

"There's a few trees left," Keaton said.

"Nothing but saplings," Samuel responded.

Lanier looked out toward the field, and Samuel stood next to him, shading his hands over his eyes as if he were out at sea in search of new land. Narsissa walked up behind them, followed by Keaton and Macon. Two sandhill cranes poked along the edge of the swamp before flying off and landing on a low-hanging branch of a cypress tree. The gray of the birds seemed to get caught up in the color of the moss that hung from the same tree branch.

Narsissa stared toward the low-lying land beyond the tree stumps where gnarled cypress trees stood with twisted thin branches shaped like witch nails. But no one paid any attention to an Indian. The neighbors kept their sights on the beautiful heroine. They took in the scene as good as any picture show they had seen at the Dixie Theatre.

12

"Mr. Gillespie, I fail to see how it can take so long for a path to be cleared. The spot I recall was hardly a jungle." The day after the fire, Priscilla Mabry stood on the porch of the inn where she and Brother Mabry were staying, covered her mouth with a hand-kerchief with one hand, and shaded her eyes with the other.

Clive Gillespie looked up from the bottom step, directly into the morning sun. He had not made it to the front door before Priscilla came out to admonish him. Even so, there was a smile on his face.

Mrs. Mercile, the manager, a stout woman who wore black shoes with thick straps and drooping stockings, pranced out of the house behind Priscilla. "I put that springwater in her bath like you said to. I put that special water in her bath, but she won't believe me." Mrs. Mercile raised her hands in the air just as if she'd been testifying at church.

When the springwater had been depleted from the barrels he

had arranged for Priscilla's baths, Clive Gillespie paid Mrs. Mercile another five dollars a week to go out into the night and fill jugs with water from the pump in the courtyard. And yet somehow Priscilla could tell the difference. "I'm so double-jointed from this impure mixture. It's a miracle I can stand at all," Priscilla had complained to Brother Mabry, who in turn voiced his frustrations to Clive.

"We didn't travel all this way to sit on a front porch and entertain every member of the clergy within three counties who shows up here uninvited," Brother Mabry said in a voice so loud that it could be heard inside the house next door. "Either get her to the spring or get us transportation back home and be done with the whole concept."

The concept was the very vision that excited Clive Gillespie to the point of needing powder remedies from the pharmacy to control his insomnia. He lay awake at night, staring at the light from the moon that seeped in from his window and illuminated the molding of his bedroom ceiling that had been handcrafted to resemble lilies. He counted in his mind the number of steamboats that would soon pour into the city and the rows of trunks from tourists that would line the deck. After he had secured Ella Wallace's property and signed the official papers securing his partnership in the inn and spa for spiritual and medicinal well-being, he would take possession of the oyster plant and then the land closest to the end of the dock, where eventually he would build a state-of-the-art warehouse. Lot by lot, foreclosure would give him the necessary means to eventually surpass the limited aspirations of his father. In a recurring dream, he stood at his father's grave and tossed twenty-dollar bills to the ground as easy as wilted moss collecting on the marble slab.

Clive motioned with his chin for Mrs. Mercile to step aside on the porch. Pushing his derby hat back to reveal his waxed hairline, Clive smiled with eyes closed. "I believe the path has been cleared now, Mrs. Mabry. Just in time to get you and your double joints straightened out."

"Praise the Lord," Mrs. Mercile said.

"But it is Sunday, after all." Clive lowered his head and looked up at Priscilla the same way he did whenever he tried to convince business owners to refinance. "Surely we can wait just one more day. I expected that on the Lord's Day you'd want to be in a house of worship, Mrs. Mabry."

She held the handkerchief with her initials embroidered in pink and waved it like a flag. "What better place to have a Sunday service than at the site of one of God's miracles? Why, I would have been good as dead by now if it hadn't been for that spring."

Since the dirt road leading to Dead Lakes was rutted and muddy from the night's rains, Clive hired his lawn boy to drive a four-horse wagon, rented from the funeral parlor, to the site of the spring. He gave Mrs. Mercile three dollars for use of her rose-printed love seat, on which Priscilla lounged in the back of the black wagon. Two women of color wearing white uniforms from their days as nannies sat on the edges of the wagon closest to Priscilla, waving heart-shaped wicker fans. "Mercy," Priscilla called out every time the wagon wheels hit washed-out places in the road.

After the fifth moan, even Brother Mabry stopped paying Priscilla any attention. His big frame sprawled across the seat behind the driver. Sweat stains darkened the back of his crimson velvet jacket. He waited until the wagon had passed the city limits before removing the coat. His baby blue shirt, dripping wet from the August sun, molded against his fat. Licking the end of a pencil, he scratched down words on the tablet he clutched in his palm. "What say you, Mr. Gillespie?" Brother Mabry roared. "Eden Everlasting."

Clive Gillespie craned his neck from the front seat and nudged the lawn boy to move his leg so he could have more room. "Beg your pardon?"

"The name of the retreat. Eden Everlasting. How does that translate?"

"Ohhh, me," Priscilla moaned, and the women fanned faster.

The wagon hit another rough patch, and Clive gripped the edge of the wagon. "Eden," Clive repeated with a reverence better suited for sacred prayer.

Brother Mabry coughed and looked back at Priscilla before addressing Clive. "I've only shared my findings with Priscilla. Hear me when I say it's confidential." Brother Mabry raised his eyebrows toward the lawn boy with the ripped straw hat that flapped with each bump in the road.

Clive reached over and squeezed the driver's shoulder. "This boy is trustworthy. You have my word. Aren't you, boy?"

The young man, who cut and raked Clive's yard and cared for his family plot at the cemetery, never looked away from the road. He only popped the reins harder.

Sweat dewed the sides of Brother Mabry's reddened face. "Hear what I say, now. If you study the book of Genesis, you will see several descriptions of the Garden of Eden that are specific. Very specific and very *strange*." Brother Mabry said the words as if he might be singing them. "All these highbrowed divinity professors have for years and years speculated where that Garden might have been located. Some say the Near East, but I say hogwash. Hogwash! Believe what I'm telling you. God wanted a sign to tie the Scriptures back to America. America!" he shouted, and the horses shook their heads. Their bridles and bits made a jingling sound.

"America?" Clive asked.

"*America.* Hear me now. Look at all the ways God has blessed this great country of ours. Why, take this war, for instance. If America hadn't stepped into this war when we did, there is no telling what sort of unbearable future those people overseas would face. President Wilson has his head on straight. America is the vehicle that the Lord is using to point the way. And hear me when I say that such was the case at the beginning of time too." Brother Mabry held up his pad and shook it. "I tell you, God is calling His people back. All you have to do is look at the newspaper. Wars and plagues . . . it's all accounted for in Scripture." Brother Mabry shifted and the wagon seat creaked. "God has put a calling on me to give people hope. I'm sent to let people know that the Garden of Eden is not some fairy tale or some outlandish place that evaporated in a desert. No, sir. It's right here before them."

"Mercy," Priscilla moaned. "I'm sure to burn to death from this sun. My parasol." The colored woman with freckled cheeks quickly popped open a pink parasol with matching fringe and held it over Priscilla.

"I see," Clive said. He lifted the derby and set the hat on his lap. Beads of perspiration dotted the nape of his neck like dew.

"Mr. Gillespie, you said you're a churchgoing man. . . ."

"Oh yes," Clive quickly said. "Baptized in the same church as my father."

The lawn boy popped the reins again. The lead horse blew dust from his nostrils.

"Well then, you'll recall from Sunday school that the Garden of Eden sat on a river that forked in four places." Brother Mabry lowered his chin. Rolls of fat glistened.

"Four places, you say?"

"Hear what I'm telling you. It's all in the book of Genesis. And do you happen to know the only place in the entire world where the river forks in four places?"

Clive looked down at the horses and then back at Brother Mabry. "Do you mean to say . . . ?"

"Search the Scriptures, and walk the globe. There's not a Harvard Divinity School professor who can argue otherwise."

Clive sat on the edge of the seat and turned completely around. When he had been contacted by Brother Mabry's New York attorney, he had only been presented a business proposition that would rival any the area had ever seen. He had been promised currency, not religion. Clive's arm was propped on the lawn boy's shoulder. "The Apalachicola River?"

Brother Mabry closed the cover on his pad. "Tell me another river in the world that forks in four places."

Licking at the sweat that tickled his lips, Clive practically cheered. "What a story! They'll come from all over . . . all over the world, even."

"Exactly," Brother Mabry said.

The freckle-faced woman standing over Priscilla gripping the parasol held the gaze of the woman who waved the fan.

"I hope you don't take offense," Brother Mabry said in a softer tone. "I took the liberty of hiring a botanist to survey the area. A fellow by the name of Listerman who teaches at the university. He came out to the spot and took samples."

"It's a blessing," Priscilla called out. "A blessing that my father found that Indian who led him to the spring."

"A blessing!" Brother Mabry roared, causing the horses to prance to the side. "I'll have all the newspapermen from across the country come see for themselves. I'll have that Listerman professor trained to speak. He'll tell it to those newspapermen in a way they can't negate. Before it's through, William Randolph Hearst himself will be coming to see."

"A blessing, yes, sir," Clive said before turning around. He laughed and brushed his hands together as if it were a winter's day. Then he leaned over and whispered instructions for the lawn boy to turn at the fork in the road.

"The long way?" the young man whispered back.

"Absolutely," Clive said in a disguised cough. He clutched the side of the wagon as the boy turned at the fork in the road. The horses high-stepped in the direction of the fishing camp where Bonaparte lived—completely skirting Ella's place.

A family of whitetail deer grazed up ahead on the side of the road. Brother Mabry leaned forward, shouting for Priscilla to muster the strength to rise and witness the sight. But the only image Clive could think about was the confirmation he had received. The note left underneath his door that morning danced across his mind. *DONE,* the note read in block letters resembling the efforts of a grade-school child. Clive lit his morning cigar, blew a ring of smoke toward the portrait of his father, and then held the amber tip to the paper. Other than the ashes of a note and charred virgin timber, there would be no official record of the man who wore brass-buckled suspenders.

At the site of the spring, Clive looked with cautious intrigue at the cleared timber off in the distance. Since the spring sat on the opposite corner of the property, past the swamp and cypress, Ella's home appeared no larger than a matchbox off in the distance.

"You mustn't jar me too much," Priscilla warned as the women and the young man tried to lift her from the wagon. "Gingerly."

"Gingerly," Brother Mabry echoed, motioning with his straw hat for Clive to help.

Rushing to offer aid, Clive was careful not to let his hands brush too closely to Priscilla's pale skin with raised blue veins or to the hands of the black workers he employed. "Yes, easy does it," he said.

Locusts roared, weeds flapped, and tree limbs snapped under the feet of the young man carrying Priscilla like she might have been his gigantic child. "You got her, boy?" Clive kept asking as the group made their way down to the embankment covered in ferns and poison ivy. A black snake slithered beneath a blanket of dead palmetto bushes. One of the women of color made a gasp that sounded like a scream. Clive glared at her, and she placed her hand over her mouth. "Easy does it," he said without looking away from the woman.

"Ohhh," Priscilla moaned and then threw her head back until she appeared to be either dead or drunk in the arms of the young black man.

"Just a few more steps, dearest. You can do it. I know you can,"

Brother Mabry yelled while sliding sideways and then rebounding by grabbing a scrub oak tree.

At the spring, the women laid out blankets that had been taken from the beds at the inn back in town. Then they tied string to trees surrounding the pool and placed white sheets over them. "See there," Brother Mabry said. "You'll have complete privacy."

The young man adjusted his weight and in the process jostled Priscilla. "Ohhh," she cried out again before demanding to be set down. He placed her on one of the blankets, and she stuck her foot up in the air. Without any direction, the freckle-faced woman went about taking the shoes and stockings from Priscilla's feet.

As Priscilla soaked, Clive lit a cigar and listened to Brother Mabry once more make the case for this being God's first place of creation. Brother Mabry swung his log-sized arms in the air and closed his eyes. Suddenly his nose crinkled and he opened one eye. "Cigar smoke doesn't sit well with Priscilla's constitution. She's allergic."

When Brother Mabry went to check on Priscilla's progress, Clive backed away and stomped across a patch of blush-colored red root growing around saplings of pines. He looked out toward Ella's house. Behind a massive oak, a palmetto bush fluttered, and a figure cast a shadow down the side of the tree.

Clive hadn't made it fifteen feet away from the tree when Narsissa stepped out from behind it. He froze, and the side of his jaw flinched as he looked back at the spring. "What are you doing?"

"I was fixing to ask you the same thing," Narsissa said.

"Well, it is Sunday. I have guests and thought that an outing to the . . . to the country would help their respiratory systems." He bit the end of the cigar and then spat it to the ground. The tobacco came to rest against a log speckled with fuchsia-colored fungus.

"Ella don't care for guests on her place unless she invites them."

"Is that so?" Clive smiled and then took a drag on the cigar.

Narsissa put the pail of red root stems down on the ground next to the palmetto bush. Before rising up, she casually lifted the silver knife out from her boot and hid it behind her back.

Clive stepped forward but Narsissa didn't move.

"We had a fire. A fire that wiped out our timber last night."

"Our?" Clive coughed out the word. "You're one step away from being down there with the others helping a pitiful white woman." Clive nodded his head back toward the colored women who were assisting Priscilla.

"I'm not scared of you," Narsissa said. "No, sir." She exposed the knife to him. The sun flickered off of the tip.

Clive flicked an ash from the cigar and laughed. He moved so close that when he exhaled, his breath caused the ends of Narsissa's hair to flutter. "Now let me give it to you straight, gal. I'll take my pistol and whip you bloody with it. Who will help you then? Ella?"

"Who says I need helping?"

Clive looked sideways at Narsissa. A nose hair twisted and turned as he breathed. "What am I thinking? Having a conversation with a gal who probably can't even sign her own name. Get on back to your shack before I knock you back there."

Narsissa didn't turn away. "You're trespassing. The law's on our side."

"Our . . . *our?*" Sunlight cracked through the canopy of vines and made Clive's waxed hair seem even slicker. "You poor old thing. Ella has manipulated you but good. You really do think that you have a stake in all of this."

"I know what I know," Narsissa said, gathering the pail before walking away.

"So sue me. Courthouse opens at eight in the morning," Clive said. His laughter could be heard long after he had tromped over the blooms of the red root and returned to the uninvited guests. The jagged sound of his amusement followed Narsissa like a haint, tormenting her all the way through the sand littered with pine stumps and to the dust that had accumulated underneath the bed where Ella mourned her loss.

The report of Clive's appearance jolted back Ella's determination as much as the raspberry-colored liquid that Narsissa drained from the skillet after frying the red roots. "It is time," Narsissa said as she forced Ella to drink the bitter concoction.

The next morning, while Narsissa hitched up the wagon, Ella gathered the breakfast plates in the sink and told her oldest son a lie. "Narsissa and I are going to town to try one more time to plead mercy with Clive." Today of all days, she didn't need a boy who thought he was a man getting into her business. After the fire, Samuel had stomped about the house, rearing and carrying on about how Clive Gillespie was to blame for all their troubles since the beginning of time. He had declared vengeance, and that night, after he had gone to bed, Ella locked the gun cabinet and hid the key in the teapot that she seldom used.

"You can't handle him by yourself," Samuel said, walking toward his bedroom to change. "I better go with you."

"No," Ella said, blocking the passageway next to the oven. "I mean it, Samuel. You are not going. Don't make me tell you again."

At the city limits of Apalachicola, Narsissa popped the reins and turned left through the outskirts of town. The shrill sound of wood meeting electric saw blades caused the mule to pin his ears back. When they came to a stop at the long wooden warehouse that served as the headquarters for Herndon Lumber, both women paused to look at the stacks of wood that covered the side yard next to the sawmill. The ground looked as if it were covered in dark-brown carpet. Colored women dressed in garments the color of pine needles stacked the lumber two at a time. Hats that reminded Ella of the ones she had seen for safaris tilted on their oily foreheads. Gloves, thick and stained with tar, protected their hands. Only a few gave a curious glance toward Ella and Narsissa.

A passel of men came out of the office doors crafted to resemble pinecones. They scattered in front of the wagon and went back to their proper places of operation.

Avery Herndon, the mill owner and a man whose waist size matched his age of forty-two, followed behind the men. He stood on the wooden step that was gnarled and peeling. Ella never noticed him. She kept her gaze toward the women and thought if only she could hire them for a week, then maybe she would have a chance.

"I know what you're thinking," Avery shouted above the roar of the saw.

Ella and Narsissa jumped in their seats.

Avery, with his hands propped on his back and his stomach protruding forward, said, "Don't hate me for hiring them." He pointed to the colored women with his knobby chin. "It's only for the time being. Until this war is over. I got twenty-seven men over in what-ya-ma-call-it fighting for Uncle Sam. Not enough men to go around if you ask me. Don't blame me for working women like they were men. Blame that sorry President Wilson."

"Mr. Herndon," Ella said, climbing down from the wagon, "may I have a word with you?"

He scratched the side of his chin. Red streaks marked the spot where his fingernails had raked. "I don't have long. I got a man from Pensacola coming by to try and sell me one of those new tractors."

"I don't have long either," Ella said.

On Avery's office desk were littered a disorganized pile of yellowing trade journals, stacks of invoices, and packages of cigarettes. He propped his hands on top of the current edition of *Southern Lumberman*. Avery nodded to each detail that Ella shared about bank notes, unexpected setbacks, and arson. He only widened his eyes and raised an eyebrow when Ella said she knew who had set the blaze.

"You know who did it just as well as I do," she said. "So I have to sell cypress. I have to cut it and sell it fast."

Avery ran his hand over the cover of the trade magazine and then looked down while flipping through the pages. A breeze from the rotating fan propped above Ella's head on the corner of a ceiling beam caused what hair Avery had left to rise. "I hate it. I really, really do." Avery shook his head, and a roll of fat that gathered above his shirt collar jiggled. "You had some good timber."

"I still do. . . . I mean, I still have good cypress. Cypress is in demand, I hear."

He shook his head again, this time faster. "Not like you might hear." He sighed and bent sideways. "Excuse me. I'm just keeping watch for that man who's bringing the tractor."

Ella leaned slightly away in the chair, giving Avery a better view of the window. Then she shifted the other way to block him. "Now, I know that cypress can be sold in Millville. Mr. Busby told me they are hiring men hand over fist to work at that new shipbuilding plant."

"Now I don't know what Mr. What-Ya-Ma-Call-Him is saying, but you take it from me. The government needs pine. Loblolly if they can get it." Avery stood up, adjusted his pants, and glanced out toward the main doors beyond his office.

Standing and looking at Avery Herndon's gray, sunken eyes, Ella never blinked. "I am not asking for favors. I'm just asking for a chance. You and I both know that I can give you some of the best cypress around here, so—"

"It's dwarf cypress, Ella. Now, I don't expect you to know the difference, but dwarf cypress just ain't in demand," Avery snorted.

"With all due respect, Avery Herndon," Ella said, "I hear otherwise."

Avery exhaled hard enough to ruffle two of the invoices stacked upon his desk. "I don't want to get into all that. . . . It's just more trouble than it's worth, all right?"

"What does that mean? I won't be any trouble to work with."

"Not you, Ella. I'm talking about the situation with Clive and the loan you got with his bank," Avery said, smiling at her sideways the way he might to a child who had tried unsuccessfully to win a game of hopscotch. "Look, Ella, like it or not Clive Gillespie carries a big stick around here. All I'm saying is I got a business to run and I'd rather not rattle that cage, if you know what I mean."

A roar and a backfire caused both of them to turn toward the entrance doors. Avery jumped up, landing his nubby fingers on the desk. "Yonder he is," he said. Avery moved faster than he had all day, bounded around the side of the desk, bumped against Ella, and trotted outside.

A stack of invoices and the edition of *Southern Lumberman* that he'd been flipping through fell to the floor at Ella's feet. Her first instinct was to stomp on them until the grime of her shoe left a permanent tattoo of her visit. When she picked the papers up like a properly trained lady, she noticed a crinkled page in the magazine. "Uncle Sam Calls on Lumbermen to Fulfill Timber and Cypress Needs."

Scanning the article, Ella could hear the cry of the tractor engine outside and the clipped pieces of male conversation. "You say it has the ground pressure of an eighty-pound boy?" Avery asked the salesman.

After reading just three paragraphs that described the new battleship *War Mystery* and the tons of cypress needed to build it, Ella used the tip of what remained of her chipped pinky nail and sliced the inside seam of the magazine. She folded the article in half and stuffed it down the front of her blouse.

Outside, Narsissa sat on the wagon and worked the reins to keep the nervous mule from running away. "The steel mule," the salesman with gray britches that were too short called the machine that sputtered and spun around the office building as Avery's foreman, a man shaped liked a square, gave it a trial run. "Take it for a run over the logs, fella," the salesman shouted. "She might look like a car, but she's got the guts of a locomotive."

The front wheels that were the size of a car's struggled over the pine log nearest the group of colored women who paused from their work only long enough to glance at the smoke that was brewing from the box-sized engine. Then the steel wheels of the back end buoyed over the log with little effort.

Before Narsissa and Ella pulled away, they heard the salesman make one last pitch to Avery. "She's the newest and greatest thing on the market. She's good for the lowlands. I guarantee you. Cypress and tupelo trees are no match for this one."

By the time the afternoon sun had cast a shadow over the store, which now had the Closed sign dangling from the window, word had made its way through the currents of Dead Lakes that Ella and her children were in the swamp, slicing at cypress trees.

"She'll wind up hospitalized and homeless, mark my word," Myer Simpson said.

"Poor thing. Never could face reality," Mrs. Pomeroy added.

"That's what you get when you let a woman run a business," Elroy Purvis, the beekeeper, said before pulling the veil down over his face.

But Neva Clarkson watched from a distance and ignored their predictions. "A survivor," she said only to herself.

At the southern end of the county, past a fork in the road, Bonaparte and the daughter who had been spared from pain said nothing. They just stood by the boat with peeling green paint that rocked on the river and listened. Their neighbor Royal cuddled a jug he had just picked up at the juke joint and leaned against the dogwood tree with the colored bottles hanging from its branches. The clinking noise caused Royal to speak louder, and the effort caused his words to slur even more. He told about a fire at the place where the healer stayed.

The troubles of the woman he knew only as a delicate figure that glided behind a store window shadowed Bonaparte's heart long after the evening lamp was turned low.

13

Earl Tucker, a man known to nurse a bottle and to disappear for long stretches of time, leaving his daughter, Ruby, to run free, showed up at Ella's doorstep with a rusted axe and a leather thermos that he claimed held only water.

"Now, Earl, I appreciate you coming out here," Ella said, swatting away sand gnats. "But I am not in a position to pay. At least not until I get the cypress up to Millville."

Tossing the axe into the ground blade first, Earl massaged the worn and broken leather on the bottle. His potato-shaped nose was covered with blisters, and the ends of his carrot-red hair hung like strands of hay at his neck. "I ain't worrying about all that," he said. "I'm here on account of Ruby. Now I ain't claiming my girl set that fire—"

"Earl, nobody here is saying such," Ella said.

Earl raised his hands and tucked his head down. "I'm not saying whether she did or didn't. I'm just here to right a wrong that's been done to my neighbor."

Stunned, Ella talked the rest of the day about how grateful she was to find at least one helpful neighbor. Narsissa reminded her how people had once come together to build barns. Samuel showed Earl how to position the gator tail saw so it could dig deeper into the cypress. "There you go, neighbor," Samuel said when Earl got it right.

But the neighborly concern didn't register with Lanier. Whether it was the way Earl nervously rubbed his mole whenever Lanier caught Earl looking at him or the questions Earl would ask three and four times in a row, Lanier wanted to keep away from this man who was only as tall as Keaton.

"Where did you say you was from again?" Earl asked the question two times before Lanier licked the remnants of water from the side of his mouth and tossed the ladle back into the bucket of fresh water.

"Georgia," he mumbled and returned to work.

"Georgia, where?" Earl took a swig out of a can that had once sat on the store shelf filled with pinto beans.

"I expect we can cut at least four more before lunch break," Lanier said, walking away from Earl.

During lunch, a crane pranced at the water's edge. Lanier could see the tail of an alligator as a splash of water called out in the distance. *If the visitor gets too nosy, there are options,* he thought.

"How come you to wind up here?" Earl said while reaching for the biscuit that Ella offered him.

Lanier sighed, and Ella looked in his direction. He smiled and this time she smiled back.

"He's family, Earl," she said. "I thought I'd told you."

"You might've. Who's to say? When you live with a girl that's slow like mine, you go half-crazy yourself." Earl laughed, but no one followed. "Just joshing a little bit," he said. "How long you reckon you'll stay in Dead Lakes?"

Keaton stopped wringing the sweat out of his shirt and turned to face Lanier. Narsissa stopped pouring water into a tin cup, and Samuel moved closer from the water's edge, dropping the wax paper still stained with mustard. Locusts buzzed the air, and no one moved, not even to strike at the mosquitoes.

They all stared until Lanier felt the back of his sunburned neck flame even stronger. When he turned to look back toward the barn, hoping for time to script a believable response, he saw them walking across the skinned field that was dotted with stumps. "Did you bring company with you, Earl?" Lanier asked.

Bonaparte led the group, carrying a rusty saw and a wooden spike as big as a rake. The others who had witnessed the disappearance of the burns on his daughter followed behind him. They fanned out across the field and for an instant looked like trees that were still sturdy and resolute.

When Lanier stood, Ella and the others followed.

"What on earth?" Ella asked.

Bonaparte kept his eyes on Lanier but answered Ella. "Miss Ella, we heard about your predicament. I expect you might not know this, but back when I was a single man, I rode the log rafts, taking the cut wood up and down to Millville."

Ella nodded the same way she might if she had been receiving Bonaparte and the men on the porch of her home.

"Folks talking about this and that and bills and so forth." Bonaparte raised his hand and tucked his head. "Now I don't mean to get in your business, but . . ."

"Six days," Ella said. "I have six days."

"Six days. All right now." Bonaparte took the saw from his shoulder and placed it on the ground. The group of men, eighteen strong, followed suit.

Ella clutched her chest and stepped backward. She stared at the men as if they were tossing out gold coins. "I can't let you . . . oh no, no, I can't have you . . ." Ella stammered and then laughed. "How can I pay . . . I mean, I can't pay right now."

"For my part, that man right there done paid the bill for you." Bonaparte pointed straight at Lanier. The men scattered down the water's edge mumbling greetings to the group. All but Earl and Ella returned to their positions.

Lanier started laughing and shook his head. He felt Earl studying him the way people examined the dolls that he made. Lanier could see the man through the corner of his view, scratching the mole on his face. He imagined words of suspicion forming into questions inside the man's scraggly head. "Well, now. Six days," Lanier said. "They tell me the Good Lord made the world in six days."

"And pray tell He sent reinforcement," Ella said, but Bonaparte had already begun showing Samuel and Keaton how to strike the ring of the cypress so that it would float properly.

Lanier tossed Ella the work gloves that she had dropped on the ground, and to his surprise she caught them with one hand. He winked at her and said, "Time for lollygagging is over."

After the sun had cast a blue streak across the horizon and the frogs had begun their steady calls from the swamp, Bonaparte rubbed his hands as if washing them. He promised Ella he would return the next day.

"I'll pay you, you know that," she said.

"We ain't worrying with that right now," Bonaparte said. His words trailed off as he looked up like there might be a script written on the tree branches.

Ella reached out and took Bonaparte's thick, gritty palm in hers. His grip grew stronger as she shook his hand. "I'm not looking for charity," Ella said. "I pay what is owed." Forcing herself to look into his dark, bloodshot eyes, Ella realized that it was the first time she had ever gotten close enough to the man to touch his skin.

When Narsissa walked up next to her and brushed her arm, Ella stood with her shoulders squared back. "My aunt always told me that people were in the world not just to observe but to impact. Each and every one of you is impacting our lives. I can't thank you enough."

As the men walked away, each spoke a pledge to return the next day. But Earl made no such promises. He walked away in a hobbled gait, rubbing the tight muscles in his shoulder. At the fork in the road where lightning had split an oak tree in half, he reached inside the dead trunk and pulled out the bottle of whiskey he had placed there that morning. By the time he had made it to the house that sat on a field where he sharecropped tobacco for Sheriff Bissell, he was certified drunk.

Lightning bugs lit up the yard where tall strands of goldenrod weeds bloomed through the gaps in a stack of cinder blocks stacked haphazardly next to the broken porch step. Ruby ran barefoot, wearing her cherry-sequined turban and carrying a chipped Mason jar. "I got another one," she said as she snatched an amber-colored bug.

"Keep at it," Sheriff Bissell said from the side of the house. He had his foot propped on a washer turned sideways on the ground, the metal wringer long broken.

"A promise is a promise," Clive Gillespie said. He walked from around the corner of the house, where he had just relieved himself. He was still zipping up his pants. "A nickel for every lightning bug caught."

Earl tucked the whiskey bottle in his back pants pocket and ran his hand through hair that was matted with sweat. His puzzled gaze shifted from Clive to Ruby.

Ruby wrapped her hand around the crumpled wax paper that covered the jar. She threw her hips to the side with each word that she spoke. "That man promised he'd pay me to catch these. He likes the way they light up his bedroom at night." Three buttons on the side of her skirt were undone, and two red blotches marked the spot on her chest where Clive's hands had groped her moments earlier.

"She's a spitfire," Clive called out. He struck a match against the weathered porch rail and lit a cigar. "I can see she's a handful."

"Got another one," Ruby yelled and jumped in the air.

"I told her to stay put," Earl said. "I tried to lock that cellar, but I knew she'd most likely pick the lock."

Sheriff Bissell kicked the piece of rotten wood on the washer and laughed. "That old rusty thing will barely hang on the door, let alone lock."

Clive blew smoke from the corner of his mouth. Dried sweat made his shirt look as crumpled as the wax paper that Ruby used for a lid on the jar. "When we pulled up here she was running free out in the field."

"She was swinging that baton like there was no tomorrow. Just a-swinging and a-singing." The sheriff laughed again.

Earl wove a path to the porch. Ruby ran toward a pile of fungus-stained firewood that was left over from the cold. No one ever cautioned her to stop climbing onto the rotting wood.

A mattress stained with yellow blotches lay on the ground next to the flower box that had last been used when Earl's wife was still alive. Horsehair from a tear down the side of the mattress invaded the flower box like gray weeds. Earl attempted to push the mattress underneath the porch with the side of his boot. But he soon grunted and gave up.

"I don't know what all the fuss is about," Clive said. "Ruby seems perfectly charming to me."

"She was just a-swinging that baton and singing and laughing. She was putting on a big show for us," Sheriff Bissell said.

"She don't mean no harm," Earl said.

"Oh no," the sheriff said and wiped his chin. "I keep telling folks that. I keep telling them but they just don't want to listen."

"Speaking of commotions," Clive said, "earlier today a man who works for me happened by the swamp, you know the piece of lowland I'm talking about, Earl. The one on the other side of the Wallace place? Just at the edge of her property?"

Earl stuffed his hands in his pockets and looked back at Ruby, who was talking to the lightning bugs she had captured. "Yes, sir."

"It's hard to see clearly through all that overgrowth, but I could have sworn there were a bunch of nigras bantering about with cross saws. My man could hear their commotion down at the edge of the property, you know, by that spring." Clive smiled at Earl and then turned his head. "I think he might have mentioned seeing you among the group."

Earl looked at the sheriff and nodded. "The sheriff probably told you. Folks is saying Ruby burnt up the timber at the Wallace place. Like I told the sheriff last night, I can manage her. I don't want no trouble. The way I seen it, if I was to go over and help out for a day, it might make things right with the Wallace woman. Maybe she won't press charges and all."

Clive squinted, and the acne scars on his forehead bunched together. "Certainly."

The sheriff used a stick to knock off mud from the corner of his boot. "Yeah, well, I want to be clear, Earl. Now I don't think I made myself clear when we first talked it over. Just because Ella don't press charges doesn't mean Ruby won't face charges."

Earl ran his hands down the sides of his pants. "Come again, Sheriff?"

Sheriff Bissell sighed. His jowls tussled about when he shook his head back and forth. "The law is the law. I took an oath to uphold the law."

"The law doesn't have cataracts, they tell me." Clive stumped out his cigarette against the peeling porch rail and tossed it at Earl's feet.

"I got twelve," Ruby said. The side of her skirt flapped in the air as she jumped.

"Folks can be so ornery," the sheriff added. "They have been after me all day to do something with that girl of yours. Everybody is scared to death she'll burn down their place next."

"She was with me all night that night." Earl shuffled his feet and placed his hand on the back pocket that hid the bottle.

"Hmmmm," the sheriff said. "And where was it again that you happened to be? I don't think being laid up drunk at the time in question will count much before the judge at the courthouse."

"Say, Sheriff Bissell," Clive said, "would it help the cause if Ruby had . . . oh, I don't know . . . something along the lines of a benefactor? Someone to support her and ensure she wouldn't do harm to the community? Someone to see after her, so to speak."

The sheriff rose on his boot heels and looked up at the first stars of night. "I expect that'd help, all right."

"Well, now," Clive said and reached inside his pants pocket. He lifted the end of a silver monogrammed money clip and pulled forth a dollar. "Ruby . . . Ruby."

Ruby ran up to the porch, still clutching the jar of lightning bugs. Greenish light from the insects flickered against the cracked, dirty glass. No words were spoken as the jar and money were exchanged. Ruby ran up the stairs and through the threshold that was missing a front door. Her giggling could be heard from inside the house. Clive held up the jar, examining his purchase. "Sheriff Bissell, if Earl is of a mind to it, then I'd be happy to serve as Ruby's benefactor."

"That's mighty white of you," the sheriff said. He stuck his tongue in the corner of his mouth, and his jowl expanded. "It sure would be a shame to lock a pretty little thing like her up in jail."

"Jail?" Earl stepped forward.

"Worst case, naturally," the sheriff added. "I expect Judge Kimball would take pity on her—her being simpleminded and all. Probably just send her over to Chattahoochee."

"Crazy hospital?"

Sheriff Bissell shrugged his shoulders. "Out of my control, Earl."

Earl kicked at a patch of sandspurs. The roots of the thorny weed finally broke free from the ground. "A doctor one time wanted us to put her in there. My wife wouldn't sign the papers." He looked Clive square in the eyes. "You hear what they do to girls like her in there?"

"Now, Earl, no need to let your imagination run wild," Clive said, raising his hand. "I'll personally see to it that things are smoothed over."

Earl stared at the patch of uprooted sandspurs. "I promised my wife I'd never . . ."

"Oh, certainly." Clive walked back and forth in front of the cinder blocks. He snatched the top of one of the weeds, and the bloom ripped. "You know, the sheriff here can attest that I esteem nothing of more importance than loyalty. Except for maybe discretion. Is that a fair statement, Sheriff Bissell?"

The sheriff pursed his lips and nodded.

"So, Earl, here's what I'm willing to do." Clive took out the money clip again and began peeling away bills. He folded the edges perfectly. "I'm going to pay you to keep showing up at Ella Wallace's place. You don't ask any questions. Fact of the matter, you don't talk beyond what is simply necessary. You just follow my instructions. You can do that, can't you, Earl?"

"Now I didn't go there aiming to work like a pulpwooder. I was just helping for the—"

Clive closed his eyes and held up his hand again. "The only worry you have right now is following instructions. Because it would be a travesty—a mortal sin, you might well say—to let that pretty daughter with the mind of a child and the body of a filly end up in the crazy hospital harnessed to the wall like a mare on breeding day."

Earl reached for the bottle again but this time didn't bother to hide it. Pulling the whiskey from his pocket, he swallowed what remained, wiped his chin, and threw the bottle to the ground. It landed against the side of a cinder block, cracking the glass right down the middle.

14

Mr. Busby picked up a vase with gold-chipped cherubs that he had acquired from a woman named Prescott in Moultrie, Georgia, who claimed that it had once belonged to Thomas Jefferson. He had stayed in the woman's carriage house with faded floral wallpaper that was missing in patches, exposing mildew on the boards. To pay for his lodging, he took a photograph of the big-hipped woman sitting on a peeling veranda, holding the granddaughter, whose face was as round as a full moon and whose hair had been tied in peach-colored bows, special for the occasion.

Inside the carriage house that night, Mr. Busby was developing film and placing pictures in thin silver frames that were scratched and dented. He was behind in his work and stayed up until well past midnight developing the photographs of people he had met on his circuit. They were different ages, sizes, and stations in life, but most were connected by the same setting: a black velvet backdrop, wingback chairs, and a bearskin rug stained with baby vomit and urine from a prized foxhound.

The photograph taken of Ella Wallace and her family was particularly clear, so he made two copies, one that he would give to Ella as a gift marking the day she finished cutting the timber and the other for his display table. Holding the eight-by-ten picture up to the light that flickered from a lamp on the small table, Mr. Busby squinted at the corner of the image. At the edge of the picture, Lanier could be seen in side profile, walking away from the group. "Look at that trash," Mr. Busby said and shook the picture that he held with small pliers. Who would want a common laborer in a family portrait? His hair, long enough for a woman, in Mr. Busby's estimation, was smeared in motion much like a fluttering of angel wings. But then the smear seemed to become something with potential.

The grime on the faces of Ella and the others was juxtaposed with enough hope in their eyes that Mr. Busby couldn't help but make comparisons of his work with that of celebrated photographer Jacob Riis. From an elderly couple in Waycross, Georgia, Mr. Busby had bartered a family portrait taken in front of their crackled, four-column house and pictures of their puny Brahman bulls for a copy of Riis's book *How the Other Half Live*. That was over a year ago, and ever since, the pictures inside the book continued to feed his dream of having his own version of the hardscrabble people published for all the world to see. He spent the hours on the road picturing his name sprawled across the cover of such a book, exacting the imaginary type copy and calculating advances from a publisher yet to be secured.

Selling himself on the idea that the appearance of Lanier—looking down at the ground with his tall leather boots in midstride—made the photograph more art-worthy, Mr. Busby stuck it inside the wet-stained leather satchel that contained his other commissions. He packed up his equipment, propped it next to a rusted chamber pot with a portrait of General Grant on the bottom, sipped from his flask of whiskey, and stripped naked before climbing into bed.

Starting tomorrow, he would display the photograph and explain to the unrefined that the smear of the man walking in the corner of the image was representational of a celestial being standing watch over the brokenhearted woman who was working like a man to provide for her children.

"Wrapping day," Bonaparte kept saying as the majority of the men who had first appeared like apparitions in the morning mist helped him drive spikes into the cypress that had been cut. Lanier and two other men dropped the chains they carried on their shoulders to the bank of the river where the cypress had been transported by the oxcart. Branches of a dogwood tree rattled with the quaking sound of the chains meeting the earth. Samuel and Keaton helped the men wrap the ends of the logs with chains until the product of their work became two rafts.

"Wrapping day," Ella repeated in a chorus. She massaged the hard callus on her index finger the same way others might rub a rabbit's foot for luck. The sun beat down on her and the mosquitoes circled. She rubbed the rough spot on her hand harder.

Bonaparte took the lead in easing the raft of cypress logs onto the water. He held the spike that he would use to help guide the raft in a way that reminded Ella of the Bible illustrations of Moses holding up a rod to part the Red Sea. Rays of the stinging sun filtered through the trees that guarded the river and sprinkled out across the dark water like a scattering of diamonds.

"Two days to go till that note gets paid," Keaton said and held on to the side rail that Lanier had built as a safety measure. No one repeated Keaton's words. The date that officially would mark whether Clive Gillespie's bank took ownership of the farm was firmly planted in the minds of all who took positions on the raft.

Narsissa stood on the front end, her rubber boots gripped to the grooves in the wood. Samuel was wild-eyed, watching Bonaparte and clutching one of the spike poles the same way he did. Keaton sat on a box that had once contained a shipment of china and now held their supply of water and food. Lanier held the rope that was all that secured the four-foot-wide raft of cypress to the riverbank. He reached up with his other hand, offering it to Ella. She licked her lips, feeling the stare of the men who remained on shore. With her first uneasy step on the log, she felt herself slipping on the slick surface of the wood.

"Easy," Lanier whispered. His breath was as hot as the sun on her neck. She got her footing before turning back and waving at the men, who grew smaller as the raft took to the river's current.

"Thank you," Ella wanted to yell. "When we come back, we'll have the party of all parties," she had planned to say that morning as they bundled the wood. "We'll burn that note and dance and drink until sunup," she tried to shout as the raft of wood rocked and moved downriver. But the words would not form on her dry tongue. The red lines she had marked on the calendar with the girl holding a Coca-Cola flashed through her mind. The remaining days between her dreams and her challenges were still wide-open spaces on paper.

Some of the men on the shore waved their hats and shouted back at Ella. Others walked away, vowing to keep Bonaparte honest in repaying the favor of helping the woman who sheltered the healer. But Earl said nothing. He walked back to the oak tree that had been struck by lightning and split down the middle. He wedged his hand inside the rotted trunk and pulled out his bottle of spirits. As he sauntered past Wallace Commissary, the Closed sign dangled sideways from the window on the door.

Reverend Simpson's Model T roared with the sound of a broken muffler, and the back wheel hit a mud puddle as the car passed Earl on the road. The floral-printed scarf that Myer Simpson wore on top of her head fluttered about in the breeze of the passenger seat. Earl darted into the shadow forming behind Ella's store. He kept his head tucked toward the ground and his hands planted inside the pockets of his pants. He fingered the sharp spikes that Bonaparte had told him to nail into the side of the raft. Instead, Earl had slipped the four-inch spikes into his pockets until they protruded from his side like a spare bone attached to his thigh, then pounded away just like he was told.

Behind the store, where an oak branch scratched against the tin roof, Earl leaned against the side of the building that was discolored with mildew. Knocking back the bottle and letting the liquid burn his throat, he cussed Clive Gillespie for making him pretend to take orders from a colored man.

In Apalachicola, Reverend Simpson and his wife, Myer, drove past the white-column Orman house with its lawn that swept down to the river.

Myer sat up straighter. "I wonder if Judge Orman will be there?"

Reverend Simpson gripped the steering wheel tighter and the automobile hit a hole in the road. "Judge Orman has more sense than us. He knows a circus when he sees one."

"Will you stop being so contrary," Myer said. "Circus or not, this man has the ear of town leaders. This man . . . this charlatan could teach you a thing or two about promotion if you'd pay attention."

"And all this time I thought I was called not to be a respecter of people," Reverend Simpson said without looking away from the road to Main Street. "And fix your scarf. It's crooked."

When they pulled up to the Franklin Inn, where the press conference was being held, Brother Mabry was standing on the porch, having his photograph made by a stringer for the *Chicago Tribune*. Just before the flash went off, Brother Mabry placed his hand on the shoulder of the man who stood on the step below him. Professor Seth

Listerman, the botanist hired to help substantiate Brother Mabry's claims. The professor, a man in his early fifties with silver hair parted straight down the middle and a protruding overbite that caused a slight slur of words, held up a long tree branch that had the length of a Christmas fir but the leaves of a fern.

"Eden, you say?" asked a young man with sagging britches held on his thin waist with a tattered belt.

"The torreya tree sample," Professor Listerman said in an authoritative, affected nasal voice that he had perfected with the aid of Brother Mabry's vocal coach. "Only a sample of the rare flora that can be traced to Eden." He held the branch higher, and an ant crawled out from one of the leaves.

"The who tree? How do you spell that?" asked a man whose belly lapped over his belt. He scribbled down the letters that Professor Listerman patiently provided.

"So, where's the apple tree?" a young man asked. The others in the semicircle laughed, and two flipped the covers over their notepads and walked back toward the dock where the steamboat awaited them.

"Hear me now," Brother Mabry said. "Genesis says nothing about an apple tree. That's man's logic. It reads that Eve plucked fruit from the *tree of knowledge*."

"Professor, hold up that branch a little more to the left," the man with the wide waist said. He flapped the pages of his notepad at the photographer. "Eden, they say?"

"Eden," Brother Mabry affirmed and then placed his hand on the lapel of his crimson velvet jacket.

"Eden?" Reverend Simpson asked as he and Myer walked toward the press corps that stood on the lawn of the inn.

"Who would believe such foolishness?" Myer asked and straightened out the wrinkles on her skirt.

"Don't you know that foolishness sells papers, Mrs. Simpson?" The flash of the photograph lit up the porch like lightning, and

Professor Listerman stumbled with momentary blindness as he walked through the front door of the inn.

Inside, Clive Gillespie had assembled town leaders and Sweetwater Jim Stephens, the Democratic machine in the Florida panhandle. Mahogany ceiling fans clipped the air that was thick with the sound of chatter and the smell of salt that drifted in through the open windows. A waiter with a lopsided bow tie served chilled shrimp on a platter covered in wilted lettuce. Mayor Cox filled his plate twice before almost tripping, making way for Brother Mabry. "Right this way, preacher." Clive Gillespie blocked the mayor and pulled Brother Mabry closer to the group assembled underneath the seven-foot sturgeon that hung on the wall.

Brother Mabry's wide hand covered the platter as he scooped up six of the shrimp in one sweep. Clive Gillespie clutched a glass of tea with a chip of melting ice. He held on to Sweetwater Jim with the other hand. "Brother Mabry, this is the man I was telling you about, Sweetwater Jim."

Licking cocktail sauce from the corner of his mouth, Brother Mabry nodded and then smiled to a couple who interrupted the introduction by wanting to share that they heard him preach once at a crusade in Chicago.

Clive gave a sudden jab of the elbow in the direction of the couple, missing the husband and hitting the wife in the ribs. The woman gasped, recoiled in horror, and darted toward the side of the room where the mayor stood. "Sweetwater Jim will make the roads possible for us," Clive said.

"Oh, yes," Brother Mabry said in a voice loud enough to be heard over the roar of a steamboat signaling its arrival at the dock outside. "Revenue generated from sales tax alone will more than cover it. Hear me when I tell you that the people will flood the gates of this city."

"Flood?" the Greek café owner asked. "No flood. No Noah's ark here."

Brother Mabry smiled while others erupted in laughter. "What would you say if I were to show you the very wood that Noah's ark came from? Wood known only to this area."

The café owner raised a bushy eyebrow and cut his eyes toward Clive, then back to Brother Mabry and back to Clive once more. "You believe this man's fairy tale?"

"Remember, at first they scoffed at Noah, too," Brother Mabry said with a wave of his finger at the café owner. A couple of people giggled, and then the room grew still. Noise from a passing car and chatter from a group of children out on the sidewalk trickled in through an open window. The crowd parted and mumbled as Brother Mabry made his way to the corner of the room where Professor Listerman stood next to a cherrywood table adorned with an object draped in red velvet. When Brother Mabry snatched the velvet cloth away, Myer Simpson gasped.

"Ladies and gentlemen, if you go back and study the Word, you'll see that the ark was built with gopher wood." Brother Mabry raised his eyebrows at Professor Listerman, who fidgeted with the red velvet material he now clutched. "Professor, keep me honest, but is this not indeed the rare—some might even have said extinct—gopher wood we found at the mysterious spot in this county?"

"Indeed," Professor Listerman whispered at first and then, when Brother Mabry lifted his hand upward, spoke louder. "Indeed it is gopher wood."

"Well, I declare," Lovey, the sheriff's wife, said. She jostled with the postmaster to get a better look at the wood, aged with crevices and discoloration.

"Now, now," Professor Listerman stammered. He spoke so fast that his lisp began to form into the rhythm of a song. "I want to just add that science speaks to the uniqueness of this place. Dr. Chapman, the renowned botanist of his day, documented his findings—solid, scientific findings—all documented in *Flora of the*

Southern United States. He was the expert of botany in his day. He was . . ."

"He was the expert of his time like Professor Listerman is the expert botanist of ours." Brother Mabry moved closer to Professor Listerman, almost eclipsing the academic with his broad shoulder and elephant-sized arm.

Sweetwater Jim's gaunt cheeks were stained with age spots, but his grip was as tight as a young man's. He reached up and spread his long, thin fingers across the shoulder of Brother Mabry. His hand looked as tiny as a child's propped on Brother Mabry's massive body. "Just when do you expect to tell people where this Eden of yours is located?"

A group formed a semicircle around Brother Mabry and Sweetwater Jim. Clive Gillespie moved to the side to let Reverend Simpson and Myer step closer. He motioned with his chin for the server to take the platter away.

"Sweetwater . . . if I may call you Sweetwater," Brother Mabry said, never looking at Sweetwater for his approval, "as a man wise in the ways of public opinion, I am sure you'll agree with me that a campaign is best launched in phases."

Sweetwater closed his eyes and nodded. "Phases."

"Hear me now," Brother Mabry said and waved his hand across the room. Cocktail sauce still marked the spot on his fingers where the shrimp had been clasped. "Eden is at your doorstep. Beauty is something to be held here in your fair port, but mysteries beyond human reasoning abound."

"Mysteries?" Reverend Simpson said.

Clive Gillespie stepped forward. "Brother Mabry, this is Reverend Simpson from the Dead Lakes community. In our county but just down the road a piece."

"Oh, Dead Lakes," Brother Mabry said and rose taller. The buttons on his pressed baby-blue shirt pulled tighter against his stomach.

"Pleasure to know you," Reverend Simpson said. "Mysteries of what order, might I ask?" Dust cast from the swirling ceiling fan danced around the crown of his head.

"The first book in the Bible tells all who believe that a river forks in four places." Brother Mabry repeated the pitch from his press conference. His powerful voice engulfed the crowd. A clanging noise rang out from the kitchen, and a horn honked out on Main Street. Myer Simpson gasped as Brother Mabry described the flora uncommon to any other spot in the world except for the basins of the Apalachicola River.

"Flora and forks in a river? But that could be anywhere," Reverend Simpson said just slow enough to reveal his lack of authority.

"Tell me, Reverend, another spot in the world where a river forks in four places?" Brother Mabry rose up on his toes and towered over the reverend.

Reverend Simpson sipped from the glass of tea. The ice in the glass had melted into slivers.

"Well, hear me when I tell you that the only other place is in Siberia."

"Siberia?" Reverend Simpson repeated, dumbfounded.

"And tell me, Reverend, what sort of exotic plants might you think grow in ice?"

The crowd chuckled, and the reverend's face grew as crimson as Brother Mabry's jacket.

"Can you believe this?" Myer Simpson whispered first to Lovey and then to Jasper Rugue, the owner of both an oyster cannery and the largest account in Clive's bank. "Can you believe what we're standing here hearing, Mr. Rugue?"

"Amazing," Jasper Rugue said and pointed to the wood. His voice was as crisp as the pressed handkerchief in his suit pocket. "Do you notice how the wood swirls with gold there in the middle? It sort of looks like a cross to me."

"You know, the Ark of the Covenant was gold," Lovey said.

The smell of Jasper's hair tonic tickled the senses of all who gathered around him. Myer Simpson squinted, looking deeper into the wood. "Amazing," she said with the same inflection as Jasper.

"Who would ever have thought that we were living right here in Eden?" Lovey asked. "Who would ever imagine?"

"Amazing," Myer Simpson said again, her word now gaining momentum.

After Brother Mabry finished delivering the words he had scripted for two days, the crowd began to talk among themselves. The sound of their voices buzzed like the electric lights on the walls.

"You know, I always said that the ferns grow bigger in my backyard than in any other spot in the county," Lovey said with a nod.

Reverend Simpson reached out to pull Myer away, but she slipped through his fingers. She stepped closer, inching her way through the men who stood like guardrails around Brother Mabry. Fingering the edges of the scarf that had protected her curled hair from the elements during the drive to town, Myer Simpson spoke as loud as the celebrated evangelist. "What do you make of healings, Brother Mabry?" Myer asked, interrupting Mayor Cox, who was asking whether Howard's Creek might be the spot where time began.

"I certainly believe in God's power to heal," Brother Mabry said as authoritatively as he would if he were standing in the pulpit. "It takes faith. Hear me now, faith that can move mountains."

"What about a man being able to heal a bleeding mule by the mere touch of a hand?" Myer ran the edges of the scarf through her fingers and tilted her chin down as if tantalizing Brother Mabry.

"A bleeding mule?" Brother Mabry asked.

"Mrs. Pomeroy saw it," Lovey said. She fanned herself with one of the cardboard fans that the funeral home had printed special for Brother Mabry's upcoming revival.

"And then there was that boy of Ella's," Myer Simpson said.

"Mrs. Simpson, we must go now," the reverend said.

"Neva Clarkson," Myer Simpson said first to Lovey and then to Brother Mabry. "She's our schoolmarm. Anyway, she said Ella Wallace's boy was sick as could be. Deathly ill, you might as well say. And then this man *kissed* him—kissed him square on the mouth—and then the boy was as healthy as you or me."

"Mrs. Simpson," Reverend Simpson said in a reprimand that Myer never heard.

Brother Mabry laughed and then seemed to search the crowd to see if it were all a joke. Clive Gillespie moved back to his spot next to Brother Mabry. "What the lady says is true," Clive said.

Reverend Simpson sputtered out the words, "Now, there's no evidence to substantiate such talk."

"And Neva Clarkson said the boy was so taken with sores in his mouth that he couldn't even eat, couldn't even breathe hardly," Myer said. "Then this man . . . this *mysterious* man . . . just showed up out of the blue, put his mouth on the boy, and kissed—"

"There was never any mention of kissing," Reverend Simpson said.

Myer Simpson raised her voice until she drowned out her husband. "The man put his mouth on the boy's mouth, and the sores were gone by sundown." She twirled her scarf across the air, seeming to demonstrate the magic of it all.

"And don't forget about that nigra girl down at the bend in the river," Lovey added with a point of the fan in Myer's direction.

"Where did this all take place again?" Brother Mabry asked, bowing down closer to the women.

"Dead Lakes," Clive answered with raised eyebrows that glistened with the same wax that plastered his hair. "Just down the road a piece."

"A knockabout place, really," Lovey said. "A quiet little community."

"Huh," Myer Simpson said and then reached for a shrimp as the waiter passed with a fresh platter. "Not so quiet after this drifter showed up and Ella Wallace took a liking to him. Just the same as if he'd cast a spell on the woman. Everything in my spirit tells me something is not right there." She pointed her chin down lower and twisted her mouth to the side. The flesh-colored mole next to her lip shifted to the left.

Reverend Simpson shook his head and chuckled. "I'm sure Brother Mabry has more important matters at hand than idle front-porch gossip." He gripped harder this time and jerked Myer away by the sleeve of her dress.

Just as Reverend Simpson was leading his wife away from the group, Brother Mabry reached out and blocked them with a hand big enough to belong to a giant. "Who did you say this man was again?"

15

Saw grass rose up and unfurled on the shore of the Wimpcoo River that ran to Millville. A white crane with a splash of fuchsia on top of its head turned and looked in the direction of the log raft before flying away.

Tall pines and patches of low-lying swamp stretched out in the distance. The side of the raft dipped down to the water, and Bonaparte pushed away from shore with the long pole he maneuvered. "Whoa now," Bonaparte said the same way he would if he were riding an agitated horse.

"We're just like Tom Sawyer and them, riding that raft," Keaton said.

"This ain't no time for dream world." Samuel stopped retying the laces of his boot long enough to roll his eyes at Keaton.

"Keaton," Ella said without taking her eyes away from the rail she was gripping. "Pay attention, now."

Keaton clung to the rail without being as obvious as Ella. He tried not to act scared. Ella had wanted him to stay with Macon at Mrs. Pomeroy's house, but he had refused. "If I worked this hard, then I'm seeing it all the way through," he'd argued until he had broken her down. Now he rocked on unsteady footing on the piece of plywood that had been secured with wooden spikes over the cypress logs.

Samuel licked his lips. He had tried to match Bonaparte's expertise with the pole but had given up and taken to checking the ends of the wood to make sure the chains that grouped the two rafts together remained secured.

Bonaparte took a pack of tobacco from his back pocket and propped the long pole up on his shoulder like a resting baby. The sharp, muddy tip dangled over Keaton's head until the raft drifted toward a low-hanging oak branch and Bonaparte lifted the pole back up. He shoved the pole down into a patch of lily pads that decorated the water like dots of green icing and grunted as he pushed the raft farther away from shore. "I used to ride these waters weeks on end, hauling wood back and forth for Mr. W. D. Moultrie. Paid next to slave wages, but he paid just the same." Bonaparte laughed, and Ella tried to laugh too before being jostled by the river current and once more gripping the rail made from saplings nailed together.

"Yeah," Bonaparte said, spitting a stream of tobacco in the oil-colored water, "we got us what they called bronzones so we could buy goods at the commissary. Met my wife in that commissary."

"Why did you stop rafting then?" Keaton asked.

Bonaparte halfway turned. Narsissa gripped the rail and then settled on an upside-down washtub that sheltered their food and water. "They had no choice," Narsissa said. "They raped the land until there was nothing but spokes of dried-up stumps left."

"Narsissa," Ella said.

"Is she making that up, Bonaparte?" Keaton asked. He studied the way Bonaparte stood erect with a confidence he didn't seem to possess out in the field.

Ella pursed her lips, shook her head at Keaton, and mouthed, "Hush."

Bonaparte ignored the question, kept his gaze straight ahead, and motioned for Lanier to check on the rope that secured the second raft of lumber. The wood swayed back and forth, sloshing the water like a toy boat being pulled in a tub.

A hawk flew out from a hickory limb and swooped down over two blue jays that pranced on the other side of the river. The bird plucked up the fattest blue jay and flew off with the other one chasing and squawking after them.

Keaton watched his mother grip the rail and try to get her footing. He wondered what Lanier would do when they had made it to Millville with the lumber and returned home on the steamboat after the sale. Would he pack back into a box and disappear? Keaton had always heard that the men gambled with cards in the back room of the steamboat. Maybe before Lanier left them, Keaton could get him to use whatever powers he seemed to have to read the cards the gamblers held in their hands and win them some more money.

The river sloshed over the sides of the raft and streamed across the floor. Watching the water rise up and then retreat, Keaton noticed two darker places in the wood. He turned his head, wondering if he was actually seeing the spot that he believed to be shaped like a heart with a line going through the middle as if Cupid had marked it as his territory. His first thought was to tease his mother, telling her that she was standing closest to the spot shaped like a Valentine heart and that the love bug was going to get her if she didn't move away.

Then Samuel shouted, "Looks like a sandbar up there to me."

"Ain't nothing but a shadow." Bonaparte spat a line of tobacco juice that discolored the wood.

Keaton looked toward the spot in the water that shimmered from the sun. Dark clouds rolled in over the low-lying water off to the right of the widening river. He watched the sunlight shift, causing the water to seem black. He looked up at the puffy clouds that began to be tinged with deep blue. A tiny thundercloud drifted over a stout white one. When they connected, the clouds took the shape of a finger pressed against pursed lips. Keaton decided that it was a sign not to mention the heart-shaped spot on the wood to anyone, especially not his mother.

Watching Lanier and his mother together was the same as looking at a picture show with two actors batting eyelashes at one another. At times Keaton would cast Lanier as the Canadian Rocky and the mule that he pulled with loads of logs as the white stallion from the moving pictures. He could see his mother jumping on the back of the horse and riding away, passing the store and the fork in the road until the screen faded to black. But that was nothing more than air castles. He kept trying to convince himself that his mother would never be swept away by a man who was not her husband.

But that night when Keaton had seen his mother in the barn, he confused the line between make-believe and reality. No matter how hard Keaton had rubbed his eyes, there was no denying what he witnessed the night he went outside to use the privy. The lantern inside the barn cast an amber light on the small space that separated his mother and Lanier where they sat on the workbench. Peering through the stalks of sunflowers, Keaton heard her giggle. He held his breath as he witnessed Lanier brushing strands of hair from his mother's shoulder. His head became top-heavy as he watched his mother sit cross-legged next to Lanier, the tip of her shoe flirting with the cuff of his pants. Keaton's breathing became ragged more from nervous shame than from anger.

Watching them there in real life made him feel just as uncomfortable as he did when sitting in the theater in Apalachicola listening to the pianist play love songs as the projector made tapping sounds, filling the screen with a Canadian lawman and a woman with hair so blonde that it looked like a heavenly light was over her. In those pictures the pieces always came together so easily that eventually he could predict the ending as much as he could the songs that the pianist played. At the picture show, Lillian Gish and the other women with lighted halos didn't seem to have to worry about lost husbands or whispering neighbors.

Squatting on the raft, Keaton looked down again at the place where he thought he had seen the heart-shaped design. Water rolled up from the river and fanned out around the sides of the raft. There was nothing but a splintered gash of wood where an axe had left its mark.

Back in Dead Lakes, Ella's youngest son, Macon, sat on Mrs. Pomeroy's porch as instructed and pacified himself by playing marbles. "You're still so puny. I can't have you going out in the yard and playing," Mrs. Pomeroy said as she swung a long swatter at an Oriental rug that was propped over a string connected to two sable palms. Dust flew around her and then drifted across the road to where Ella's store stood with the Closed sign on the door.

"I'm fine now. I was out there helping girdle the cypress," Macon said and grabbed the cat's-eye marble that had rolled to the edge of the porch where a bird had left its mark.

"Do what? Girdle?" Mrs. Pomeroy swung the swatter again and coughed as dust scattered.

"Bonaparte taught us."

"Who?" Mrs. Pomeroy turned around to face Macon. Strands of hair had escaped her hairnet. They veiled the side of her face like a spider's web.

"The colored man that lives past the fork in the river. He showed us how to slice the tree just right so that the gum drains out of it. That's so it can float on the river to the mill."

"Mercy, me. I'm just glad that Ella's aunt didn't live long enough to witness all this." Mrs. Pomeroy coughed and shook her head. "She's spinning in her grave right now, I have all idea."

"You know, Mama won't care if I shoot these marbles in the dirt." He stood up with the marbles and stepped on one porch step and then tentatively down another.

Mrs. Pomeroy hit the rug again, and the loose flesh on her forearms jiggled. "I don't care what your mama will or will not allow. After all you've been through with your weakened constitution. And now you want me to let you fool around out here in my yard, out in my dirt? Next thing you know you'll wind up with worms and all sorts of ailments. That man might not be able to jibber-jabber and make you better a second time. Then the next thing I know you'll be laid out in your mama's living room in a pine box. No, sir, I won't have that on my conscience." A cloud of dust enveloped Mrs. Pomeroy.

Next door, Myer Simpson came out of her house carrying a watering pail purchased from Ella's store. Before Harlan ran away, Myer had paid extra for Ella to paint the red roses that were now fading on the side of the tin. As she watered the ferns that sat on white columns on her front porch, Sheriff Bissell's automobile made its way around the bend next to the store and parked right in front of Mrs. Pomeroy's house. Water dripped from the fern on the porch and gathered on Myer Simpson's shoes. She leaned against the porch rail, peered down at Mrs. Pomeroy's yard, and continued pouring water into the overflowing fern.

Sheriff Bissell's hat was cocked to the side as he exited the car. He held the back door open, and Clive Gillespie stepped out. Clive held up his hand as if expecting to assist another passenger. Instead, Neva Clarkson made her way out the door on the opposite side of the automobile. She squinted, pulled at her skirt, and followed the sheriff and Clive through the front gate, which was shaped like a pineapple.

Mrs. Pomeroy tucked strands of her hair back into the hairnet and fumbled around with the rug swatter before propping it against a sable palm tree. She folded her arms and shifted her weight as the sheriff explained the reason for the unscheduled visit.

"I don't know," Mrs. Pomeroy said, rubbing her fingers against a frayed corner of the rug that hung on the line. "Can't this wait until Ella gets back?" Her eyes scanned first the sheriff, then Clive, then Neva. She turned around and looked up at the Simpson home, where Myer Simpson waved.

"Is anything the matter?" Myer called out.

The sheriff never looked away from Macon, who was standing on the bottom porch step. "Everything's fine. Go on back to your watering."

"No," Clive said. "It cannot wait." He stepped forward and then stopped. "Can it, Sheriff?"

The sheriff pushed his hat back, wiped his brow, and moved past Clive and Mrs. Pomeroy. Neva Clarkson looked back at the pineapple-shaped gate when Sheriff Bissell picked Macon up. Macon, too big to be carried any longer, arched away from the sheriff's stained shirt. His feet dangled at the sheriff's bent knees, and the cat's-eye marble slipped from his hand. Clive reached down and retrieved it. He twirled the marble between his fingers, playfully stuck it in his pocket, laughed, and then handed it back to Macon. "She's a beauty. What you say, sport? How about we go inside for some lemonade and have a little chat?"

Inside the house, Macon sat cross-legged on the cool marble by the fireplace. The clock whose face was painted to resemble a sundial ticked and kept beat with the questions that the sheriff asked about the night Lanier had brought breath back into Macon's lungs.

"Now, son, we want you to be honest and straightforward with us," the sheriff said. He sat on a Victorian chair that was too small for him and pulled at the pants that gathered at his crotch. "Nobody's in trouble or nothing like that."

"Oh, no." Clive sat and reached up for the glass of lemonade that Mrs. Pomeroy offered. "We're just curious is all."

"Curious," Mrs. Pomeroy repeated. She looked at Clive and then at Macon. Her smile faded when she saw Neva Clarkson staring at the floor and fidgeting with the hem of her skirt.

Neva sat on the brocade love seat closest to Macon. "And why are we so curious?" Neva asked.

Macon looked up at Neva and then back at the sheriff. Sheriff Bissell fanned his hat as if erasing Neva's question. "Now, son, what did the man do exactly when he bent down over you?"

Macon rubbed the marbles that bulked out in his pants pocket. "He just breathed on me."

"Breathed like this?" The sheriff inhaled and then exhaled so deeply that the peacock feathers in the vase next to the fireplace swayed. Macon laughed, and then the others followed, even the sheriff. "Good gracious alive," the sheriff said. "No, but Macon, I'm just trying to get me a picture of how this all took place. Did he do it that way?"

Macon shook his head. "No, he got up real close on me. It scared me at first."

Clive Gillespie sat on the edge of his chair and placed the glass down on the floor. "It scared you?"

Sheriff Bissell halfway turned and gave Clive a disgusted look. "It scared you, you say?"

Macon nodded and rubbed the side of his pants pocket. "I sort of felt . . ."

"Nothing to be ashamed of, son," the sheriff whispered. "We're all friends. You felt what?"

"Lanier's my friend."

"Oh yeah," the sheriff said. "He's been a good friend. But what I'm wondering is, when he put his mouth on top of yours the way he did, did it . . . well, did it bother you?"

Macon looked up at Mrs. Pomeroy, who used her stumpy hand to fan her face. "I felt kinda scared," he whispered.

"You felt scared. I bet you did. I would," the sheriff mumbled. He leaned down closer to Macon before getting down on the floor where he was knee-to-knee with him. He groaned, and his back made a crackling sound. "Just me and you talking now. Man-to-man," the sheriff whispered and motioned for Neva to move aside. She sighed and patted her shoe on the floor before getting up and moving to the other side of the room, where Mrs. Pomeroy stood next to an oval-shaped photograph of her taken last year in Ella's store.

"Did he put his mouth on you the way a husband might do with his wife?" The sheriff's words were low, and he tilted his chin when he said them.

Macon looked over at the peacock feathers that were still swaying from Neva's movement.

"Come on now, man-to-man. Just me and you talking," the sheriff said in a voice only loud enough for Macon to hear.

Clive Gillespie leaned closer, his buttocks balanced on the edge of the chair cushion.

Macon slid away from the sheriff, knocking the vase and shaking the feathers yet again. "He . . . uh . . . am I in trouble?"

"No," Neva said and stepped forward. "Macon, you're not in any trouble whatsoever."

Clive stuck his arm out, blocking her. "Let us leave the sheriff to do his job."

"Now, there's nothing to be ashamed of," the sheriff said and patted Macon on the shoulder. "It wasn't your fault, now. We know that. Just tell me one thing. Did he put his mouth on you the way men do the women in the picture shows you see in town?"

Macon looked down and bit the corner of his lip. It only took a nod of his head to cause the sheriff to rise up from the floor. The clock ticked, and the sheriff's knee made a popping sound.

"You sure I'm not going to get in trouble?" Macon asked again before Mrs. Pomeroy sent him outside to draw circles in the dirt underneath the sable palms.

"I'm not comfortable with one bit of this," Neva said.

"Sit down," Clive said without looking at Neva. "Sheriff Bissell, what are next steps with this matter?"

The sheriff rotated his head back and forth, and more joints popped. "Oh, let me figure on it. I expect we'll need to put a formal investigation together. We'll need to talk to the nigra girl too."

"I am not comfortable with this at all," Neva said louder. "Now I want to know what law gives you—"

"And I want to know what teacher can hear about perversion . . . such unnatural affection toward a child, and not report it to authorities?" Clive tilted his head and raised his eyebrows at Neva.

"There was . . . there was nothing perverse about what I was told. Unusual, yes, but . . ."

"Like I told you before, Neva, as a school board member I will not—let me say I *cannot*—let this go uninvestigated."

Neva jumped from the seat. "Investigate what? Rumors and innuendos?"

"Really, Miss Clarkson. I would think if I were in your position about right now, I'd be worried about my employment. Or maybe you'd prefer to work at the cannery, shucking oysters?"

"All right, all right," the sheriff said. "Let's not get carried away." His words were drowned out by the hour chime on the clock that played "Way Down upon the Swanee River."

"More lemonade, anyone?" A glass pitcher wobbled in Mrs. Pomeroy's grip. Sweat ran down the sides of the pitcher.

As her guests stood outside at the front gate, Mrs. Pomeroy stood by the rug that was half cleaned and ran her hand down the side. The sheriff started to open the driver's door to his car, then shook his head and laughed. He held up the glass that now contained only a shriveled lemon and half jogged back to where Mrs. Pomeroy stood.

"I expect you didn't mean for me to drive off with your glass," he said as he handed it back to her. The sheriff looked down at Macon, who was sitting on the ground, cleaning off his marbles. "And I appreciate you, young man, for telling the truth." He reached down and rubbed Macon's head the same way he might if Macon had been Mrs. Pomeroy's yard dog. "You're helping us. You're helping your mama, too. She'd be proud."

The sheriff took three steps and then turned back toward Macon. "That fella, Lanier. I never did hear how he was to end up here in Dead Lakes."

Macon tossed the marbles into the ring that he had drawn in the dirt with his bare finger. He took the cat's-eye marble that Clive Gillespie had fancied and put it in his pocket. "He just showed up one day is all."

The sheriff chuckled. "Just like that, huh? Just like magic."

"Showed up to help us out. He's my daddy's cousin." Macon repeated the script exactly the way Ella had instructed him and his brothers the night after Lanier arrived.

Mrs. Pomeroy clutched the line, weighing down the rug until the fringed tips of the carpet were tangled in crabgrass. The back of her hair was tangled in perspiration.

The sheriff grunted as he knelt down on the ground. He scooped up a wayward marble that was in a clump of dried moss and tossed it back into the circle marked in the dirt. "Well, I be dad-gummed . . . just like magic."

After the visitors had driven away, Mrs. Pomeroy never seemed to notice the rug as it drooped lopsided on the line or the dirt on Macon's arms as he lay on his stomach shooting marbles. She could only lean against the sable palm and stare across the road at Ella's store.

"You promise I'm not going to get in trouble?" Macon continued asking until Mrs. Pomeroy, unable to summon enough energy to lift the rug swatter, retreated to a wicker chair on the porch and threatened to switch him if he didn't hush with his questions.

By the time Mr. Busby crossed the river bridge into Bainbridge, Georgia, the woman who ran the café had already pulled the tray of peanuts she roasted that morning out onto the sidewalk. A chalkboard advertising the blue plate special was propped sideways on the tray. After adjusting the tray on a card table that dipped in the middle, she stepped away to examine her display. Her hands were placed on two sharp bones that stuck out from the sides of her dress like the handles of concealed pistols. The smell drew the attention of everyone who journeyed by foot, car, or wagon, including Mr. Busby. A man paused to scoop up a handful of peanuts before walking inside.

Busy watching the customers who filled the café, Mr. Busby did not see the group of men who paused in the median, trying to cross the street. "Whoa now," one of the men yelled just as Mr. Busby pulled the reins, fighting to stop his wagon.

With each step across the street, past the furniture store, and by the market window with fresh chickens and guineas hanging from silver hooks, they shook their heads and cussed. One of them took off his cowboy hat and flapped it at Mr. Busby as if he were a gnat. "Watch where you're going, junk man." They laughed, scooped up peanuts, and nodded to the café owner as they entered.

Two men with matching gold timepieces dangling from their pockets walked out of a building with stained glass on its doors. The noon sun hit the glass in such a way that it seemed to flash in rays of pink and gold light. Temporarily blinded by the brightness, Mr. Busby looked to the left of the window and noticed that all of the others on the building had been painted black. The man with the broadest shoulders pulled the watch from his pants pocket, flipped open the face, and glanced up at Mr. Busby before hiding it back inside his trousers. He never acknowledged Mr. Busby's nod or the group of other workers who filed out of the building and walked ten paces behind him.

The horses slapped the brick street with their hooves and whinnied when a whistle from the warehouse roof blared. Looking up at the roof of the building, where statues of owls were perched, Mr. Busby noticed for the first time that the top of the building had a faded illustration of a cartoonish smiling moon with block letters that spelled out, *Blue Moon Clock Company, Established 1872.*

16

An eagle flew out of the woods and above the river with a piece of bear grass hanging from her beak. She soared over a patch of lavender water hyacinth that dotted the shore and swooped down as a snapping turtle jumped from a log into the murky water. The bird finally came to rest on one of the broken pines that populated a small island in the middle of the river. Tucking the thick, rope-looking grass into the top of the tree that had long ago been ripped away by a hurricane, the eagle pecked at the makings of a nest. She sat on the twigs and limbs that were beginning to take the shape of a crown and tilted her head down to where the rafts of logs were coming into view around the river's bend.

"See there how that tree limb is sticking up out of the water." Bonaparte stood at the front of the raft and pointed with a fistful of cornbread to a shrub oak that seemed to rise up from the river at the edge of the island. "See there," he said to no one in particular.

"Yeah," Ella said.

"I see what you're talking about," Samuel added and gripped the pole he held tighter.

"I don't see it," Lanier said.

"Up there to the right," Bonaparte said and took a bite of the cornbread. Flakes of cornmeal sprinkled the tops of his boots. "That means there's been freshets flooding the place. The flash floods, I'm talking about. Everybody pay close attention." Bonaparte wiped the remaining crumbs from his hands and picked up his pole. He held on to it the same way he might if he'd been carrying a gun. "The current is fixing to change on us."

Lanier copied Bonaparte's stance and took position at the opposite side of the raft. Narsissa secured the washtub over the supplies and screwed the tops on the water canisters. "Keaton," she said and motioned for him to sit next to her. He turned his back toward her and faced the island that was coming up ahead.

The plywood floor of the raft shifted with the changing river current and made a whining sound as it sloshed against the cypress logs that were secured underneath. Ella gripped the rail and then let go before easing closer to Bonaparte. "What should we be doing?"

"Hold on tight." He never turned to face her.

"Should we check on the other raft?" Ella asked, reaching out but never touching Bonaparte's arm.

"I'll check it," Samuel said. He handed his pole to Ella and then straddled the back of the raft.

"Be careful," Ella yelled.

Samuel stuck his hands out to balance himself. His legs were wobbling when he shouted, "I got it. You be careful."

The chain that connected the two rafts together sloshed and kicked up a spray of water against the shifting current. As Samuel moved, the raft jostled to the side, and Ella yelled once more, "Be careful." She watched him hunch down over the chain. His body swayed with the way the raft seemed to fight against the change of stream. Samuel soon leaned down and balanced himself with his fingers spread out against one of the logs.

Samuel squinted as he looked toward the front. "Bonaparte. Hey, Bonaparte, one of these spikes is sticking out sideways."

"Just one spike?" Bonaparte yelled without turning around.

Samuel shook his head and peered down at the spikes, hunching down over the back of the raft. "All of 'em."

The raft made a creaking sound again and jerked toward the tall, wheat-colored grass at the edge of the island. Samuel hovered over the back with a hand positioned on either side of him, seemingly ready to pounce and tackle the raft that was bouncing and thrashing behind them.

"Samuel," Ella said. "Samuel. Get away from . . ." Her words were drowned out by a loud crackling sound. Her first thought was that Samuel had set off firecrackers and that at any moment he would fall backward in a fit of laughter. They would all jump, and then she would chastise him for scaring her. It would be the sort of thing they would talk about during family gatherings for years to come. But there were no fits of giggles from childish pranks, only the explosion of wood as the rear raft broke apart.

"Samuel!" Ella screamed as she watched her son fly up in the air like a rag doll, flailing forward and then backward nearer the edge of the raft. She screamed as the other raft shifted to the side and an iron spike that had secured wood was hurled upward, barely missing Samuel's head before landing in the water. Ella scrambled on hands and knees toward him, never feeling the splinters that wedged into her palms.

Samuel tumbled backward, past Ella and toward the front of the raft. His shoulder struck the tub where Narsissa sat, knocking her to the floor. Narsissa scrambled upright and pulled Samuel's arm away from the edge of the raft where he was sliding. Like cards being shuffled on the water, cypress logs in the second raft behind them snapped free from the deck and flew up in the air along with the iron spikes that rained down like oversized nails.

Bonaparte staggered backward and gripped the pole tighter until the muscles in his forearms stretched the patches on his sleeve. "Push 'way from that island," he hollered. Lanier shoved his pole over the top of the leaves of the shrub oak that bobbed above the water like hair on a dead man.

The sound of chaos as they scrambled to protect their work broke the tranquility of the river. Cypress soon spread out across the river surface. In the days to come the sight would burst in Ella's mind in flashes, the same way the kaleidoscope that her aunt had once entertained her with would explode into colors with a playful twist of the hand.

When they had made their way past the island and regained their footing, they stood in silence watching half of their shipment scatter like misplaced pencils, drifting farther down the river. Ella was the first one to step away from the end of the raft. She sat on top of the overturned washtub, gripped the side that was now jagged at the corners, and stared as the water rode up over the edge of the raft and slapped at her boots.

Lanier stepped toward her, casting a shadow across the spot on the floor that held her downward gaze. She never felt the thorn that lodged in her palm or the touch of Lanier's hand when he reached down and caressed her shoulder.

Mr. Busby started his day by brokering a deal with the furniture store owner to let him set up his studio inside. For a complimentary portrait of the staff, Mr. Busby even got to set up a display table on the sidewalk in front of the store.

When the woman who ran the café argued that Mr. Busby was stealing the spot that she used to entice customers with her roasted peanut table, he promised her a portrait if she'd leave him in peace to unfurl his torn black velvet tablecloth over two sawhorses and a piece of plywood. "Madam, we all have a job to do," he said and unpacked framed photos from his satchel and placed them on the display table.

He was careful to cover the torn spot of the velvet tablecloth with a portrait that people would not pick up and examine. Looking inside his bag, he pulled out the photograph of Ella and her family on the day of the timber cut. With the image of the man Ella had hired to help her tucked in the corner of the photograph like a blurred ghost, Mr. Busby knew he was safe in using that frame to hide the tear. The South Georgia crackers would not see the work as art but rather as a smudge of film. They would look at it and blink before turning back toward the photos at the front of the table. Pictures of women wearing wide-brimmed hats long out of fashion and men with handlebar mustaches wearing blank stares—these would be the pictures that would catch their fancy. They would hold and inspect the black-and-white pictures, smudging the glass surfaces of the frames with their working-class fingers. They would not have an inclination toward any documentation of a woman dressed in men's work boots standing in front of a stack of cut pine alongside a Creek Indian and three dirty-faced boys. The reality would be too harsh and familiar.

A woman with a mouth shaped in a permanent upside-down V stood over the table of photographs. She clutched the folds of her stomach like there was money tucked inside. "Do you charge by the number of people in the picture?" the woman asked. Mr. Busby shook his head and turned his attention to one of the men he had seen yesterday upon his arrival. The man was broad-shouldered and wore a black jacket that was snug at the sides. A gold chain hung from an inside pocket and draped down to the man's waist. He jostled the chain and slowed his step when he walked by, glancing down at the table.

The man paused long enough to give Mr. Busby hope that a man of wealth might be interested in his services. "Pictures are living memories," Mr. Busby called out. But the man hastened his step and crossed the street, turning the corner toward the spot underneath a streetlamp where he kept his freshly washed automobile.

At the end of Main Street, coal from the noon train engine blanketed the air the same way the smell of roasted peanuts had the day before. Steam poured from the side of the engine that had just pulled up to the depot where an advertisement for Coca-Cola covered the outside wall. Ignoring the No Parking sign that was nailed beneath the painting of a Coke bottle, the man parked his shiny car and then made his way up to the train platform. He stood next to a wooden bench, fingering the chain on his watch and observing as depot agents stacked luggage on the deck.

J.D. Troxler made his way down the steps of the first-class railcar. His shoulders were broader than the younger brother who waited for him at the station platform, but a similar gold watch chain dangled from his waist, shaking with his every move. Shifting his weight as he walked down first one step and then another, he waved away the assistance of the colored steward who stood at the bottom stair. A woman with a sky-blue dress that formed tightly at her waist came out of the train behind him and nodded to him before disappearing into the smoke and crowd of townspeople who lined the depot, waiting on travelers.

"That one is a looker. Did you bring her back with you from Atlanta?" the younger brother, Parker, asked as J.D. walked up to him.

"Only a hangover," J.D. said. He scratched the stubble of whiskers and the scar that ran down the side of his jaw, a permanent medal from the days of his youth when he had been foolish enough to wager a bet that he could fight a bear in a circus cage.

"You got the deal, I understand," Parker said, running his fingers up and down his watch chain. He paused only long enough to motion for a porter to gather J.D.'s luggage.

J.D. looked a moment longer at the spot where the woman had

stood. Then he turned and shook his head at Parker. "What are you doing? Wandering around town, waiting for my train? You're so lazy you wouldn't breathe unless you just had to."

J.D. shook his head while Parker rattled off excuses and numbers of production achieved while J.D. was in Atlanta securing business and exerting his freedom from family.

When Parker maneuvered the car back into his assigned spot as vice president of Blue Moon Clock Company, the president made his way toward the café, where he snatched up a handful of peanuts every afternoon. It was the one time he allowed himself freedom from the desk that sat below a mounted head of a wild boar he'd killed and oil portraits of his father and deceased sister, Octavia. He had personally retrieved the painting from her home after her murder and had driven the nail into the plaster with the butt of his pistol, vowing to unseat the sheriff who couldn't deliver justice. "Calamity is not the same as commitment," his father had written in the letter to J.D. before he tied cinder blocks to his ankles and jumped into the Chattahoochee River. The man who had started the Blue Moon Clock Company and held part interest in a textile mill in Columbus and a department store in Macon never owned peace. The official obituary would call his death a drowning due to a fishing accident. For the Troxlers, there was no such thing as suicide.

"Where are the peanuts? Where's Lula?" J.D. eyed Mr. Busby with suspicion and then turned in a half circle.

The café owner came out of the door with a white napkin. The smell of the roasted peanuts drifted from the tie at the top. "Here you go, Mr. Troxler," the café owner said before handing the napkin to him. She pulled at the edge of her skirt and almost curtseyed. "This picture taker is just borrowing my spot for the day. Tomorrow I'll be right where I've always been."

J.D. bit into a peanut and glanced down at the table before turning to step off the sidewalk.

"Pictures are living memories," Mr. Busby cried out. He reached up and grasped at the air. "Uh, sir, just so you know . . . I take business portraits too. Lots of businesses are forgoing the old-timey painted portraits and going for the celluloid. I can make portraits any size you want them."

J.D. turned and spat a peanut hull. The broken shell landed at the corner of the table where the photograph of Ella and her family was displayed. The sun cut across the side of the table and highlighted the broken tip of the picture frame. Flecks of the silver frame sparkled, and J.D. Troxler stepped closer to the table. Mr. Busby massaged his hands in anticipation of a corporate order.

Peanut crumbs from J.D.'s fingers scattered across the frame as he held it up. The torn spot in the black velvet tablecloth was revealed for all to see.

"Now, that is not representative of my work," Mr. Busby said while placing his hand over the torn spot in the cloth. "That was just a favor I did for a neighbor lady . . . an experiment, so to speak. This batch of photographs might be more what you had in mind." Mr. Busby tried to hand J.D. a photograph of the mayor of Eufaula sitting in a wingback chair.

Stuffing the napkin of peanuts into his pants pocket, J.D. Troxler brushed away the crumbs on the frame and pulled the picture inches away from his eyes.

"That's not representative of my corporate work," Mr. Busby said again, dancing around him, daring to reach for the photograph. "That's artistic flair. . . . That blur is artistic license."

J.D. held it up higher toward the sunlight and pondered the picture. He moaned and cursed Lanier Stillis all in the same breath.

J.D. motioned for his brother to move out from the street and yelled, "Parker, get over here and tell me if I'm seeing things." J.D.'s voice could be heard all the way to the dock, where bales of cotton were being loaded onto a steamboat.

17

As dusk settled over the Millville timber yard where the remaining cypress would be sorted by government men and shipped to a Texas shipyard, Ella stood on the deck of the last steamboat heading toward Apalachicola. She stepped over the low-hanging rusted chain with the crooked-lettered sign reading *No Passengers Allowed*. She was tired of following the rules and exhausted from pretending that all was not as bad as it seemed. She moved to the edge of the boat, where faded life jackets were stacked haphazardly. Leaning over the railing, she looked out at the riverbank that once seemed jeweled with Spanish moss hanging from tree limbs. The landscape she had once painted with her aunt now seemed like snarled wood dipping out over the water like fingernails discolored with gray fungus.

Massaging the check she had safety-pinned to the inside of her pants, she wondered what sort of God would tease her and then fling her pleas away. "The worst is over with for now," Narsissa had assured her when they boarded the boat that would take them home. If it hadn't been for Keaton, who was standing by the boat steward and watching her board behind Narsissa, she might have rolled her eyes and cursed futile optimism. Instead, Ella simply nodded and accepted the hand of the steward who assisted the female passengers on board. It was only after she boarded that she wondered if the man had felt the callused and wounded places on her palm.

Now, standing away from the others on the top level of the boat where coal-colored smoke danced from the stack pipes, Ella was too numb with exhaustion to continue her act. She listened to the darkness that whispered that her financial struggles would never be over. Feeling the vibration of the engine on the wooden railing that protected passengers from falling into the water, she wondered what was the next catastrophe that awaited her on this journey of life that was so foreign from the one mapped out for her by her aunt. She pictured the check becoming undone from the pin and inching up the waist of her pants. It would take flight in the humid breeze and skip across the churning water below. The check would disintegrate into pieces, falling down to the river bottom, covering the lost cypress like flakes of snow.

Leaning over the rail, she let her head drop and dangled there with her hair swaying from side to side like black silk on the dress hem of a dancing woman. Watching the water churn below and feeling the boat railing that supported her weight press into her abdomen, Ella wondered if she could stay here all night. There was security in being hidden from the others, slumped over toward the dark water while feeling the blood rush to the top of her head, proving to her that she was still alive, still vital.

"Are you all right?"

Ella flinched at the sound of Lanier's voice. Rising upright, she felt Lanier's hands around her waist, helping her back into place. She twisted away from him and folded her arms. "I'm fine. . . . I was just . . . I was just looking down at the water."

"Well, I wondered where you'd slipped off to."

When she turned away from him, she kicked over the life jackets that were stacked next to the railing. They fanned out across the boat deck like a boundary between Ella and Lanier.

"Didn't mean to scare you," he said. The dirt and stubble on his face made his eyes seem greener.

"You didn't. . . . I just wanted some time by myself to think."

"Everything okay?"

Ella stared at him and then glanced back at the woods that lined the riverbank.

"What I meant was—"

"Fine. Everything is fine."

The sound of an out-of-tune piano being played in the dining hall rose up from the floor below. Ella kicked at the life jacket that had fallen next to her boot. The inside of the life jacket got tangled on the tip of her boot and when she kicked harder she slipped backward, landing against the rail.

Lanier reached out, gripping her arm.

The water churned and the whistle sounded as the boat turned a bend in the river. Ella snatched her arm away from him and raised her head up to the first star of the night. She felt as jumbled together as the weathered life preservers that littered the boat deck. Fighting against her emotions, she tried to brush away the tears with the back of her callused hands. The piano played on, and Lanier moved closer. "Don't," she said.

"I was just . . ."

"Don't. Don't come over here and comfort this poor *little lady*."

"I wasn't," he said and moved to the side, stepping on top of one of the life jackets. "I just know something about what you're talking about."

"Oh, you know something about living hand to mouth? Is that it? I guess we are kindred spirits, you and me. Two vagabonds wondering where our next nickel will come from. Well, no thank you. I don't want your way of living."

"Now, you're just exhausted. You're upset . . . you're . . ."

Ella balled her fists and shook them up toward the star. When she looked at Lanier there was wildness in her eye that had yet to be broken. "I said do not patronize me. Do you even *know* what that means?"

He shook his head, wiped the corner of his mouth with his thumb, and then turned to leave. "Now who's the one patronizing?" When he got to the chain with the sign prohibiting access, he walked back to her.

She could smell the musky odor that she long thought she'd grown immune to. His top lip was blistered by the sun. He stood so close to her that she felt the fury of his words.

"Has anybody ever told you that you have a mighty high opinion of yourself? With your education and your past that you pet on like some lapdog. Puffed-up memories of some old-maid aunt. Let me guess, she brainwashed you into thinking that you have royal blood from England or Scotland or someplace too."

"I'm sorry?" Ella scowled.

"Not as sorry as you try to make out to be. I just can't figure out how somebody so smart can be so pitiful."

"Pitiful?" Ella stepped forward and then looked up when the steam whistle blew.

"Mighty pitiful," he said as spit landed on Ella's shirtsleeve. "All right, you lost half the wood. You ought to be happy you didn't lose the whole lot. You still got money for the other half. Ella, you're straddling somewhere between petted and pitiful."

"I am not putting up with this," Ella said. "Just as soon as we hit land, I'm paying your passage on the next boat out of here."

"You don't have the money to buy yourself passage, let alone anybody else. Man alive. I knew better than to stay."

"You stayed because I let you stay." Ella folded her arms and moved back until the screws pressed against her spine.

"No, ma'am. I stayed because you needed me to stay."

"You stayed because you needed refuge."

"Spoiled and prideful, too, I see."

The waters churned below, and the boat tilted slightly before making the curve of the river. Ella stared at him, and when the steam whistle overhead blew, she did too. She balled her fists in the air and screamed until the veins in her neck protruded like fingers. "Leave!"

"I've listened to you boss me just about long enough," Lanier said, leaning against the box where the life preservers had been stacked.

"I said leave."

"No." He folded his arms and cocked his head to the side. "I've decided to stay put."

Ella pulled at the sides of her dungarees the same as if she'd been wearing a ball dress. "This is not appropriate. You need to get back downstairs right this minute. People will talk. They will say . . ."

"Let 'em!" Lanier laughed and then grunted. "If I had a plug nickel for every time I heard *they* . . . They don't mean nothing to me. And if you ever plan to live your life—I mean really live it, not for nobody but yourself—you won't care what *they* say."

"Well, I can't just up and run like some people. I have responsibilities. I have children. What is said about me impacts my sons, and that matters to me."

Lanier blocked Ella from walking away. A streak of moonlight illuminated part of his angular face, making him appear to be wearing a mask in the darkness. "When are you going to quit hiding behind your boys?"

"Oh, I don't think I'd bring up the subject of *hiding* if I were you."

"Let me ask you something, and then you won't have to worry with me no more. What has caring about those people got you?

Forgive me for speaking plain, but the only ones I saw show up and help you was a drunk, Bonaparte, and some of his neighbors."

"I'll have you know that I am respected in Dead Lakes."

"That's not what I asked."

"And what makes you think you know what I need? What I need is for you to leave me alone."

A woman's playful scream rose up from the dance floor below, and laughter followed.

"I don't believe you." A cloud shifted across the moon, and as it did, the light strayed away from Lanier's face.

Ella looked at him as though a mask had just been removed. "Just who do you think you are?"

"I know more about you than you think I do." Lanier's eyes narrowed in a way that was anything but playful. "I see somebody who's scared and running from a past that won't let her go. I see somebody who's lived her life trying to please people that ain't worth pleasing."

Ella looked around at the life preservers that scattered at her feet and caused her to feel blocked in. The dam of fear unlocked from her mind and flooded her system, causing her to tremble. Stuffing her hands deep into the pants pockets, she cocked her head to the side, hoping to bluff away her unease.

"Whether you like it or not, you know I'm speaking the truth." Lanier's breathing became haggard. He moved closer, and when Ella looked away, he placed his hand on the back of her head, forcing her to face him. "You know how come I can tell you all this? Because when I look at you, I see the person I used to be."

Ella could make out the chatter from the people below. Their words intertwined with the piano music and made her feel light-headed. Lanier's grip tightened on her skull, cupping her, scaring her. The memory of the low-seated fainting sofa with its cherry-printed material that her aunt kept close to the front door for times of bad news floated across her mind. Pushing away from Lanier, she thought of calling out for Samuel. "Do not ever put your hands on me again," she yelled. Jabbing an elbow into Lanier's side, she broke free and stumbled, landing on top of a wooden box stamped with the boat's name, *John W. Callahan*.

"I'm not the enemy," he said. "No matter what *they* say."

He stood over her with his back to the moon that was now unencumbered by the veil of clouds. A breeze drifted in off the river, and strands of Lanier's hair tangled around his jagged ear. Moonlight anointed the back of his head. *"Angels and demons are often dressed in the same cloth,"* her aunt called out in her mind. But there was a pleading in Lanier's eyes that settled her, hypnotized her into believing his words.

When Lanier reached his hand down to help her, she ignored the offer and instead gripped the side of the rail. Upright, she looked him in the eyes and tried to form her conflicting thoughts into words. There was no sensible explanation for the current of fear and attraction that caused her mind to race and her heart to hold on to faith in him. Everything in her told her to let go.

Lanier brushed his hands against his pants and stepped to the side, letting Ella return to her place by the rail. "When we get to Apalachicola, I'll get me a ticket to New Orleans, and we'll be done with it."

Ella folded her arms and looked down at the scattered life jackets. "Fine. That's just fine. Quit."

"From the best I can tell, you already quit for the both of us."

His words caused her to step backward, once again feeling the sharp bolted places on the rail. Even before Harlan, her greatest fear was winding up a broken woman like her aunt, a woman who'd prefer to dream life away rather than walk through the pains of the present.

When Lanier got to the spot where the chain separated the deck from the stairs that led to the public area below, Ella moved forward, fueled by anger if nothing more. Feeling drunk from exhaustion and the floating music of the piano, she pulled Lanier toward her and kissed him. She dug her fingers into the side of his head, pressing her nails into his scalp until she was sure she had drawn blood. She kissed him with the same intensity with which she wanted to slap him.

A large white tent, fit for a circus, sat in the center of Lafayette Park in Apalachicola. With the bay waters glistening in the background behind him, Brother Mabry walked back and forth across a makeshift stage. One of his thumbs was tucked under the lapel of his crimson jacket. Sweat ran from his head and discolored his baby-blue shirt, but he never seemed to notice. He balled up his fist the same way he had seen President Teddy Roosevelt do when making his points in the newsreels. "Hear me now. Evil is wise. As wise as the serpent. The days we live in are evil, people."

The tent was filled to bursting. Those able to fit inside sat on wooden benches with shoulders pressing one against another. Children stood balanced on the rails of the park gazebo, peering at the man who was as big as a walrus.

Moths fluttered around the tent lanterns. A flickering glow danced across the faces of the audience. A pale woman wearing an upturned, faded brown hat clutched her three-month-old baby closer. Two older women sat next to her on the bench. They looked at her and then fanned their faces faster with the cardboard fans that Collins Funeral Home had given away at the tent entrance.

And then Brother Mabry's voice fell to a whisper. The echo of his last words could still be heard when he walked to the edge of the stage and bent over, his low-hanging stomach rolling down to his knees. "And what else does the Word say about these horrific days? Horrid days, people. Hear me now."

An old man wearing a wilted magnolia blossom in the lapel of his overalls cupped his hand to his ear. The woman holding the baby jostled him in her arms and swung her leg with nervous energy. Brother Mabry reared back and roared.

"There will be false prophets. Impostors, I say. Charlatans appearing on the scene, fooling the people with so-called miracles. People, hear me now. I'm not telling you a nursery rhyme." Brother Mabry stomped to an oak podium and held up a Bible bigger than most of the family Bibles the audience had in their homes. "Go read the words for yourselves. False prophets will populate this land. They will claim to heal. Hear me now, some will claim to heal like sweet Jesus Himself." With his other hand, Brother Mabry grabbed the local newspaper that would be released the next day. He held it as high as the Bible.

Brother Mabry dramatically brought the newspaper to his eye level. He dipped his head and peered out at the audience over the top of the headline "Miracle Signs and Wonders in Dead Lakes." While Brother Mabry read the story about a drifter appearing at Ella Wallace's farm and healing her son, a mule, and a colored girl in that order, the woman in the second row could no longer jostle her baby enough to keep him from crying. The mother slipped out into the aisle, pulled the blanket over the top of the baby's head, and walked on tiptoes to the back of the tent. She passed Gil, the freckle-faced newspaperman who was now on Clive's payroll.

The Adam's apple on Gil's neck bobbed as Brother Mabry read his article. The crowd was dangling on every word he had written. When he saw Clive leaning against a tent pole smiling at him, Gil flinched.

Brother Mabry had been enamored with this young newspaperman with the enthusiasm and freckles of a teenage boy. Deciding to give the local paper an off-the-record scoop of the exact location of Eden, Brother Mabry had sat on the side porch of the Franklin Inn and grown flush as the young newspaperman pointed out discrepancies in deeds from the courthouse archives claiming exactly who owned Eden. One stamped paper with the seal of Franklin County declared Clive Gillespie as the owner, and the other, dated several weeks later with the witness's signature torn away, named Harlan Wallace.

Smoking Cuban cigars in the privacy of Clive's home, Brother Mabry was assured that the discrepancy would soon be a footnote. Clive slid the folded newspaper that contained the cash across the coffee table and the newspaperman yanked it up. "For good faith," Clive told him. "We'll need someone to be our publicity man when this thing takes off. I'll even blot that little loan you took out for a new press from the books." All had been forgiven.

The revival audience murmured about the story in the paper. Their voices swept across the tent like swarms of bees. Brother Mabry stomped his size-fifteen shoe on the stage. The plywood buckled, and flames in the lanterns that hung on the poles wavered. "Don't be like Eve. Don't be taken in by the serpent who deceives. Hear me now: guard your hearts and minds. The devil strikes the hardest where the Lord is working. And make no mistake, ladies and gentlemen, He is working here. The footprints of God are on your very soil."

18

By Monday people from all points in the county had walked through the doors of Ella's store, searching high and low. While they pretended to look for cans of peaches or bottles of aspirin, it was the man with the healing powers they came to inspect.

Leaving Narsissa to manage the store, Ella rode in the wagon and fiddled with the purple beaded purse that secured her future.

In Apalachicola, the side of the revival tent flapped against the midday breeze. A crumpled flyer advertising Brother Mabry's week-long crusade rode the wind that was kicked up by a steamroller heading down Main Street. The black machine, resembling a small train, was operated by a colored man wearing overalls and an ancient straw hat. He stood atop the roller, shoveling out oyster shells that were crushed and ground into the street bed. Gray smoke from the machine veiled the driver. As Ella and her sons passed by on the wagon, the driver glanced up and nodded. He would be the only one that day who didn't stare at them.

A man dressed in a checkered hat that was turned sideways honked as Samuel, Keaton, and Macon crossed the street. The door of his two-door Bearcat car rattled as he passed. Ella stood across the way on the block where the bank stood. She shaded her eyes with her hand and watched as the boys purchased their tickets. Keaton glanced at the poster that hung on the theater wall advertising Charlie Chaplin's new film, *A Dog's Life*. Samuel moved past him and swung the door to the theater open. Just before he turned to follow, Keaton glanced back at Ella. She waved in an animated way that might be more appropriate for a cartoon and motioned for him to go on inside the movie house. A gust of wind rolled in from the bay and lifted the ends of her black hair until the strands fanned across her face, but she could see her son perfectly. Keaton had worried about her long enough, she decided. Today she was determined to let her sons just be boys.

The pawnshop was located two blocks away from the Dixie Theatre. The stenciled letters on the store window were peeling away and a cat sat on the window ledge. A cowbell on the front door called out as Ella entered. She pulled back two dented kettles that hung low from the ceiling with penciled price tags. "Mr. Sawyer . . . Mr. Sawyer?"

A short, bald man with gray eyebrows as thick as caterpillars rose from behind a glass counter that was covered in dust. He groaned and leaned on the side of the counter. When he lifted his elbow from the glass, an imprint remained. "Uh, huh . . . look what the cat drug in."

"You never lacked for words, did you, Mr. Sawyer?" Ella held her purse in one hand and then the other. She tried to smile, but Mr. Sawyer was too busy examining a watch face clutched in his hand to register her awkward gesture.

"Looky," he said and held the watch up. "A man from Nashville who owns one of the boats hired me to fix this jim-dandy for him.

Said he would give me a pretty penny if I could get it in working order. Plans to trade it when he goes to New Orleans."

"How nice," Ella said and massaged the clasp of her purse.

"What can we do for you?" Mr. Sawyer asked, returning his focus back to the watch.

One of his cats cried from the top of a rafter. Ella jumped when the cat landed on the cherrywood table closest to her. The cat stretched down on his front paws, seeming to bow at the painted figurines that lined the table.

"Well, I decided to take your offer."

Mr. Sawyer stopped shining the watch and turned his head in amusement. "Oh. Busby couldn't beat my price, could he? You ought to know not to let amateurs handle your business."

Ella stepped forward and laid her purse on the counter. Dust scattered and attached to the bag's purple beads. "No, that's not the case. I never discussed your price with Mr. Busby."

For the first time, Mr. Sawyer stopped looking at the watch and turned his full attention toward Ella. "Is that a fact?"

Pulling the sapphire-blue ring circled with tiny diamonds from the inside of her purse, Ella didn't hesitate in handing it to Mr. Sawyer. There was no need to inspect the ring that Harlan had placed on Ella's hand when he promised to love and keep her in front of the justice of the peace. Mr. Sawyer already knew its value, and so did Ella. He had given her two estimates, and this time she was demanding the higher offer. Even though the value of the ring would never have been the saving grace in paying off the loan, it would now help clear her name. Combined with Narsissa's money and the proceeds from the cypress she managed to get to market, selling the ring would leave Ella with three dollars and ten cents and a marriage that belonged to a woman she no longer knew. "Mr. Busby refused to take it when I offered it to him on consignment," Ella said. "He said it was the last thing to remain of me."

"You don't say. Never knew him to be that much of a poet," Mr. Sawyer said, squinting his left eye and examining Ella the same way he had examined the ring months ago when she first came to get an appraisal.

"Mr. Busby feared I'd have regrets."

"Huh," the old man said with a gargled sound. "He fears your husband will come back and there'll be a higher price to pay." Mr. Sawyer held up the ring between two fingers with shredded cuticles. Leaning over the counter, he looked back and forth at the sapphire in the ring and at Ella's eyes. "Well, I'll be . . . this stone matches your eyes. I reckon that's how come your husband picked it for you."

The smell of Mr. Sawyer's soured words caused Ella to blink and recoil. She looked at the cat that was licking his paw next to a clock adorned with two gold angels. Then, thinking she might seem vulnerable, she looked directly into the clouded gray eyes of Mr. Sawyer. "You can make the check out to Gillespie Savings and Loan, please."

Mr. Sawyer opened up his ledger and dipped his old-fashioned quill into a bottle of ink to write Ella a check. The cat jumped down and sauntered away with his back raised. Ella looked at the ring, which didn't sparkle in the cramped confines of Mr. Sawyer's place. She tried not to think about the evening that seemed like a lifetime ago when Harlan gave her the ring that even her aunt admitted was beautiful. The first few weeks after Harlan vanished, Ella had lain in bed staring at her ceiling that was painted robin's-egg blue. She'd stretched out across the spot where Harlan had once slept, painting scenes in her mind of her husband returning with a bounty from the marathon poker tournaments he took part in during his travels.

The cat's meow sounded more like a hiss, and Ella turned as if someone had just called her name from the door of Mr. Sawyer's shop. Her aunt had been wrong. There was no such thing as an heirloom too valuable to part ways with. When the cat reached up and slapped his paw at the hem of Ella's dress, she kicked him hard enough to make him cry out and hide underneath the table covered with items that were at one time valuable to those who walked through Mr. Sawyer's door.

Before entering the bank two blocks away from where she sold her wedding ring, Ella rearranged the clasp of the necklace that Narsissa had made for her from gar fish scales. She fought the temptation to repaint the past into a magical, sentimental memory and instead rubbed the edge of one of the scales, reciting in her mind Narsissa's promise that wearing the necklace would give her power.

The redheaded teller who worked below a large, iron-faced clock that hung on the wall did a double take when Ella came inside the lobby. He walked from around the teller booth. The collar of his otherwise-pressed shirt stood out from his neck in disobedience. "Miss . . . Mrs. Wallace."

Ella could see the silhouette of Clive Gillespie through the frosted glass of his office door. He appeared to be talking on a phone. "I am here to see Clive." For good measure, Ella smiled.

"He's tied up at the moment. May I help you with something?" The young man folded his hands in a manner that reminded Ella of a funeral parlor owner.

"I'll wait."

"It's going to be a while. He's being connected to long distance."

"How long could that possibly take?" Ella copied the teller's stance.

"It is all the way to *Atlanta*. . . . It takes the operator as long as fifteen minutes just to connect him."

Nerves boiled under the surface of skin too old to be a girl's and too young to be an elder's. The calm way Ella had scripted the presentation of the check crumbled with anger. "Has he been connected to the call yet?"

Without unclasping his hands, the teller halfway turned and glanced at the big clock behind him. "Well, seeing that he just picked up the receiver before you walked in, I'd say it will be some time, so why don't you—"

The leaves of the potted palm in the lobby shook as Ella brushed up against the plant and circled around the teller. "Well, then, in that case I have time to stick my head in and say hello. I won't be long."

"Now hold on. Mrs. Wallace . . . hold on there. This is long distance."

When Ella made it to the office door, the teller made one last attempt to stop her. His smile had been transformed into pursed lips. Ella slipped her hand around his waist and turned the brass door handle. "I'll be out the door in no time."

Clive was standing behind his desk, holding a cigar in one hand and the black phone receiver in the other.

For the past six weeks Ella had tried to picture what Clive Gillespie's face would look like when she brought the money and laid it on his desk. Sometimes she conjured up the image while swinging an axe in the woods or maybe while pulling out the ticks that had managed to slip under her work hat and into her scalp. During those times his mouth would appear as a mocking grin. When she washed her hands with kerosene to strip the pine tar from her skin, his mouth was usually pictured open, fully displaying his shock. At night as she sat on the edge of her bed, spreading salve across the blisters that broke and bled, his mouth was always twisted in anger. But when reality arrived, she saw nothing on Clive's face to indicate emotion, and that scared her the most.

"I told her you were . . ." The teller raised his hand in protest.

"Ella," Clive said, putting the phone receiver down on his desk. He drew on the cigar, and smoke rolled from the corner of his mouth as he said, "This is an important call. I'm holding for long distance to Atlanta."

"So I hear," she said and opened her purse. She extended the envelope with the endorsed checks, and when he ignored the offer, she settled for placing it on his desk. "It's there for you right down to the penny." Ella turned slightly and nodded at the teller, who was still standing at the door. "Young man, you're the witness to all this. It's paid in full."

When Clive waved him away with the cigar, the teller followed orders and closed the door behind him.

Clive placed the smoldering cigar on the side of an amber-colored ashtray. He stepped from the side of the desk. The pages of a big calendar with an illustration of a lush pasture fluttered with the rotation of the overhead fan.

Placing her hand underneath a corner of the desk, Ella willed herself not to move. The smell of Clive's hair tonic was stronger than the scent of the cigar. Smoke rose and twirled behind him. When he stepped close enough for her to count the number of acne scars on his face, she held the small purse up to her waist. He turned his head, smiled, and reached his hand out like he might brush the side of her hair but stopped. "You might want to keep watch over your time in the sun. You're beginning to acquire something of a red neck."

Ella felt her face grow flush and her heart race. "I'll want a receipt, naturally."

When he laughed, Ella smelled the coffee and tobacco that lingered on his breath.

"Receipts and deeds. Now, precious, all that legality between such old friends?" He winked and reached out like he might stroke her neck with the back of his hand.

Ella stepped farther away, pressing herself against the side of the spooled-back chair meant for guests. "A receipt," she repeated.

He went back behind the desk and took another draw on the cigar. With a defeated groan that seemed to mock her, Clive opened a drawer and pulled out a large ledger bound with layers of gold strings. He slowly opened the book and began writing the receipt. "Receipts? Between such longtime friends?"

"You know, my sons are over at the picture show right now. Clive, I think you missed your calling. You'd make a wonderful dramatist."

"Well, let me get to it, then. It seems there's a matter with the deed that I have to bring to your attention." Clive picked up the phone, listened into the receiver, and then set it back on his desk. He squinted until the acne scars on his face all pinched together. "Pardon me. I'm still waiting for the connection."

"What is it now? What deed are you even talking about?"

"You can verify what I'm saying at the courthouse, but there appears to be a matter of confusion over the deed to that parcel of land that your husband swindled . . . well, some might say stole from me."

"The only confusion I have is why you're so bent on doing me in."

"No need to become disagreeable. This has nothing to do with you, precious." Clive laughed again. "Harlan taught you well. You have a poker face if ever I've seen one."

"Look, Clive . . ." Ella raised her hands in frustration but not surrender.

"You really don't know. I can tell."

Ella licked her lips and looked away at the square blocks with red numbers on the calendar. If only she could go back in time.

"While you've been running around chopping down trees with your boyfriend, there's been a windstorm of excitement. It turns out your little place is smack-dab in the Garden of Eden." Clive laughed the same way he had months earlier when the broker who represented Brother Mabry had first contacted him with the proposition to bring Apalachicola world acclaim.

Ella folded her arms and tucked her purse where Clive couldn't see it. She reached for the door handle. "And I took you for just being crooked . . . not crazy."

"Listen. I don't give a second thought to your timber or your little store. That spring where your Indian gal frolics around, and probably where a whole generation of Injuns is buried, is right where Brother

Mabry—yes, *the* Brother Mabry—where Brother Mabry believes that the Garden of Eden once sat." Clive shrugged and rolled his eyes. "Who's to say? Is he sane? I don't much care. But one way or another there will be a slew of people flocking to this place. They'll bathe in that spring. . . . They'll pray. . . . They'll spend."

"Eden . . . Camelot . . . whatever you want to claim is on my place, the reality is I've paid the note, and that land belongs to me."

Clive flicked the long ash of his cigar and cleaned his front teeth with his tongue. "Precious, you're half right."

"If you call me 'precious' one more time, I'm going to jump across that desk and finish cleaning your teeth with the tip of that cigar."

He pointed the cigar at her, grinned, and shook his head. "I always said you were a live wire. I guess people see that now. Now, *Mrs. Wallace.* You know, there was a great deal of . . . shall we say spirits consumed the night that your husband and I tossed around cards for that piece of land. Spirits . . ." Clive chuckled. "Excuse the pun, but we were tight to say the least. And when the cards were all laid out and the victor decided, we fumbled around with some piece of paper that the steamboat captain gave us. . . . Captain Seavy, you remember him?"

"And the fumble turned out to be mine." Ella turned and opened the door. An auburn-haired boy waited in the lobby for his father to complete a transaction. The boy watched as a green balloon secured at his wrist bobbed in the air. His giggles echoed in the high ceilings of the building.

"Maybe it is, maybe it isn't. We'll let the court decide."

When Ella turned to face Clive, he was sitting down at the desk, flipping through a ledger. "Court?" She stepped back toward him, but he didn't look up.

"You don't think I'm about to give up Eden itself over something as trivial as a drunken poker match. Of course I'll take you to court. Property lines are such complicated matters." As if nursing an injury, he rubbed the top of the ink pen against his acne-scarred chin. He winked at her. "I'll ride you in court until you go from being the filly that you think you are to the old nag that everybody knows you to be."

A garbled voice came out of the phone receiver. Clive stood to attention. The pages on the calendar continued to sway with the motion of the fan, and cigar smoke rose and twisted toward the ceiling painted with gold flowers. Just as Clive announced his name into the receiver, Ella walked to the side of his desk. With a raised eyebrow and drooping shoulders, Clive cupped his hand tighter over the phone receiver and looked up at Ella with a semblance of caution and confusion. She yanked the ledger toward her, and a stack of folders scattered across the desk and tumbled to the floor. The muddled voice called out once more through the phone, and Clive didn't bother to respond. Ripping her receipt from the ledger, Ella stomped over the folders, folded the receipt in half, and never looked back as she left his office.

Only the boy took time to notice Ella walking across the bank lobby. Outside, exposed in the sunlight, she felt her knees buckle and saw dots that made her walk with an unsteady gait. She made it to the corner where the hardware store sat before nausea overtook her. Darting into an alley that smelled of rotten meat and urine, Ella fanned her hand across the fish scales on her necklace.

Next to a pallet stacked with empty paint cans and broken glass, she leaned against a rusty barrel that had been turned into a trash can. Looking inside, she saw the crumpled words printed by the newspaperman. The paper was layered with grease and bits of crushed eggshells. Ella read as much as she could about miracles and false prophets before finally vomiting on the picture of Brother Mabry.

19

The oxen stood in their pen, staring at the people who congregated in front of Ella's property. Strands of hay fell from their mouths as they watched their masters further barricade themselves against the packs of people who chanted, screamed, and pleaded for miracles found by a dip in the spring or a touch of the man who slept in the barn.

The crudely painted No Trespassing signs that Samuel and Keaton had placed on the clearing of land that held the spring didn't do any good. The placards painted by Ella's own hand were eventually knocked aside and stained with muddy shoe prints. People walked, crawled, and if necessary were carried to the spring in hope of cures. Wagons lined the edge of the road like a stalled funeral procession for a celebrated figure. Cars unable to reach the final destination on tires meant for better roads ended up in ruts, their owners taking a plunge in the water before hiring the nearby farmers who waited in their wagons and took advantage of the ignorance by charging top dollar to pull the vehicles to safe passage.

Sheriff Bissell finally took pity on Ella and placed a deputy at the store and another by her front door. Ronnie, the deputy whom Ella favored, kept watch while sitting on a swing with an unloaded shotgun propped between his knees. Torchlights that the pilgrims carried colored the night from the edge of Ella's store down to the edge of the land where the spring had bubbled up since the beginning of time. After three days, the store had sold more than it had in three months. Narsissa began telling the people that each night Lanier would walk through the store touching all of the goods. She told them what they wanted to hear and, satisfied, they would return home and lay the items on the sick.

"Umm . . . umm . . . umm." Myer Simpson clucked her tongue. "I want you to look at this foolishness," Myer said to Neva Clarkson as they made their way through the crowd gathered at the store entrance.

Inside, Myer pushed back against a bent-over woman who carried a sack of flour like it was a baby. "Brother Mabry said that in the last days people will follow false prophets and there will be plagues. Now what did I tell you about those military boys dying from the flu? Huh? What did I say? I said it was a plague," Myer Simpson said while holding her wicker basket that carried more sugar than the government allowed during times of war. She clucked her tongue again just before a man with two handfuls of cloth that was rumored to have been touched by Lanier pressed up against her asking, "How much you want for these rags that the fella blessed?"

Neva Clarkson was jostled against a shelf of kerosene bottles, and Myer rode a wave of customers away from her, farther toward the back of the store. A girl wearing a leg brace and carrying one of Lanier's wooden dolls walked toward the checkout register. Neva slipped past her and out through the back door that led to the loading dock. Outside she made a path toward the home of the woman she had once shared a room with at school.

"Afternoon, Miss Clarkson," Ronnie the deputy said. He scratched the day-old stubble on his chin and looked at the front door of Ella's house before looking back at the teacher.

Neva nodded. "Ronnie." She paused and folded her arms before taking a step up the porch.

"You here for a healing?" Ronnie laughed, and the folds of his stomach vibrated against the shirt patched with the seal of Franklin County. "I haven't seen the likes of this since they quit having the horse races in town."

"I was hoping to see Ella," Neva said.

Ronnie rubbed his chin again and looked out toward the road. Conversations drifted to the porch with the buzz of a beehive.

"I, uhh . . . I need to speak with her about the boys coming back to school next month. I told the superintendent I'd figure out a way to keep this circus away from the children. They don't need to disrupt their lessons."

"It's a circus, all right," Ronnie said before giving her passage.

"Public service is never dull, is it?" Neva nervously laughed.

When Neva was on the same level of the porch as him, Ronnie flicked his front tooth with his tongue. "Yeah, it's something working for Uncle Sam like you and me do. Or maybe I ought to say working for Uncle Clive?"

Neva looked twice at Ronnie before knocking on the door.

Inside, Neva sat on the floral-printed love seat the same way she did when she delivered Macon his lessons whenever he was sick. Ella fidgeted with her hair before flipping it behind her neck and adjusting her seat so that she would not have to look out upon the people who camped on the road.

"The stress of all this . . ." Neva's words trailed off as she leaned sideways, peering toward the hallway. She wrinkled her brow and pointed toward the back bedrooms.

"They're out at the store, helping Narsissa. Macon is out back with Lanier."

"Oh," Neva said and shifted her weight on the sofa. "There was such a crowd in the store . . . well, I must have missed them."

"No worries. One of the deputies is in there with them," Ella said in a clipped tone.

Neva crossed her legs, uncrossed them, and finally settled on tucking her feet under the edge of the sofa. She looked up at the fireplace the same way she would if there was a script printed on the brick. "Well, how is this affecting . . . How are the boys?"

Ella attempted to make a case for the sanity of her boys and then decided to let them make the case for themselves. "They're doing about as good as I am. Holding their own." Ella folded her hands in her lap, rubbed her nail over the callused spot, and then locked her fingers into a ball. She never realized that she was rocking back and forth. "Keaton said the other day this reminded him of the pressure Jesus must have had on Him with all the people begging for healings."

Neva brushed her hand in the air. "Oh, Ella, I don't think I'd go around saying that."

Ella stopped rocking. "Well, naturally he didn't mean it. He was just . . . you know . . . oh, what does it matter? They'll think what they think anyway."

"That's exactly why it matters a great deal." Neva sat on the edge of the sofa and leaned closer to Ella. Noise from the crowd out on the road competed with the sound of Ronnie humming out on the porch. "Ella, I feel absolutely awful. I have been worried sick about you ever since . . ."

Ella stood up, and the peacock feathers in the vase on the fireplace mantel swayed. "I am threadbare from caring what people think, so please don't worry about my good name because—"

"I'm worried because I've done something awful." Neva balled her fists tighter and looked at every corner in the room except for the spot where Ella stood. "I've run my mouth and put you in jeopardy."

Ella's face became flushed and then crimson. All she could think was that on the evening of their return from the sale of the lumber, Neva must have passed along the road in front of the house. She must have seen Lanier give Ella the paint kit he had bought her. She must have witnessed their embrace just beyond the barn door. Ella steadied herself against the fireplace mantel, jostling the feathers with her arm.

Listening to Neva confess how she had shared news of Macon's healing with Reverend and Myer Simpson, Ella saw a frailty in Neva that she had forgotten. Neva kept cupping the material of her skirt until her hem crept higher.

"I wish a thousand wishes that I could take back my words that day at lunch with Reverend and Myer," Neva said. "I wish I could just run off sometimes. Start my own school where I don't have to kowtow to the likes of Clive Gillespie. And when I think about what he did to that poor Ruby . . . I should have spoken up."

"It wouldn't have done any good. He's above the law, evidently. Did you know Clive is now saying that he'll sue me over this property? Now, tell me one single lawyer who isn't locked in his grip."

Neva moved to the edge of the seat. Her brow softened, and her eyes lit up with excitement. "My cousin practices law in Pensacola. He's a suffragist. Pro-woman. I can get you an appointment. I can help."

Neva's enthusiasm was not contagious. Ella smiled and nodded. Hope seemed as far removed as her ability to make sense out of this new world.

The women sat there looking at each other, casting their own thoughts in the comfortable silence of established friendship and shared histories. A child's squeal from the crowd outside caused Neva to jump and look away toward the window.

"If I'd known I'd go through all of this I might not have broken it off with Clive way back when," Ella said. "I could have married him, slipped him some rat poisoning in his coffee each morning, and watched him die a slow, agonizing death. Widows still get sympathy, you know."

When Ella laughed, Neva shook her head and laughed too, the same way they had as girls at Miss Wayne's school. "You always had the most outlandish dreams." Neva's words dissolved into a nervous cough. Noise from the crowd outside grew stronger.

Neva rolled her head up to the ceiling and sighed long and hard. Sunlight from the windows illuminated the dust that scattered about the room. Neva's shoulders released, and for the first time her back was actually reclining against the sofa on which she sat. "Do you remember back in school how upset you became when Miss Wayne lectured about those Salem witch trials? You couldn't even sleep in your own bed, you were so tormented by those dreams. You came into my room and slept on the floor every night until we moved on to the next lesson. Miss Wayne said it was the artist in you that kept those images in your mind. Those poor people hanging the way they did." Neva wrapped her arms around herself. "Now I'm the one who can't sleep. Ella, you need to know something. The board of elders have pressed Reverend Simpson to hold a town hall meeting. Some sort of gibberish about the man you have here and the need to protect our children."

"I can't believe . . . I mean, Neva, who do they think they are?"

As Neva laid out the details of the hearing that would take place in the house meant for worship, Ella didn't bother to hide her shaking hands behind her back. She walked in circles around the footstool stitched with her aunt's monogram. Neva's final question caused her to finally sink and sit still. "Is that man really who he claims to be?"

"Neva, you don't mean to tell me that you actually believe . . ."

"I just wonder . . . I'm sorry—I just wonder if the man really is the person he claims to be."

"He is an innocent man. He has a letter from the sheriff where he came from," Ella said with the same conviction as Brother Mabry. "Neva, he has done nothing . . . nothing. The fact of the matter is he wants none of this . . . this spotlight. That's why he won't even see those people out there. Just imagine if he wasn't a better man. He could make a mighty fine dollar off of them. . . . He could set up a tent like that preacher in town." Ella stood up again. The burnt-orange carpet with stitching shaped like pears gathered and wrinkled as she walked back and forth across the parlor. "Listen, Neva. I can't explain all this . . . can't begin to. But that man showed up here when I was this side of a nervous breakdown . . . about to lose my son, my home. When everybody else offered pity, he pushed me. Because of him I still have a home. I might be fighting a never-ending battle with Clive, but because of that man, I'm fighting just the same. My boys need to see that. Neva, I need to see that."

Nodding, Neva glanced around the room as if she were forgetting something. She held her hands out like she might hug Ella but then withdrew them behind her back. "You know, last year I had a precarious situation. One of those Sullivan boys, the oldest, came to school with a letter from his father. It was typed and very official. The letter said that he wanted the boy dismissed on days when I talked about creation and evolution. I'll never forget it. The note said that I might come from a monkey but his boy certainly did not."

"That bunch of Sullivans," Ella said dismissively.

Neva looked down at the floor and with her shoe straightened the corner of the rug that was flipped upward. "Come to find out, the father didn't write the letter after all. The boy did. I felt such a fool for never questioning it."

At the door, Ella squeezed Neva's wrist, a wrist so thick that it would have been better suited on a much larger woman. "I've seen enough bad men to know a good one. Don't worry." Ella spoke the words for herself as much as for Neva.

"It looks like rain," Deputy Ronnie said as soon as the front door cracked open and Neva stepped out onto the porch. Ronnie looked out at the crowd and then up at the dark clouds that rolled in the eastern sky. The humid air seemed as thick as wool.

"It must be nearing three o'clock, then," Neva said as she walked down the stairs and patted the perspiration on her brow.

"The rain will make them people scatter soon enough." Ronnie's laughter trailed Neva down to the driveway.

Neva waited behind the rope that until last week had harnessed Ella's mule. The deputy with a hard look unclipped the rope that was stretched between two fence posts with the No Trespassing signs nailed to them. Neva thanked the officer, who didn't seem to care one way or the other. She apologized to the stout woman who bumped into her. The woman was clutching a rosary and chanting. "Antichrist," yelled an old man who smelled of body odor and fresh whiskey. He hurled his fist in the air, and Neva turned away, running into a gaunt-faced man who wore a baggy Army uniform. "Forgive me," Neva said. The young man had an oversized glass eye that was iridescent blue and a fresh scar that zigzagged across his cheek and over his nose. When he sneezed, he tried to no avail to cover his mouth. A man wearing a leather driving cap backed into the soldier, and his arm jerked up in the air. A spray of spit slapped Neva's face. Nudging against the crowd with her shoulders, Neva Clarkson pressed forward until she could make out the pineapple-shaped gate of Mrs. Pomeroy's house on the other side of the road.

Out behind Narsissa's cabin, a clap of thunder rang out, and Lanier called the game of marbles. "You win," he said.

"One more game," Macon said, scraping the marbles into a pile and drawing a fresh circle in the dirt.

The deputy with hips the size of a teenage girl's chomped on a sliver of sugarcane and spat a chewed-up stalk at the side of the vegetable garden. The used-up portion of the stalk landed on the string that sectioned off a row of butter beans.

Lanier looked up and found Ella peering at them through the kitchen window. He met her smile and forced himself not to break away. When she turned toward the other side of the room where he could no longer see her, Lanier followed the sound of feet crunching the oak leaves that scattered the back of the cabin.

Bonaparte pulled at his pants and walked forward, never taking his eyes off the deputy.

"The man down there by the road let me pass." Bonaparte handed the deputy the red slip of paper that the other deputy by the driveway had given him.

"I know him," Lanier said. His reassurance didn't keep the deputy with the sugarcane from eyeing Bonaparte up and down.

"That's Bonaparte," Macon said, brushing the dirt from his pants.

Nodding toward the circle of marbles, the deputy said to Macon, "Why don't you go back to the store and fetch me a Coca-Cola."

Macon kept picking up marbles until the circle was filled. Giving up, the deputy tossed the rest of the sugarcane into the garden and made his way into the store. "I figure your boy yonder will protect you," he yelled and pointed at Bonaparte.

"We got trouble," Bonaparte said in a stage whisper. He planted his hands on the sides of his pants.

"You're a little late with that bit of news." Lanier bent down, picked up a tiger's-eye marble, and thumped it into the ring. Macon jumped around to the side of the ring and licked his lips.

"I ain't playing with you," Bonaparte said. "These folks mean business. I got a family. I got to make a living 'round here."

Macon shot another marble out of the circle and moved around to the other side. "Lanier, your turn."

Bonaparte's oily face glistened in the sun. "The sheriff and Gillespie came out to the house. Talking about bringing us to the church for some meeting. Telling me that my girl better say such and such or I be bucking justice."

Lanier stared up at the window where Ella had stood.

"Folks is saying that Gillespie knows you the one keeping Miss Ella from selling this place to him. He got them saying you're a devil. Not me but other people, you understand. Not me."

"Lanier, do you want me to play your turn?"

Without looking away, Lanier nodded, and Macon shot a cat's-eye marble across the border of the circle.

"Do you hear me talking to you?" Bonaparte asked. "The sheriff says I best protect my own before I start protecting you. Now I got to do what I got to do. You can up and leave here. I can't."

"I'm tired of leaving."

Bonaparte shifted his weight, dug his hands into his pockets, and stared down at the marbles like they were miniature crystal balls.

At the kitchen window, Ella appeared again and leaned sideways. Her hair gathered at the nape of her neck. This time she did not attempt to wash away reality with a smile.

That evening, after she had dried the supper dishes the same as if it were just another night, Ella once again stood at the kitchen window. She looked out at the light from the lamp that seeped through the cracks in the barn wall, then glanced toward the parlor, where she could hear the boys arguing over a game of gin rummy. She was grateful for their argument. At least it kept the noise of the outside shut away for one night.

Without telling a soul, Ella took one of Samuel's khaki rain jackets that hung on the hook next to the back door and slipped away. She glanced at the calico cat that jumped from her porch and jetted off toward the woods that was now just a field, sliced and jangled with stumps.

The deputy with the bald head looked down at her from the front porch as she made her way toward the barn. One more to discount her reputation, she thought before she could stop herself.

She didn't bother to knock before pulling the door open, slowly at first and then with force. *It's still my property,* she thought.

Lanier stood shirtless with the waist of his pants flapping partway open.

"Oh," Ella said and covered her face like a schoolgirl before turning her back to him. "I didn't know you weren't decent."

"I'm decent," he said as he finished dressing.

The barn smelled of barley and dampened dust. The mule that was getting fat in the stall lifted his head and returned to his hay. He never bothered to kick at the stall door.

Lanier sat down at the table he had made out of two sawhorses and a piece of discarded plywood cut for the raft. He had repaired the leg on the stool that had once been used by Harlan when he was a racehorse jockey. "Won't you have a seat?" He swept his hand across the chair the same way he might if he were in a grand inn. "It's my parlor."

Ella couldn't help but laugh. The laughter cut the tension in the room as much as it did the tension in her mind.

"You make me laugh."

"That's a good thing."

She folded her arms and then swung them free. "I tend to drown in blue spells. You rise up and laugh."

"I've had practice." He ran his hand across the top of the plywood. "I've had my sinking spells, believe me."

"Lanier . . ." Ella's words came out in a sigh.

"I know." He looked up from the table, and for the first time she saw tears in his eyes. "I'm sorry," he whispered.

The deputy out on the porch coughed, and some of the small group of people who had not yet given up on seeing the healer laughed. Ella turned toward the noise, and then stepped closer to Lanier. This time she made sure that the table separated them.

"You know Neva Clarkson, the teacher, the one I told you about who was in school with me? Well, she came by today." Ella tapped the table with the fingernail that was growing back after being cut for common labor. "I assured her that all would be fine. I told her not to worry about this so-called meeting at the church. I told her that you are a good man."

Lanier looked up as if the crowd had just burst through the door.

"I told her the truth," Ella said and tapped the table. "I told her the truth, didn't I?"

He sat down on the stool and stared at a hoofprint that the mule had made on the ground. "That means a lot. I expect people are wondering why you don't make me leave or why I don't run on."

Ella's neck tensed at the thought of the conversation drifting in the direction of the moment they had shared on the steamboat. Her heart didn't want to discuss his leaving, but her mind told her it was the right thing to do. "But now you know, at the meeting they will be publicly stating what has been whispered. They will ask about the healing. They will ask, and I have to go answer."

"Have to?"

"Have to," Ella repeated. Her hand was laid flat on the table. "I want to stand up there and tell them what I told Neva. I want to tell them that you are a good man. A trustworthy, decent man. I want that, Lanier."

"I am," he said, walking around the wagon wheel that was in need of repair. "I'm all that."

"But I need answers. I respect your abilities . . . your gift . . . whatever it might be. And up until now, I haven't pointedly questioned you on it. I have always felt that faith is a private matter. You told me you weren't into darkness, and I took your word for it."

"I think you ought to know that by now."

His words settled over Ella, and for the first time since she had walked through the door, she breathed deep enough for her belly to expand.

"When my granny told me that I had the gift . . . being a fatherless son and all . . . she said never to tell what I was praying when I touched people. It's how I was raised in the mountains up in Georgia."

"And the North Georgia mountains are far away from here," Ella said.

"It rips me up inside," he said. "I'm tempted to just let the next person pull out the fire, cure the thrush, heal the whatever. And they tried to tell me it was a gift. Then how come it feels like a curse?"

Ella folded her arms. "Curse?"

Lanier ran his hands through his hair, and strands fell down over his face. "Don't worry. The witches aren't flying in on brooms just yet."

"All jokes aside, I trusted too much already."

"I understand," he said.

"Now they are congregating at that church, and I'm going to be publicly skewered. This thing you have . . . this whatever it is that you have to make people better . . . Lanier, you need to tell me how to explain it to people. You owe me that much."

"Faith."

It was the quiet way he said the word that caused Ella to take her hand from the stall door. He moved closer, and she could smell the musky scent that only he gave. The smell that caused her to feel unbalanced, frozen. She wanted him to put his arms around her again, but when he lifted his arm, she stepped to the side.

"You know, Neva mentioned that letters can be doctored up all sort of ways to look official."

"What are you saying?"

"I don't know you, Lanier. I mean, I really don't know you. It's not just the healings. I'm very open-minded . . . more open-minded than most. But all this talk that we're so similar. Well, I'm learning that emotions are one thing. Reality is another." Ella folded her hands behind her back. "A letter is only a piece of paper."

"That letter I have from the sheriff is certified."

Ella tapped the wood with her fingernail. "The story behind the letter is what I'm getting at."

Lanier sat back down on the stool. His legs were wide, and his arms rested on his knees. "You've trusted me more than anybody would have. It's how come I have these thoughts, these feelings. . . ." His words trailed off, and he looked down like he might be praying. "My wife, Octavia . . . she had . . . problems. Mental problems."

"You told me that much already," Ella said.

"I had a son, Nathaniel. He was three when she drowned him."

Ella stepped backward, pressed against the stall. She tried not to move, not to even breathe as he spoke his words. A dirt-dabber bug fought against a mound of dirt and then wiggled into the hole he created, disappearing for good.

"We wrote Nathaniel's passing off as accidental. Accidental drowning. Octavia said she was distracted by a bell ringing and left him in the tub just a minute too long. I knew different. The girl, Rosie, who kept house for us knew different. The problems . . . the mind problems didn't come on until after Nathaniel was born. Octavia claimed having Nathaniel caused her to be the way she was. Her family claimed it was me. No matter how hard I tried to wash up or learn the way they wanted me to think, I never could suit them."

Even as the mule stuck his head out from the stall door and nudged her shoulder with his nose, Ella never moved.

"My brother-in-law is heartless. You might as well say evil. People said one time him and his brothers strung up a colored man for looking twice at J.D.'s wife." Lanier shook his head and stared down. "Like Camilla would be interested in a man to start with. Poor Camilla. J.D. had no business marrying that girl. She wasn't supposed to marry. Anybody could see that. He married her for her money. Her daddy owned most the land in the county and a sawmill in the city. Umm . . . I guess Camilla was really the one who had no business marrying. Pressured, I reckon. By her family. By the community. Who knows. But she gave in just the same. She married him when she was thirty-one. They'd been married for a few years when I came into the picture.

"For a year or two, I just thought they were close . . . Octavia and Camilla . . . like sisters or something. Then, after Nathaniel . . . well, I'd have to be blind not to see it. A touch of the hand. A sideways glance that turned into a stare. Hugs that went on too long, even in public. Even after the funeral, weeks after we buried Nathaniel, the only person Octavia would let into the room was Camilla. I was numb to it all . . . my baby boy dying . . . then here comes Camilla. The only reason I agreed for her to move in with us is because she managed to make things quiet in the house again.

"I always wondered what J.D. thought about his wife packing up and moving in. He had her inheritance in the bank. I reckon he didn't need her in his own house. And I always wondered about Rosie. Did Rosie ever know what was going on?" Lanier stared across at an orange and black spider that hung from a broken web on the stall gate.

"Rosie had worked for the Troxlers for years. She was polite to me, but like the rest of them she was distant. When I was able to save Nathaniel from the croup, she seemed to get scared of me. So see there, I've had some experience with all this . . . all this judging."

Ella tried to smile, but Lanier was too far away in his mind to notice. He hugged himself and rocked forward. Muscles in his forearm twitched.

"The morning . . . the morning it all happened, I heard them talking in the kitchen. Camilla's voice was low, but Octavia yelled, 'Take me away from here or I'll take myself.' I figured she wanted to go to Atlanta for a day or two. They'd do that now and again.

"It must have just happened right before I got there for lunch. Rosie hadn't made it back from the market yet. I liked to eat late and then shut my eyes for a little bit. Like always, Rosie left my lunch in the heating cabinet up over the stove. I came in the house. Funny, all I remember hearing was the screen door creak and the birds chirping outside. Not even a clock ticking . . . nothing but birds . . . happy-sounding.

"'Octavia,' I called out. Easing down the hall, walking past the table that I'd made for her on our first anniversary. The first thing I remember seeing was a black shoe sticking out from the door. It was turned toward me. The buckle strap was bright silver . . . brand-new. Not a scratch on it. I never had paid any attention to Camilla's shoes. It all still comes to me now and then like flashes . . . like lightning you can shelter from but can't stop from happening. Camilla had on a black skirt. And cherries. Cherries on her blouse—all these little cherries sewn on it. The top part was covered in blood from where a pistol had ripped her chest wide open. The gun right there by the foot of the bed . . . my pearl-handled gun . . . the one Octavia bought for me when we got married. The barrel was even still warm.

"Octavia was on the other side of the bed. Blood was all over the wall. All over the oval picture frame that held Nathaniel's photograph. Everywhere was blood on my side of the bed." Lanier folded his arms and tucked his hands inside the folds of his biceps. "All over my hands. The blood got on me when I lifted Octavia's head, thinking I'd be able to stop it from happening or something. Just like I could fix it."

Ella shifted her weight and then slid down against the stall door until she was resting on her knees. The ends of her skirt ballooned over the bits of hay that covered the ground.

"Rosie made it back in the house carrying her groceries. She made it back just in time to look in the door and see me holding the pistol. . . . I was just sitting on the floor looking at the gun the same way I would if the gun could talk and tell me that I'd failed to stop all this. Naturally she went to screaming and then ran out of the house. But not me. I just kept squatting there over them . . . holding that gun and staring over at the woman who loved my wife in a way I never could. None of them believed what Octavia wrote about her and Camilla in that note she left on the dresser. 'There's such a thing as being driven to the point of crazy,' J.D. told me when he struck a match and lit that note right in front of me in jail."

"Jail? So there was a trial?" Ella whispered.

"If you can call it that. I had the sense to hire a lawyer from Columbus. He said I had the good favor of having a new medical doctor do the autopsy—a fella straight out of Emory who was still too fresh to be bought. He declared it was a murder-suicide. Murder-suicide, pure and simple. But all the Troxlers heard was murder."

Neither of them said any more. They just sat there staring off in different directions. At the barn door, Ella whispered the words with the same force that she might have if she were yelling them. "I'm so sorry."

He only nodded and then reached down for a blade of straw. He drew rows of lines in the dirt.

"The truth." She brushed the dirt from her skirt. "The truth is what matters here. Truth about your wife . . . the truth about this healing business. As long as you're telling me the truth, then we'll be fine."

Ella eased out of the barn door with a reverence she would have shown if she were leaving in the middle of a church service. Before she could close the door behind her she pretended not to hear Lanier say, "Don't be so confident in the truth making things right." She walked back to the house without ever putting the coat back over her head.

Before he left town, Mr. Busby once again stood in front of the marble desk in the lobby of the Blue Moon Clock Company in

Bainbridge, Georgia. The young woman who wore red lipstick too strong for her fair face told him twice that Mr. Troxler was not in the building. A mural of a blue moon was painted on the wall behind her, and the ticking of the grandfather clock in the corner echoed.

When Mr. Busby's charm gave way to frustration, the young woman met the volume of his voice. "For the last time. He is not here."

Straightening the tie that he had put on special for the occasion, Mr. Busby pushed his weight against the iron door of the building, crossed the street to where the café owner was assembling her roasted peanuts, and made his way to the sheriff's office.

A lanky deputy with imitation snakeskin boots greeted him. The man kept saying "Yes, sir" to Mr. Busby's story about meeting the man he thought would offer a corporate contract but then took the photograph with Ella Wallace and her sons standing in front of the pile of cut timber.

"It is a piece of art," Mr. Busby said. "I can fetch my price for it at any gallery in Atlanta."

"Yes, sir," the deputy said and sat on the edge of a wooden desk cluttered with discolored files.

"It has a blur in the corner that makes it gallery worthy. That man stole that piece of art from me."

"He stole it?" the deputy asked and lowered his head. "You're talking about Mr. Troxler?"

"Yes," Mr. Busby said.

"I see," the deputy said with folded arms and pouty lips. "You're saying Mr. Troxler stole one of your pictures."

"He asked if he could take the photograph with him. It was that man in the corner of the picture. A regular bum if you ask me . . . a no-count with hair as long as a woman's."

The sheriff, an older man with pointed ears and thinning gray hair slicked down on the side and a wine-colored birthmark on his temple, stepped from out of his opened office door.

Mr. Busby looked at his audience and adjusted the knot of his tie. "The older one—J.D. Troxler they said his name is—he kept staring at the smudge. He asked his brother if he recognized the man. The younger brother went about cussing in a manner that probably ran off my customers. I should get payment for that offense too."

"Yes, sir. I see," the deputy whispered.

"I told the gentleman—and I use that term loosely—that I didn't even consider the man in the picture a model for my work. He was just a mistake. Just a smudge that scurried away from being photographed. On the shy disposition. The type who runs away when the camera comes out."

"Yes, sir."

"Well, then the older Troxler, the one who runs that business, he just walked off as good as you please with the picture in hand. Walked right across the street with that brother cussing and carrying on behind him. They walked into their big warehouse as pretty as you please and never once paid me a cent. I work with people on consignment. Naturally I knew he was good for it. But it's been two days, and I'm thinking that he skipped town without paying me. Now I know he can afford my prices."

The sheriff squinted and cocked his head sideways so that the birthmark pointed directly at Mr. Busby. "Come again," the sheriff said. He motioned for the deputy to quiet the inmates who yelled behind the iron gate framing a row of cells. "Tell me again about the woman who owns the place."

An inmate down the hall of the jail cussed, and the deputy hollered back at him.

"Ella Wallace?" Mr. Busby's voice was laced with disdain. "What does she have to do with the Troxler man stealing my photograph?"

The sheriff closed his eyes and raised his head, chin up. He had handled threats against his life, a shotgun blast through his front door, and even a burning cross on his front yard for stopping a lynching. Mr. Busby's outrage was nothing more than child's play. "Pacify me a little bit."

Against the clanging noise of a billy club running down the iron cages and the shouts of the deputy from behind the gate, Mr. Busby talked of Ella Wallace in terms of an artist, painting her in the best light possible.

The sheriff grabbed a writing tablet from the desk. "And spell the name of the place where this picture was made?"

Mr. Busby walked around the desk. He faced off with the sheriff and didn't seem bothered when the inmates down the hall cried out. "Is my friend in some sort of danger?"

The sheriff touched the end of the pencil to his long tongue and steadied his hand on the paper. "Depends on how fast you can spell."

20

Brother Mabry wanted to meet Clive away from the prying eyes of the skeptics and the faithful. Gil, the local newspaperman, drove Brother Mabry along the street that ran down the river and emptied into a dirt road dotted with broken shells and crushed pinecones. As the car came into the marsh pasture where Clive kept three horses he raced, the pine limb that hung out over the road scraped against the top of the car.

A colored man, not more than thirty, cracked a whip in the air as younger boys rode the backs of the horses in the marsh where sable palms and saw grass lined the banks. Water came halfway up the hind legs of the animals, and the boys rocked back and forth as they sloshed through the marsh in a trot.

Clive stood on top of a massive stump, all that was left of an oak struck down by lightning the summer before. The hot, sticky afternoon breeze swept across the field and caught the ends of the pieces of his hair that weren't waxed flat to his scalp. He called out when Brother Mabry opened the car door. The preacher's low-hanging belly poured out in front of him. The automobile tilted and swayed as he struggled to get out.

The man with the whip glanced back at them and then popped the frayed ends in the air. One of the horses threw its head up, sniffed the air, and whinnied.

"Beautiful horses," Gil said. He put his hands in his pockets before settling on folding them in front of his waist. "Beautiful piece of property."

"I come out here practically every Saturday. Even in winter."

The chestnut-colored horse shook and whinnied again. Water flew from his mane, and the rider leaned down over the horse's neck.

"The water strengthens their legs," Clive said, offering a cigar to Gil before striking his own match. "It's just a hobby, more or less." Clive looked at Brother Mabry as if there was an explanation needed for the horse racing.

"I'm not Catholic," Brother Mabry said in a clipped tone. "There's no call for confession."

Clive laughed and Gil joined in. A horse whip cracked the air, and Brother Mabry pulled at the front of his baby-blue shirt, trying to ventilate himself.

"Mr. Gillespie, if there is one thing I pride myself on, it is having answers to questions most other people can't figure out. That said, I'm growing rather agitated at not being able to answer the simplest of questions. My wife is asking me daily, if not hourly, when will the spring be hers?"

Clive drew in the tobacco and blew the smoke in the direction of the horses. "How is Mrs. Mabry holding up with all of the commotion over the revival?"

"I'll tell you how she's doing. She's all to pieces." Brother Mabry's voice grew into a boom, and the horses jerked sideways in the water.

"Hear me. . . . I have no answers for my wife. I do not delight in handing my wife empty promises."

"The matter of the deeds will be settled in no time. Now, I know for a fact the woman doesn't have the money to fight it out in court."

"Court draws drama," Brother Mabry yelled. "Drama draws scrutiny. I've never seen any good come of having more than two lawyers in the same room."

Clive tried to stand taller. "It won't come to all that. It's just idle threats."

"And if anybody should be suing around here, it's me," Brother Mabry roared. His face was reddened by anger and the heat. His breathing became haggard. "You brought me down here under false pretense. Claiming that you owned that land outright."

"I do," Clive answered, rising on the tips of his shoes. "Sir, make no mistake . . . the land is mine."

"I'm not going to stand here in the blazing sun and argue the particulars for the umpteenth time with you. You told me you'd correct the matter, and that's exactly what I expect you to do." Unfurling a burgundy handkerchief from his pocket, Brother Mabry dabbed at the perspiration that gathered in between the folds of his neck. "I don't like confusion. You hear me? The devil's in the middle of confusion. You get that land so the deal is ironclad, or be done with it altogether."

"Ella's being disagreeable. She's a typical woman. She's high-strung. Let me work it my way. Her hand will be forced soon enough." Clive looked at Gil, smiled, and then drew on the cigar.

"There's something about to happen," Gil said, his voice growing in confidence as he spoke. "Now, Clive and I have about got it figured out."

"Figured it out, huh!" Brother Mabry said in a snort.

"The community is having what you might say is a hearing . . . a meeting."

"A town hall," Clive corrected.

"A town hall," Gil repeated and folded his hands back across his waist. "The pressure of running a place that size will turn her head around. I'm betting Reverend Simpson will help us too. Folks listen to him."

"He'll help when he sees a dollar or two," Clive said, brushing away a piece of lint from the leg of his pants. "There's always a collection plate that needs filling."

The horses strained against the water. The riders hunched down, wrapping their arms over the wet manes. Sounds of sloshing water and the baritone voices of the riders rose up to the dry land where Clive and the others stood.

"Gil's article painted the perfect picture. And of course, you've painted a scary picture yourself. I mean with all this talk of the Antichrist and end times." Clive laughed.

Brother Mabry spun around and towered over Clive. "You find God's Word humorous, Gillespie?"

A hot breeze swept over the marsh, and the smell of salt grew stronger. "Absolutely not," Clive said, chopping his hands at the air.

"I speak the truth," Brother Mabry said with even more conviction than he had on the stage. "This is more than a business deal to me and certainly to God."

"Certainly," Clive said and tucked his head. "It's a calling."

Brother Mabry looked at Gil, who looked over his shoulder at the horses being unsaddled.

"I'll have you know I didn't walk away from civilization and meander down all this way to the backwoods for a dollar," Brother Mabry yelled.

"Certainly not," Clive said.

"When I say it's God's work, that's what it is," Brother Mabry shouted. "It's a conviction, not a religion."

"Not a religion?" Gil asked.

"A conviction," Clive repeated.

"A conviction that this is sacred ground." Brother Mabry held his fist higher than the horse trainer's whip. "A conviction that my wife doesn't take lightly either."

Out in the thick oaks and cypress that lined the marsh, a crane flew out and landed a few feet away from the horses that were being led in a circle by the riders. The sweat and water on their coats glistened.

Brother Mabry shook his head. "I might as well be speaking Greek." He turned to walk back to the car but then stopped. "Gillespie, mark my word. God won't be mocked. He told me to build this retreat and to make His land known to His people. The healing powers of the water on that land have no ownership other than that of God."

Standing back on the tree stump, Clive watched them drive away. He didn't move, hardly breathed, until they had made it through the open gate that was usually chained shut. Then he tossed his head back and stomped his foot and howled with a guttural laugh that rolled up over his body like a wave. His roar swept down to the marsh bank, and the crane took flight back into the woods.

The crane landed next to a rotting log that was tangled in thorny vines. The bird turned in the direction of Earl, who was hunched in the position of a warrior or an ape.

Hidden in the woods tucked adjacent to the marsh where the prized horses exercised, Earl watched through a curtain of vines. The colored man popped his whip as the horses trotted off away from the marsh in a prance of freedom.

Behind Earl, a snake slithered across the damp ground that was carpeted in gray dead moss and brittle leaves. Earl pulled from inside his pants waist a long-barreled pistol from an earlier generation and stretched his arm out, pointing the gun in Clive's direction. Crumpled leaves rustled as the snake slid across them. Distracted,

Earl looked down at the three-foot-long snake that now was inches from his boot. The head was round. It was just a blacksnake, not a moccasin. He lifted the heel of his boot and waited until the snake was perfectly aligned before slamming his foot down, crushing the snake's head. While the body of the snake flailed and flapped around Earl's ankle, he set his sight back toward his real target. But the tree stump where Clive Gillespie had stood was now bare. The riders were teasing each other with boyish taunts and beating the horse blankets dry against the sides of the corral that held the horses. "Keep your mind on your business," the colored man yelled at the boys and twisted the frayed end of the whip before tucking it into a storage bin by the feed trough.

The engine of Clive's car came to life. When the car passed through the gate of the pasture, it took up speed on the main road. Only the scent of cigars and a faint puff of exhaust fumes proved that he had ever really been there.

J.D. Troxler sat in the first-class section of the train with his legs crossed and his hat balanced on one knee. He had grown weary of his brother's descriptions of how he would take Lanier Stillis bone by bone and serve his skin to the buzzards. He set his sights out toward the dense timber that lined the edges of the track like rows of bars in a jail cell.

His brother Parker sat next to him, caressing the pistol that was inside his jacket. The man they hired for the job—Jack-Ray, the one they always hired to take care of business too dirty for their hands— sat in the row across from them with his mouth open as he slept. With each turn and bump of the train, Jack-Ray's head teetered.

"You reckon he tied one on?" Parker asked, motioning toward Jack-Ray with his chin.

"Makes no difference," J.D. replied. "He can split a man like a hog and sleep like a baby. He's loyal to a fault."

J.D. stared at Parker long and hard. Parker once again stroked the shape of the pistol that protruded from his jacket. J.D. smiled and looked out the window. A shanty sat between pecan trees in the middle of a field. "Maybe I should've had Jack-Ray run for sheriff. He'd be more competent than the ignoramus we have in there now," J.D. said.

"I don't figure Jack-Ray made it past the fourth grade," Parker said, stretching his arm across the top of the train seat.

J.D. shook his head and brushed lint from his shoulder. "Backbone counts for more than book sense. If I'd had my way when Lanier first showed up on Octavia's arm, we wouldn't be in this fix." J.D. leaned down with his forearms pressed against his knees. He raised his eyebrows until one arched higher than the other. "Don't you remember I wanted Jack-Ray to take care of him way back then? Eh, don't you? But Daddy wouldn't have any of it. Said we had to keep peace in the family. Said he was just glad Octavia found her a man. Said we'd dress Lanier up. I kept telling him, Daddy, you can polish cut glass till kingdom come but it won't make a diamond. All he could say was he didn't want a scandal." J.D. huffed and flakes of dust floated away from the window. "Well, we got us a scandal all right."

A boy not more than ten tried to make his way up to the front cabin. He gripped the edge of the seat where the hired hit man was stretched out. The boy slipped around the boot that had fallen from the seat and hung down in the aisle. The sun hit the side of Jack-Ray's face, illuminating the rudimentary branding on his right cheek. It was the letter *J* and had been put there by his father when Jack-Ray was not much older than the passenger trying to pass by.

Parker laughed and J.D. looked at him, cross.

"It tickles me. All this time we can't catch him, and some old, beat-down picture taker winds up leading us right to him," Parker said. From his other coat pocket, he pulled out the folded picture of Ella in front of the pines and the blurred image of Lanier. Parker held the picture up to the window and stared at it. His laugh transformed into a sigh. "I reckon we shoulda paid the old man something for that picture. You know, a reward or something."

Ignoring his brother, J.D. continued to look out the window at the pecan trees that lined a field where a two-story clapboard house sat. "Lanier would have to go and make this as inconvenient as possible. Who ever heard of a place you can't even reach by train?" He pulled out the gold pocket watch his wife had given him on their first anniversary, back when he was confident theirs was a traditional marriage. J.D. stared as the second hand ticked away the hours to justice. "I'd just as soon stay on this train and not take that steamboat. I don't care for water. Never have."

By the last night of the revival, the crowd had grown until the benches buckled and the scent of clammy body odor laced the air. They fanned for relief, seeming to stir the contagious notion that they were living in original paradise. Clive Gillespie stood underneath a lamp at the back of the tent just as he had been doing for the past few nights. He scribbled down Brother Mabry's words on a pocket pad the same way Myer Simpson, who had taken to sitting on the third pew—the position she took at her own husband's church—marked notes in her Bible. Both pretended to verify, but only one came to believe.

Only a few of the people noticed Ruby. She sat on the end of the bench nearest to the middle. She had eased through the open tent flap right after the accordion player and pianist had led the congregation in a hymn. Mrs. Pomeroy was the first to notice her and stopped fanning long enough to nudge the woman who sat next to her. "Be ready to hightail it out of here. She's a fire starter."

The light from the lantern that hung on the tent hook over Ruby's head caused the sequin cherries on her turban to glisten. Ruby sat cross-legged, Indian style, tapping her toe on the bench. Finally a man dressed in a tie that ended at his sternum motioned for her to quit.

"Eden was meant to be a perfect place," Brother Mabry shouted. A large circle of sweat stained his crimson coat. It spread out so that the discoloration looked as if someone might have shot him in the back. "But man ruined it. Sinful man destroyed it. Well, hear me now. . . . I'm here to help restore it. I'm here to show all of God's people how to find healing of the body and soul. I'm building this retreat so people can see the good God intended and flee from the sin of the mind that pollutes and destroys the body. Hear me now. . . ."

Ruby did hear him. She sat so still that she never even bothered to wipe away the sweat that slid from beneath her turban and snaked down the sides of her face. She didn't even stand when Brother Mabry gave the invitation to come to the front and seek forgiveness. But when the accordion player stopped and Brother Mabry stood back up out of the tall wooden chair that creaked with his weight, Ruby shot up from the bench. Before Gil, the newspaperman, could stop her from walking up the small wooden steps that led to the stage, she was already standing next to Brother Mabry. He reached out his hand like he might touch her, but she darted to the side. She dashed to the front of the platform and through tears screamed, "I'm a sinner!"

Mrs. Pomeroy nudged the woman next to her, and they raised their eyebrows at the same time. "What did I tell you?"

"I've sinned. I've sinned."

When Brother Mabry stepped toward her, she ran to the other side of the platform and looked out into the audience. Her arm was outstretched, pleading with the congregation. She yelled in a voice so mighty that others would later speculate if she was not demon possessed. "I'm with child. I'm carrying Clive Gillespie's baby child."

At first no one said a word, not even Brother Mabry. Murmuring from the front of the tent rolled all the way back to where Clive stood. The benches groaned and popped as people turned around to look at his face, which was growing as red as Brother Mabry's coat. Clive licked his lips and thumped his pencil on his notepad. Rising up on his toes, he chuckled and shook his head.

Before Ruby could be pulled off the stage by an officer, she threw her head back and screamed, "He paid me. He paid me to fornicate with him."

Mrs. Pomeroy fanned and leaned closer until the folds of her hips hung over the side of the bench. Myer Simpson swayed as if she might faint. Her Bible tumbled out of her lap and onto the sawdust-covered ground. Then she jumped up and squinted, wanting to see Clive's reaction.

"She's gone and completely lost her mind," Clive kept repeating about the girl they had all seen lead imaginary parades.

As the officer gripped her forearm and pulled her down the aisle to the back of the tent, he could not stop her from jumping up in the air and kicking Clive sideways. The jolt caused the officer to lose control, and before anyone could move from the last pew to protect Clive, Ruby had knocked him to the ground. She pounded her fists and swung her head, saying words that caused mothers to cover the ears of their children.

Two men jumped over the bench and helped the officer pull Ruby up and drag her out. "My baby ain't a bastard," she screamed until her voice sounded nothing more than a whimper.

Gil, the newspaperman, hovered over Clive and offered his hand. Wiping the blood from his lip, Clive declined. Instead, he balanced himself on his free hand and rose back up. Even though he acted as if nothing out of the ordinary had occurred, there was no denying that his hair had broken free of the wax and flopped over his eyebrows.

As the meeting broke up, people walked out carrying their Bibles and looking at each other with wild-eyed shock.

"They tell me she's one of them fire starters," the woman who sat next to Mrs. Pomeroy reported to the hardware store owner. "She could've killed everybody in here. There's no telling."

A girl wearing a flowered dress made from a feed sack broke away from her mother, who was busy speculating about the revelation with her neighbor by the center tent pole. The girl squatted down and scooped up the cherry-sequined turban that had landed underneath the bench. She brushed off the dirt and sawdust before putting it on her head. Running out of the tent, the girl squealed all the way to the gazebo where the other children played hide-and-seek behind ancient oak trees that had weathered many storms.

21

After Clive publicly denied all charges and was assured that Sheriff Bissell had obtained a judge's order that Ruby be locked up for her own protection, Ruby's father, Earl, sat on the broken step of his house. He intermittently sipped whiskey and looked down at the faded, crumpled picture of his wife that he kept in the back of his pants pocket. Having Ruby taken away to the institution in Chattahoochee was the remaining vow to his wife that he had been unable to keep. He might have been a drunk or a bum in the eyes of the good people of Dead Lakes, but he was a survivor. Growing up the middle child of a brood of eleven in a house built out of mud and pine logs, he had learned early on that if he was going to have enough food to satisfy the hunger pains, then he was going to have to provide the kill. He shot and dressed his first deer at age eleven. As a man, whiskey might have clouded his vision, but his sight was still good enough to hunt when he needed to.

Looking at the stained mattress on the front porch, Earl pictured Clive Gillespie rolling around on it with his daughter. He tossed his head back and drained the last remaining drop from the bottle. Pulling his arm back, he threw the bottle at the mangled and misaligned cinder blocks stacked in his yard. "You might be ignorant, but you're naturally born hardheaded. When you set your mind to it, you can get water from a rock if need be," his mama had said when he brought the first deer he killed home by dragging it through the swamp by the hind legs. Somewhere between determination and disappointment, that boy had died. He thought of Ruby thrashing in a cell wearing a straitjacket and wiped his mouth with his stained shirtsleeve. Most likely she'd be knocked out and given an abortion to hide the evidence. The images that flashed in his mind resurrected the boy inside him. It wasn't a deer or a trout line that he was after this time. It was Clive Gillespie.

Dead Lakes might have been a quaint hamlet tucked in the corner of Franklin County, but there was nothing simple about the inside of the church where Reverend Simpson ministered. A cross made from glazed cypress hung on the wall. The altar glistened in the light of candles that had been arranged on candelabras, a gift left behind to immortalize a deceased benefactor.

As the townspeople filled the church until wooden folding chairs had to be placed at the ends of the pews, everyone wondered where Reverend Simpson had taken off to in his automobile. They clipped the sweet smell of cypress with their fans and patted sweat from their lips with their handkerchiefs.

"He's delayed," Myer Simpson said, sitting in the front row in the lilac-colored dress she had sewn special for the occasion. "He went out to the old salt mine to question the nigras once more. To gather all the facts for the discussion, you know." She tried to smile and fan at the same time. The fact of the matter was that Reverend Simpson had left long before supper. His plate of vegetables and cornbread soaked by the turnip juice that swam on the plate was long past room temperature. Before dressing, Myer had tossed the food out the back door for the stray dogs that wandered through town at night.

The beekeeper and the head elder walked back and forth at the foot of the altar. The beekeeper kept pulling his pocket watch. A murmur, just as strong as the one heard at Brother Mabry's revival, began to rise up to the wood ceiling. The beekeeper motioned for the organist. "Play 'How Great Thou Art' or something." The organist, who wore a hat with a wilted daisy tucked in the side, ignored the request.

The fervor only faded when Ella and Narsissa walked through the doors. Heads craned and a buzz rose when they sat down on two folding chairs at the back of the church. Neva smiled and squeezed Ella's hand. Crickets sang out beyond the open windows, and Myer Simpson fanned faster.

"Well, if there's one good thing to come out of all this, it's the fact that Ella Wallace has been forced back to church," Myer said to the organist.

"And to think she brought the Indian with her too. I wonder if that thing has ever even been to church," the organist whispered.

"We've had a delay," the beekeeper yelled, and the crowd quieted. "Myer assures me it's a momentary delay." The beekeeper thumped the face of his pocket watch.

Myer fanned and tucked her head down until her chin brushed the collar of her new dress. "Slight delay."

"Perhaps we could all sing a hymn. . . ." The beekeeper pointed to the organist again.

"I don't think that's appropriate," the organist said first to Myer and then to the beekeeper. "This isn't a church service, you know."

The beekeeper's face flushed, and he stammered. The roar from a car engine outside momentarily drowned out the chirp of the crickets.

Reverend Simpson came through the side door of the church. His white beard stood out at full attention as if electricity had struck him. He left the door partially open. Bonaparte was standing just outside with his hands on his daughter's shoulders.

The murmur amid the crowd returned, and the sweat stains underneath the arms of Myer Simpson grew wider.

Reverend Simpson stood next to the beekeeper and motioned with his hands for the crowd to hold their tongues. When that didn't work, he brushed against the beekeeper until the man moved to the side. Then he proceeded to have his say. "Ladies and gentlemen. Now I know there is excitement . . . dare I say intrigue involved in our meeting tonight. Some of you have come for pure curiosity, others out of genuine concern."

"Concern for the children," the blacksmith with the puffy black beard yelled out from the middle section of the church.

"Amen," the beekeeper said.

Reverend Simpson once again pushed his hands down in the air, trying to guide the crowd to silence. "Let's not forget that we are in the house of the Lord."

A toddler screamed, and a woman got up from her pew, slipping past the crowd and into the night with the fair-haired child in her arms.

Reverend Simpson's voice grew louder over the feedback from the crowd. "I've been a minister for going on twenty-seven years," he said. "I've never seen emotions run as high as what I've witnessed the past month." Reverend Simpson walked up the steps to the pulpit, where a white flag stitched with a gold sacrament cup hung. He took his place below the flag with a confidence few of those who belonged to the church had seen before.

"In these twenty-seven years, I have made mistakes and learned lessons. And the biggest lesson I've learned is that faith based on fear and emotions is usually a faith that won't hold. Emotions ebb and change with the direction of the sun . . . dare I say, with the voice of popular opinion. But true faith is another matter entirely. I don't have the answers. I don't make such claims."

The crowd buzzed again, but Reverend Simpson's voice grew stronger.

"After all, faith is made up of things hoped for and things not seen. I venture to say that if any man claims to understand all matters of faith, well then he probably never understood faith at all."

"Now hold on," the beekeeper said and rose from his seat.

"I've been troubled," Reverend Simpson said with a rising voice. "Yes, even grieved at how our community has turned propaganda into proof. And yes, I am grieved even more to stand before you and say that I too have been strung along."

"Strung along?" the blacksmith yelled.

"Jesus told His disciples that indeed they would be able to do miraculous works in His name. Did He not? And yet, I wonder, if we were in another time and place, would we even be here tonight? Indeed, if we were in the days directly proceeding Jesus, maybe not. Maybe healings were commonplace." Reverend Simpson shrugged his shoulders and opened his palms. "But now, if we were in the days of the settlers of this country . . ." Reverend Simpson paused, looked down at his wife, and then moved to the opposite end of the altar. "You see, our daughter was prone to convulsions when she was a girl. The fact of the matter was her condition made her a spectacle. She'd fall out in fits at the market or out in the street. Our beautiful child became a spectacle beyond her own control."

Myer Simpson's face grew flush with anger. She fanned faster until the thin handle of the fan split in two. Not even the organist could comfort her.

"The doctor treated her with tonic and said she'd grow out of it. Praise be, she did. But I wonder now . . . especially now. What if we would have been in the age of witch trials and the like? What would have been said about the circumstances that rendered my daughter out of control and left my wife and me with questions and doubt? Would she be the subject of a meeting like the one tonight? Would she have been burned at the stake for simply being different?"

The beekeeper sat down, and Myer Simpson wept into a lace handkerchief meant for show, not tears.

"Do I understand miracles? Have I ever seen one? I don't know. I certainly saw my prayers answered with my daughter. But I do have faith enough to believe that all things are possible, with or without my understanding. And I understand enough to know that accusations of evil, without substance, are repugnant. And I've sinned."

Stunned silence fell over the crowd and then a sharp intake of air from Myer. She cocked her head to the side and dug her fingernails into the seat of the pew.

"I have taken part in such discourse . . . gossip, to be exact. I ask your forgiveness as well as God's."

"What in the world?" the organist whispered when the reverend called Bonaparte and his daughter into the church with the crook of his finger.

The girl took a step into the sanctuary before stopping and looking up at her father. Bonaparte waited until Reverend Simpson smiled before he ushered the child into a domain that up until this night had been forbidden for the people down at the old salt mine. Shocked gasps within the congregation transitioned into agitated grumbling.

"This is not appropriate," the organist said, sliding to the edge of the pew.

"You've gone too far with it now, preacher," the beekeeper said.

"I want them out of here." Mr. Olsen, the head of the school board, yelled. The beige suit vest that he wore bowed out when he stood up.

"It's your free will to leave if you wish." Reverend Simpson raised the volume of his voice until he drowned out the disapproving chants. The minister placed his hands on the same place on the girl's shoulders where Bonaparte's hands had rested.

"The Wallace boy has given us his account," Reverend Simpson said. "He was drowning in his own fluids practically, and this man— this Lanier Stillis, if you haven't taken the time to meet him—this man healed him. The boy didn't hear any words. He just knew he had been healed. But this young lady . . ." Reverend Simpson patted her shoulders. "This young lady heard."

"Heard what?" Mr. Olsen called out.

"She heard words of supplication."

The little girl pulled at the sleeves of her best dress, a thin, faded pink shift. When Reverend Simpson patted her shoulders a second time, she turned and sought confirmation from her father. Bonaparte nodded assurances, and Reverend Simpson called the beekeeper up to the altar. "In case there should be need for a witness," he explained.

"Tell us. Don't be bashful." Reverend Simpson grunted and knelt down. His bended knee brushed against the hem of the girl's best dress. "Tell us what the man said when he bowed over you after you'd been burned."

The woman returned back inside with the towheaded child in her arms. She settled in the back of the church next to a man wearing a lopsided red bow tie. A cough rang out, and people moved to the edge of the benches, trying to at least read the girl's lips that at first whispered.

She pulled at her sleeves and rocked back and forth on her heels. "He says something about his Father." Her sleeves were pulled half-way down over her hands.

The old man who had stood on the box out in front of Ella's home held up the crudely painted sign with the word *Antichrist*. "What did I tell you? He's a-saying he's Jesus." He had his say three times before the blacksmith and church elder grabbed the man by the elbow and escorted him outside.

"Speak up, girl," a man cupping his ear shouted, and the little girl jumped.

Reverend Simpson rubbed the girl's shoulders and looked right into her eyes. "One more time. Strong and courageous."

"In the name . . . ," the girl said. Her hands were now completely hidden under the dress sleeves. "He says in the name of the Father," she said with the conviction of a grown woman. "In the name of the Son and Holy Ghost."

The congregation was at first reverent, as if the girl had said a prayer. Then Mr. Olsen stood up. The crumpled end of his white shirt snaked out from the waist of his pants.

"You mean to tell us that's the best you can do," Mr. Olsen said. "Drag some nigra child up here to make a case for that man."

"That's right," Reverend Simpson said. "Just a child. She has the faith of a child. The same sort of faith we're called to have."

The reverend held up his black, leather-bound Bible and then laid it open across the top of the pulpit. "If you're ever going to listen to me, listen now." He flipped through the pages and pointed twice at the words before him and read. "'And heal the sick that are therein, and say unto them, The kingdom of God is come nigh unto you.'" He held the opened Bible up as proof. "The words of Lord Jesus Christ."

Narsissa brushed her finger across Ella's hands that were clasped together in prayerlike fashion.

Reverend Simpson unfurled a paper from the inside of his jacket pocket. "I don't claim to know the ways of the mountain people. Never had the pleasure of visiting the mountains. It's a way of life that I venture to say is foreign to us. As I'm certain our ways are equally foreign to them. After all . . . who would eat mullet and call the trash fish delicious."

A few laughs rolled out from the audience, and Bonaparte's shoulders relaxed a bit.

"This man, this Mr. Stillis, he holds true to the traditions of his people," Reverend Simpson said. "Traditions that I don't believe I'll ever completely understand. But let it be said that I don't understand the power of the living God, either. The God who says His ways are not our ways."

Reverend Simpson popped the paper in the air and then smoothed it out against his chest. "After telling me that he felt convicted, Mr. Stillis wrote down the words he uses when he heals. When I read the verses, they caught my eye." Reverend Simpson held the paper up in front of him and cleared his throat. "'And when I passed by thee,'" he read, "'and saw thee polluted in thine own blood, I said unto thee when thou wast in thy blood, Live; yea, I said unto thee when thou wast in thy blood, Live.'"

Ella wiped away a tear but kept her eyes on Bonaparte.

"Sixth verse, sixteenth chapter of Ezekiel. Praise be the Word of the Lord," Reverend Simpson said the way he did every Sunday after Scripture readings. He held up the paper before handing it to the beekeeper for further inspection.

"Praise be to God," Ella whispered.

22

After the last pole from Brother Mabry's tent had been taken down and stored and the last hymnal in Reverend Simpson's church returned to its place in the back of the pew, the sun rose over Ella Wallace's property the same way it always had.

Ella sprung out of her bed, holding on to the dream that seemed so real she half expected to see waves from the Gulf of Mexico cresting outside her window. Peering through the open curtain, she noticed the blue and pink colors that swirled together above the oaks around the store. When she stuck her head out the window, she was stung by the heavy heat of just another summer day. Across the road Mr. Pomeroy was opening the pineapple front gate of his yard, about to go around back of his house like he did every morning and pick what vegetables remained. Everything was the same, Ella told herself and pulled her head back inside. She dressed and repeated the reassurance, but nothing in her being would let her accept the words. Nothing would ever be the same again.

The crowds had dissipated. Many had made their way to the county line, to Martin Kessler's farm, where a calf had been born next to a dried-up well. Three black crosses perfectly blazed on the calf's side. Martin declared it the sign of the Trinity. His wife claimed that the cross-shaped markings had only appeared after the calf came back to life after being born dead. Even the old man who had stood on a milk crate at the entrance to Ella's property and held the sign that read *Antichrist* had left. Now they all stood behind the new fence that Martin had painted white and offered to pay good money just to touch the side of the calf.

When Ella stepped outside, she noticed Narsissa sweeping off the stoop of the store the same way she did upon waking every morning. Dust swirled up around Narsissa until she looked like an apparition that might disappear without warning. Pausing, Ella took a step toward the store but then stopped. Fearing that she would be called a fool, Ella decided not to share her dream with Narsissa.

Walking through the obstacle course of tree stumps, those that had gained profit and those that had been destroyed out of greed, Ella let the feeling of melancholy blanket her. She was having a difficult time remembering just how thick the trees on her property had once been. Maybe it was best to forget.

When she got to the edge of the ravine that led to the coveted spring, she noticed Lanier standing by the spring, looking down into the waters the way he might if he could look into his future. It was only when she stepped on a limb and it snapped in two that he looked up. "Morning," he said.

"You're up early," Ella said. "I didn't expect to find you down here."

"That barn was starting to feel like a prison. Besides, you know how us serpents like the Garden of Eden."

Ella laughed. "So you came down here to tempt me?"

Lanier laughed and pulled at his injured ear. When his neck turned red, Ella stammered. "What I meant was . . ."

"So what's next?" Lanier's smile never wavered.

"For once I'd like to wake up and not have to think about that question."

"Then I expect that's when we'd put you in a pine box. I'm learning life is nothing more than a bunch of 'what's nexts.'"

Ella held on to the way he said *we*. "How did you rest last night?" She asked not out of social grace but in desperation to change the course of the conversation.

"Better," he said, hitting his ear, trying to knock water out. "You?"

"Wonderful," Ella repeated twice. She pulled at the ends of a red-berry vine, careful not to touch the thorny places. Smiling, she started to speak but then shook her head.

"What is it?"

"Nothing," she said and shook her head faster.

"You can't do me like that. What is it?" This time Lanier laughed right along with her. The sound echoed across the swamp and was entangled with the sound of locusts roaring.

"I had the most vivid dream." She looked up at the sunlight, holding the blaze until it was too much and she had to close her eyes. In her mind's eye she could still see the images that had washed over her last night. The time when Macon was still a toddler and Harlan was still the man she hoped he could be—a sober man who had not yet been blemished by the opium. They had taken the ferry to St. George Island for an Easter afternoon. Emerald waves crashed on the white sand beach while the children tromped through the sand searching for hidden Easter eggs. Ella could still feel the taut muscles of Harlan's arm as she reclined against him on the blanket. Soft breezes swept through the tops of the trees that lined the shore, and the squeals from her sons, still playful and young, tickled her ears. She held that memory and was grateful for the chance to relive it if only in her sleep. It was too valuable to give away.

"Nothing, nothing." Ella fluttered her hands like she might be a bird ready to take flight. "I just woke up thinking about St. George Island, just across the bay. There was a time when people were talking about it becoming something big. A resort, you might as well say. A man by the name of Saxon was going to build a club and lease lots on the beach."

Lanier bent down and scooped up a handful of springwater. He held up the water and let it cascade over his head and down the front of his shirt. Ella turned away from him and watched as a lizard ran round and round up a small oak tree.

"It all sounded so wonderful . . . so magical . . . this resort Mr. Saxon talked of. He wouldn't sell the land. He wouldn't hear of it. He would only lease the lots on the island. I wanted one of those lots. Oh, I wanted one like nobody's business." Ella laughed, and the lizard seemingly disappeared. "I had notions of having a cottage over there like something I'd seen in *Harper's Magazine*. I'd paint day in and day out while my boys swam and fished and got tanned as pecans."

"Sounds nice."

When Ella turned back to face Lanier, water was dripping from the ends of his hair, and his face seemed to glisten. "It was one of those air castles. Harlan couldn't come up with the $250 lease, and Mr. Saxon wasn't interested in handing out credit. At least not to Harlan. But the whole idea, the whole concept, always intrigued me. I'd never heard of people leasing land like that before . . . not the way Mr. Saxon had in mind. You'd have it the same as if it was yours, but it would be leased for ninety-nine years. He would always be the outright owner."

Lanier planted his hands deeper inside his pockets, and the wet material on his chest spread out wide. A patch of black hair from his chest rose up out of the shirt. "Those eyes of yours are narrowing."

Ella moved closer to the spring and looked down at the water, wondering if it really was magic after all. "What?"

"Those blue eyes are getting narrower and narrower. I noticed that's how you look when you work your way around a problem."

Ella deliberately widened her eyes. "Now if you'd listen, you'd understand what I'm trying to tell you. I think I might have found a way to beat Clive Gillespie at his own game."

Lanier's eyes were the ones now narrowed. He tilted his chin back and studied her.

She stepped closer to him, and the branches of a palmetto bush scraped the backs of her legs. "That ninety-nine-year lease idea . . . If Clive is going to fight me in court, I might as well make a little money off the land while I can. I won't be giving it up. It'll still be mine. Clive Gillespie knows I'm not worldly, but he doesn't know that I'm wise."

"Oh, I know you are. Wise as a serpent." Lanier chuckled and sat down on the bank of the spring. A sliver of sunlight fell upon him, making his hair seem blonder, more youthful than before. "You're gonna have that preacher and banker clawing at each other like two trapped rats with one piece of cheese between them."

"I think I'll pay Brother Mabry a visit."

"I'll drive you."

Ella held up her hand. "Not today."

Together they sat on the bank of the spring, side by side, and never even bothered to consider what anyone passing by might think. They watched the water bubble and rise to the surface and scripted a future out of reach of their past. Without ever signing a contract, they outlined a partnership that would never really let him walk away.

After Samuel took Keaton and Macon down to the river to fish like they used to do on carefree days before the note came due, Ella dressed in her Sunday best. Out behind the barn, away from where anyone could see, she tried three times to get the bit in the mule's mouth before she slapped him on the side of the head. "Now, straighten up," she yelled. The mule opened his mouth and snorted a stream of mucus that covered Ella's sleeve. Not bothering to change clothes, she hitched the wagon and popped the reins as hard as she could. When she passed by the parsonage, Ella gripped tighter and kept her eyes on the cows that crossed the road ahead of her.

Myer Simpson was sweeping off her porch stoop when Ella passed. Myer stopped her chore long enough to shade her eyes with her twisted, arthritic fingers. "After everything that's happened, I'd think your man friend could at least drive you to town," Myer said. Her voice trailed behind the wagon. "Ella, I'm worried about you. Where are you going?"

Ella popped the reins, the bridle jingled, and the mule trotted faster. Neither Ella nor the animal looked away from the road before them.

By the time Ella made it to the city limits of Apalachicola, the town had come to life. A line of elementary-age schoolgirls, dressed in their uniforms of matching navy dresses, walked out of Miss Wayne's school and down the sidewalk to the library. A black dog with white paws trotted across the street and in front of Gillespie Savings and Loan. The bank clerk with red hair and a ruddy complexion paused to look at Ella before turning away as if he had never known her.

Tying the wagon to the hitching post at the corner of the Franklin Inn, Ella straightened the best hat that she could find in her closet and dabbed perspiration from her lip. Inhaling as deep as she could manage, she walked inside the mahogany-paneled lobby and placed her arm on the reception desk.

A woman with a crooked nose and tiny slits for eyes greeted her. "Mrs. Wallace."

Ella blinked and tried not to show her surprise that the woman should know her name.

"Good morning," Ella said with all the confidence she could manage. "I need to get a message to Brother Mabry."

"Brother Mabry?" The woman dropped her chin and her eyes looked bigger. A breeze came in through the open door of the inn, and the pages of the newspaper on the counter ruffled.

"He's your guest, isn't he? I'd like to speak with him, please."

"Do you have an appointment? I mean, Mrs. Mercile, our manager, has been taking care of them personally."

"He'll want to see me. Take my word for it," Ella said, trying to hide her dress sleeve soiled with mule mucus underneath the counter.

That evening Clive Gillespie stood on his front porch, leaning against one of the stone pillars that was shaped like a pyramid. He bit the end of a cigar, spat the tip at a rose bed below the porch, and stared off toward the bay. He watched as the string of lights on the bow of a steamboat grew stronger as the boat made its way to port. The sound of the boat's whistle momentarily interrupted the symphony of the crickets, locusts, and bullfrogs that filled the night air. Reaching down to the porch rail, Clive picked up the crystal tumbler he had filled and finished it off in one sip.

The water near the dock bathed in the blue light of the moon. The oyster cannery building at the corner of the dock blocked Clive's view of the passengers who were disembarking from their journey. He could hear the sound of the colored men who unloaded the cargo and called out the names of the passengers whose bags were being tossed to the deck for retrieval. He heard the name Troxler but paid about as much attention to it as he did the name Smith.

The Troxler brothers and their hired man had taken the train as far as they could and then picked up the steamboat to Apalachicola. J.D. Troxler was never one for boat travel and arrived in ill humor.

Clive kept his watch on the dock, seemingly hypnotized by the people who moved along the dock as shadows. Clive struck a match against one of the stones on his porch and cupped his hand to light the cigar. He studied the cigar like he might a lover. He was too preoccupied in his visions of tourists flocking to the spring that would soon be his to glance across the street at the park where children had played earlier that day. If he had, he might have seen Ruby's father, Earl, crouching behind an oak tree or the barrel of the rifle he held that was aimed straight at the cigar Clive held close to his chest.

The sound of heavy breathing caused Clive to look up. Brother Mabry, dressed in sweat-drenched linen pants that bunched in thick folds around his thighs, paused at the corner to catch his breath. "Gillespie," he yelled with one big exhale.

Tossing the cigar to the rose garden below the porch, Clive slicked down his hair with his hand. "Brother Mabry. What a pleasant surprise. What has you out this time of night?"

Brother Mabry grunted as he pulled himself up one step and then another by gripping the porch rail. His face was reddened with anger as much as from physical strain.

Clive slicked down his hair one more time and reached out to help Brother Mabry.

"Get inside the house," Brother Mabry shouted like he might to a misbehaving child. "It's time for an altar call."

23

Before the rooster crowed, Clive Gillespie was up with a pistol strapped in a holster inside his suit jacket. He walked down the sidewalk toward the bank as if it were an ordinary day. Clive passed the tavern with an illustration of a beer mug on the window and tapped on the glass. The owner, a hawkish-nosed man whose property Clive had just threatened to foreclose on, looked up in time to see Clive offer a tip of his hat and a raised eyebrow. People on the street watched Clive glide downtown with a peacock strut that caused them to wonder how a man who had been humiliated by a simpleton like Ruby Tucker could still be so arrogant. They could never possibly realize that this morning it was anger, not self-importance, that put him in motion.

At the corner near the courthouse, Clive made a sharp left in the opposite direction of the bank. When he reached the entrance of the Franklin Inn, he brushed against the shoulders of the Troxler brothers and their hired man who had just paid their overnight bill and were setting about their business. "Mind your step," J.D. Troxler said with a toothpick stuck in the corner of his mouth. Never pausing to render an apology, Clive marched forward past the reception desk and into the restaurant that was off to the side. Two potted ferns on marbled columns marked its entrance.

In the restaurant the morning sun streamed in through lace curtains and fanned out across the bamboo floor. Clanking silverware rang out along with a chorus of conversation among the regulars. Mayor Cox and the new owner of the oyster cannery hunched over cups of steaming coffee. The cannery operator, a young man with a wayward shirt collar that poked straight out from his neck, occasionally turned to look back at the café entrance. At the table next to him, a steamboat captain sipped coffee with a slurping sound and read yesterday's newspaper.

Across the room in the corner nearest the swinging kitchen door, Sheriff Bissell sat with his back to the room. A napkin stained with coffee was tucked inside his shirt collar. He was mixing scrambled eggs in the ketchup he had just poured onto his plate.

Just as the sheriff was sticking the fork into his mouth, Clive came up from behind and slapped him on the back with a thrust that was less than friendly. "Morning, Sheriff," Clive said.

Sheriff Bissell groaned, flinched, and turned to look at Clive with an angry scowl. He took the edge of his napkin and dabbed his mouth. Drops of blood were next to the coffee stain on the napkin. "You just caused me to jab my mouth with that fork."

Clive tossed his hat onto an empty seat before taking his place directly next to the sheriff. "You're just lucky I didn't come over to your house last night and jab you with a pitchfork."

"Got up on the wrong side of the bed, did we?"

Clive planted his hands on the table, knocking over a red and green porcelain cup that was filled with sugar. "Last night I had a little visitor, or should I say a gigantic visitor. Brother Mabry showed up at my front door, ranting and carrying on."

"Was he drunk?"

"Drunk with rage. And I must say that it's catching."

Sheriff Bissell dabbed at his mouth, looked at the bloody spot on the napkin, and then raised an eyebrow. "Now, look, Clive. I can't see how any of this involves—"

"Charlie Bissell, I want you to hear what I'm saying and hear me good." Leaning closer to the plate, where a slice of bacon puddled in grease, Clive spat as he spoke. "I've been patient with you. I've trusted you. I've included you. And what do I have to show for it? Uh? That man is still on Ella's place, and now he's putting all sorts of foolish ideas in her head."

Sheriff Bissell raised his hand, trying to get the waiter's attention. "You need a cup of coffee."

Clive gripped the sheriff's hand and placed it down on the table. "Coffee makes me nervous."

"Go on and give me your gripe. What you got for me today?"

"It seems that Ella has got it in her head that she can lease the land to Brother Mabry . . . lease it without selling it. She'll even let him put his little retreat on the land right next to the spring."

"Oh," Sheriff Bissell said.

"*Oh* is right. *Oh,* and I'll be out of the deal altogether. *Oh,* and you'll be back to working security on the steamboat, looking for children who are hiding underneath roulette tables and cleaning up after drunks who can't handle their liquor." Clive licked the corner of his mouth and waved across the room to the steamboat captain. A waiter refreshed a pot of coffee at a busing station where decanters of honey sat.

"Now, I've had it with you, Charlie Bissell. I told that nutty preacher I'd see to it that he owned that land outright—told him he didn't want to fool around with the whims of a woman who changes her mind from one day to the next. But he's about to go along with what she's offering."

"This whole mess has got way out of hand," the sheriff said, balling the napkin up and tossing it in the pool of grease on the plate.

"It only got out of hand when that hobo showed up at Ella's. I told you," Clive hissed. "I told you he'd be trouble, but you continued to look the other way."

"Now, may I say this," the sheriff said while leaning back in his chair. "I might owe you a great deal, but . . ."

Pulling at his brass-plated suspenders, Mayor Cox made his way around the room, greeting the diners. He glanced at Clive, who was still hunched over Sheriff Bissell's plate, and simply nodded.

"Now look, Clive . . ." Sheriff Bissell used his finger to drag the napkin around and around the plate. The napkin grew heavier and darker with the grease that it collected.

"No, you look. You look me directly in the eye and tell me that you don't owe me your job. If you know what's good for you, you won't forget it."

The sheriff raised his right hand as if being sworn into office. "Fair enough. But I owe the law something too."

Clive smiled, chuckled, and then laughed so loud that the waiter across the room stopped wrapping napkins around silverware and stared.

"I don't see nothing funny about that," Sheriff Bissell said.

After finally regaining control, Clive wiped away tears of laughter.

"I just can't go around putting people in jail, you know."

Clive flicked his front two teeth with his tongue. "Tell me something. How long has this man been at Ella's?"

Sheriff Bissell rubbed his neck, tilting his head from side to side. Pepper on his plate scattered when he sighed.

"Now, need I remind you that we have an agreement." Clive picked a piece of lint from the shoulder of his jacket and then tossed it in the air. "You help us secure that land, and you'll get your cut when the deal comes through. But right now, the deal is out of our control. And I don't do well with losing control."

"Clive," Sheriff Bissell said, staring at the lint that shifted and floated in the air. "Don't you think there comes a time to move on?"

"Give up, you mean? That's what you're really saying."

The sheriff raised his shoulders and twisted the side of his mouth. "I'm just saying . . ."

"And I'm just saying that you don't want to buck me. Not now. If I go down with this thing, bless pete, you go down with me. Why, I declare. I bet you couldn't even get a job working back on that steamboat with a charge of bribery slapped on you."

The sheriff shrugged once more and tapped his boot at the spot where the lint landed next to his chair.

"Let me tell you one thing, Charlie Bissell. You might not care about this town, but I do. This place used to be something, and now look. . . ." Clive motioned with his hand toward the window. The curtain moved against a breeze. A lot where a warehouse had sat twenty years ago was a weedy cavity in the mouth of the city. "Tell me. Do you think I enjoy these foreclosures? Do you?"

Sheriff Bissell was gripping the ends of the table, staring at the plate. "I don't think much about it, to tell the truth."

"With this preacher, we have the chance to put Apalachicola back on the map. And what about our plan to bottle that springwater, hmm? Ship it around the world. From here to kingdom come. It's your chance to make some real money for a change." Clive leaned down closer. The end of his tie lay across the table. "So if you have to take that hobo and jail him for suspicion of jaywalking, you do it. And you do it today."

The waiter appeared and tentatively motioned toward Sheriff Bissell's plate. "Go ahead, he's done," Clive said. "We were just leaving."

Upstairs, above the restaurant, Mrs. Mercile, dressed all in white, brought the morning tea and coffee on the same tray she had used every day since Brother Mabry and his wife, Priscilla, had occupied the room on the top floor. The white uniform was only a recent request from Priscilla. It reminded her of back home, where servants knew their place.

Once the tray was set on the table Mrs. Mercile eased into the bathroom, carrying the teacup. She walked on the black-and-white tiled floor on her tiptoes, so as not to disrupt the guest. A roll of fat gathered above the belt of her freshly pressed uniform.

Priscilla's bony frame was silhouetted behind shower curtains that turned the porcelain tub into an island all to itself. Without saying a word, she reached her bony hand through the gap in the curtains. Mrs. Mercile turned and looked away as always instructed. Priscilla sipped the tea and sloshed in the water that was meant to give her healing. "This tea is lackluster warm," she protested.

"Is it?" Mrs. Mercile rolled her eyes. "Do you want me to run down and get you another?"

"By now I'd think you'd know my stomach becomes ornery if I don't have my morning tea."

When Mrs. Mercile walked back through the room, she almost curtseyed in front of Brother Mabry, whose hair was still wet and perfectly parted on the side. The look made him resemble a fresh-faced schoolboy on picture day.

"Shall I send this week's bill to Mr. Gillespie again?"

Brother Mabry rubbed his eyes. "I never heard of a place charging by the week like you do." He looked out through the white curtains and onto the street below.

"I just can't afford to keep groceries in the house with the amount you . . . Will you be staying on with us much longer?"

Below, Clive Gillespie and Sheriff Bissell got in the sheriff's automobile with the official seal of the county painted on the door. Sticking his head out of the window, Brother Mabry yelled,

"Gillespie. Gillespie . . . I've made up my mind. I want a word with you."

"Must you be so vivacious this early in the day?" Priscilla called out from the bathroom.

Brushing against Mrs. Mercile and causing the tray to wobble, Brother Mabry stomped down the burgundy-carpeted stairs two at a time. In the lobby a woman wearing a sleeveless dress meant for someone far younger than her years trailed behind him. "Brother Mabry, Brother Mabry. I couldn't make it to the last service, but I heard . . ."

Out on the porch, Brother Mabry shoved through a group of men wearing matching pin-striped hats. "And he calls himself a man of the Word," one of the men said when an apology was not rendered.

Earl came from around the corner where he'd been waiting for Gillespie. When the sheriff started the car, Earl purposely walked toward the old automobile that belonged to one of the men Brother Mabry had offended. After the men shook their heads and mumbled, they went on about their business in the inn's café. None of them paid any mind to the preacher or the deadbeat drunk who slipped inside the automobile and cranked the engine.

In the street, Brother Mabry spread his legs wide and once again shouted, "Gillespie, I want a word with you."

Earl wove the automobile around Brother Mabry. Once he'd cleared the obstacle that stood in the middle of the road, he followed the path of the lawman's car.

Everyone on the sidewalk paused to look at Brother Mabry, who stomped and shouted, but no one responded. The sheriff's automobile had already turned the corner at Main Street.

Down the street, past the park, and next to the shipping dock, Deputy Ronnie carried a thermos of coffee and whistled as he approached the station. The smell of sea salt and rotting fish laced the air.

Ronnie jingled his keys and dropped them when he saw the sheriff from Bainbridge standing outside the door. The man was standing next to a street post where a faint smoke from the steamboats hovered. "Morning," the sheriff said with a serious nod.

"Morning. Can I help you with something?"

The sheriff looked around and paused to notice a group of colored boys who laughed and frolicked on their way to the unloading dock. He reached out to shake Ronnie's hand and ended up gripping the thermos. "Sheriff Loring from Bainbridge, Georgia. Is your sheriff on the premises?"

"No, sir. He's at breakfast, I imagine."

"Well, I need to talk with somebody with some authority," Sheriff Loring said and scratched his ear.

"All right," Ronnie said while shifting his weight.

"I'm afraid there's fixing to be some trouble. And somebody's liable to wind up dead before it's through with."

In Ella's kitchen, the morning heat began to stir through the open windows, and the smell of fried ham still clung to the clothes of all who sat at her table.

"I'm going to work on the garden some today," Narsissa said.

Lanier looked at Samuel, who sat at the table across from him, and then reached for one of the last biscuits on a plate painted with seashells.

"The store needs restocking," Ella said and sipped coffee. "Samuel, can you help with that?"

If he heard his mother, Samuel never indicated. He put the last bit of ham into his mouth and then scooped out another serving of grits from the bowl.

"We need to order school supplies too," Keaton said.

"When's school?" Macon wondered.

"Next week." Ella pointed with her fork to Macon's plate. "Now eat all your ham. You'll be hungry before noon."

"I don't want to go back to school," Macon said and picked at the ham.

"You sure wanted to go when you were laid up in bed sick," Samuel said and then glanced up at Lanier.

"I don't know about y'all, but I'm going to have to get another slice of that bacon," Lanier said. "I mean, unless anyone has any objections to that."

Narsissa, never bothering to put down the biscuit she was eating, motioned with her elbow toward the platter of bacon next to the pitcher of milk.

When he stood up and turned, Lanier looked out through the kitchen windows. He half stood over the table, his hand frozen above the plate of bacon.

Outside, in front of the azalea bushes, J.D. Troxler climbed out of the back of the old Ford Model T pickup that he had paid Mrs. Mercile, the inn manager, five dollars to borrow. He placed the black derby hat cock-ways on his head, and his brother Parker spat a stream of tobacco out of his mouth and onto the side of the truck's passenger door. Jack-Ray stood up in the flat-board bed and never lost his hat from his head as he leaped to the ground.

Lanier moved so fast that he knocked over the kitchen chair. He whirled around the kitchen door and into the dining room, where he leaned against the wall closest to the windows.

"Lanier?" Ella said. She was the first to stand, followed by Samuel and Narsissa.

"They're out there."

"Who?" Ella asked, playing with the collar of her shirt.

"The Troxlers."

Only Ella knew the significance of that name. Narsissa stared up at Ella, who bit her lip and shook her head.

The oxen mooed outside, and the sound of automobile doors slamming rolled inside the house.

"Who?" Samuel asked.

"Where's the key?" Lanier said, pulling at the locked gun cabinet in the dining room with the panicked look of a trapped animal. "We got to get to the guns."

"Now listen," Ella said. She took a step forward. "First let me try to talk—"

Lanier turned and looked at her with a ferociousness she had not seen from him. "Get back!"

Samuel tore into the dining room. "Hey—nobody speaks to my mama like that."

Lanier gripped the boy by the neck until his veins popped out and his face contorted in pain. Ella gasped, and Narsissa reached for the butcher knife that was still on the kitchen counter. Leading Samuel into the hallway like a captured bull, Lanier spat the words in Samuel's ear. "Now you want me to kill you or do you want them to do it? Because one way or another you're fixing to die unless I get the guns."

"Keaton, go get the key," Ella said, moving to block Samuel from Lanier. "It's in the good teapot."

Keaton ran into the dining room and used the turned-over kitchen chair to climb up to the top of the dining room cabinet. He fished a key from inside a fragile iris-blue teapot.

Ella looked at Narsissa. The pulse in the side of Ella's neck was evident when she stroked her fingers across the fish-scale necklace. Keaton ran into the hallway and fumbled with the key before Lanier snatched it from him. He unlocked the gun cabinet and pulled wads of gun shells from the drawers. Lanier nodded at Keaton. "Start handing out the guns. Hurry it up!" Lanier tossed shells to each one, including Narsissa.

"Lanier . . . Lanier," Ella kept saying. "You're scaring me."

He stopped to look at Ella before throwing the shells in her direction. She let go of the necklace, missed catching the first shell, and then scrambled on the floor to recover it. Lanier's eyes were electric green, and the steadiness she had relied on was now replaced with fear. "Well, you should be scared."

Ella pushed Macon toward the back bedroom. "Run, get under my bed. Don't you move until I call for you. Do you hear me?" Macon stared up at her. His eyes were glazed and wide. Ella grabbed his shoulders, shook him. "Get."

"Hello!" J.D. yelled twice before circling the truck and shading his eyes with his hand and staring off toward the barn. He called Lanier's name the way he might call the name of a missing hound during a hunting trip. No one in the front part of the house moved. The only sounds were the footsteps of Macon as he ran down the hall.

"Lanier," Troxler yelled. "Is there a Lanier Stillis on the place?"

Samuel pumped the shotgun. A breeze came in through the open living room windows, and the yellow curtains playfully danced about. Everyone stared at Lanier. And Ella could no longer ignore the way that his lower lip was quivering. Lanier motioned for them to line the wall in the foyer. From where Ella stood she could make out the truck that was parked sideways. The left front corner of the truck was pressed into the bushes in such a way that it looked like branches of the shrub were growing about the headlight.

Out in the yard, Parker Troxler leaned against the side of the car and pulled two pistols from his jacket. Jack-Ray reached down inside the back of the truck and rested his hand on the rifle that sat on the floor of the bed. J.D. made his way up the porch steps with his hands tucked inside his jacket, massaging the silver handles engraved with his father's name.

"Hello, Wallace family," J.D. said as he made his way onto the porch. He knocked on the door, and Ella caught her breath. "I can smell the bacon and ham a mile away," he said and began a slow back and forth on the porch. J.D.'s bootsteps echoed inside the house. Ella watched the silver tips of them glisten in the sun. She heard the creak of the porch swing when he pushed it with his boot. She caught the restrained eagerness in his voice. "Lanier Stillis." J.D. bent down and looked through the window at the end of the living room, closest to the fireplace mantel. The curtain fanned back and forth across his face.

Just when Ella thought he would crawl inside, she looked past him and saw Sheriff Bissell's automobile pull up her driveway.

"Thank the Lord," she said, moving toward the door.

Samuel tried to pull her away. "What are you doing?" he hissed in a whisper.

"Sheriff Bissell is here. It'll be fine. The sheriff will take care of this."

Samuel blocked her path and stood at the foyer entrance with his legs spread far apart. "You are not leaving this house."

Lanier turned and pointed the shotgun right into Samuel's chest.

"Watch yourself," Narsissa said, holding a pistol aimed at the base of Lanier's skull.

Lanier never moved the gun away from Samuel. "Ella, go on out there."

Ella looked at Samuel. The Adam's apple twitched in his neck, and his eyes darted back toward the hallway to where she could find safety.

"Don't you do it, Ella," Narsissa said. "You're liable to get shot." Her aim never left Lanier.

"If you're ever going to trust me, now is the time," Lanier said in a deep, monotone voice. "If you don't go out there, we'll all be shot."

When Ella walked out onto the porch carrying the shotgun that shook in her grasp, the Troxler brothers and Jack-Ray looked at each other and grinned.

"No cause for that, ma'am," J.D. said, pointing at Ella's shotgun and taking off his hat all at the same time.

Ella stepped forward, and J.D. moved backward, one step at a time. The roar of Sheriff Bissell's car coming up the drive caused him to turn and partly stumble down the last two steps.

"You're trespassing. We have . . . we have a sign out front." Ella gripped the gun tighter and motioned with the barrel toward the sheriff's automobile.

J.D. nodded. "I'm J.D. Troxler. I believe my former brother-in-law, Lanier Stillis, is hiding on your—"

"Sheriff Bissell," Ella shouted over and over as the sheriff and Clive climbed out of his car.

The sheriff never bothered to put his hat on. He pulled at the crotch of his pants and looked at the men with the same suspicion as Ella did. "What's all this?"

"This man was poking his head in through my living room window. I keep telling him that he's trespassing, but he won't listen."

Sheriff Bissell motioned toward Ella but never looked away from J.D. "Now put that gun down before you hurt somebody."

J.D. extended his hand and smiled. "Sheriff, I'm J.D. Troxler from Bainbridge, Georgia. I'm afraid there's a fugitive on the premises here. I came looking for the man who owns the place."

"I figure she's looking for him too," Sheriff Bissell said, using his thumb to point at Ella. "This is the Wallace place. Who's this fugitive you're talking about?"

"Lanier Stillis," J.D. said. He withdrew his empty hand from the inside of his jacket. "About six feet or six-one. Blond headed."

"Hair as long as a woman's," Parker, the other brother, called out.

Sheriff Bissell looked up at Ella, and Clive Gillespie made his way behind the sheriff.

"Well, I do know," Clive murmured.

"What you want with him?" Sheriff Bissell asked.

"Murder," J.D. said.

"Well, now," Clive said before turning toward Ella. "Murder. That's a mighty big charge."

"Ella, where's the man? In the barn?" Sheriff Bissell asked.

All of the men were looking up at Ella, who still held the gun clutched to her chest. "There's no need to know where he is."

Parker spat a stream of tobacco at the tire of the truck. "Ole Lanier always could catch the eye of the ladies." Jack-Ray moved toward the barn, but none of them seemed to notice.

"I can tell from the looks of it he found another one to swindle. Just like he did my sister," J.D. said.

"There's no swindling," Ella said and held the gun higher. "He's worked here."

"Oh, so he *is* here," J.D. said.

"Ella," the sheriff said. "Either you put that gun down, or I'll come up there and take it from you."

She slowly lowered the shotgun and propped it, barrel up, against the side of the door.

"There you go," the sheriff said. He looked back at J.D. and squinted. "Fella, I think you need to fill us in on exactly what brings you here with these big accusations."

J.D. Troxler stepped forward and placed his hat in open palms like an offering. "First, I want to say to the lady that I completely understand her confusion right about now. I am sure she had no idea what she was getting into. Neither did my sister."

Ella eased to the center of the faded circle that Macon had drawn with chalk.

"Now, Lanier Stillis, the man you've been keeping, he was once my brother-in-law, sad to say. . . . He killed my wife and my sister."

Parker massaged the pistols in his coat pockets and chewed on a wad of tobacco. He seemed more concerned about running his finger inside his mouth to loosen stray bits of tobacco than he was with hearing J.D.'s story.

Ella forced herself to stand up straight. "I know about your wife and your sister. I know all that."

"I bet you do," J.D. said. "I bet he painted a vivid picture." J.D.

rotated the hat in his left palm and used his other hand to circle over it the same way he might if he'd been holding a crystal ball. When J.D. stepped forward closer to the porch rail, Parker and Jack-Ray spread out across the yard. "My wife . . ." J.D. looked up at the white clouds that hung so low they looked like they might touch the ground. "My wife, Camilla, had a gift. The gift of caregiving. When she saw my sister hurting the way she was, she took to her like any caregiver naturally would. But Lanier . . . well, Lanier tried to make something perverse out of it. By then he'd already found himself a sweet little thing, and he wanted to get rid of my sister."

Ella ran the tips of her fingers up and down the side seam of her dress. Then she reached over and caressed the rusted tip of the gun barrel.

"An adulterer and a murderer, you say?" Clive asked with his head bowed in reverence.

"Lanier controlled my sister . . . built her up with his words and then tore her down after their boy died. I never could figure it. He took my sister, who was always a spirited young woman, and turned her into a limp washcloth who couldn't get out of bed. Some who worked around the house claimed he doped her up with potions he made. Some claimed he was evil. Some claimed—"

"Some claimed your wife was in love with your sister," Ella said.

The sheriff pulled at the seat of his britches. "Now, Ella. That's not talk fitting a lady."

J.D. raised the hat toward Sheriff Bissell. "No, no. That's quite all right. That's what you were told, I bet. He went around telling anyone who'd listen. He wanted it that way. It would make for a more convincing story when he killed them and took the money my sister had inherited. You take that plus the life insurance, and, well . . . that whittler from the mountains who could barely read and write when I first met him was sitting pretty."

Clive clasped his hands like he might be praying and squinted up at Ella. "Open your eyes. The man is a con artist. A criminal, no doubt."

J.D. Troxler pulled a set of yellowed, crisp documents from the inside of his coat. "And do you want to know where he learned how to whittle?"

"The mountains are full of those who do such," Ella said, wondering if what she said with such authority was true.

"And so are insane asylums." J.D. Troxler opened up the papers as if Ella could make out the letters from where she stood up on the porch. "All this talk about crazy . . . did it ever come to mind that he painted such a good picture of my wife being crazy because he learned it firsthand? In the sanatoriums they learn from each other. One crazy man becomes a case study for another. They even teach the crazies how to weave baskets. They call it therapy. Lanier didn't take to the baskets. He learned how to whittle with a dull spoon that one of the nurses who took to his looks gave him."

Parker Troxler snickered. "How come you think he got his ear cut off? He read about some artist doing it in one of his books and got it in his mind that he'd try it too." Parker twisted his mouth until the plug of tobacco visibly pressed against the side of his cheek, and then he spat it out. "I'd hate for him to get in one of his spells and cut your ear off that way."

Ella glanced at the front door and picked at a loose thread on the sleeve of her dress.

J.D. put the papers back inside his coat and toyed with the gun that was protruding from underneath his jacket. "You take a mighty fine picture, by the way."

"You see now why I had the sheriff come out here?" Clive said. "Now do you see, Ella? We're concerned for your welfare."

Ella could only see spots of color, like the kaleidoscope that her aunt used to let her look through on Sunday afternoons. She gripped the back of the porch chair, looked out toward the barn and then down at the shotgun that rested next to the front door.

The sheriff held up his hands like he might be preaching. "Now, Ella, you're not in trouble. We just need to talk to the drifter."

Jack-Ray eased down the side of the barn and behind the patch of sunflowers. He pulled from his pants waist a long-barreled pistol with the letter *J* engraved on the handle.

"Listen to us, Ella," Clive said. He walked up the stairs. His words were as soft as his steps. "I want to help you. I really do. Now a schoolgirl crush is one thing, but harboring a fugitive is quite another. Listen to this man. He knows what he's talking about. His sister and his wife were killed by this man friend of yours. You don't want to be the next victim here. Now if I didn't truly care about you, I'd—"

The popping sound was shrill and the flash crisp. The noise came from the side of the pasture where Earl sat on a tree stump, steadily holding his hunting rifle. Like a streak of lightning, the bullet ripped through the side of Clive's head. Blood and gray mixed together and flew in the air like paint being thrown on a canvas. It splattered the side of the porch and the length of Ella's dress. The eye that was left in Clive's head looked at Ella in shocked wonder before he tumbled down and landed across the stair rail.

The front door flew open. With the butt of his gun, Samuel knocked Lanier against the foyer wall. He ran out of the house, hunkered down and firing. A bullet shattered the headlight of the Troxlers' car, and another ricocheted off the grille. Ella screamed at Samuel but it was too late for words. Only deeds mattered now.

Jack-Ray ran into the patch of sunflowers, and Parker took cover behind the car. Sheriff Bissell looked toward the field and raised his arm in self-defense. A bullet grazed his forearm and left a burned spot on the sleeve of his shirt. He had just taken the gun out from his holster when Earl fired a second shot, piercing the left side of Sheriff Bissell's chest. Bits of khaki cloth and fatty skin flew up in the air and dotted the circle of sand where Macon had played earlier that morning.

Lanier reached out from the open front door and jerked Ella inside. All the while she was screaming and clawing at this madman she should have feared all along. Lanier then grabbed the shotgun she had propped against the doorjamb. "Get inside," he yelled to Samuel.

J.D. Troxler bent down on one knee behind an azalea bush next to the porch and fired the shot that blew out the glass window above the door. Glass rained down on Samuel, and he dropped the gun, covering himself with his hands. Slithering around on the porch to reach the gun that was lodged under the leg of the porch chair, Samuel left a trail of blood flowing from his cut hand. Rising up with his pistol gripped in one hand, J.D. Troxler aimed directly at Samuel. The scream of bullets pierced the air. With a lurch forward, J.D. dropped his gun and gripped his neck. His body tilted back and forth while the branches of the azalea bush shook. Blood ran from the cracks of his fingers and down onto his pressed white shirt. He landed backward, spread across the hood of the truck, his gaze slightly downward toward the door where the shot had been fired.

Lanier stood at the door with smoke coming from his shotgun. Reaching down, he yanked Samuel by the collar of his shirt and pulled him inside.

Inside the house, glass popped and sprayed across the room while Keaton and Narsissa scrambled to the side of the dining room. They took positions under the open windows. Narsissa stuck the rifle barrel through the opening and fired, missing Jack-Ray but slicing a branch from the azalea bush.

Ella was kneeling in the foyer, looking at the glass like she thought she could piece it back together. She grabbed the gun that was lying on the floor and pointed it straight at Lanier. Her hands twitched, and his eyes pleaded. "I'm a good man," he yelled before a bullet ripped through the wood of the front door and caused him to tumble on top of her. She pulled herself out from under him and scrambled for the shotgun.

Outside Jack-Ray eased down the rows of sunflowers and then ran unnoticed toward the back of the house. Stationed behind the car, Parker Troxler fired at will and shattered the glass out of the living room windows. Pale-yellow curtains danced in the breeze, the top portions dotted with bullet holes. When he rose up behind the car and positioned his gun on the roof, Earl moved out from the pasture and trotted toward him. Parker fired a shot that shattered the window where Keaton hid. The boy then lifted himself up and had glass tangled in his hair. He screamed in a high, pierced way—a boy caught between manhood and youth. His shot hit the rear window of the car and caused Parker to fall to the ground. Rolling over, Parker gripped the gun with both hands. Keaton was still looking back at the car, not noticing that his threat had moved.

As Parker pulled back on the trigger, he glanced up to find Earl standing over him. His lanky shadow cast across Parker's face and shoulders. The shot was clean and quick and merciful, the way a farmer might do to a mule that had foundered and was no longer workable. A small hole pierced Parker's blond hair. Blood seeped out under his head until it took the shape of a pillow.

Inside the house, smoke from the bullets lingered. Everyone lay still and silent. A muffled cry streamed out from the bedroom where Macon lay under the bed, gripping the bedposts and crying.

"Is it over?" Samuel yelled from the living room. Macon's cries from the bedroom echoed throughout the house and tangled with the sound of the oxen calling outside.

Ella looked down at the blood on her hand and wondered if it was hers or Clive's. There was no noise, only the sound of birds chirping in the distance and the flap of curtains through the open windows.

"Is it over?" Samuel yelled again. He tried to stand, but Lanier reached over and pulled him down. He motioned for him to stay quiet.

Narsissa rolled onto her side, and slivers of glass crunched at her weight. She looked back into the kitchen and saw Jack-Ray standing at the doorway. Before she could reach for her gun, he put a bullet through the center of her chest. Keaton scrambled through the glass and landed on one foot in the foyer before sliding into the living room. He lined the wall with the others and let Ella grip his head against her chest.

Smoke was still billowing from Jack-Ray's gun when he turned toward the room where Ella had at one time hoped to have social gatherings. The sound of his boots echoed down the hallway. Lanier leaned against the wall that separated the foyer from the living room and stuck his gun out and fired. The bullet missed Jack-Ray and broke a lantern that hung on the wall. "You know what they say about dead or alive," Jack-Ray said as he walked over glass.

When Jack-Ray made it to the edge of the living room, the floor creaked against his weight. The sound of the family's jagged breathing seemed to fill the room the same as the echoes of bullets that still remained. Samuel jumped from behind the love seat and fired. The oval picture frame holding the photograph of Ella and Harlan on their wedding day shattered into pieces. Ella saw the panic on Samuel's face and the methodical way that Jack-Ray walked toward him with his pistol drawn, inching forward the way he would stalk a rabbit that was perched on a stump ready to be shot. Ella screamed, "The one you came for is over there." She pointed toward Lanier, who stood in the corner of the room next to a coat rack. When Jack-Ray turned to fire, Ella lifted the shotgun and shot a hole through the side of his pants. He bounded over a small coffee table and kicked the gun from her hands.

Turning his gun in Ella's direction, Jack-Ray stared at her and calmly pointed the gun at her. There was neither pain nor fury in his eyes. There was only a blank darkness, the same as if someone had cut out his eyes and replaced them with pieces of coal. When Lanier fired, Jack-Ray leaped sideways, never losing the grip of his gun. Lanier lifted the gun to fire again, but it only clicked, empty of bullets. Keaton scrambled across the floor for his gun. Jack-Ray aimed right for Lanier's temple and grinned when he did it.

The firing of the gun caused his head to jerk backward in a snapping motion. When he landed on his knees, Jack-Ray was missing the portion of his face where the letter *J* had been carved. Lanier struggled to breathe. Blood, like sores, covered his face as he kept gathering unused bullets that were scattered on the floor. He never noticed Earl, the father of a simpleton locked away for the town's safety, standing in the foyer. All any of them could see that day was the smoke that billowed from the room, the bullet holes that riddled the walls, and the blood that would forever stain the floor of their home.

Against the weight of his boots, broken glass crackled as Earl walked out of the splintered front door. He eased down porch steps speckled with flesh and headed deeper into the woods, where sane people knew better than to venture.

24

Narsissa was buried on a Tuesday, the day after Clive Gillespie's funeral and two days after the town dressed in black for Sheriff Bissell's service.

The small group, made up of neighbors and Neva Clarkson, assembled in the section of the cemetery segregated for Indians. Moss and rotting tree limbs littered the plot of land. Ella stood next to an anthill and listened to Reverend Simpson piece together a woman he only knew from what others in the community said about her. The magnolia casket that Lanier had stayed up for two days working on now gleamed in the afternoon sun. Ella rubbed the ends of the fish-scale necklace and wished that it really had magical properties. If so, she would turn back time and turn Lanier Stillis away from her farm.

"Jesus promises peace not like the world gives, but eternal peace." Reverend Simpson closed his Bible and looked straight at Ella. "May your beloved Narsissa have peace." Then he reached for Ella's hands. "May you finally have peace."

Lanier did not join the group that circled around the casket he had made. He chose to stay behind, telling Ella that he didn't want to draw more attention than had already been given. "I'm an innocent man," Lanier kept saying long after Sheriff Loring had returned to Bainbridge, taking the bodies of the Troxler brothers to the cemetery where their sister and father awaited them in death. The yellowed papers that J.D. claimed verified Lanier's mental instability were found, torn from bullets, inside his coat jacket pocket. They were the death certificates of his wife and sister—war tokens, more or less.

Earl's argument for innocence would turn out to be as riddled with holes as Ella's home the day he walked out of it. After Deputy Ronnie took testimony from everyone, he wrote up the whole affair as "self-defense and justifiable homicide." Sheriff Bissell would be memorialized in popular opinion as a fallen hero who had been ambushed by the brothers from Bainbridge. Judge Takerton, the man Clive Gillespie had helped elect, split the report the deputy wrote right down the middle with a pewter envelope opener. "Justice is blind in my courtroom. She has equal balance. A crime is a crime is a crime," he said the day he signed off on the verdict to send Earl to Raiford Prison.

Even after the bodies were identified, the floors cleaned, and the curtains and windows replaced, the events of that day would hover over Ella and her sons like an estranged relative whose memory never truly goes away.

Riding in the wagon back home after Narsissa's funeral, Ella and her sons were trapped in their scattered thoughts. A fox darted out in front of them before running back through the high grass that led to a broken-down farmhouse. The gray, rotted porch floor was cracked right down the middle.

Samuel popped the reins a little too hard, and the mule shook his head.

"It's not his fault," Ella said.

Samuel popped the reins again, and once more the mule shook his head, causing the bridle to make a jingling noise.

"Samuel, you're too rough with the reins."

The wagon wheel dipped into a rut, and Ella was jostled up against her oldest son. His muscles were taut, and he snapped the reins again, harder, until the mule called out.

Snatching the reins away, Ella shouted, "Stop it."

He balled up his fist like he might hit her, but she never turned away. Ella only gripped the reins tighter and leaned away from her son.

Samuel kicked the floor of the wagon, folded his arms, and simmered until they reached the corner of their property.

Lanier was at the water pump, priming the handle, when the wagon headed up the path toward the barn.

"Samuel," Ella yelled.

Before the wagon could stop, Samuel had leaped from the seat.

Lanier halfway turned and was knocked backward toward the sunflowers by Samuel's fist. Sunflower stalks bent in submission.

"You killed her," Samuel yelled through gritted teeth. He slammed his fist on Lanier's head twice before Lanier rebounded and swung his weight, flipping Samuel down on his back. Samuel, pinned to the ground by Lanier's grip on his wrists, kept yelling. "You killed her. You killed her. You killed her."

Beneath Lanier's weight, Samuel writhed and jerked like a wild animal being held captive. "You killed her," he screamed.

Ella pulled Lanier off her son, and Keaton tried in vain to hold his brother back. Samuel bounded forward and bumped into Ella as he tried to get to Lanier. "I said stop," Ella shouted. When Samuel failed to listen to her, Ella pushed her way in between the two of them.

The hat she wore was knocked askew, and a reddening spot showed where Samuel's shoulder had landed when he bumped her aside to get to Lanier. Ella kept pulling at Samuel's face, trying to hold his head still. He thrashed and spat, cursing Lanier. When words failed, Ella struck him square on his face. The crimson shape of her fingers remained on his cheek.

"He killed her," Samuel said, heaving out the words. "He good as killed her." Slumping to the ground, Samuel cried harder than he had since his father disappeared.

No one took Lanier his supper that night, and he didn't venture out of the barn to request it.

Ella opened the door of Narsissa's cabin. The hinges creaked when it opened, and for a moment, she stood there in the darkness, taking in the smell of herbs that Narsissa kept in the dresser that Ella had given her as a hand-me-down. Never bothering to close the door, Ella lit the lamp and looked in the corner where Narsissa's bed sat.

The pattern quilt that Narsissa had made out of discarded baby clothing worn by Ella's sons was laid neatly across the mattress. Ella folded the quilt the same way a soldier might handle a flag and sat down on the edge of the bed. The picture of Narsissa with the man who was once her husband was next to the small nicked and stained nightstand that Ella had replaced in her own home with a nicer version. She looked at the picture and tried to imagine the woman Narsissa must have been at that time. A woman who would follow a man to a distant land. A woman, not unlike herself, who was at one time intoxicated with a love that leaves the mind and spirit hungover. Pressing the quilt against her, she inhaled the scent and for the first time cried harder than she had when Harlan deserted her.

"I'm sorry." Lanier stood in the doorway with the light striking the side of his body in a glow.

Ella jumped from the bed and wiped her eyes.

When he stepped inside, an owl called out beyond the door. Ella moved to the other side of the room. "Everything's fine." She looked around the cabin, seeking a distraction.

His words were crisp and excited, like a schoolchild seeking approval. "I made some more dolls. They're in the store. Just inside the door."

A hot breeze stirred through the open door, and the light in the lamp swayed. "There must be a thunderstorm heading our way," she said and ran her hand across the quilt. "Narsissa could predict the weather as good as any steamboat captain."

"I'm sorry," he said yet another time. "Out there today in the yard . . ."

"The shipment from Pensacola came in today. I'll need to start restocking tomorrow." She stared down at the woven rug next to the bed that covered Narsissa's secret compartment.

"I'm sorry . . . about everything."

"Your dolls are still selling, healing or no healing," Ella said and then sighed. "I guess everybody is still holding out some hope."

"I'm sorry."

"Hush!" Ella shouted.

Crickets and bullfrogs called out as a distant symphony. Stepping backward, Lanier turned to go but stopped. "Know one thing. . . . I never meant to bring you trouble."

"It's more complicated than apologies."

"I hate it. I just wish I'd kept going on to New Orleans."

Ella sat on the edge of the bed and looked at the open door. She didn't want Lanier to come any closer but didn't want to tell him so either. "We both know that if you hadn't ended up here, my sons and I would be in the poorhouse, begging for our next meal. My son might even be dead. You know that. Just the same as if Narsissa wouldn't have wound up here, I'd be in the poorhouse. I couldn't take care of myself. I guess I never have."

"Yes, you could have."

Her mouth twisted to the side. "No, I couldn't have. I needed you just like I needed Narsissa. She paid the price in all of this."

"The price?"

"I cost Narsissa her life by not being able to manage. If I was as strong as her, we wouldn't be in this situation. I would have let you stay the night in the barn and then Samuel would have taken you to the steamboat the next morning. You'd be in New Orleans, and Narsissa would still be here."

"This has nothing to do with you. It was . . . I don't know, timing. . . . Fate. . . . Whatever you want to call it."

"Of course it's about me. It is *always* about me. Always has been." Ella fluttered her hand and then balled it into a fist. "I've been dependent my entire life. I've been selfish . . . just waiting for the next person to swoop in and take care of me." Her voice broke again.

He took a step closer, and she slid farther down the bed. "Don't," she said.

"I wish I'd left after we made the cut."

"You wouldn't have," she said. "Because I wouldn't have let you."

"Because we're partners."

"Partners? I'm married."

"Partners in business, is what I meant to say."

Ella dropped her chin and looked at him in a way that would not let him circle the truth.

Lanier ran his hand through his hair. "Look, I feel terrible about all of this."

"I'm still married. The law won't let me forget it. And people won't either."

"I ain't gonna stand here and let you beat yourself up like this." The light illuminated the back of his head. "You helped me just like you helped Narsissa."

"I helped you all right." Ella toyed at a loose thread on the quilt before twisting it around her finger and yanking it free.

"Ella, do you want me to leave? Is that what you're aiming for?"

"What I want and what I need are two different things."

He reached out and stroked the back of her hair. This time she didn't move. "Ella, deep down, what do *you* want? Be honest, now. If you're ever going to be honest with yourself, now's the time." The box springs on the bed squeaked when he sat down.

For the first time that evening she exhaled long and deep. Part of her wanted to fall back on the bed and sink into the feather mattress. "I might not care what these people around here think of me anymore, but I still care about the opinion of my boys."

"There were no boys in my question."

"The truth is, Lanier, I want you to stay."

Lanier's fingers brushed against her shoulder.

"But right now a bigger part of me wants you to leave."

The sting of her words etched across his face.

Ella lay across the side of the bed with her back to Lanier. She could feel the shift in the mattress and the creak of the springs when he got up. Tucking her hands underneath the heavy quilt, she forced herself to stay still. She heard his boots tap on the floor as he made his way out the door. The crunching sound of his weight against the broken limbs and leaves outside the cabin was soon overpowered by the cry of the owl. Up until now, she had never thought of the bird's call as mournful.

Fog canopied the road in front of the store, and dew sprinkled like diamonds across the grass on Ella's yard. Clouds hung so low that the earth and sky became one. Ella stood at her bedroom window and could only make out the azalea bush at the edge of her porch. A spider's web, dotted with drops of water from the mist, hung from the corner of the porch banister. Ella studied the intricate design that looked like lace and wondered how long it had been there without her ever noticing.

Slipping on her robe, Ella felt the cold surface of the floor on her bare feet and hoped the sensation would jolt the numbness that blanketed her mind. The hallway floor creaked, and she knocked on the door of the boys' room. "Morning," she said without opening the door. She said the greeting again, this time forcing herself to add a cheerful lift to her voice.

In the kitchen she pulled the skillet from the cabinet and scooped out the lard that Narsissa had put into a canister. *Today will be a good day,* she told herself and then prayed for the strength to make it so.

After the boys had dressed for school and eaten, they went about their morning chores. Ella cleaned the kitchen and watched them from the window. They wove in and out of the fog like they were actors coming on and off a stage between scenes.

Scrubbing the skillet faster and faster, Ella jumped when Keaton called her name. He was standing at the back door of the kitchen, his hands placed on the sides like he was holding up the frame. "Mama," he said. His eyes were as wide as they had been the day Lanier climbed out of the box. "He's gone."

Holding the grease-stained rag, Ella looked at him. Her full lips parted slightly as if she were in the middle of forming a word that was now locked in her throat.

"Lanier's gone."

Out in the barn, they all stood around the spot where Lanier had made his bed. They stared at the ground the same way they would have if he had shrunk and they were seeking him in the scatter of hay. The mule looked up at them with slivers of hay hanging from his whiskers and then returned to his breakfast.

Macon was the one who found three twenty-dollar bills tucked underneath an oak box that rested on the workbench. He tried to open the lid but Samuel took it from him and completed the job. Inside there were pencils, tubes of paint, a canvas, and three long paintbrushes. "He must have ordered this with that shipment he unpacked yesterday," Samuel said. He pulled out a piece of parchment paper. With one of the pencils, Lanier had written a note that Samuel read out loud. "I've said enough. I've done enough. I appreciate everything that has been done to help me but it's time for me to set out to where I started. I'm going to New Orleans to start fresh. I hope you all will think of me from time to time. Not about the bad things but about the good ones. We natural-born worked, but we did it. We did it. Paint a picture and think of me sometime."

"That's all?" Keaton asked.

"What's in the box?" Macon asked.

"Paint," Ella stammered.

"Paint?" Macon said.

Samuel handed the box to Ella. "We got to head on. We'll be late for school."

"He just left?" Keaton said. "He just up and left without telling us bye?"

"Is he coming back?" Macon asked and then pulled the box lower so he could get a look inside.

"No," Samuel said. "He won't be coming back."

"He just left without saying anything to anybody?" Keaton looked back down at the spot where Lanier had slept.

Ella let Macon hold the box of paints and then looked straight at Samuel. "It's for the best."

"Samuel was right," Keaton said, kicking the spot where Lanier had slept. "He's nothing but white trash."

"Mind what you say about Lanier," Ella said.

"He's still our friend," Macon said, looking up at Ella for reassurance. She pulled him close to the fold of her underarm but didn't reply.

"It's for the best," Samuel said and handed the money to Ella. When his fingers brushed up against hers, Ella squeezed them before he had a chance to pull away.

Standing alone at the barn door, Ella watched her sons disappear into the fog and make their way to school. She clutched the box of paint to her chest and heard Lanier in her mind. *"Let the art free your mind.*" Rubbing the surface of the plywood box, Ella felt she was drowning in the darkness that she pictured as a yoke around her soul. She imagined herself walking into the mist and folding inside the empty feeling that tormented her until she would eventually vanish.

She thought of her aunt and the way she would often wrap her arms around herself and shudder. "I'm just so nervous and melancholy today," her aunt would say. Ella would quietly walk about the house and peer into the bedroom where her aunt rested during bright spring days with the drapes completely drawn. Her aunt had spent so much of her life behind closed curtains. A shiver ran down Ella's spine, and she forced herself to step out of the barn and into the damp mist that covered the air. The time for tears had come and gone. "It's for the best," she said twice more before forcing herself to take one step and then another back to the house.

25

A late-September thunderstorm swept over New Orleans and broke the heat wave that had left the French Quarter cooking in a brew of bodily fluids and alcohol that heavied the air. Lanier welcomed the momentary relief that came with the rain. The one-bedroom flat that he rented in the brick row home with the broken black lamp above the door lacked ventilation. It was owned by Miss Prideaux, a mulatto woman with a red mole above her right eye. Her dark skin made the spot look more like a ruby on the Indian women Lanier saw in one of the heavy books he studied at the library. She would hear none of Lanier's comparisons. "I'm 100 percent French, or I'm nothing at all," Miss Prideaux said.

Mr. Pelham, an aging illustrator with a yellow-tinged goatee, sold silhouette drawings to the people who passed by his stand at Jackson Square. The old man told Lanier that Miss Prideaux was a prostitute. In turn, Miss Prideaux whispered to Lanier in the courtyard where dead banana leaves were embedded into the broken pebbles that Mr. Pelham had come to her doorstep from an insane asylum. It was fitting, Lanier thought. For so long back in Georgia with the Troxlers, he had worried about his reputation and his associations. Now he had no reputation whatsoever.

Mr. Pelham's stand was right next to the one Lanier set up just to the right of St. Louis Cathedral. Most days he would share po-boy sandwiches with Mr. Pelham, but he never consumed his gossip. Lanier had found his niche carving dolls and wooden puppets, complete with playful expressions and strings that controlled their every move. The less he said, the better off he'd be. A woman from the Garden District whose husband was the head of the Cotton Exchange had bought dolls for every room in her home, for friends who had given social favors, and even for her maids. She spread the word about his wares. Those below her on the social rungs quickly followed her example. Soon Lanier was so busy that he was able to trim back his hours at the United Fruit Company, where he unloaded cases marked with exotic seals from Cuba, Argentina, and Hawaii. He preferred the stench of the Quarter to the smell of the rotting fruit on the deck.

Walking back to his flat on Burgundy Street, Lanier watched as a woman with a low-cut top dropped a bucket down on a rope from a second-story window. A boy not more than twelve with a wool cap turned sideways placed a sack with a loaf of bread sticking out of it into the bucket. The woman held on to the rope and yelled down, "You got the gin in there?" The boy hit the side of the bucket with his hand and nodded. Lanier stood against the street post and watched the boy saunter away with his hands in his pockets. There was something about his gait and the way that he turned his head to the side like he was contemplating an important idea that caused Lanier to think of Keaton. Then, just as easily, his mind drifted to Ella. He shook his head as if he could dislodge the memory of her and walked across the street.

Lanier unlocked the iron door that led to the courtyard of Miss Prideaux's boardinghouse. He could make out an argument behind the door at the end, the peeling door with a one-eared lion's head as a doorknocker. The couple in that room had moved in two weeks ago, after the man had been discharged from the Army. From all appearances, he battled the bottle as much as he did the ability to walk on one leg.

Juggling the croaker sack filled with the dolls and puppets he had failed to sell that day, Lanier looked up in time to see Miss Prideaux on the ledge above him. Her long hair hung over her shoulder, and her left leg was propped up on the top of the iron railing. Soap covered the bottom part of her leg, and the evening sun caught the tip of the silver straight razor that she held. "Sell anything?" Miss Prideaux asked just like she did every day.

No, have you? Lanier thought but didn't ask. He smiled and shrugged with the bag slung over his shoulder. "You know, a little here and a little there." If she heard him, Miss Prideaux gave no indication. She just slowly dragged the blade across her shin and bit the tip of her tongue.

His room was made up of a bed, a broken desk, and an olive-colored sofa with horsehair spilling out from a tear. Lanier retreated into his imagination the way he had ever since coming to New Orleans. He had made the mistake of being an open book once and would not make it again. Besides, it had to be this way. Life had dictated it. It was for the best.

Opening the pages of a novel about a woman striking out on her own to California, he read the description of the woman three times. He was determined to read the books that the librarian, a man with a missing tooth in the front and a speckled nose, told him were worthwhile. But this book had been more than an obstacle. It had been a trigger for bad feelings that he no longer had the discipline to shove aside. No matter how many times Lanier read the description of the

New York woman and tried to see her as a redhead or a blonde, he kept seeing her the way she was presented, a woman with dark hair and iris-colored eyes. A woman like Ella.

Ella clouded his sleeping hours as much as she did his daydreams at Jackson Square. Often he dreamed the same visions. He would see her in the square, circling the vendors, wearing a hat covered in purple peacock feathers. She turned her head and smiled that pouty way she had, but her eyes never fell upon him. She was looking just to the right, where Mr. Pelham drew illustrations of human faces. In those dreams Lanier would leave his wares and fight through the crowd to reach her. Bobbling in the crowd, Ella would never stay in one place. She would only smile and cast her eyes about the people as if she were looking for someone other than him. And like always, he would awake gasping for breath and hearing the sounds of the French Quarter beyond his open window: a scream of ecstasy or fear, a fading trumpet, a bottle breaking, or a couple fighting. He never once heard the sad sound of the whip-poor-will that seemed to own the night air at Ella's farm.

By the time the sky in Dead Lakes transitioned from the pink of late summer to the lighter blue-green that heralded cooler nights, the main lobby of Brother Mabry's retreat was complete. He had gladly signed the lease Ella had proposed and then set forth clearing a road that would allow his wife Priscilla to lounge in the spring at leisure. "I own the land," Ella said to him on more than one occasion. "You're free to build your center, but you'll lease the land. That land stays in my name." To ensure safeguards of her privacy, Samuel was on hand the day the stone fence was erected around the spring, verifying that none of the pilgrims who would come from points unknown would encroach on their way of life. But in spite of good intentions and careful oversight, life was never completely the same.

A gravel road replaced the red-dirt one that ran in front of the store. Iron gates marked the entrance to Eden. A comfortable sixty-room lodge made out of virgin pine and Georgia marble was the place that gave comfort to those in search of a cure. The faithful lounged in hospital chairs around the spring that never changed temperature and prayed with Brother Mabry's associate staff of seven.

By early October the newspapers had lost interest in Brother Mabry's crusade and had busied themselves with the business of tracking the end of the war and the flu that was sweeping across the Northeast.

In the most severe cases, the influenza was leading to pneumonia. In search of cures if not protection, the wealthy of southern New York, where Priscilla had social and financial ties, spent days traveling to Apalachicola. Their trunks lined the docks as colored boys eager to make a quarter stood in a line to take care of their traveling needs.

Mr. and Mrs. Pomeroy's son, Zach, came home from the war after spending time in a New Jersey military hospital for burn wounds to his lower torso. "If only that man was still here," Mrs. Pomeroy said in the store. "I know he could do Zach some good, like he did with that colored girl. Do you ever hear from him?"

Ella glanced at the string puppet shaped and painted like Uncle Sam that had arrived from New Orleans in a fruit crate. She handed Mrs. Pomeroy her change and pointed out a two-for-one sale on sponges at the opposite end of the store.

Reverend Simpson preached his sermons as if Ella had never leased her property to the acclaimed evangelist. The only difference was that now Ella and her sons occupied the back pew from time to time. Bonaparte collected oysters from Apalachicola Bay and sold them to the head chef at Brother Mabry's retreat. Neva Clarkson taught Macon his times tables, and Keaton mapped out the state capitals. He could better relate to the locations in the Northeast from having met some of the citizens of those states. The sojourners came into the store chattering about the quaintness of the locale and the freshness in the air that empowered their lungs. At the time, most everything in Dead Lakes seemed to have stayed the same—at least that was what the locals told themselves without ever speaking to the fresh supply of Eden seekers who arrived at Brother Mabry's iron gates in a bus with his name on the side of it.

"I need a bottle of aspirin," Mrs. Pomeroy said on one autumn afternoon. "Zach's running a fever. I can't keep it down, and the doctor is at a loss. If only that man was still around." Mrs. Pomeroy pulled at her sweater. She looked up at Ella with hopeful curiosity.

Ella waved her hand in the air, wanting to dismiss Mrs. Pomeroy as much as her reference of Lanier. "Miss Potter said everybody in Apalachicola is down with it too," Ella said. "Just a bug, more or less. It'll pass." Ella didn't mention how Brother Mabry's dire predictions of plagues and Myer Simpson's first report of the flu months earlier had caused her now to wonder, if not worry. It was a fleeting thought, but just the same, it was there. Maybe Lanier had brought curses to the town.

Ella waited until Mrs. Pomeroy had left before she turned back to the Panama City newspaper. The lead story was about a funeral parlor in Philadelphia that couldn't buy caskets fast enough. By that evening Ella's teacher from days gone by, Miss Wayne, was dead from pneumonia. Three days later, the Pomeroys would buy a casket for their son, Zach. "He fought a war in some blasted place I can't even pronounce, but he got taken by the flu," Mr. Pomeroy yelled at Reverend Simpson during the wake held in the parlor of the Pomeroy home. "What kinda God is that?"

Brother Mabry called the citizens of Franklin County together in a prayer rally. People showed up at his Eden with handkerchiefs tied around their mouths. Inside the cathedral with its shiny ceiling made from cypress wood and its amber-colored glass windows as tall as a man, if anyone sneezed they were escorted out by one of the elders who wore matching green suspenders.

"Jesus said if we have enough faith we can move mountains," Brother Mabry said and pulled at the button of his crimson velvet jacket. "But enough faith is the key. Hear me now. . . . If . . . *if* we have enough faith, we can pray down this flu." The crowd grew silent when Priscilla stood up in the front row that had been quarantined by red ropes that kept everyone else two pews away from her. She reached up her hand like she might be testifying to all that Brother Mabry spoke. A trickle of blood ran from her nose and fell to the stone floor. Without so much as letting go of her handkerchief, she collapsed. The crowd scattered outside as she was cradled away in Brother Mabry's massive arms. Guests quickly changed into their long swimsuits and sectioned off to the gender-specific bathing areas at the spring. Water splashed and the faithful proclaimed protection.

When the pool of water failed to keep the first victim in Eden, a twenty-three-year-old woman from Greenwich with hazel eyes too big for her face, from catching the influenza that turned her milky-colored skin black, the faithful couldn't find enough colored boys to lug their trunks back onto the steamboats that would lead them home.

The day after Priscilla's body was embalmed and packed in a crate for burial at her family's New York estate, Brother Mabry stood on the bow of the *John W. Callahan* steamboat with a handkerchief monogrammed with his initials tied around his face. He watched the land that he once believed to be his spiritual homeland drift farther away. As the warehouses that lined the dock became nothing more than dots on the horizon, he took off his velvet jacket and tossed it in the wind. The crimson-colored coat landed on the cresting waves, the wide sleeves outstretched the same way they would be if they were filled by the arms of a drowned man.

In New Orleans the flu that the papers had declared an epidemic showed no boundaries. The wealthy of the Garden District were struck down with the same force as those who lived in what many considered to be the slums of the French Quarter. People stayed away from Jackson Square and took refuge in the bars as much as they did in the churches.

Lanier walked through the cobblestoned alley that led to his rented room. At the end of the damp, littered space, a cat with eyes that seemed bigger than its bony head clawed through a box of trash. The cat moaned in a gurgled way that caused Lanier to stop. Then, before he could take another step, he saw the wagon of the undertaker pass. Bodies were stacked in the back of the wagon the same haphazard way that he had stacked logs back at Ella's place. A child's hand hung over the tailgate of the wagon. The blackish-blue hand flopped about as if it were waving. Turning away, Lanier quickly walked back to Jackson Square.

Inside the church, Lanier sat on the edge of the back pew and watched the faithful light candles, make the sign of the cross, and kneel. The faithful stream of attendees, usually old women with lace around their heads, had become a sea of people from different classes and ages. A young boy touched the foot of the statue of Jesus that stood in the corner while a man about Lanier's age cried in front of the Virgin Mary. Lanier looked up at the main altar, where candles cast a yellow glow around the crucifix. The thorns on Jesus' head and the blood around His forehead and ribs seemed brighter than before. *By his stripes we are healed.* Lanier knelt on the pad in front of his pew and wrestled with feelings of betrayal. The words of his grandmother, a woman with strands of coarse gray hair that dangled over her right eye, echoed in his mind. *"It's a gift. If you was to ever tell the words that we speak over them that needs healing, then you ain't fitting to have it. The Lord will take that gift from you because you squandered it away to man."* He wanted to walk right through the church doors and run. To run and hide in the bushes. To keep his eyes turned away from the houses that had black ribbons tied around their doorknobs, indicating the places where the flu had visited. Lanier thought of his son and the hand of the child he had seen in the back of the death wagon. He wanted to run out into the night and inhale with all his might. He wanted to run as much as he wanted to die.

A broad-shouldered woman who swayed from side to side as she walked lifted the edge of the gauze mask that she wore and wiped away tears. Her soft cry echoed in the high cathedral ceiling and landed upon Lanier, filling his spirit until he trembled and wondered if he had finally caught the fever. He watched the woman wobble up to the altar, light a small candle, and cross herself as she knelt in front of the image of Jesus.

Long after the candle melted, Lanier was still there. He stayed until the church bell chimed three times.

Lanier followed a slump-shouldered nun out of the church. He stared at the tassel that was attached to the end of a rope tied around the folds of her stomach. The white ends of the tassel seemed new, crisp, and pure. The sister shoved the massive cathedral door with both hands, and the muffled cries coming from the makeshift hospital tents outside seemed louder in Lanier's mind. He covered the side of his scarred ear with his hand and followed the tassel that flapped back and forth around the nun's calves. It was easier to stare at the object that reminded him of a Christmas tree ornament than to look at the blood-splattered white shoes that the nun wore. When she turned left and stepped around a distraught woman holding a baby whose face was covered with a soiled handkerchief embroidered with the sign of the cross, Lanier copied her steps. There was nothing that awaited him back at Miss Prideaux's but books and memories whose endings he couldn't change.

When the nun flipped open the door of the tent nearest a banana tree, Lanier moved forward. The nun never noticed him as she busied herself with tying a soiled apron around her waist, covering the tassel of the rope belt she wore. The stench of human waste, alcohol, and dried blood overtook Lanier. He recoiled but never ran away. Part of him wanted to inhale the scent deep and hard. Influenza would be a destiny of sorts.

"Are you one of the volunteers?" A sister wearing a white habit and an apron printed with a red cross approached him. She held a murky basin of water like an offering. Wiry chestnut hair poked from underneath her ears. Her voice was jagged and sharp, native New Orleans. "The bishop promised more volunteers." She handed him the basin and pointed toward the tent flap. "Toss that and fill it with fresh water." Before she walked away, the nun snapped her fingers at pails of water that were stacked on top of a portable steel table. "Then get busy applying wet gauzes to their heads."

The nun hovered over a boy who shook and kicked until the sheet over him balled at his waist, revealing bony knees. White sheets covered the other patients, who lay in cots lined perfectly in three rows. The placement of the cots reminded Lanier of the mausoleums placed side by side in the local cemetery. He lifted the tent flap, tossed the water, and obeyed the nun's instructions.

Applying fresh gauze to a young woman who coughed until ligaments protruded from her skin, Lanier stared into the panic in her eyes. She reached up her hand, clawing the air with sharp, dirty fingernails. Thinking that she might cough easier if she were elevated, Lanier cupped his arm under the woman's knotty spine. Her fingernails landed into his forearm and scratched his skin. A gurgle formed in her throat. Lanier rubbed her back until he felt her body grow limp and her hand slip away from him. Standing over the woman, now dead, whose eyes and mouth were still open, he felt the breeze of the nun as she worked around him. She yanked the sheet over the woman's body and pointed to the next patient, a redheaded man who hadn't yet outgrown his freckles. "Just keep moving."

By the time Lanier reached the third row of cots, he had comforted a wailing woman who stood at the foot of the cot containing her youngest daughter, gripped the hand of a teenage boy who thought Lanier was his father, and refreshed four more basins of water. The shortest nun of the group, an older woman with protruding teeth, walked up and down the aisle carrying a red-and-white tin filled with a yellowish paste. "This will help ease the pain," she whispered as she dipped a strip of gauze into the tin and then tried to tuck it underneath the leg of a girl who thrashed, swinging her head from one side to the other.

"Here," Lanier said, moving to the side of the girl's cot. He set down the basin of water and gently rolled the girl to the side. "Now see if you can get it underneath her."

"Thank you," the nun whispered.

Lanier was looking at the girl, trying to smile and comfort her when he heard the voice from his childhood call out.

"Get away from me, woman."

A loud clang rang out, and the nun helping the girl stopped long enough to look toward the end of the row where the commotion brewed.

The nun who had instructed Lanier gripped a bowl filled with yellow paste. With a wide stance, she leaned over the man who flailed about in his bed. "It's just mustard seed and buckwheat."

The man screamed as if he were deaf.

"It'll help with your skin blisters."

The man cursed her, her God, and her concoction all in one ragged breath.

The nun looked at Lanier and twisted the side of her mouth. "That man has been nothing but trouble. Out of his mind by the time they brought him in here. Not only does he have the flu, but he's coming off dope too." The nun gritted her oversized teeth and then turned her attention back to the girl.

After Lanier had picked up the basin of water, he moved slowly to the last cot. The nun was looking at the remaining paste in her tin and mumbling words Lanier could not understand. When he stepped closer, Lanier saw the gaunt, sore-riddled face of the man who had once mesmerized him as a boy. "Harlan?" Lanier said, once in a whisper and then louder.

"He's talking out of his head," the nun said in her nasal voice. She stopped worrying over the ointment and studied Lanier. "Do you know this man? The police brought him here yesterday."

Lanier stared at Harlan's thick-bearded face. Bloody red sores grew from the sides of Harlan's mouth. They were similar to the sores that Lanier had healed on his youngest son. "Harlan Wallace?"

Harlan's coal-colored eyes stared up at the ceiling of the tent. His shaking fingers clawed the seam of the sheet. Thin skin revealed bluish veins along the base of his neck.

"Do you know this man?" the sister asked again.

Shaking his head, Lanier turned to leave. A priest was standing at the end of a cot, making the sign of the cross and mumbling last rites. Lanier never apologized for bumping into him. The wife of the redheaded man reached out to him as he passed by and requested a fresh towel. By the time he'd made it to where the fresh water was kept, Lanier tossed the basin to the side without looking to see if it landed on the table.

"Will you come back?" the nun called out, trailing him to the door flap of the tent. "The bishop promised us volunteers. Do you hear me? I'll be praying for you to come back."

The nun's words and the vision of Harlan tormented Lanier long after he had locked the door to his room at Miss Prideaux's and turned out the flame of his lamp.

26

In the Apalachicola cemetery, heaps of freshly tilled dirt took the shape of giant ant beds. Keaton held on to the side of the wagon that Samuel drove and noticed two men with gauze masks digging one more. Pressing his nails into the plank of wood where he sat, Keaton looked down the empty Main Street and out toward the water. At least the steamboats still bobbed at the dock with clouds of black coming from their stacks. Watching the boats and the few men who paraded around the dock carrying crates of supplies, Keaton felt relieved at some sight of normalcy.

The wagon Samuel drove made its way through the downtown that was cleared of people. The only person in a block's radius came out of the pharmacy. Examining the bottle of tonic in his hand, the man never looked up as he crossed the street. If Samuel hadn't stopped the wagon in time, they would have run over him.

At the dock three colored boys, younger than Keaton, made

straining faces as they carried crates stamped with the logo of a supply company from Atlanta. He nodded at them and planted his
hands deep in his pockets outside the warehouse where Samuel paid
for the stock for the store. The steamboat that looked like it was
bowing in half, with the end portions rising higher out of the water
than the middle, blew its whistle. Keaton jumped at the sound, and
the colored boys laughed. The water splashed when an olive-skinned
man cast a fishnet from the pier. His long, skinny arms stayed in the
air, frozen in the position until the weighted net floated deeper into
the water.

Keaton inhaled the scent of salt, sweat, and seafood that lingered.
Then he held his breath, hoping that by doing so he could filter out
the flu that kept most of the town behind secure doors. He should
have worn the mask like his mother wanted him to.

A bowlegged man with gray hair parted down the middle stared
at Keaton from the bow of the *Crescent City* steamboat. Then he
bounded down the plank that was secured to the dock. Keaton
looked back toward the net that was flying in the air again.

"You the one they told me about?" the man asked. He raised his
leg and brushed away the bits of cotton that clung to his pants.

"Sir?"

"You the one they hired to be my boy?"

Keaton looked around the dock and shoved his hands inside his
pockets again.

"My other captain's boy is eat up with that flu. They told me they
had me another lined about and I was figuring . . ."

"No, sir," Keaton said before looking at the cans of oysters that
were stacked at the end of the boat under a blue awning that was
tattered and faded.

"Well, you have any experience on the boats?"

Keaton studied the way the smoke from the steamboat danced in
the breeze. The colored boys walked back by him, and one of them

snickered. Keaton waited until they had passed before he answered the captain. "I, uhh . . . I rafted wood downriver."

"Is that so?" The man picked at a fresh scab on the side of his chin. "That's hard work. Man's work."

Keaton nodded and then glanced over his shoulder toward the warehouse, wondering how much longer Samuel would take inside.

"Captain Marcum," the man said.

Keaton stuck out his hand and gripped the captain's hand before the man had a chance to initiate the handshake himself. "Keaton Wallace."

"I pay three dollars a week. Not a cent more. You clean my quarters, run messages back and forth between me and the engine room. . . . We don't need business spread all over the boat, so you have to be discreet. . . . You get to see new places and so forth and so on." The captain reared back so that his stomach protruded forward. He looked Keaton up one side and down the other. "And just so you know, I got no use for know-it-alls."

"Yes, sir," Keaton said.

"Let me know if you're interested, or if you're not, pass the word on. I got no use for lollygaggers." Before the captain walked back to the boat with his knees turned out to the sides, he said, "You'd think there was a plague around here. I never seen such a racket made over a bad cold."

When Samuel came out, Keaton gripped the side of the crate containing the supplies needed for their store and shuffled with the others who carried the crate to the wagon. Keaton gritted his teeth and stared at the colored boy who held the box on the opposite side.

On the ride home, he never mentioned meeting the steamboat captain to Samuel. He kept his eyes away from the gravediggers at the cemetery and wondered if his father had ended up doing that sort of work—steamboating, not gravedigging. Maybe Lanier was riding the boats up and down the river too. Maybe he had never left at all and was living on the boat, waiting for the right time to come back.

After they had returned to Dead Lakes and put the sacks of grain, cans of seasonings, and boxes of gauze masks on display in the store, Keaton walked toward the school that had been turned into a makeshift hospital. Easing around to the side where he had once smoked a cigar he had snuck out of the store with his friends, Keaton peeked in through the open window that had been cracked by a rock thrown by a girl who moved to town.

Inside the classroom the desks had been stacked in the back next to the coat closet. Cots lined the side of the wall nearest to the blackboard that still had the numbers that Miss Clarkson had written for their math quiz. The doctor who shuttled around the area counties tending to the sick was bent over from exhaustion as much as from bad posture. His thin white hair stood out from his head like he had been shocked. There was a shortage of doctors in the area. The younger, more adventurous, and some said more patriotic doctors had joined the war effort overseas and on military bases.

Miss Clarkson, Mrs. Pomeroy, and Ella circled around the cots, dabbing mouths that foamed with blood and saliva. Coughs from the patients jarred the opened windowpanes from where Keaton watched. The door to the school swung open, and Keaton saw Reverend Simpson straining to carry his wife, Myer, into the room. She was stretched out on a cot. It was the first time that Keaton saw the grayish-brown hair that up until then was always kept under a hat and tied up in a neat ball.

The sound of tapping and laughter caused him to move from the window and to the back of the school, where wildflowers grew. Next to the outhouse painted with a half-moon over its door sat five caskets stacked on top of one another. Macon and two of his friends, two fair-haired boys who belonged to the owner of a fish camp down the road, climbed up and down the caskets like they were stairs leading to a magical kingdom. The youngest boy stood on the highest one and smiled so wide that he showed two missing teeth. "Walk the plank," Macon shouted and sliced the air with a stick as thick as a sword.

"What are you doing?" Keaton yelled as he ran toward them.

Macon was standing at the bottom casket, waiting his turn. He was wide-eyed and seemed intrigued rather than scared.

Before Keaton could reach them, the boy lost his balance. He landed against the casket and then fell like a domino down the rest of the stack. The top casket fell sideways to the ground. The swollen body of Grayson Marshall, the blacksmith, rolled out onto the grass.

Keaton slapped Macon across the back and shook the wonder out of his eyes. "We were just playing," Macon kept crying. "We didn't know." Before Keaton could grab the Wakefield boys, they scattered, running back toward their home.

Four days later the younger of the two would be placed in a casket half the size of the one that he had pretended was a pirate's plank.

In her dreams Ella would find herself standing in the middle of the classroom, surrounded by cots. They grew until they were stacked on top of each other like bunk beds. "Where's the man?" a man with yellowed teeth would ask and reach up to Ella from his cot with bloodstained fingernails that were turning black at the tips. Turning in circles, Ella would call out for Lanier to come and save them. Every time she had this dream, she would see him standing outside the door next to the place where the undertaker stacked the caskets because room at the funeral home had become scarce. He would look at her with serenity that she thought no one was any longer capable of possessing. Pulling the gauze mask from her face to yell to him, Ella would only find another mask and then another. She would jolt awake clawing at her face until scratches lined her cheeks like acne on a teenage girl.

Before leaving the house to relieve Neva for the early-morning shift at the makeshift clinic, Ella opened the door and peeked at

Macon, who was sleeping with his back to her. She counted the breaths that he took as his back rose and contracted. After the casket had overturned and the Wakefield boy had died, Ella quarantined Macon to his room. His constitution was weakened enough from respiratory ailments. But from the accounts of all the healthy who passed her way, the concern was unwarranted. She heard their speculations in clipped whispers. "You're lucky you let that man stay with you," Mr. Pomeroy finally said right to her face at the entrance of her store. "I just imagine he put a shield of protection around your place before he left. Maybe that's why the rest of us who did him wrong are suffering," Mr. Pomeroy said in a hiss. Ella ran her hand through her hair and could think of nothing to say. Watching Mr. Pomeroy walk across the road to his home, shuffling his bag of goods from one arm to the other, she started to call out to him but returned to her sweeping. Dust flew up from the porch steps. She only paused long enough to remind Samuel, who was now running the store, to put on a mask.

At the schoolhouse door, a nurse wearing a stained apron came out carrying a bedpan. Ella didn't recoil the way she had when she first came to help. She stepped to the side, held her breath, and entered the place that was now haunting her nightly dreams.

Neva Clarkson wrung a hand towel in a tin dishpan filled with murky water. She placed it on the head of the beekeeper's daughter. When Neva looked up at Ella, her eyes were cradled above dark purplish circles and her face was flushed. The gauze mask she wore was turned sideways.

"You need to go on and get some rest," Ella said and then placed a mask over her own face.

"Bonaparte was here a moment ago," Neva said.

The girl with the towel on her head coughed, and the others on the cots followed. Myer Simpson's eyes turned red, the blood vessels bursting from the constant strain of coughing and gagging. The girl next to her called out for her father, but Neva and Ella paid her little attention. There were too many scattered about the room who were worse off, and fever caused most of them to hallucinate.

"It seems the doctor set off to Bay County without going to the salt mines like he told me he would," Neva said.

"Are there many sick out at Bonaparte's place?"

"His wife," Neva whispered and pulled off the apron that, once pristine white, was now splotched in aged blood and gold-colored mucus.

"What about the daughter? What about Geneva?"

"Healthy as can be. Running and playing. What to make of it?" Neva gave Ella a knowing glance. Ella hoped that she would not mention Lanier and question whether or not his blessing rendered the girl immune.

"I'm going out there this afternoon," Ella said.

"Ella, you can't . . ." Neva's words softened. She folded the apron and put it in the barrel with the rest of the dirty sheets and used masks that were burned every evening in a sand pit that had been dug behind the school. "You can't be doing that." She started to leave and then spun around. The bright sun streamed in from the tall windows and illuminated blue veins in Neva's neck. "I'll go with you," Neva said.

By the time Myer Simpson left this world, her mouth gaped open like she had one last word to say. Lines of phlegm zigzagged the corners of her mouth like a perfectly shaped spiderweb. Ella tried not to stare, but she couldn't help but wonder if the caked mucus on Myer's lips trapped parting words asking forgiveness. Ella pondered whether she would have given it to her.

Before Myer's body could be wrapped in a sheet and removed, Ella felt the start of a slight headache. "Just a bad case of nerves." Neva repeated reassurances and fanned her fingers across her back. "Your head hurts, and my back is in knots. It's nervous strain. How much can one person take, I ask you." Neva turned to place a damp cloth on the forehead of the next patient, but Ella didn't move away from the spot where Myer lay. She was paralyzed not by the tension that Neva reasoned, but by a dizziness that caused her ears to ring.

Ella didn't mention anything the next day when stiffness settled in her neck. Going to bed that evening, she held on to the words spoken over her by Mr. Pomeroy and pictured a net, the type that kept mosquitoes away, hanging in all corners of her property and draping the top of her roof. When the sun rose and sunlight stretched like fingers across her bed, Ella tried to get up, but the chill of a fever kept her pinned down.

Outside Ella's bedroom window, at the corner of the store, girls whose brother had just died skipped the new jump rope that their mother had bought them out of guilt for believing she never showed the son enough love. Their singsong chant tickled Ella's ears and tormented her mind:

I had a little bird.
    Its name was Enza.
    I opened up the window, and in-flu-enza.

27

When Ella fell ill and took to her bed, Samuel assumed full responsibility for running the commissary. Macon became the reluctant assistant to Neva Clarkson, who cared for Ella. The boy would run and fetch fresh pans of water, lay washcloths across Ella's face, and even empty the chamber pot. But it was Keaton who felt that it was up to him to keep Ella from dying.

After Neva Clarkson had given Ella the cocktail of turpentine and sugar that Bonaparte claimed helped his wife recover, she showed Keaton how to measure out the dosage. "How are you holding up?" Neva asked before closing the door to the bedroom where Ella's sleep was broken by coughs.

Keaton kept his eyes on the rising of his mother's chest against the sheet. When he shifted his weight in the straight-back chair next to the bed, the floor creaked.

Keaton looked out the window, watching Miss Clarkson walk away with a wicker basket dangling at the crook of her elbow. The washcloth that was drooped across his mother's forehead slid down over her right eye.

Easing the dresser drawer open, Keaton flipped through the pants that his mother kept folded inside. He had seen her put the card that came with the puppet that Lanier sent into the drawer. Although she had never told any of them that the puppet was from Lanier, Keaton had suspected. The wooden toy was painted with the same almond-shaped eyes as the miniature versions he had crafted in the barn. When Ella was at the store, Keaton had found the postcard under the pair of khaki pants that were permanently stained with turpentine. Keaton had said nothing to his brothers about the card. Part of him was fearful that Samuel would use the card against their mother and further his talk that she had been carrying on with Lanier.

Holding the postcard with the black-and-white photograph of a streetcar idling toward the camera, Keaton looked at the address and then over at Ella. Her chest rose and sank with her gasping breath. Tucking the card inside the waist of his pants, he looked out the window and watched the people move about their business as if it were any other day. Only the masks on their faces indicated what they were hiding from.

At daylight when Samuel opened up for business, Neva Clarkson took her place in the chair in Ella's room. With everyone distracted, Keaton went to his bedroom and pulled out the empty seed sack that he had taken out of the storeroom the day before.

Careful not to stand in view of the windows that lined the side of the store, Keaton walked directly under them, brushing his shoulder against the splintered wood of the outside wall. Mr. Busby's wagon was tied to the hitching post by the corner just like it was every last Friday of the month, influenza or not. Mr. Busby had spent the day before busily photographing those who had been reluctant to have their picture made. "Pictures last forever . . . long after our souls have left the bodies," Mr. Busby had told them, scaring them into letting him position them against the black velvet and securing celluloid proof that they had ever existed. "Off to Apalachicola and down to the dock tomorrow to photograph a dead man they're shipping home to New Orleans," Mr. Busby said the day before when Keaton came in to get another stick of peppermint for his mother to suck on. "Lots of people wanting portraits of the dearly departed all laid out in their Sunday best. Business is up twofold. But it's a shame how it came about, of course."

After the beekeeper walked from the store with the veil of his hat hanging down the back of his neck, Keaton lifted up the tarp over the wagon that had once been bright red but was now faded orange from exposure to the sun. Inside the moldy-smelling wagon, Keaton put the sack of clothes under his chest and pushed away the sharp ends of a candelabra that poked at his leg. Lodged between a torn screen printed with hand-sewn blue jays and a chunk of green marble that had once been a fireplace mantel, Keaton listened to the chatter of those who went about their business and waited for the man who would unknowingly secure his passage to New Orleans.

When Mr. Busby's wagon stopped at the post office in Apalachicola, Keaton waited until he heard Mr. Busby grunt as he climbed off and tied the horses up to the hitching posts. The sputter and then roar as an automobile gained speed and passed by on the road tangled with the sound of Mr. Busby pitching his services to a woman on the sidewalk. The woman sternly said, "No thank you," and Keaton could make out her steps as she walked away on the wooden sidewalk. Keaton counted to fifty and figured that had given Mr. Busby enough time to make it inside the post office. He slowly lifted the edge of the tarp. A boy not much older than himself nailed a leaflet to the side of the hitching post and then darted across the street, not realizing that two of the leaflets had fallen to the ground. *Dover's Powder for Pain: Do Not Fear When Fighting a German or a Germ.*

Keaton slipped out the back of the wagon, pausing only long enough to untangle the end of the croaker sack containing his belongings from the leg of a broken chair.

Keaton skipped down the sidewalk with the sack over his shoulder, wondering if anyone would try to stop and question him. He kept looking back, but not even the colored man who swept the boarded walkway outside the inn noticed him. The man kept his head tucked and only occasionally stopped sweeping long enough to straighten the red handkerchief that was secured over his face like a bank robber's. Once Keaton made it past the first intersection, even Mr. Busby's white horses stopped watching him and began biting the post where they were tied.

At the dock, Captain Marcum came down to greet him only after a toothpick-thin man named Silverton, who Keaton was sure was named such because of a silver front tooth, skeptically sized him up.

"You came back, did you?" Captain Marcum said with his gray hair perfectly parted down the middle. The ends of his hair hung just below his ears and fluttered with a breeze that drifted off the water. A flock of seagulls hung in midflight over a bucket of fish heads. The yellow in Captain Marcum's hair seemed brighter in the morning sun, and the seagulls scattered as he passed. "What makes you think I'll still have you? You did say you're fourteen, didn't you?"

Keaton looked down at the bucket of fish heads and nodded, wondering if the captain would figure out that he was only thirteen. The fish head closest to the top had a swollen eye that seemed to be staring right back at him as if the dismembered fish knew that he was lying. "Sir, I can promise you this. I'll outwork any man you got on this boat," Keaton said with an assuredness that caused the captain to tilt his head the same way the seagulls looked at the fish heads.

"If that's true, then I'll pay you three and a quarter a week. If you're not man enough for the job, then you find yourself looking at a one-way passage back from New Orleans."

Keaton decided that he wouldn't remind the captain that he had originally told him he'd pay three dollars a week. The less said, the better. Silverton pointed to a narrow stairwell that led to the deck below and hollered, "Room at the end. Right over the hull." He laughed before he walked toward three men who were tossing bales of cotton to one corner of the cargo area.

Down below, the smell of the hull—a tonic of oil and human waste—overtook Keaton, and he pulled the collar of his shirt up over his nose. At the end of the dark, narrow hall, he found a cramped room with blotches of mildew stamped on the wall. Keaton put his sack on the corner of the soiled hammock that he would sleep on. The whistle rang from the top deck, and he jumped.

Back up on the storage deck, Keaton dodged passenger trunks as men with shirtsleeves rolled up to their biceps tossed the cargo around as easily as he and Macon thumped at their marbles. He listened to Silverton go over his primary responsibilities such as keeping the captain's cabin clean, delivering messages between the engine room and the captain's perch, and preventing an overflow of the waste in the hull. "We don't need passengers fretting and getting all in our business," Silverton told him. The whistle blew once more, and both of them locked their stances, trying to stay balanced as the steamboat pushed away from the dock and headed out into the bay.

Keaton recited in his mind everything that Silverton was telling him. He tried not to let the man that lisped with the piece of silver in his mouth notice that he was gazing off just above his right shoulder. He had about as much control over the boil that stirred in his stomach as he did over his fear that he was making a mistake. Nodding at Silverton, Keaton pictured Samuel reading the note that he had left for him under his pillow. Samuel would probably make fun of him for leaving a note like a lovesick girl. He preferred to think of it that way as opposed to Samuel vowing to beat him for running off the way their father had. *I'm not running off,* Keaton kept repeating to himself as he mumbled "umm-hmm" to Silverton's mandates.

"Are you hearing a word that I'm saying?" Silverton asked. A spray of his spit landed on Keaton's arm.

"Yes, sir," Keaton answered. But he never turned his eyes away from the sight of Wefing's marine hardware store that stood majestically on Water Street just over Silverton's shoulder. Long after Silverton had tossed him the broom to sweep pieces of cotton from the deck, Keaton stared at the building until it became a tiny square on the horizon. Moving behind the tallest bale of cotton at the front of the bow, Keaton gripped the broom, looked away toward the Gulf that was unfolding like a clean, gigantic blackboard, and bit his tongue, struggling not to cry like a scared little boy.

Lanier stayed away from the influenza tent as long as he could. Every time he closed his eyes he saw Harlan's face with the sores covering his lips and the bones of his cheeks under yellowed skin so thin it seemed like it was already decaying. Lanier tried to rub away the chill that never left his system after seeing the inside of the tent. Each time he did, he felt the broken skin where the woman had clawed him in a dying fit.

Lanier kept telling himself that Harlan was not worth saving. In fact, he made it a point to walk three blocks out of his way to work at the United Fruit Company just so he wouldn't have to pass Jackson Square. Buckling his pants and pulling on his boots, Lanier never noticed the first light of day that cut through the thin curtain and fell upon the stacks of books. Reason might agree that Harlan Wallace was better off dead, but Lanier's heart told him otherwise.

Standing at the tent in the square, Lanier listened as the bells of the cathedral struck six times. Not even the clanging from the steeple could mask the sound of the coughing.

Sunlight bled through the tent ceiling and caused the nuns tending patients in the second row of cots to shield their faces when they called out for supplies from the volunteers. The nun with protruding front teeth came up to Lanier with damp towels balanced on her upheld arm. "Thank you for coming," she whispered and then whisked past him toward the basin table. The scent of rubbing alcohol and body odor accompanied her.

A man with an unknotted black tie and a teenage boy wearing a golf cap tied the ends of two sheets. On the cot before them lay a four-year-old girl, her eyes wide with anticipation, just like the dolls that Lanier made. It was only when Lanier reached the foot of the bed that he realized she was dead.

Cries from a woman were shrill and then grew fainter as a nun escorted her out of the tent.

Lanier eased toward the pole that held the corner of the tent up. He leaned down over Harlan, debating what sort of greeting he should offer. He opened his mouth but no words would form.

"Wylie Stillis," Harlan hissed through the space where his front two teeth were once located. His voice sounded more garbled, as if he were speaking underwater.

Lanier flinched at the sound of his father's name. "No," he stammered. "No, it's Lanier. Wylie's . . . Wylie's son."

"Wylie," Harlan said and turned his head. A patch of hair was missing from the side of his scalp, and a fresh V-shaped scar was in its place. "Wylie. You got out of prison, did you?"

"I'm Lanier," he said. "Lanier."

Harlan coughed, and a rope of phlegm wormed out his mouth and onto the sheet. He gasped and exhaled his words. "Wylie, how come you raped that girl and sliced her up?"

"I am not Wylie. Now look at me. It's Lanier. I'm your cousin."

"I don't claim you." Harlan hacked and the cot vibrated. His fingers trembled as he tried to touch the sores on his lips. "You sliced that girl up like a hog." Harlan's body convulsed as he coughed and tried to speak. Phlegm and damnations flew from his mouth.

Lanier felt the shame wrap around him tighter than the sheet that was stretched up to Harlan's neck. "I'm Lanier. *Lanier.* I'm trying to help you, if you'll let me."

"If anybody needs helping, it's you." Harlan tried to lean up on his elbow. For a second Lanier thought that he might sit up in bed. "You rapist and murderer. You left your wife and boy to beg for handouts. You'll rot in hell."

Lanier gripped Harlan's arm through the sheet. It felt like the hind leg of a day-old calf. Harlan kicked until the sheet untucked from the cot. Gnarled yellow toenails broke free and poked Lanier. Jerking away, Lanier lost his balance and landed on one knee.

"Now listen. I tried to help your family just like I'm trying to help you. You left them, Harlan. Do you remember that?"

Closing his eyes, Harlan lifted his hand long enough to crook his finger and motion. Lanier leaned closer. "Wylie, get me my pipe," Harlan said with haggard, pungent breath. "I got to take my medicine."

Lanier felt rage building at the base of his skull. It boiled him the same way he imagined the fevers afflicting those in the tent. Everything he'd felt about his father was placed on Harlan. Gripping the side of the cot, he shook it hard enough for Harlan to open both eyes. "Don't cast stones when you don't have the rocks to throw."

Harlan coughed again and arched his back. Balling his fist, he contorted against Lanier's grip and then released. "Come nearer," he whispered. Lanier moved closer until he could make out the film that clouded Harlan's dark eyes. They were dead to the spirit like the eyes of the horses that were forced to pull the carriages around the square.

Harlan raised his wobbling head and managed to grin before spitting a stream of green phlegm straight into Lanier's face.

A nun screamed orders. Two volunteer medics rushed forward with leather straps. While they tied Harlan's arms to the sides of the cot, he laughed and gagged all at the same time. None of the rest of them could make out what Harlan was saying, but Lanier understood him perfectly. "Wylie, I reckon to see you in hell."

It was Macon who found the note that Keaton left on Samuel's bed. He ran into Ella's room and jostled Samuel, who sat sleeping, slumped to the side of the rocking chair. Rubbing his eyes, Samuel read the note, silently mouthing each word. *I've gone to find Lanier so he can help us. Be back soon.* Samuel looked at Macon, cursed Lanier Stillis, and then balled the note into his fist. He propped both hands on Macon's shoulders and led him out into the hallway, feet away from where Neva Clarkson slept in a state of exhaustion on the living room sofa. Squatting before Macon, Samuel looked him straight in the eye and whispered, "Don't you worry about Keaton. I'll let the law know tomorrow. He's big enough to fend for himself until they find him. We got enough to worry about with Mama. And I want you to promise me you won't tell Mama a word about this. Now is the time we got to be strong. We got to get Mama better. She can't get better if she's worrying about Keaton."

Macon nodded, and tears welled up in his eyes.

"No matter what happens, I won't leave you," Samuel whispered. "You understand? I'll never leave you."

Nodding faster, Macon reached to hug Samuel, but he had already slipped back into Ella's room. Running back into the bedroom, Macon threw himself on the bed that Samuel had not occupied for two days and landed facedown on the spot where the note had rested. He buried his face deeper into the covers and cried harder than he had the day his playmate died.

The next morning, an hour after the sun rose, Neva stood over Ella and pressed the moist rag against her friend's forehead. Macon sat cross-legged at the doorway of Ella's bedroom. When he saw his mother stir in the bed, Macon ran and grabbed the big wicker fan shaped like a palmetto leaf and began waving it across her. Samuel moved from the edge of Ella's dresser where the postcard from Lanier had been hidden and grabbed the top of the fan. He slowly shook his head at Macon and motioned for him to move back to the door. Macon took a few steps and then settled against the dresser with his arm propped on top of the crocheted doily that his great-aunt had made.

A cool breeze drifted in through the open window. The sheer curtains twisted and turned like dancing ghosts.

Ella opened her eyes. As if they were connected, the boys and Neva moved closer to the bed as one unit. "You're better now," Samuel said. It was more of a command than a question. "You're better. I can tell. Listen to me, I can tell." Neva draped her long fingers over his shoulder and squeezed and then patted.

Ella stared at the swirls of yellow in the curtains that twisted against the wind that came in through the bedroom windows. Swimming in the fever that cooked her body, Ella's mind dreamed in bursts of illuminating color. Color as bright as the kaleidoscope that her aunt Katherine had allowed her to look through on Sunday afternoons. Indeed, her aunt had come to her through the window last evening and told her that colors abound and beauty would never fade with the sun. Ella pretended to know what she meant, but before she could ask any questions, her aunt moved behind the curtain that bowed out of the room with the current of the breeze. The curtain fell back against the window, and there was nothing there but the high-backed chair with the seat made of black-and-white cowhide that Ella used as a place to lay out her robe each night.

Ella rolled her head against the pillow and looked toward the door. She tried to reach out for Macon, but the weight of the sheet locked her down like restraints. She tried to smile.

Samuel nudged Neva. "See, I told you she was better."

The attempt was lost on Macon. He peeked through the gap between Neva and Samuel. His eyes were as frightened as they had been when the thrush had nearly killed him.

Come here, son, Ella wanted to say, but the words hung in her throat, blocked by the walls of secretions that Neva constantly wiped out of her mouth. When she tried to reach her arm out to him again, Macon slid his shoulder against the wall and stepped backward out of the room.

At the door she saw Lanier and tried to sit up. Lanier's hair was as bright as the curtains, and his eyes were stronger than she remembered. He held his hands up over Macon's head and ran his fingers over the boy's shoulders as if he were playing a game with him. Macon turned away and slipped down the hall. His departure didn't seem to bother Lanier. He just stood there, dressed in a white linen shirt that dangled at the waist of his denim pants. Ella recognized the tenderness in his eyes that caused her to trust him when common sense dictated otherwise. She tried to rise and greet him. In her mind she beckoned Lanier to stay, but Neva pushed her back against the bed that was contoured and damp from her suffering. "Rest now, Ella," Neva whispered. "You belong to rest."

The curtain swept up in the air again, and when Ella looked out the window, she saw Harlan standing in front of the sunflowers. He was wearing a derby hat and a gold chain that dangled from his vest pocket. His shoulders were as broad as they had been before the addiction ravaged him. He moved toward the house with the same purpose Ella had seen when she first met him. The deep-gutted laugh that rolled out like carpet announcing his celebrated arrival caused Ella to shake. Neva replaced the damp rag with a fresh one and then placed a chip of ice on her broken lips. The cool sensation tickled Ella's senses, and she tried to open her mouth wide enough to take in all of the relief.

Ella jerked her head back toward the door, wanting to warn Lanier that Harlan was coming back for his possessions. But this time when she looked at the doorway, all Ella saw was the chalk mark, shaped like an apple, that Macon had drawn on the door when no one was watching.

28

Silverton and the other men who worked in the engine room of the steamboat were drunk by the time the last passenger disembarked at the pier in New Orleans. Captain Marcum never told Keaton not to follow them. He just lit a pipe and told Keaton to use the big-handled brush that was lying on the nightstand in his cabin to clean off his black suit coat. Wood covered the walls, floor, and ceiling. It reminded Keaton of a box, and he thought how Lanier must have felt trapped in an even smaller version.

"The beams," the captain said and pointed to the wood molding that lined the ceiling. "You dusted them, did you?" The brass lanterns on the wall had been cleaned too, but Keaton decided not to point them out.

"I'm going to have me a steak dinner and paint the town red," the captain announced and slipped on the coat Keaton had prepared. Captain Marcum looked at Keaton and laughed in a way that made him feel ashamed. "Boy, you know what 'paint the town red' means?"

"Yes, sir," Keaton said and fidgeted with the torn place on his shirtsleeve.

Before leaving the cabin, Captain Marcum turned the photograph of a doughy-faced, ringlet-haired woman in a pewter frame facedown on the nightstand. "Well, then. I reckon I don't need to caution you about wayward women on the streets who are eager to take your wages." The captain paused at the door of the cabin and pulled at the ends of his beard as if he might be pulling off a disguise. "I'll tell you like I tell all the others. Don't get so tight that you can't work tomorrow."

Standing on the deck of the boat, Keaton watched the captain disappear into the wave of people that flowed around the pier. Rows of crates lined the dock that stretched longer and wider than the one he knew back in Apalachicola. Sounds of breaking glass, exotic accented words, shouts of anger, and peaceful chimes from the cathedral intoxicated the air. Above a warehouse painted with the words *United Fruit Company*, Keaton saw Venus shimmering in the sky, the same way he knew it was doing over their barn in Dead Lakes.

Loneliness wrapped around Keaton until he couldn't move. He pictured himself being swept up in the crowd and drowning, tossed about the foreign land, never to be heard of again by his family. He thought about the Bible story of Jonah being swallowed by the whale and thrown up in a distant place because he didn't do the job that God intended for him to accomplish.

Stepping forward and walking down the plank that was tied to the pier with knotted ropes frayed at the ends, Keaton wobbled on the wood that shifted with the weight of the men who exited in front of him. He tried not to grip the side of the plank and look vulnerable.

Out in the street that was sectioned off by warehouses on each corner and a bar where the sound of trumpets echoed, Keaton put his hands in his pockets and forced himself to stand up straight. If he could pretend that he knew where he was and what he was doing, then maybe everyone else would believe it.

He circled the square three times and looked the other way when he saw a man and a woman locked together and pressed against the wall inside an alley. The money he'd put in his shoe caused him to walk like a pebble was lodged under his sock. Tripping over a missing cobblestone in the street, Keaton landed just shy of a car that passed by, honking its horn at him. A group of young men not much older than him laughed and passed around a bottle of whiskey underneath a building where a woman's feet dangled outside a second-story window. A ruby-colored shoe covered one of them; the other one was streaked with dirt.

By the bar, crumpled newspaper and empty bottles littered the foot of a scrub oak. A woman with bushy auburn hair parted on the side had her arm propped against the tree. Her elbow pressed against the trunk like she was part of the natural growth. A jade ring, too big for her index finger, caught Keaton's attention. The woman flicked it with her thumb, and the cut glass that lined the ring glistened against the gas streetlight. Two men wearing sailor uniforms vied for her attention by pounding their chests and fanning money between their fingers. "This here ain't cheap," the woman said in a laugh. Giving up, the men went inside the bar. They circled around a young girl who was sitting on a stool wearing ripped black stockings.

When the woman by the tree looked toward Keaton, he quickly turned his head. Just as he was about to cross the street, the woman tapped him on the shoulder with the ringed finger. "You with Captain Marcum's boat?"

Keaton looked back at the bar. Now the sailor with pants too short for him was leaning down over the young girl as if consuming her. "I, uhh . . . yeah . . . yes, ma'am."

"There ain't no ma'am around here. I work for myself." The woman laughed and then coughed. Keaton stepped backward.

"Ain't nothing but cigarettes. Don't you go thinking I got the influenza or nothing. I'm clean."

Keaton dug his hands deeper into his pockets and wondered if she thought he was fiddling with his money.

The woman brushed her hand across his brow, and the ring pulled against his hair. She smelled of damp cigarettes that had long been stomped out.

"You're a cutie pie. Just a regular little cutie pie."

"I'm not that little," Keaton said.

The woman laughed and then coughed again. "This your first time? First time in New Orleans, I mean."

The young girl at the bar shrieked and threw her head back. The sailor bit her strand of pearls and the trumpet inside hit a shrill note.

"Well, anyway," the woman said. She pulled a cigarette out from the top of her low-cut dress. Her chest was blotchy and more freckled than her face. Like a magician she pulled a match out of the bushiest side of her hair. Keaton went flush when she put her hand on his shoulder, balanced herself, and struck the match on the sole of her shoe. She blew smoke from the corner of her red-lipped mouth and held his glance when he found the courage to look her directly in the eye. "You know, if I wasn't a good woman, I could take advantage of you."

Excitement and fear lit Keaton the same way her cigarette gave light to the night that was settling over the street. A car rattled past them. Exhaust caused Keaton to cough. This time the woman moved away. "There's some around here who'd take you to service and then knock you in the head. They'd take everything you had, and you'd wind up not knowing where you was . . . or who you was for that matter."

"I'm here on business."

"Ain't we all," the woman said in a graveled laugh.

"I'm looking for somebody."

"Uh-huh." The woman took a draw on the cigarette and stuck the hand with the ring out to him. "I'm Ivey," she said with the formality of a business owner.

"Pleased to meet you, ma'am. I'm Keaton Wallace from over in Dead Lakes, Florida."

"Hey, I mean it. Knock it off with the *ma'am*." She tried to laugh but it lazily turned into a cough. "I figure I ain't much older than you."

Keaton felt his face grow warm with embarrassment and glanced back at the bar. The young girl and men were now gone. The bartender was wiping a dingy towel across the table where they'd been. He was looking out at the street where Ivey and Keaton stood.

She blew smoke from the other side of her mouth and talked all at the same time. "What sort of business you got here anyway? Fresh-off-the-farm boy like you ain't got no business here, if you ask me."

Keaton pulled from his pocket the postcard he had found in his mother's dresser drawer. He smoothed out the spot where he had folded it before showing the picture of the streetcar to Ivey. She flipped it over and studied the words. "A streetcar. Boy, you come all this way to ride a streetcar?"

When she handed the postcard back to Keaton he pushed it back into her hand. "No, not the streetcar. The address on the back. That's where I need to go."

Ivey pushed the card back at him. "The light ain't too good. I can't make out what them words is saying."

Keaton studied the card with Lanier's swirled penmanship. He could make the words out perfectly fine and wondered if he would insult her by reading them aloud. "It's right here," he said, pointing to the top corner of the card and handing it back to Ivey.

She fanned the postcard away with her cigarette and wouldn't even look at him. "Look, I need to get going. It's prime time and . . ."

Before she could walk away, Keaton read the words on the card as fast as he could. By the time Ivey got to the corner of the bar she turned around. "What was that last part again?"

"Lanier. Love, Lanier." Keaton felt burdened inside, like he was carrying the sin of his mother and betraying her secrets.

"Baby, I ain't interested in no love. I'm talking about the street number. What was that street you was saying?"

Keaton held the postcard up to catch a sliver of light from the street post. "209 North Burgundy Street." He repeated the address once more, only slower.

Ivey ran her tongue around the edge of her mouth. "If I was to take you there, you reckon somebody will pay me for my time?"

"You know where Lanier . . . where this man's staying at?"

"I know the gal who claims she owns the place. Letticia Prideaux. Nothing but trash. Cheapest whore in the Quarter."

29

The taxi wagon Keaton and Ivey rode in was driven by a Chinaman. The man at first pretended not to understand English until Ivey slapped him against the back of the head. At the edge of the French Quarter they passed a pharmacy. A poster board with an illustration of a lamp-sized silver fumigator hung from the store window. *Stop Influenza Infections with Sanitas Fumigators*, the sign read. Keaton made a mental note of the name of the equipment and for good measure closed his eyes and etched out the letters in his mind.

At the gate of Miss Prideaux's courtyard, dead leaves from a banana tree scattered the chipped walkway. Ivey told Keaton she'd wait at the corner by the street post. "If she sees me then that whore won't tell you a thing. She's always been jealous of me."

The woman who answered the door wore a short silk robe that was probably new five years ago. The top portion was stained, and the color was the same as the red mole on her forehead.

"I'm looking for Lanier," Keaton said in a stammer and rose up on his tiptoes to appear taller.

Miss Prideaux dressed him up and down with her eyes. "The question is, is he looking for you?"

"I know he is, ma'am," Keaton said with a confidence that would even impress Ivey.

Keaton found him in the courtyard of St. Louis Cathedral where during normal times Lanier would sell his carved dolls and puppets. Now the spaces for artists and street vendors had been taken up with khaki-colored tents. A carnival, Keaton first thought. Then a nun dressed all in white walked out one of the tents. She tossed a pan of urine out into the briar patch and palmettos that grew near the corner. Inside the tents, gurgled coughs and moans caused Keaton to lift the top of his shirt up over his nose.

He walked through the passageway lined by tents. Nurses with hollow eyes glanced at him but never questioned. The chimes on the cathedral rang ten times, and a new shift emerged from the cathedral doors. Keaton could make out the flames from candles inside and the shadows of the faithful who lined the nave waiting for confession.

A young man wearing a loose shirt with a brown patch sewn to the pocket came out behind several nuns. When the man put his cap back on his head, he stepped away from the line of care- givers, and Keaton's heart felt like it had momentarily stopped. Lanier shuffled around the young man and then broke from the group. He walked toward the last tent and then circled the bushes where the bedpan had been emptied. Trotting toward him, Keaton bumped into a nun carrying fresh towels and mumbled apologies. At the end of the line he looked both ways but saw nothing other than a funeral home carriage making its way down the street and a dog whose coat was ravaged with mange darting underneath the covered sidewalk.

A cough rang out from the last tent, and then Keaton froze at the sound of the voice that had called to him all those times in the woods. The buzzing rang in his ears like the sound of a hive being disturbed. Keaton started to open the tent flap but was stopped by a nun with skin that clumped on the sides of her eyes like handlebars on a bike. "Young man, this is off-limits," she said.

"I know that man," he said.

"I don't care who you know. This is as good as a hospital and we follow hospital orders. This is quarantined. Do you want to go and get yourself a case of the flu?" She folded her arms and moved close enough for him to smell the scent of stale coffee on her breath. "You don't know what you're getting into."

Before she could pull his arm away, Keaton jerked open the tent flap. Inside, the scent of death almost knocked him backward. Lines of bodies filled the tent that seemed to run for a street block. The sisters who were wearing white habits fluttered about the area with stained skirts. They moved about like doves that had been bloodied and dazed in crossfire. A young girl, about his age, stared up at him from the cot where she lay. Her blue eyes were only made brighter by the dark stripes that spread out over her cheeks, broken blood vessels that had turned black.

Lanier rose from the side of the cot containing the silhouette drawer, Mr. Pelham. "Keaton . . . Keaton?"

Keaton stammered before realizing that his mother might already be like these people by now. She might even be dead.

"Where did you . . . ? What are you doing here?" Lanier said, jerking Keaton's arm as he led him outside.

The nun who had cautioned Keaton now reprimanded him. "It's because of such carelessness that we're in the state we're in with this influenza. People like you who have no common sense about them." She stomped off toward the tent.

"Son, what are you doing here? This is no place . . ."

"I don't care what you did. . . . I don't care about none of that from the past." Keaton flung the words out of his mouth so fast that Lanier grabbed his arms.

"Now get ahold of yourself. What are you talking about?"

"I don't care why you left, but I need for you to come back."

"Now settle down." Lanier tried to level his hand on Keaton's shoulder but Keaton brushed him away.

"Mama's sick. She needs you."

A bat swooped down before flying up and hiding inside the bell tower. The cries from a woman in the tent behind them overpowered the coughs of the other patients.

"Now, son, just calm down."

"You can make her better." Keaton grabbed Lanier by the shirt and pulled him closer. "I didn't come all this way to watch you make these people better. I know all about you and her and everything. Just make her better. Please. You can't let her wind up like that." Keaton pointed to the tent where the woman was retching and coughing. Silhouettes of the nuns moved about inside, gathering around the cot and trying to hold the woman down. The woman's thrashing legs were illuminated against the side of the tent. She kicked the air the same way she might if the nuns had been trying to amputate her.

Lanier looked away from the tent and up at the top of the cathedral. Keaton felt the glare of the nun who had lectured him. She tossed bloodstained towels into a wicker basket and stood with her feet wide apart and her arms held out as if she were about to hold a baby. With the resilience of a grown man, Keaton stood face-to-face with Lanier. "I'm not asking you, Lanier. I'm begging you. Please come back and help her."

Ella's aunt Katherine sat on the edge of the bed. It was the first time since she had been visiting that Aunt Katherine had been that close to Ella. The light from the lantern on the bedroom dresser cast a soft glow behind Aunt Katherine's head. She looked more beautiful than Ella had ever seen her. Her hair was not gray but thicker and blacker. The coal-colored eyes that always made Ella think her aunt could look right through her were so rested, so serene. Over Aunt Katherine's shoulder, Ella could see Neva, slouched sideways in the high-backed chair that Aunt Katherine's father had made for a future wedding day that never arrived. Trying to touch the hem of her gold embroidered dress, Ella could only manage to scratch the sheet. Breathing had become a harder chore than cutting the timber, and at times she dreamed she was tossing deep in the spring that supposedly had no end. She would look up and see the surface bubbling above her and the evergreens that surrounded it, but no matter how hard she kicked she could never reach the top and find air.

Aunt Katherine seemed to know that Ella was struggling. She put her hand on top of the sheet and squeezed Ella's hand underneath it. "You're tired," Aunt Katherine whispered. The voice, high-pitched, almost better suited for a little girl, gave Ella comfort. She said the words the same way she would whenever she admonished Ella to take afternoon naps. "A lady needs rest to keep her skin firm and rosy," she would say. Ella tried to smile, but the cracked and chapped lips caused her too much pain.

"You need to come along with me," Aunt Katherine said. "There's something better than this waiting for you."

"My boys." Ella forced the words out in a wheeze.

Her aunt patted her hand. The touch was light and cool. "They'll be fine. They'll be watched over."

"Where will we go? Back to your house?" The home had been ravaged by a fire the year after Ella wed Harlan. But in her mind the home's smell of licorice and gardenia perfume still thickened the air. Ella gasped, but her aunt didn't seem alarmed like the others.

Aunt Katherine closed her eyes and smiled. Her lips were the color of rubies. Ella wheezed and tried to reach up and touch them.

"Come now," Ella's aunt whispered. "Don't dally." When she stood up, the gold brocade dress with an A-line skirt fanned out across the room. Ella thought it was the most beautiful garment she had ever seen. She wanted to rub her fingers against the dress and once again feel the outline of the tiny woman inside of it. For the first time since her childhood, there was only light inside her mind. The darkness that ushered fear and unease had been washed away by the wave of peace that settled over her.

"It's time to go home," Aunt Katherine announced. She held out both hands and leaned back as if she might be ready to dance. Forcing her hands free from the sheet that held her down, Ella clasped her aunt's hands. The skin that she had remembered as dry and cold was now smooth and welcoming. Ella glanced at Neva, who seemed like she was in a stupor. Neva's mouth was gaping, and her chest rose and sank like a baby pacified from warm milk.

The curtain flew up and welcomed the breeze. Her aunt smiled and waved her hand like she might be welcoming a visitor. "We'll go this way, as not to disturb the others." Aunt Katherine pointed toward Neva, who slept in the chair.

Ella stood at the window and felt her head swimming at the ease with which her aunt, a woman who had once refused to walk through a freshly painted store door for fear of staining her clothing, climbed out of the window. Aunt Katherine stood on the porch on the other side and laughed. The swirling curtains framed her like she was an actress on a stage. She giggled lighter than Ella knew she could and motioned for Ella to follow. "Ella, for goodness' sake. I raised you to be a lady. And a lady knows when it's time to excuse herself and leave."

Brushing the curtain aside, Ella stepped forward and stuck her hand out of the window. She waited for her aunt to grab it and was comforted once again by the soft, dewy touch of Aunt Katherine's fingers. She led Ella the same way she had all those times before when Ella, the orphaned girl, could not take care of herself. Bending her head down, Ella leaned out through the window and took the final climb toward freedom.

30

The morning Lanier paid for their passage back to Apalachicola, he took Keaton to Holt Cemetery at the edge of the city. Broken clouds hung over the only place in New Orleans where bodies were buried below the ground. Lanier never told Keaton that it was a pauper's graveyard.

At a mound of dirt marked with the paw prints of either a small dog or a cat, Keaton stared at the wooden cross that Lanier had hand-carved for Keaton's father. Keaton knelt down at the edge of the damp dirt and ran his finger over the *W* on the wood like he might have been carving the word Wallace himself. The passing roar of a train vibrated the earth. Afterward Keaton glanced up at Lanier. "When you saw him, did he ask anything about us?"

"Oh, yeah," Lanier said. "Sure. He wanted to know all about y'all. He especially wanted you to know how sorry he was. He said he wished he'd never started taking that opium. He cried just like a baby over it." Lanier presented the story the way he'd hoped it would be, not as it was. He would never tell Ella or her sons how Harlan had cursed him, God, and life itself. He would never let on that Harlan lost his faith long before he stumbled into the tent of death on Jackson Square.

Keaton thumped the marker with his thumb and forefinger. He stood up, but dirt remained on the knee of his britches.

"He told me something else, too," Lanier said. "He said he was sure proud of you. He told me that you've always been there for your mama. He told me you could do anything you made your mind up to do. He told me that you—"

"We need to go if we're going to make the boat," Keaton said, brushing past Lanier. He stepped over a rusted angel figurine that sat lopsided on the grave next to his father's. A broken necklace of cut glass hung from the angel's neck. Keaton looked down at the decoration like he might examine it but then hurried down the ragged path that led to the street corner. He didn't say another word until the boat was far from the port of New Orleans.

Lanier didn't pressure Keaton to talk. He respected him more than that. He left the boy staring out into the Gulf through a boat window that was layered with salt and black soot from the smokestack. Lanier stayed at the stern of the boat for most of the trip. He leaned against a rust-covered piling and stared out at the paddleboards that clipped the water. The movements seemed so slow and fatigued. He closed his eyes and stepped forward so the sun could cover him. Images of Ella in various stages of influenza like those he had witnessed in the tent flashed through his mind. Panic boiled up inside him, and he wondered if he was making a mistake. He didn't want to bear another loss. Could her boys stand losing both of their parents? He couldn't finish raising them by himself; there was no use even considering such a notion. Lanier stared down at the wheel of the steamboat. The paddles circled and churned the water, over and over.

Lanier watched the water foam and splash at the slap of the paddles. He stared until his head swam with dizziness. He barely knew Ella. She had been right, they were nothing alike. But Lanier bought his own lie about as much as Keaton had accepted the story that Lanier made up about Harlan's deathbed confession. The time for lies had come and gone.

Lanier stood upright and looked out into the wide-open space of the Gulf. Momentarily blinded by the sunlight, he saw nothing but dots jumping on the horizon. "I never wanted this . . . this gift. Never asked for it. Take it from me. Go on, take it. Just don't take her," he shouted at the choppy, endless waters. Looking up into nothing but brightness, Lanier stretched his arms out wide and breathed deeper than he had since running away from his past in the middle of the night.

When the boat blew its whistle and eased into Apalachicola Bay, Lanier was once again at the stern with his hands dug into his pants pockets. He could make out Wefing's hardware store and the colored boys who emptied wheelbarrows full of sponges that they collected from the boats. The sponges cascaded onto a ship anchor that was propped against the corner of the store. As the muffled sounds from broken conversations on the dock drifted closer, Lanier felt a wave of nausea and wanted to turn right back around toward New Orleans.

Deputy Ronnie, who had been appointed sheriff until a special election could be held, was leaning against the hood of the sheriff's car that still had a spray of bullet holes across the top. A picture of the latest battle surge in France was plastered on the front page of the newspaper that Ronnie read. When he popped the paper and turned the page, Keaton and Lanier walked straight toward him. Ronnie jumped from the car the same as if electricity had run through him. A section of the paper fell to the ground and got swept up in the breeze. The page with the obituaries wound up stuck to a piling at the edge of the dock.

"What the . . . ?" Ronnie said, standing upright. "You got some gall running off. Folks have been looking for you. Boy, you shouldn't worry your brothers that way."

"I went to find Lanier. He's gonna help Mama," Keaton said, tossing the croaker sack of clothes onto the oyster shells that scattered the sand.

"Boy, you ought to be ashamed of yourself for running away." Ronnie didn't wait for him to explain. "Especially with all your family is going through right now. Dead Lakes is hit hard. It was a loss . . . for everybody."

Panic snipped at Lanier. His heart pounded until the pulse seemed to roar in his ears. All he could hear was the word *loss*.

Keaton's voice cracked the way of a boy transitioning into being a man. "Is Mama dead too?"

Looking crossways toward the boats docked, Ronnie spat a stream of tobacco that landed next to one of the sponges that had rolled away from the pile. "Bunches of them gone. . . . Myer Simpson, the Pomeroy boy. Just a shame."

"Mama?"

Shaking his head, Ronnie wiped his mouth. "No, not your mama." Then he folded the paper and lightly tapped it on Keaton's shoulder. "But they tell me she's in bad shape. I ain't going to lie to you."

"We need a ride out there right now," Lanier said. When Ronnie stared at the trunk of goods that Lanier carried, he added, "I can pay you. I got money."

"I ain't running a taxi service." Ronnie ran his thick finger inside his mouth and pulled out a plug of tobacco. He tossed it to the ground and motioned for Keaton to pick up his bag. "Now this is just between you and me. I can't just haul every tomcat there is around the county."

Putting the trunk into the back of the car, Lanier felt Ronnie standing behind him, breathing heavy on his back. "And I want to tell you right now, I don't need another carnival. Fact of the matter, I won't put up with a carnival with your healings and so forth."

Turning to face him, Lanier said, "I never aimed to put one on the first time."

On the drive out to Dead Lakes, little was said. Lanier was lost in his thoughts, and Keaton sat in the front passenger seat, leaning against the open window as the cool autumn breeze swept his hair up in sections.

Passing the pastures along the way, Lanier found comfort in the signs of life that dotted the road. A batch of cattle made Ronnie stop so they could freely cross over to a field blanketed with amber-colored Indian grass and goldenrod. But when the car came to the first sign of human existence, Lanier had the same panic that he had when his friend nailed him into the Blue Moon Clock Company box. Past the house where Neva Clarkson lived, the schoolhouse was still surrounded by wagons and a couple of trucks. If anyone unfamiliar would have wandered into the community, the person would have thought that there was a town celebration. Through the side door of the school that students would exit to make their way to the outhouse, two men wearing gauze masks and work gloves carried a dead body that was wrapped in a sheet, rust-colored with dried blood.

When they pulled up in front of Ella's place, the beekeeper's wife met Keaton at the car door. "When in the world is the store going to open?"

Ignoring her, Keaton ran with the sack on his back toward the house.

While Lanier struggled to get the trunk out, Mr. Pomeroy bolted from his house across the road. He had three days' worth of beard on his face and liquor on his breath.

Tapping Lanier on the shoulder, Mr. Pomeroy folded his arms across a shirt stained with lard. "Where have you been?"

Ronnie stepped in front of them and tossed his head back. "All right, Pomeroy. None of that."

"With folks dropping like flies around here, you decide to run off. When you could really help some people, you run away."

Lanier felt the sting of his words and wanted to run once more. Gripping the handles on the trunk, he looked toward the house and debated where to place his belongings. He ended up walking toward the barn.

Mr. Pomeroy yelled, "My boy died, you know. He fought for his country but died from what? A cold . . . a flu bug." Mr. Pomeroy's words were shrill and sharper. "You saved a mule but you didn't save my boy."

"All right, Pomeroy," Ronnie said. "We don't need more trouble."

Mr. Pomeroy's last words sent a chill down Lanier. It was the impression he feared most.

"If you'd been here, my boy would still be living."

"I'm not a savior. Never claimed to be," Lanier said without turning back to face them. "I'm just a man."

Ella's three sons stood at the open door. Lanier tried to form his words as he walked up the porch steps. He had quit on them the same way he had quit on himself. Even though he wanted to run from them as much as he wanted to run from the gift that he had been given, he nodded and brushed against Samuel's shoulder as he climbed up the last step.

Macon ran out of the door and hugged him around his waist. For the first time since his son died, emotions escaped Lanier's control. Tears fell from his face as freely as sunflowers swayed against the cool evening wind. Keaton led Lanier by the finger and past Samuel, who looked embarrassed and nodded. Never saying a word, Keaton brought Lanier to Ella's bedroom and pointed. Ella was propped on two pillows, her mouth was open, the black hair was matted to her scalp, and a gurgle rose up from her lungs. The long fingers that were draped on top of the sheet were beginning to darken into the color of fresh bruises.

Neva Clarkson appeared paler than usual. She stood to greet Lanier like he might be a dinner guest. "Let me go out to the water pump and get some fresh water," she said before walking out with the ceramic bowl painted with cherubs.

The wind made a whistling sound as it seeped in through the open windows and tangled the curtains. When Lanier stepped into the room, the wood floor creaked against his weight. Keaton moved beside him.

"Miss Clarkson said Mama got out of bed night before last," Macon said. "Must have been sleepwalking or something. Crazy from fever, they say. When Miss Clarkson woke up she found Mama trying to climb out of the window. 'My boys.'" Macon looked up at Lanier. "That's what she was a-saying. 'My boys.'"

"You can make her better, can't you?" Samuel said from the doorway. He stepped inside the room and never looked at Lanier, only at his mother. "Please."

Lanier leaned down next to the bed. He gripped the fingers that he had held all the times before and pretended that they were wed to him. Tears fell from his face and landed on the sheet. He buried his head against the side of her leg that was tucked underneath the cover. Never asking the boys to leave, he prayed the words that he'd been given so long ago. He prayed them with a faith as if he were saying them for the first time. Ella coughed, and the bed shook. A rattling sound rose from her full lips that were outlined in dried blood. He prayed six times and then ten more. He prayed until he felt that every cell of life in him had been given up for her welfare.

By the time he had finished, each of Ella's sons had taken different positions in the room. Keaton was across from him on the other side of the bed, his hands clasped in prayer. Macon stood behind the curtain closest to Ella's head. The silhouette of his body behind the sheer yellow material resembled an apparition. Samuel was in the opposite corner of the room, staring at the bed, guarding it. Only Neva Clarkson went about her business. She skirted around Lanier and continued applying the cold compresses to her friend's scalp. Each time she touched her hot skin, she prayed in her own way.

When Ella's breathing became nothing more than gasps of gurgling noises—the death rattle, as Lanier knew it to be called—he moved back until the doorknob pressed into his lower back. The others in the room moved forward and took their places around her. Macon, without warning, threw his head back and screamed in a tortured grief that caused Neva to engulf him in her arms and Lanier to turn away.

Outside the house, he could still hear the boy's cries. Lanier walked faster and then began running toward the barn. He swung the door open and then, trying to block the sounds from the house, he jerked the barn door closed. The mule whinnied, and a wood spider ran across a web that now hung over the spot where Lanier had slept.

His breathing was ragged, and he wrestled with the confusion, guilt, and torment of not being able to save the woman he had grown to love. *Why didn't I fight harder before now?* he thought. He reached down and dug his hands into the hay-littered dirt. Rocking back and forth, he prayed once more and fought the disbelief that defeat was his to own and that God had turned His back on his prayers. *"It's a gift. If you was ever to share the words, then you're the same as cursed."* His grandmother's face, lined with wrinkles so deep they looked like scars, flashed through his mind. The cries of the witch from the creek who cursed him as a man after his father's own evil heart switched his soul. He could hear her as loud as he had that day at the creek. Pulling clumps of dirt and hay, he covered his ears. Flashes of his past fluttered through his mind like a picture show flapping about on a broken machine. Octavia smiled and then screamed. Gunshots echoed. His son, dressed in the christening gown, took his first steps once more. The sound of pounding nails filled his ears and then he smelled damp, aged wood as he was pinned into the box and loaded onto the boat.

When the light from the sun hit him, Lanier raised his arm up as a shield. At first he thought that the end was at hand and that hell was about to burn him. When he looked up the door swung open with a squeaking noise and for a second he was unable to see anything but forms of bodies.

Standing at the forefront, Ella, still dressed in her damp nightgown, wrapped her arms across her chest. Sunlight illuminated the curve of her thighs through the thin material. Her hair was matted and her face gaunt, but there was life in her eyes. She blinked and said his name in a graveled, weak voice. "Lanier."

Behind Ella, her sons and Neva Clarkson formed a semicircle that made Lanier think of the shape of a cloud, ready to cushion her and prevent a fall. Without caring what the others might think, Lanier jumped up and grabbed Ella with the force that he had wanted to use before he left. Her body, light and fragile to the touch, folded into him. There were no words of condemnation or curses. He just stood there, holding her, smelling her, memorizing her as if memory itself was a form of art.

31

The school burned on a Friday. It was a controlled burn that some had tried to turn into a party with stalks of sugarcane passed out to the children and bottles of whiskey passed around to the men. Those left in Dead Lakes gathered at the crossroads across from Ella's store and watched as members of the school board stuck blazing torches under the foundation.

"It's for the best," the beekeeper said. "We can't have any germs left in that place coming back to haunt us."

Neva sat on the end of the store porch with her feet dangling like a schoolgirl herself. A few of the horses hitched to wagons darted and snorted when the roof began to blaze. The children cheered and pranced in the street.

Samuel kept watch over the customers inside the store and even wore the black-and-white striped apron that had remained hanging in the coat closet after his father left. He had become good at reading customer needs and at ordering on speculation what he thought he could sell.

A fresh coat of blue paint covered the walls of Lanier's new home. He had moved into Narsissa's cabin only after settling on a fair rent to pay. "I'm not staying here like a freeloader," he protested. In honor of the original occupant, he painted a white letter *N* over the front door. Ella dressed it up by painting lavender-colored blazing star, Narsissa's favorite wildflower, around the corners.

Painting had become something more than a hobby for Ella. She began selling her paintings, weathered farmhouses set on landscapes covered in Indian grass and marshes dotted with palmettos and sand pines. Guests arriving at the Franklin Inn found her work greeting them in the lobby and hanging on the walls of the dining room.

Macon came running into the store and ignored Samuel's order to slow down. "Mama, come quick. The school roof just caved in two."

She leaned down to him, and her long, feathered earrings brushed against his cheek. "I don't care to see that school destroyed. And you shouldn't either. I'll tell you like Aunt Katherine used to tell me. People can take your house, your money, all your belongings, but they can't take away your education."

If Macon ever heard her, she wouldn't know it. He ran back outside and joined the other children parading down the road.

By early November, the charred remains of the school had been cleared. No one thought to wear a mask. The only masks they were now concerned with were gas masks and the effects of the mustard gas that had ravaged the soldiers in the war.

On November 11, church bells chimed, and people cheered in front of Ella's store. Reverend Simpson had just returned from Apalachicola with official word that the war to end all wars had finally come to a close. "Peace," he declared out in the street while standing on the bumper of his car. "There's peace in the world."

A week after she had recovered from the flu, Ella rocked in the porch chair that Harlan had special ordered for her and stared at the sunflowers. She listened as Lanier shared the details of Harlan's death.

"I want you to know I did everything that I could but it just didn't take," Lanier mumbled. His words buzzed around her like bees to a new bloom. Lanier sat on the porch step and stared up at her as if expecting Ella to cry, scream, or question. Creaking filled the space in the air as Ella rocked in the chair. Her eyes never ventured away from the flowers she had planted long ago to block the view of Harlan's store from their home.

After Lanier retreated back to the cabin, Ella slowly got up and walked into her bedroom. She pulled Harlan's tailor-made white shirt out from the bottom dresser drawer and wadded it into a ball, cussing the material and the man who wore it. For days afterward whenever she would boil over with emotion for all that Harlan had cost her and himself, she would take the shirt out and cover her mouth, muffling her screams.

The following Sunday the church was filled as if it were Easter. Everyone but Lanier occupied a pew. "I think I'd better stay close to home," he said when Ella asked him to join them.

An American flag was draped from corner to corner behind the pulpit and underneath the cross that hung on the front wall. Reverend Simpson lifted his arms high toward the congregation and smiled. "Armistice Day. Let us give thanks to God."

"What does *armistice* mean?" Keaton whispered and pulled at his shirt collar.

"The end of hostilities," Ella said. She felt her words.

That morning before the armistice service and after the breakfast dishes had been cleared, Ella took Harlan's shirt and eased outside. Wearing her best lavender dress, she picked up a shovel and walked until she reached the base of the spring. There between a cedar tree and a pine stump, she had buried the shirt and with it dreams better suited for a girl.

At the church altar Reverend Simpson stood before the congregation wearing a coat that was too big for the thinner man he now was. He seemed hopeful though somber. His voice, just as majestic as before, was more tempered. "We celebrate the end." His words echoed, and a few in the church were heard crying. "This year gave us end of life and end of war. We've seen destruction. And now we hear of peace."

At the back, Lanier slipped in through the church door. The man standing closest raised an eyebrow and motioned with a felt hat for him to move away from the door. Ignoring the instruction, Lanier licked his lips and searched the crowd.

Turning his neck side to side and stretching his arm out into the aisle, Samuel looked back and saw Lanier. Without saying a word to Ella, he stood up, turned his back to the altar, and faced him. Samuel nodded and then motioned for Lanier to come forward. At first, Lanier looked over his shoulder at the church door, but there was an urgency in Samuel's eyes, one Lanier had not fully recognized before, that called him to take one step and then another. Slowly moving forward, Lanier tried not to look at those who filled the church pews, staring at him, still trying to place him in their individual boxes of expectations. Easing into the pew next to Ella, Lanier turned to thank Samuel, but Samuel had already made his way to the back of the church, occupying the spot next to the door.

"I've long said we are not human beings having spiritual experiences," Reverend Simpson said. The beekeeper shifted his weight against the front pew, and a baby cried. Mrs. Pomeroy nudged a sleeping Mr. Pomeroy with her elbow. He snorted, opened one eye, and then ignored her reprimand. "We are more or less spiritual beings who have a human experience. I can't explain the events of this year or the events of life for that matter. And I can't deny the grief we've all shared or the bickering that could have torn us apart. But I know for certain that I can find hope in the darkest hour. Our little village might be called Dead Lakes, but make no mistake, there's certainly nothing dead about our faith."

At the end of that year, Brother Mabry, vowing to never again step foot on land that he now cursed, had the gates to the Eden retreat bolted and the doors sealed. Eventually presented with an opportunity for publicity that he couldn't refuse, he sold the retreat facility to the county for the sum of one dollar. He gave a two-paragraph quote to newspapermen who recorded his generosity and marveled that a building meant for spiritual enlightenment would now be a school. There was never any mention in the press release that Ella Wallace owned the land or that the county would be taking over Brother Mabry's lease on the property.

When Miss Wayne's school for girls closed upon her death in the epidemic, many of her students became full-time boarders at the new school in Dead Lakes. After two semesters none of the students even seemed to remember the evangelist who had built the building which now served as their school. With the additional students, two more teachers from the women's college in Tallahassee joined the faculty, and by Easter break, Neva Clarkson was named principal.

During the break, Mrs. Pomeroy came into the store while Ella was opening up a supply of oil paints and a box of canvases. The basket on Mrs. Pomeroy's arm dangled, and she dropped a bag of sugar into it. "They tell me," she said in a singsong voice, "that our dear reverend has been bit with the love bug."

Samuel dropped a crate of hammers on the floor in the back of the store, and Mrs. Pomeroy jumped.

"They tell me," she continued, "that he met some rich widow woman at a church conference in Panama City. And to think, poor Myer hasn't been gone a year. Reverend Simpson is making a fool out of himself, acting like a silly schoolboy. Can you imagine?"

Never looking away from the tins of pastel paints spread out on the counter before her, Ella said, "I can imagine it perfectly."

Ella and Lanier sat on her front porch and watched the sun cast an orange glow over the marsh where cypress still grew in patches. Lanier chirped about business proposals with the same steady rhythm as the locusts that called out from the field.

"Now, Lanier, I just don't know about that," Ella said, flicking a piece of dried paint from the side of her finger.

"Hear me out," Lanier said. "I saw in the paper where that state chemist who passed through Apalachicola—the governor's man, the one going around talking about new ways to work the land—"

"Mr. Rose, I believe the paper said his name was. I read the article. Something about a heat wave causing a shortage of wheat."

"Well, did you notice what he said about this place being a natural fit for growing rice? I got an idea that we can plant rice right down there." Lanier leaned over and pointed beyond the porch toward the low-lying water. "Right where we cut the cypress." He stopped the chair in mid-rock and rubbed her hand. "What you think?"

It was not the first time that he had mentioned the proposition. Since the newspaper article about the prospects of new planting, Lanier had talked of little else. Ella listened to his words but up until now hadn't engaged him. The details swirled in Ella's head, and she struggled with the idea of it all being a risky gamble. She looked out across the land where saplings dotted the sand and down to the edge of the water where cypress stumps rose up like jagged thumbs. "Rice down here? Whoever heard of such hogwash?" she had heard the beekeeper say in the store the day the article appeared in the paper. "An ignoramus government man, if ever I heard one. Show me what sort of rice can grow past the Georgia line," Mr. Pomeroy had added.

A storm of nervous energy rumbled inside the core of Ella's being.

She scraped her fingernail across a gnarled, weathered spot on the arm of the chair and then put her hand on top of Lanier's. "At the end of the day, I hate to say that I never tried," she said.

"We'll make a pretty penny on this one, you just wait and see." Lanier studied her with intense examination. The light that was left in the day caught the small amber circles in the center of his irises. They penetrated her like a fire melting the double-locked gate of fear—the fear of failure and the fear of public opinion about their unconventional arrangement. "We're partners. Fifty-fifty," Lanier said.

As the sun sank lower and the sky turned darker blue, a half-moon formed over the horizon. A strand of clouds illuminated pink by the setting sun hovered over the tops of the oak trees, the church steeple, and the tin roof of the store. What was left of the clouds on that day formed the shape of a spine, like the one that had once hung on a skeleton in the laboratory at Miss Wayne's school. Toward the east, faint wisps of clouds scattered across the sky. To Ella they looked like thin ribs stretching out and then crumbling toward the evening star. The scent of Lanier clung to the crisp air of early evening, and for a moment, Ella breathed deep until her stomach stretched out wide. She purposely exhaled slowly, savoring the scene before her. The sounds of laughter rose up from the spring down in the woods and tickled her ears like wind chimes.

Girls who had transitioned from Miss Wayne's school giggled as they frolicked along the edge of the spring that some in town still claimed was magical. But the girls added their own stories about the spring, about Indian princesses who frequented its bank at midnight and those who grew stronger by daring to bow down and brush their lips against the water's surface. With school uniform dresses hiked up to their knees, the girls dipped their feet into the spring and sipped from the bottles of Coca-Cola they purchased from the commissary. They wished, hoped, and dreamed.

And all the while, Ella Wallace lived.

About the Author

A fifth-generation native of Perry, Florida, Michael Morris knows Southern culture and characters. They are the foundation and inspiration for the stories and novels he writes.

Michael started his career as a pharmaceutical sales representative and began writing in the evenings. The first screenplay he penned is still someplace in the bottom of a desk drawer.

While studying under author Tim McLaurin, Michael started the story that would eventually become his first novel, *A Place Called Wiregrass*. The debut book won the Christy Award for Best First Novel.

Michael's second novel, *Slow Way Home*, was compared to the work of Harper Lee and Flannery O'Connor by the *Washington Post*. It was nationally ranked as one of the top three recommended books by the American Booksellers Association and named one of the best novels of the year by the *Atlanta Journal-Constitution* and the *St. Louis Post-Dispatch*.

Michael is also the author of a novella based on the Grammy-nominated song "Live Like You Were Dying," which became a finalist for the Southern Book Critics Circle Award. His essays have appeared in the *Los Angeles Times*, the *Dallas Morning News*, and the Minneapolis *Star Tribune*. In addition, his short stories can be found in Sonny Brewer's *Stories from the Blue Moon Café II* and in *Not Safe, but Good* volume 2, an anthology edited by Bret Lott.

A graduate of Auburn University, Michael also holds an MFA in creative writing from Spalding University. He lives in Alabama with his wife, Melanie. Visit him online at www.michaelmorrisbooks.com.

Reading Group Guide

A Conversation with the Author

What inspired you to write *Man in the Blue Moon*?

During my early years, I lived next door to my maternal grand-parents. I spent a lot of my childhood in their home. Every evening my grandmother's widowed sister would join us for supper. While the meal simmered on the stove, the two sisters would sit at the table and talk about local news that never seemed to make the newspaper. Most of the time I'd sit in the hallway, eavesdropping on their tales about the townspeople I knew and picturing the scenes I heard as a movie in my mind.

My grandfather was also a "talker," and whenever he'd enter the room, he'd share in the conversation, disputing some of the women's stories and adding details to others. He was the best storyteller I have known.

One story from my grandfather's childhood has long fascinated and haunted me. In 1920, when my grandfather was ten, he and his older brother were sent to pick up a delivery that was arriving from Bainbridge, Georgia, by steamboat down the Apalachicola River to their home in Florida. Since their father owned a mercantile in a crossroads community, such a request was not unusual. The boys were always being sent to Apalachicola, the county seat, for deliveries.

After the dockworkers had loaded a crudely constructed box onto their wagon, my grandfather and his brother traveled back home guessing what was inside. My grandfather bet his brother that it was a grandfather clock.

Back at the family store with the box now unloaded from the wagon, my great-grandfather used a crowbar to pop the lid open. As a boy, my grandfather was so scared at the sight he saw that he stumbled and fell backward, tearing the seat in his britches. A man, soiled with filth and caked with mud, climbed out of the box.

The man who had been nailed shut inside was shipped during the night to his cousin, my great-grandfather, for safekeeping. The man was on the run for supposedly killing his wife. Even though the court had exonerated him, the wife's family sought vengeance. They had made it known that they would hunt him down and kill him.

My grandfather and his brothers were instructed not to ask any questions, and if they were asked by the people in the village, they were told to simply say that the visitor was a worker their father had hired. After about four months, my grandfather awoke one morning and the man was gone. They never heard from him again.

Man in the Blue Moon has been more than just another novel— writing this story has been a calling, a way to give back to my grandfather the story that he first presented to me. After months of research, I began writing the first draft of the novel on his ninety-ninth birthday. When I would visit with him, he would ask about "the box story." Then he would lean over and caution me that I must never reveal the name of the man who was originally shipped to his house when he was a boy. "I promised my daddy I wouldn't talk about it," he'd say in a stage whisper.

Brother Mabry is a fascinating character—sort of a cross between P. T. Barnum and Billy Sunday. What inspired his character? How does he compare to Reverend Simpson in your mind?

I've often heard writers say that some of their characters appear out of nowhere—that right when they are focused on some aspect of the story, these unplanned characters appear in their minds. Up until this novel, I had never experienced anything like that. Before I write the first sentence of a novel, I like to develop detailed character sketches, so while the story might go in a different direction than planned, the characters typically remain the same. But Brother Mabry threw me for a loop. He literally walked into the story and held court.

Brother Mabry's appearance helps to further the conflict in the story. He is in direct contrast to Reverend Simpson, who at first tries to ignore the public outrage over Lanier's ability to heal. However, as time goes on Reverend Simpson realizes that he can no longer sit by and watch the town persecute Lanier. I think because of Brother Mabry's arrival and the hysteria that he ignites, Reverend Simpson comes into his own and becomes more courageous. While Reverend Simpson is perhaps more authentic in his beliefs, from a writing perspective Brother Mabry was the most fun to write!

The setting is an integral part of the story, often echoing the themes and arcs of the different characters' stories. Why did you choose this part of Florida?

As a fifth-generation Floridian, this is the area I know best. All of my grandfather's stories revolved around West Florida, where he grew up. He lived to be 101, and during his growing-up days, Florida was still a rough, untamed world. When he was a boy, my grandfather once witnessed a man walk into his father's country store and shoot another man in the back of the head. The man who fired the shot claimed that the other man had stolen his cattle. When the charge was proven true, the crime was deemed justifiable homicide.

As I began to research for *Man in the Blue Moon*, I was struck by the complicated details of the area where my grandfather was reared. It was a part of Florida that had known excessive wealth before the Civil War when the port of Apalachicola was the third-largest exporter of cotton on the Gulf of Mexico—the French government even had a consulate there. Apalachicola now has around 2,500 citizens. The town is still a beautiful place with a large number of homes and buildings on the historical register. Whenever I start a new novel, I go there for inspiration. It's one of my favorite places and seems to find its way into almost every story I write.

One thing reviewers consistently comment on is the authenticity of the voices of your characters. Is that something you're constantly studying and perfecting, or is it something that comes naturally?

Like all writers, I am always listening and observing. Sometimes when I am sitting at a restaurant or waiting in line at an airport terminal, I'll hear someone say something in a unique way and I'll jot it down. I have lots of paper napkins and torn pieces of paper tucked inside a shoe box. Then, when I start a new story, I'll scatter the sayings out on the floor and go through them, pulling out good ones to use for dialogue.

Do you see *Man in the Blue Moon* as similar to your previous novels, or does it mark a departure in your writing? How so?

Even though my previous novels are not historical, some of the themes are the same, such as the close ties of community in a small town and the Southerners' love affair with the land. My work tends to focus on characters who are facing "life hurricanes" and how they come out the other side. At the end of the day, I just want to write a novel that is one I'd like to read.

What's next for you?

I'm looking forward to the release of my next novel, *The King of Florabama*, which is about the longest-serving sheriff in Alabama, who must confront the circumstances behind a forty-year-old murder that has splintered his relationships with his children. And like the other novels, Florida plays a part in the story.

Discussion Questions

1. Ella's boys all have different reactions to Lanier, both when he first arrives and throughout the story. Discuss the differences in their personalities and responses. Why do you think each boy reacts as he does?

2. Ella often idealizes her aunt Katherine yet admits she was "a broken woman . . . who'd prefer to dream life away rather than walk through the pains of the present." What does that say about Ella? Would you characterize Ella as a weak or strong woman? Why? Do you think that changes over the course of the novel?

3. Why is Ella so determined to keep her land? Do you agree with her decision to fight for the land, or do you think she was foolish not to sell at least part of it? Why? How does the fact that she has three boys to feed impact your answer?

4. Lanier has a gift he often wishes he hadn't been given. Have you ever felt that way about a gift or talent? How did you decide to handle that gift?

5. After they cut down the last pine, Ella finds she can't embrace the joy everyone else feels. "Somehow it was easier to stay in the shade of doubt rather than give way to the momentary light of wishful thinking," she muses. Have you ever felt this way? How did you overcome those feelings?

6. What is revealed about Clive Gillespie's background? How does that play into his actions? How much do you think our past shapes who we become later in life?

7. Narsissa holds on to a belief about her husband for a good portion of the story, but she later admits she was only fooling herself. Why does it take her so long to realize this, or at least to admit it? In what ways is Narsissa like Ella? In what ways is she different?

8. Did Reverend Simpson's speech in chapter 21 surprise you? Why or why not? Did it change your opinion of him? How would you have handled the situation?

9. Both Ella's land and the larger area of Apalachicola are an integral part of the story. Discuss how the land reflects the journey of the main characters and almost becomes a character itself.

10. The people of Dead Lakes are easily swayed by public opinion and quickly skeptical of anyone who is different. Give some examples. Why are they quick to judge Lanier though they easily accept Brother Mabry's rather outrageous claims? How can we balance belief with healthy skepticism? Where do you draw the line between faith and discernment?

11. In chapter 20, Brother Mabry says, "The healing powers of the water on that land have no ownership other than that of God," and he later proclaims, "Hear me now. . . . If we have

enough faith, we can pray down this flu." Discuss the irony of his statements in light of other events in the book. Would you characterize Brother Mabry as crooked or merely misguided? Do you think he is well-intentioned? Why or why not?

12. Discuss the symbolism of Brother Mabry's act when he last appears in chapter 25.

13. When influenza sweeps through Dead Lakes but spares the two children Lanier had already healed, Mr. Pomeroy suggests the town is being punished for the way they treated Lanier. What does that say about how he views God? What is the danger with that line of thinking?

14. Which character or event in the book surprised you the most? Which did you find the most tragic? Triumphant?